Days

Days

James Lovegrove

Copyright © James Lovegrove 1997
All rights reserved

The right of James Lovegrove to be identified as the author
of this work has been asserted by him in accordance with
the Copyright, Designs and Patents Act 1988.

First published in Great Britain in 1997 by Phoenix House

This edition published in great Britain in 1999 by Millennium
An imprint of Orion Books Ltd
Orion House, 5 Upper St Martin's Lane, London WC2H 9EA

To receive information on the Millennium list, e-mail us at:
smy@orionbooks.co.uk

A CIP catalogue record for this book is available
from the British Library

ISBN 1 85798 841 8

Printed in Great Britain by
Clays Ltd, St Ives plc

What are days for?
Days are where we live.
Philip Larkin, 'Days'

Prologue

The Seven Cities: according to Brewer's *Reader's Handbook*, seven cities are regarded as the great cities of all time, namely Alexandria, Jerusalem, Babylon, Athens, Rome, Constantinople, and either London (for commerce) or Paris (for beauty).

5.30 a.m.

It is that time of morning, not quite night, not quite day, when the sky is a field of smudged grey, like a page of erased pencil marks, and in the empty city streets a hushing sound can be heard – an ever-present background sigh, audible only when all else is silent. It is that hour of dawn when the streetlamps flicker out one by one like heads being emptied of dreams, and pigeons with fraying, fume-coloured plumage open an eye. It is that moment when the sun, emerging, casts silvery rays and long shadows, and every building grows a black fan-shaped tail which it drapes across its westward neighbours.

One building casts a broader shadow, darkens more with its penumbra, than any other. It rises at the city's heart, immense and squat and square. Visible for miles around, it would seem to be the sole reason for which the houses and tower blocks and factories and warehouses around it exist. Hard rains and hot summers have turned its brickwork the colour of dried blood, and its roof is capped with a vast hemispherical glass dome that glints and glimmers as it rotates ponderously, with almost imperceptible slowness. Hidden gearings drive the dome through one full revolution every twenty-four hours. Half of it is crystal clear, the other half smoked black.

The building has seven floors, and each floor is fourteen metres high. Its sides are just over two and a half kilometres long, so that it sits on seven hundred hectares of land. With its bare brick flanks it looks like something that weighs heavy on the planet, like something that has been pounded in with God's own sledgehammer.

This is Days, the world's first and (some still say) foremost gigastore.

Inside, Days is brackishly lit with half-powered bulbs. Night watch-

1

men are making their final rounds through the store's 666 departments, the beams of their torches poking this way and that through the crepuscular stillness, sweeping focal haloes across the shelves and the displays, the cabinets and the countertops, the unimaginably vast array of merchandise that Days has to offer. The night watchmen's movements are followed automatically by closed-circuit cameras mounted on whispering armatures. The cameras' green LEDs are not yet lit.

Across the sea-green marble floors of the store's four main entrance halls janitors drive throbbing cleaning-machines the size of tractors, with spinning felt discs for wheels. The vehicles whirr and veer, reviving the marble's oceanic sheen. At the centre of each entrance hall, embedded in the floor, is a mosaic, a circle seven metres in diameter divided into halves, one white, one black. The tesserae of the white half are bevelled opals, those of the black half slivers of onyx, some as large as medallions, some as small as pennies, all fitted intricately together. The janitors are careful to drive over the mosaics several times, to buff up the precious stones' lustre.

At the centre of the gigastore, tiered circular openings in each floor form an atrium that rises all the way up to the great glass dome. The tiers are painted in the colours of the spectrum, red rising to violet. Shafts of light steal in through the dome's clear half, reaching down to a fine monofilament mesh level with the Red Floor. The mesh, half a kilometre in diameter, is stretched tight as a drum-skin above a canopy of palms and ferns, and between it and the canopy lies a gridwork of copper pipes.

With a sudden hiss, a warm steamy mist purls out from holes in the pipes, and the tree canopy ripples appreciatively. The water vapour drifts down, growing thinner, fainter, sieved by layers of leaves and branches, to the ground, a loamy landscape of moss, rock, leaf mould and grass.

Here, at basement level, lies the Menagerie. Its insects are already busy. Its animals are stirring. Snarls and soft howls can be heard, and paws pad and undergrowth rustles as creatures great and small begin their daily prowling.

Outside Days, armed guards yawn and loll blearily at their posts. All around the building people lie huddled against the plate-glass windows that occupy the lower storey, the only windows in the building. Most of them sleep, but some hover fitfully in that lucid state between waking and dreaming where their dreams are as uncomfortable as their reality. The lucky ones have sleeping bags, gloves on their fingers, and shawls and scarves wrapped around their heads. The rest make do with blankets, fingerless gloves, hats and thicknesses of begged, borrowed or stolen clothing.

And now, at last, as six o'clock approaches, over at the airport to the west of town a jet breaks the city's silence. Its wingtips flaring like burnished silver in the low sunlight, it leaps along a runway, rears into the air and roars steeply skyward: the dawn shuttle, carrying yet another fuselage-full of émigrés westward, yet another few hundred healthy cells leaving the cancerous host-body of the motherland.

The echo of the plane's launch rumbles across the rooftops, reaching into every corner of the city, into the deeps of every citizen's mind, so that collectively, at four minutes to six, as is the case every morning, the entire population is thinking the same thing: *We are a little bit more alone than yesterday*. And those who continue to sleep are troubled in their dreams, and those who come awake and stay awake find themselves gnawed by dissatisfaction and doubt.

And still the day remorselessly brightens like a weed that, no matter what, will grow.

1

The Seven Sleepers: seven noble youths of Ephesus who martyred themselves under the emperor Decius in AD 250 by fleeing to a cave in Mount Celion, where, having fallen asleep, they were found by Decius, who had them sealed up.

6.00 a.m.

The brass hands of the alarm clock on Frank Hubble's bedside table divide its face in two. The perfect vertical diameter they form separates the pattern on the dial into its component halves, on the left a black semicircle, on the right a white. A trip-switch clicks in the workings and the clock starts to ring.

Frank's hand descends on to the clock, silencing the reveille almost before it has begun. He settles back, head sighing into duck-down pillows. The roar of the departing shuttle is now a distant lingering murmur, more remembered than heard. He tries to piece together the fragments of the dream from which he was summoned up by the knowledge that the alarm was about to go off, but the images spin elusively out of his grasp. The harder he reaches for them, the faster they hurtle away. Soon they are lost, leaving him with just the memory of having dreamed, which, he supposes, is better than not dreaming at all.

The street below his bedroom window is startled by the sound of a car's ignition. The window's russet curtains are inflated by a breeze then sucked flat again. Frank hears the timer-controlled coffee machine in the kitchen gurgle into life, and moving his tongue thirstily he pictures fat brown droplets of a harsh arabica blend dripping into the pot. He waits for the sharp odour of brewing coffee to creep under the bedroom door and tweak his nose, then, with a grunt, unpeels the bedcovers and swings his legs out.

He sits for a while on the side of the bed gazing down at his knees. He is a medium-sized man, well proportioned and trim, although the years have worn away at his shoulders and put a curve in his upper vertebrae so that he suffers from a permanent hunch, as though he is saddled with a heavy, invisible yoke. His face is as rumpled as his pyjamas, and his hair is a grey that isn't simply a dark white or a light black but an utter absence of tone. His eyes, too, are grey, the grey of gravestones.

In a bathroom whose midnight-blue walls are flecked with stencil-led gold stars, Frank urinates copiously into the lavatory bowl. Having pushed the flush and lowered the lavatory lid, he fills the basin with steaming-hot water, soaks a flannel and presses it hard against his face. Though his skin stings in protest, he holds the flannel in place until it cools. Then he lathers on shaving foam from a canister marked prominently with the same back-to-back semicircles of black and white as on the dial of the alarm clock, and with a few deft strokes of a nickel-plated razor he is unbristled. He has his shaving down to such a fine art that he can leave his face smooth and nick-free without once consulting the mirror in front of him.

Frank fears mirrors. Not because they tell him he is old (he knows that), nor because they tell him how worn and weary he looks (he has resigned himself to that), but because, of late, mirrors have begun to tell him another truth, one he would prefer not to acknowledge.

Still, it has become part of his pre-breakfast ablutions to confront this truth, and so, resting his hands on the sides of the basin, he raises his head and looks at his reflection.

Or rather, looks *for* his reflection, because in the mirror he sees nothing except the star-flecked, midnight-blue bathroom wall behind him.

Fighting down a familiar upsurge of panic, Frank concentrates. He is there. He knows he is there. The mirror is lying. He can feel his body, the organic life-support machine that keeps his mind going. He knows there is cool floor beneath his bare feet and porcelain basin in his hands because nerve-endings in his skin are reporting these facts to his brain, and fitted tightly and intricately into that skin is the configura-tion of flesh and bone and vein and sinew that is uniquely Frank Hubble. The air that slides over his lips as he breathes in and out tells him that he exists. He feels, therefore he is.

But the mirror continues to insist that he is not.

He fixes his gaze on the point in space where his eyes should be. His mind is descending in an express lift, swooping vertiginously down towards a dark well of insanity where writhe not gibbering demons but wraiths, a blizzard of wraiths who float soundlessly, mouth hopelessly, twisting around each other, oblivious to each other, invisible to each other. Neither guilt nor shame, the common demons, terrify Frank. What he fears most is anonymity. The nameless wraiths flutter like intangible moths. Nothing is appearing in the mirror. Today, of all days, may be the day that he is finally swallowed up by the emptiness inside him. Unless he can visualise himself, he will be gone. Lost. Forgotten.

He has to remember his eyes. If the eyes fall into place, he will be able to piece together the rest.

Gradually, with considerable effort, he makes two eyes emerge from the reflected wall, first the grave-grey irises, then their frames of white.

He makes the eyes blink, to prove they are really his.

Now the lids appear, purple and puffy with sleep and age.

Now he shades in two eyebrows of the same smudgy, forgettable grey as his hair.

His forehead follows, and quickly the rest of his face falls into place – fisted nose, fettered jaw, furrowed cheeks, foetal ears.

Below his chin he has a neck, below his neck a collarbone that reaches to both shoulders from which drop arms that end in basin-bracing hands. The stripes of his pyjama jacket are sketched out in jagged parallel lines. On the breast pocket a stitched monogram of the divided black-and-white circle manifests itself.

He can see everything of himself that is visible in the mirror. The struggle is over again for another day.

But it is not with relief that Frank turns away from the basin. Who knows – the moment he takes his eyes off his reflection, perhaps it vanishes again? Behind our backs, who knows what mirrors do?

It is a question Frank prefers not to ponder. Leaning over the bath, he levers up the mixer tap, and a fizzing cone of water spurts from the head of the shower. The mixer tap is marked with a black C on a white semicircle next to a black semicircle with a white H. Frank adjusts the water to a medium temperature, divests himself of his pyjamas, and steps into the bath, ringing the shower curtain across.

The shower curtain, the flannel Frank uses to scrub himself, the bottle from which he squeezes out a palmful of medicated shampoo, his unscented soap, all sport the divided-circle logo, as do the bathmat he steps out on to when he has finished showering, the towel with which he dries his body off, and the robe he drapes around himself.

The logo, in various guises and sizes, appears on no fewer than forty-seven different fixtures, fittings and items of toiletry in the bathroom. Even the treacherous mirror has a coin-sized one etched into its corner.

Warm-skinned and tinglingly clean, Frank shuffles into the kitchen, using his fingers to comb his hair into a lank approximation of how it will look when dry. The timing of the ritual of his mornings is so ingrained that as he enters the kitchen the last few drips of coffee are spitting into the pot; he can pick up the pot and pour out a mugful straight away.

Blowing steam from the rim of the mug, he opens the blinds. Staring out at the hazy silver city, he takes his first sip of coffee.

Usually Frank admires the view for all of three seconds, but this morning he takes his time. Even though the present position of every building, thoroughfare and empty rectangle of demolished rubble is familiar to him and forms part of a detailed and constantly updated mental map, he feels that, for posterity's sake, he ought to make a ceremony out of this act of observation, so that in years to come he will remember how every morning at 6.17, for thirty-three years, he used to stand here and stare.

He suspects that all day long he will be highlighting mundane little moments like this, tagging the regular features of his daily routine which under normal circumstances he would perform on autopilot but which today he will fetishise as a long-term convict whose sentence is coming to an end must fetishise his last tin-tray meal, his last slopping-out, his last roll-call. Though it will be sweet never to have to do these things again, it will also be strange. After thirty-three years, routine has become the calipers of Frank's life. He hates it, but he isn't sure that he's going to be able to manage without it.

So, consciously and conscientiously, he gazes out at a view that he has seen thousands of times before, either in the dark or in the false dawn or in broad daylight. He observes the thick-legged flyover, the spindly section of elevated railway along which a commuter train crawls like a steel caterpillar, the whole treeless, joyless expanse of flat-roofed concrete estates and crumpled, clustered houses. As with all employee accommodation, the windows also offer him a view of Days, the distant store's upper storeys lying like a lid over the city, but by lowering his head just a little he can block it out of sight behind the rooftops.

Now he feels he has gazed enough. Into his otherwise tightly timetabled rising ritual he has factored two minutes of slack so that, unless there is a major hold-up, he is never late leaving the building. He has used up one of those minutes, and it is wise to keep the other in hand in case of emergency.

It vaguely amuses him that he should be worrying about arriving late for work on what he fully expects to be his last day at Days, but a habit of thirty-three years' standing is hard to break. How long will it take, he wonders, for the robot in him to adjust to life after Days? Will he wake up punctually at six every morning until he dies, even if there is nothing to get up for? Will he continue to take his coffee-break at 10.30, his lunch-break at 12.45, his tea-break at 4.30 in the afternoon? The patterns stamped into his brain by years of repetition will be difficult to reconfigure into something more suited to a leisurely lifestyle. For more than half his life he has been locked into a groove like a toy car, travelling the same circuit six days a week. Sundays have been days of disjointed lethargy: waking at six as usual, he passes the hours snoozing, reading the newspapers, watching television and generally feeling sleepy and out of sorts, his body unable to assimilate the hiccup in its circadian rhythm. Is that what his life will be like after he resigns? One long chain of Sundays?

Well, he will have to deal with that when it happens. For now, he has today – a Thursday – to contend with.

He inserts a slice of bread into a chrome pop-up toaster which, with its vents and lines, calls to mind a vintage automobile. On the counter beside it sits a portable television set, which he switches on. Both toaster and television, needless to say, have the back-to-back D's of the Days logo stamped on their housings.

The television is programmed so that whenever it comes on it automatically tunes in to the Days home-shopping channel. A pair of wax-faced women of indeterminable age are rhapsodising over a three-string cultured-pearl choker from the Jewellery Department, while a computer-generated simulation of the interior of the world's first and (possibly) foremost gigastore planes sea-sickeningly to and fro behind them.

With a click of the remote control, Frank cuts to a news channel, and watches a report on the construction of the world's first terastore in Australia – official title: the Bloody Big Shop. Intended to serve not just Australia and New Zealand but the Pacific Rim countries and

South-East Asia as well, the Bloody Big Shop is an estimated eighteen months from completion but still, in its skeletal state, challenges its immediate neighbour, Ayers Rock, for size.

The toaster jettisons its load of browned bread. In one corner of the slice a small semicircle of charring backs against an uncooked counterpart. This is the corner Frank butters and bites first.

Frank does not eat much. He doesn't even finish the toast. He pours himself another coffee, turns off the television and heads for his dressing room.

Down a high-ceilinged hallway he passes doors to rooms he seldom uses, rooms whose immaculate and expensive furnishings would be under several inches of dust were it not for the ministrations of a cleaning lady Frank has never met. Shelves of books he hasn't read line one side of the hallway, while on the other side paintings he barely notices any more cover the wall. A fussy-fingered interior decorator from Days chose the books and the paintings and the furnishings on Frank's behalf, making free with Frank's Iridium card. Frank has not yet paid off the sum outstanding on the card, so when he resigns he will have to surrender almost everything he owns back to the store. This will be no hardship.

His Thursday outfit is waiting for him in the dressing room, each individual item hung or laid out. Frank put the trousers of his Thursday suit in the press the night before, last thing before he went to bed. The creases are pleasingly sharp.

He dresses in an orderly and methodical manner, pausing after each step of the process to take a sip of coffee. He puts on a cool cotton shirt with a blue pinstripe and plain white buttons, and knots a maroon silk tie around his neck. He dons a charcoal-grey jacket to match the trousers, and slips a pair of black, cushion-soled brogues built more for comfort than elegance over the navy socks on his feet. Then he addresses himself to the full-length mirror that stands, canted in its frame, in one corner.

Patiently he pieces himself in.

The clothes help. The clothes, as they say, make the man and, decked out in the very best that the Gentlemen's Outfitters Department at Days has to offer, Frank feels very much made. The crisp outlines of the suit fall readily into place. The tie and shirt and shoes fill out the gaps. Frank's head, neck and hands are the last to appear, the hardest to visualise. God help him, sometimes he can't even remember what his face looks like. Once it manifests in the mirror, its familiarity mocks his faulty memory, but in the moments while he struggles to recall just one feature, Frank honestly fears that he has finally winked out of existence altogether, slipped sideways into limbo, become a genuine ghost as well as a professional one.

He makes a point of fixing the time – 6.34 – in his mental souvenir album. At 6.34 every workday morning, give or take a minute, he has stood here newly dressed in an outfit every piece of which carries a label into which is woven a matched pair of semicircles, one black, one white, above the washing and ironing instructions. Tomorrow morning he will not be standing here. In one of the dressing-room wardrobes a packed suitcase waits. The fluorescent pink tag attached to its handle bears a flight number and the three-letter code for an airport in the United States. A first-class plane ticket sits on top of the suitcase. Tomorrow at 6.34 a.m. Frank will be aboard a silver-tinged shuttle jet, soaring above the clotted clouds, following the sun. One way, no return.

He pauses, still unable to conceive how it will feel to be hurtling away from the city, all connections with the only place he has ever called home severed, no certainties ahead of him. A tiny voice inside his head asks him if he is crazy, and a larger, louder voice replies, with calm conviction, *No*.

No. Leaving is probably the sanest thing he has ever done. The scariest, too.

Returning to the kitchen, Frank pours himself his third coffee, filling the mug to the brim as he empties the pot of its last drops.

Halfway through drinking the final instalment of his breakfast-time caffeine infusion he feels a twinge deep in his belly, and happily he heads for the bathroom, there to succumb to the seated pleasure of relieving his bowels of their contents, which are meagre, hard and dry, but none the less good to be rid of. Each sheet of the super-soft three-ply lavatory paper he uses is imprinted with ghostly-faint pairs of semicircles. When he was much younger, Frank used to treat the Days logo with almost religious reverence. As an icon, its ubiquitousness indicated to him its power. He was proud to be associated with the symbol. But where before he might have balked at such an act of desecration, now he thinks nothing of wiping his arse on it.

In the bedroom again, he straps on his sole sartorial accessory, a Days wristwatch – gold casing, patent-leather strap, Swiss movement.

Before he slips his wallet into his inside jacket pocket, he checks that his Iridium card is still there, not because he expects it to have been stolen but because that is what he has done every morning at 6.41 for thirty-three years.

He slides the Iridium from its velvet sheath. The card gleams iridescently like a rectangular wafer of mother-of-pearl. Holding it up to the light and gently flexing it, Frank watches rainbows chase one another across its surface, rippling around the raised characters of his name and the card number and the grainily engraved Days logo. Hard to believe something so light and thin could be a millstone. Hard to believe something so beautiful could be the source of so much misery.

He returns the card to its sheath, the sheath to his wallet. Now he is ready to leave. There is nothing keeping him here.

Except . . .

He spends his second 'spare' minute wandering around the flat, touching the things that belong to him, that tomorrow will not belong to him. His fingertips drift over fabrics and varnishes and glass as he glides from room to room, through a living space that, for all the emotional attachment he has to it, might as well be a museum.

How he has managed to accumulate so many possessions, so many pieces of furniture and *objets d'art* is something of a mystery to Frank. He can vaguely recall over the past thirty-three years handing over his Iridium to pay for purchases which took him all of a few seconds to pick out, but he is hard pressed to remember actually buying the individual items – this Art Deco vase, say, or that Turkish kilim – let alone how much they cost. No doubt the Days interior decorator was responsible for obtaining and installing many of the pieces Frank has no memory of acquiring, but not all. That is how little the transactions have meant to him, how unreal they have seemed. He has bought things reflexively, not because he wants to but because his Iridium has meant he can, and now he is mired in a debt that will take at least another decade of employment to work off.

But as he cannot bear the thought of another day at Days, and as what he owns has no value to him, not even of the sentimental kind, he feels no qualms about his decision to tender his resignation today. To quit, as the Americans would say. (So direct, Americans. They always find a succinct way of putting things, which is why Frank is looking forward to living among them, because he admires those qualities in others he finds lacking in himself.) He has calculated that by repossessing the flat and all that is in it, his employers ought to consider the debt squared. And if they don't, then they will just have to come looking for him in America. And America is a very big place, and Frank can be a very hard man to find.

His tour of the flat is complete. It is 6.43, and he has pushed his timetable to its limit. There can be no more procrastinating. He takes a black cashmere overcoat from the coat rack by the flat door and flings it on. The door clicks softly open, snicks snugly shut. Frank steps out on to the landing, part of a central stairwell that winds around a lift shaft enclosed in a wrought-iron cage. He keys the Down button by the lift gate, and there is a whine and a churning of cogs from deep down in the shaft. The cables start to ribbon.

2

The Corporal Works of Mercy: in some Christian denominations, seven specific acts of charity that render physical aid

6.52 a.m.
It takes Frank five and a half minutes to walk from his building to the train station. In his first few years at Days it used to take him four. Age hasn't slowed him. He still has the legs of a twenty-year-old. But his stride has lost its spring.

At the station's automated newsstand he inserts his Iridium into the slot and makes his selection. The newspaper flops into the chute and he extracts it. His Iridium is debited and ejected. A similar procedure buys him a return ticket and a styrofoam cup of coffee.

Through the turnstile he goes, and up the stairs to the platform, where a dozen commuters are standing and every so often casting hopeful glances along the tracks. Like Frank, they all have newspapers and hot beverages and invisible yokes. Their faces he knows well, and he has learned names to go with some of the faces by eavesdropping on their desultory conversations. He and they are old warriors, brothers and sisters in arms who have fought this daily battle for more years than they would care to think. To his surprise, Frank is saddened to think that this will be the last time he will be sharing their company. He moves along the platform, murmuring an inaudible goodbye to each person under his breath. One or two of them glance up from their newspapers as he passes, but the majority do not.

He takes his place by a wooden shelter whose burnt-ivory paintwork has been almost entirely obliterated by graffiti. A chilly breeze stirs the grit on the platform's asphalt surface and sends discarded sweet-wrappers and crisp-packets scuttering. Weeds shiver fitfully between the rust-encrusted iron sleepers. Finally an incomprehensible announcement burbles from the loudspeakers that sound as if they are made of soggy cardboard, and, to everyone's relief, the tracks begin to sing.

The train comes rollicking in, grinds to a halt, and gapes its doors. Frank finds himself a seat. The doors close, and the train hunks and clanks away from the platform, cumbersomely gathering speed. The rolling stock is so old it could probably qualify as vintage. The carriages squeal and sway, their wheels shimmying on the rails; the seat fabric smells of burnt oranges, and the windows are a smeary yellow.

Frank knows he has thirty-one minutes, barring hold-ups, to read his paper and drink his coffee, but today he delays doing either in order to cast his eye around the carriage and fasten details in his memory. The tattered corner of a poster advertising a Days sale long since finished. The empty beer can rattling to and fro across the dun linoleum flooring. The slogan scrawled in blue marker pen, 'fuk da gigastor' – a sentiment Frank has some sympathy with. The synchronised jerk of the passengers' heads, mirrored by the twitch of the handstraps that hang from the ceiling. The sulphurous glide of the city.

He will not miss this. He will not miss any of this.

The daily paper no longer contains much to interest him, if it ever did. He buys and reads it out of sheer habit. Nothing that happens in this country concerns him any more. All the news seems old. The unrest, the disputes, the crime, the prevaricating of the politicians, the pontificating of the clergy, the intriguing of the royals . . . it has always been this way for as long as he can remember, and longer. Nothing in the news changes except the names.

But America – something is always happening in America. A hurricane that leaves thousands homeless, a serial killer who leaves dozens dead. A trial that spectacularly acquits the defendant, a civic official who spectacularly turns down a bribe. Huge salaries, huge tragedies. Everything on a larger scale. *Two* gigastores, for heaven's sake! Not that a gigastore is necessarily a mark of greatness, but as the only continent to sport two of the things North America has to be marvelled at. And, what's more, they are open twenty-four hours a day.

Frank expects that he will visit both Blumberg's, N.Y., and Blumberg's, L.A., if for no other reason than professional curiosity. He intends to traverse the entire country coast to coast in trains and cars and buses, secretly observing the nation and its people. In a land that size, losing himself will not be difficult; nor will it be unprecedented. America teems with lost souls who rove its emptiness, who love its emptiness. Perhaps among them, among a secret sub-nation of nobodies, he will find fellowship and a home.

As for so many other people, *this* country is used up for him. Dried out. Husked. As for so many other people, there is nothing here for him any more except years of work, a brief retirement, and an unremarked death. This country has grown mean in spirit. This country has lost nearly eveything it used to have and has become fiercely, greedily protective of the little it has left. This country, fearing the future, has turned its eyes firmly on the past. This country is no longer a home to its inhabitants but a museum of better days.

A voice that manages to sound bored even though it is only a recording announces the name of the approaching station twice. The train slows and comes to a halt, carriage banging into carriage like a queue of cartoon elephants butting up against one another's behinds. A scrawny girl in torn jeans and an engulfing anorak enters the carriage. She ambles along the aisle and plumps herself down in the seat next to a matronly woman. By means of a snort and a peremptory flap of her gossip magazine, the woman conveys to the girl that there are plenty of other perfectly good seats available, but the girl is not intimidated. She does not move, merely looks sullen and cunning.

Frank, feeling a familiar prickling at the nape of his neck, watches.

Sure enough, the train has hardly begun to move again when the girl's hand sneaks across the chair arm towards the clasp of the matronly woman's handbag. The girl's face remains a slack mask of indifference, her bored gaze elsewhere. She is good, Frank will grant her that. She has learned her job well, and probably the hard way, from beatings she has received when her fingers have not been nimble enough or her feet fleet enough. He knows what she is after, too. Sell a Days card on the black market and you will be eating well for a couple of weeks. (Sell one to an undercover police officer and you will be eating prison food for a couple of years.)

Peeking surreptitiously over the top edge of his newspaper, he follows the progress of the theft. The girl's hand, as it steathily undoes the handbag clasp and delves in, seems not to belong to her. It seems to be operating of its own accord, an independent, spider-like entity. The matronly woman remains unaware that her handbag is being rifled, its contents being blind-assessed by expert fingertips. She is completely absorbed in the article she is reading and in the hangnail she is doggedly chewing.

Frank waits until the girl's hand emerges. There! A glimmer of silvery-grey plastic flashing across the chair-arm, vanishing almost the instant it appears.

Frank stands up, sets his newspaper down in his seat, strides across the aisle, grasps a handstrap, and bends down over the girl, fixing her with his grey gaze.

'Put it back,' he says.

She looks at him blankly; in that blankness, defiance.

'I'm giving you one chance to put it back. Otherwise I pull the communication cord and summon the transport police, and you can explain to them what this woman's Days card is doing in your pocket.'

At that, the matronly woman frowns. 'Are you talking about *my* Days card?'

'Well?' says Frank to the girl, not breaking eye-contact.

She continues to glare back at him, then slowly lowers her head and sighs. Reaching into her pocket, she produces the card.

'S'only a crappy old Aluminium anyway.'

The woman gasps, although it is unclear whether this is in surprise at the sight of her card in the girl's hand or in mortification at the broadcasting of her status as the holder of the lowest denomination of Days account. She snatches the card off the girl and hastily thrusts it back into her handbag.

The train is slowing. The name of the next station is announced twice.

'Get off here,' says Frank, stepping back.

The girl gets up and hipsways along the aisle towards the nearest door, tossing her hair.

'And you're just going to let her walk away like that?' the woman demands of Frank. 'She stole my card. She should be arrested. Stop her!' She addresses herself to the whole carriage. 'Somebody stop her!'

No one makes a move.

'You got your card back,' Frank says. 'If you want her arrested so badly, stop her yourself.'

The doors open and, insolent to the last, the girl gives Frank and the woman a cocky little wave before alighting.

'Well!' the woman exclaims.

Frank heads back to his seat. The doors close and the train begins to pick up speed. A sudden lurch catches him off-balance and he sits down heavily, crushing his newspaper. He slides the paper out from under his backside and smoothes it flat on his lap. Before he resumes reading, he glances back at the matronly woman.

She is staring at him, shaking her head. Only after she feels he has been exposed to enough of her scorn does she turn back to her magazine and her hangnail.

No, there really is nothing for him here.

3

Pride: one of the Seven Deadly Sins

7.24 a.m.
Linda Trivett has been lying awake since shortly after five, watching the glow that frames the bedroom curtains brighten. It is too late now to pretend that she is going to go back to sleep. She is far too excited for that, anyway. In fact, she did not think she was going to get off to sleep at all last night and took a couple of pills to help her, little expecting them to work, but they did. Gordon, not surprisingly, needed no pharmaceutical assistance. As if it were just any other evening, he closed the book Linda had borrowed for him from the library (a self-help manual on assertiveness) after, as usual, managing less than a page of it, then set the book down on the bedside table, placed his spectacles on top, turned out the bedside light, rolled over, and started snoring almost straight away.

He is still snoring now, a grating suck-and-snort rhythm that Linda has almost, but not quite, trained herself to ignore. Lying there with a pillow bunched up under his head, a lock of his thin, sandy hair snagged on one eyebrow and a line of drool leaking from his slack mouth on to the pillowcase, he looks like a child. Sleep has eased years from his face.

Linda, experiencing a twinge of tenderness – but not love; she knows Gordon too well to feel love for him – reaches over and gently brushes the lock of hair back into place.

She climbs out of bed carefully so as not to disturb him, even though it would take a near-miss with a Howitzer to wake Gordon once he slips into REM. Putting on a velour dressing gown over her nightdress, she goes down to the kitchen and makes herself a cup of tea.

She can scarcely believe that today has finally arrived. She has been looking forward to this morning ever since, just over a week ago, she and Gordon learned by post that their application for a Days account had been accepted and that their Silver card would be arriving later that same day. Linda cancelled her hairdressing appointments and stayed home just so that she could be there to greet the courier when he came. *That* was an event to set the neighbours' tongues wagging: a Days courier pulling up in front of their house, resting his motorbike on its kickstand, unbuttoning the holster on his sidearm and with wary glances to the left and right walking up the garden path to knock on the front door and hand over the bulky, securely wrapped parcel he was carrying in the pouch slung over his shoulder. Linda saw net curtains twitch all along the street as she signed for the package and the courier strode back to his bike, doing up the chin-strap of his half-white, half-black helmet.

How she managed to hold off opening the parcel until Gordon came home from work Linda has no idea. Her self-control astounded her, and disappointed Margie and Pat and Bella, all of whom dropped by that day on various pretexts, hoping to catch a glimpse of an honest-to-goodness Days Silver. Margie and her husband had applied for an Aluminium and were still waiting to hear if they had been accepted, so she was the one who stared at the package with the greatest envy.

'A Silver,' she sighed. 'We'll never manage Silver on Tim's salary.'

It occurred to Linda that on the amount the packing plant paid Tim they would be lucky if they could manage Aluminium. It was a touch smug of her to think that, perhaps, but if she couldn't be smug then, when could she?

She said, 'Well, the bank did give Gordon a small pay-rise recently, and add to that what I get from my hairdressing . . .' She shrugged, as if that was all there was to obtaining a Days Silver.

It wasn't. Her shrug belied five years of struggle, of hard graft, of sacrifice and self-denial and self-discipline, of pennies pinched and corners cut and weekends worked. Five years of clothes mended to last beyond their natural lifespan, of evenings spent in instead of being enjoyed out, of winters endured with the thermostat turned down low, of Christmases without a tree or decorations and with only the most modest of gifts exchanged. Five years of repeatedly postponing the decision to have children, children being such a financial liability. Five years, until she and Gordon had at last scraped together the minimum collateral required to qualify for a Silver. (They could, of course, have opened an Aluminium account as soon as the new grade was introduced, but Linda decided they should continue saving up for the Silver because a Silver was what they had set their hearts on and, more to the point, an Aluminium was common, in both senses of the word.)

And was it worth it? Of course it was! Anything was worth the moment she and Gordon sat down together, tore away the parcel's plain brown wrapping, and took out a Days catalogue and a slim envelope.

The catalogue was vast, as thick as three telephone directories, with the edges of its onionskin-thin pages colour-coded in six rainbow bands, one for each of the six shop floors still in service, Red to Indigo.

Gordon straight away began leafing through it. Linda, meanwhile, carefully slit open the envelope with a kitchen knife, delved in, and extracted a Days Silver.

A Days Silver with their names on it in embossed capitals.

The ecstasy she felt then as she held the card in her hands, angling it from side to side and watching the light flash across its surface and across the ridges of the letters that spelled out GORDON & LINDA TRIVETT – oh yes, any amount of hardship was worth *that*.

She proposed that they visit the gigastore the very next day, but Gordon pointed out that, until they had signed and returned the disclaimer form enclosed with the card and had received acknowledgement of its receipt from the store, they were still not permitted to pass through the doors of Days.

He read out the form aloud, mumbling as he skated over paragraphs of dense legal jargon, which he promised to look at more closely later. Basically the form seemed to be saying that Days could not and would not accept liability for anything that might happen to the Trivetts while they were on the premises, and that should the Trivetts break any of the rules mentioned 'heretofore and herein' they would not be in a position to seek indemnity or reimbursement from the store.

Linda listened patiently but none too attentively and, as soon as Gordon finished reading, signed her name next to his on the dotted line at the bottom of the form with a thrilled, quivering hand.

The next morning she posted off the form, along with the passport-sized photographs of herself and Gordon required for security purposes. The acknowledgement slip came back two days later.

That was last Saturday morning, and the moment the acknowledgement slip arrived, Linda suggested to Gordon that they visit the store right then. If they left immediately, they could be there by opening time. Gordon said he wasn't ready. He complained of a headache. He had, he said, had a hard week. And besides, he had heard stories about Days on a Saturday. Stories about packed floors and wrestling crowds, scuffles and riots and even deaths.

Linda replied that she had heard stories like that about Days on *every* day of the week, and had chosen to discount them as rumours, or at any rate exaggerations of the truth spread by people without Days accounts who are all too ready to condemn what they cannot have. But she had to admit that Gordon *did* look a little pained and weary, so she gave him the benefit of the doubt and proposed that they go to Days on Monday instead. Gordon pointed out that he couldn't afford to take a day off work, not if they were to maintain the level of income necessary to keep the use of the card, so therefore if they went, it would have to be on a Saturday or not at all. Linda replied that Saturdays were her busiest – and therefore most lucrative – hairdressing days, and that if *he* took a day off sick he got paid, whereas she did not. And anyway, had he not just objected to visiting Days on a Saturday on the grounds that it would be too dangerous? He couldn't have it both ways. Either they risked the Saturday crowds or they went on a weekday.

It occurred to her then, although she did not comment on it, that Gordon seemed to be making up excuses not to go at all. Surely he wasn't getting cold feet? After all this time and effort?

So she suggested Tuesday. She could, she thought, just about hold out till Tuesday.

Gordon, predictably, repeated his claim that he couldn't under any circumstances take a weekday off, to which Linda, her patience wearing thin, retorted that in that case she was going to go on her own. Much as she wanted Gordon to come with her on her first trip to Days, she simply could not wait until next Saturday.

That did the trick, as she had known it would. No way was Gordon going to let her loose in Days on her own with their card. He sighed and suggested a compromise: this coming Thursday.

And so Thursday it was, and Linda, magnanimous in victory, took her husband by the hand and, giving her best approximation of a knowing, lascivious grin, led him upstairs to the bedroom and there bestowed on him the Special Treat usually reserved for his birthday and Christmas Eve. And though the deed, as always, left a bad taste in her mouth (both figuratively and literally), it was worthwhile. When she returned from having rinsed out with mouthwash in the bathroom, Gordon was looking less defeated, more contented, as he lay flat out and naked on the bed.

And now, as she sits in the kitchen sipping her tea on this Thursday morning which she thought would never arrive, Linda feels like a child on Christmas Day. In about an hour she is going to call her scheduled two blue rinses and a demi-perm and tell them that Gordon has a virulent 'flu and that she feels she ought to stay home and look after him. Then she is going to call the bank and tell the manager the same story: Gordon will not be coming in today, the 'flu, probably that twenty-four-hour strain that has been doing the rounds, he should be fine by tomorrow if he stays home today and gets some rest. She would ask Gordon to make the call himself, but he is the world's worst liar and would only make a hash of it, umming and ahhing and interspersing his sentences with feeble, unconvincing coughs. Besides, coming from the concerned wife, the lie will possibly sound more authentic.

Gordon hasn't taken a day off sick in as long as Linda can remember, not even when he has genuinely been feeling under the weather. These days no job is safe, and even if, like Gordon, you work as a loan adviser at a small local branch of a large national bank – money-lending being one of the few growth industries left in these days of high unemployment and low income – missing a day can still mean the difference between employment and the dole queue. Not only that, but for the past few weeks Gordon has quietly been trying to curry the manager's favour. The assistant manager is leaving soon to take over the running of another branch, and Linda has her eyes firmly set on the vacated post for her husband. He, however, instead of simply going up to the manager and demanding the promotion (which he fully deserves), has adopted the tactic of working hard and waiting and hoping. No matter how many times Linda has told him that nothing comes to those who wait and hope, that at the very least he should be dropping hints, but that preferably he should just come right out with it and *ask*, he has so far failed to pluck up the courage to do anything so forceful and positive. He would much rather believe that his diligence will be noted and duly rewarded. The poor, deluded innocent.

The Days catalogue is lying opposite Linda on the kitchen table. She heaves it towards her, marvelling yet again at the size of it. It needs to be this large, since it purports to list, and in many instances depict, every single item available at Days.

Every single item? Linda, in spite of herself, finds the claim hard to swallow. Days is supposed to be able to sell you anything you can possibly want, anything in the entire world. That is the store's motto, which can be found on the cover of the catalogue beneath the name of the store and its famous logo, in small type: 'If it can be sold, it will be bought, and if it can be bought, it will be sold.' That is the principle on which Septimus Day founded the store all those years ago, and the pledge which Days upholds to this day. (Linda has read the potted history of the store on the inside front cover.) But how can a catalogue, even one as immense as this, contain *everything*, every piece of merchandise in existence? It just isn't possible. Is it?

In the week that she has had the catalogue Linda has been able to peruse less than a quarter of it, but she has managed to pick out a number of items she would like to buy. She hoists the huge tome open and flips through to a section she has bookmarked with a slip of paper. Ties. Dozens of men's ties blaze up at her from a photo spread that illustrates just some of the thousands of items of men's neck apparel listed on adjacent pages. Linda has circled a dark green silk kipper with a repeating pattern of coins and made a note of its serial number. Gordon needs to jazz up his image. When it comes to clothing, his penchant for the plain and the simple is all very well, but a bit of excitement, a dash of colour to offset his sartorial conservatism, would not go amiss. She may never be able to persuade him to wear, say, a bright shirt, but she might just manage to get him to try out an interesting tie, particularly if, like the one she has chosen, it has a thematic connection to his job. And who knows, perhaps the tie will alert the branch manager to a facet of Gordon's character that Linda has for a long time known exists, or at any rate believed exists, or in fact (let's be honest here) *hoped* exists. She is sure Gordon used to be an exciting person once. When they were courting, and in the early days of their marriage, he was bold, spontaneous, impulsive, even dashing . . . wasn't he? Surely he was. And still is. It is simply that over the years this side of him has become buried beneath an accretion of responsibilities and concerns, like a ship's hull becoming encrusted and weighed down with barnacles. Now that they have their Days card, that is about to change. Everything is about to change.

She flips on through the catalogue to the Clocks section, where she finds another item which she is fully intent on buying today.

In itself the carriage clock is nothing special. A reproduction of an antique, its brass casing boasts sections of Gothic filigree laced over panels of dark blue glass, and instead of feet the clock rests on the backs of four winged cherubs, whose stubby arms hold trumpets to their lips and whose cheeks bulge with the effort of blowing. These are nice enough features, but there are many other more ornate and more beautiful examples of horology on display. However, the clock happens to be an exact copy of one that Linda's parents once owned, an heirloom that had been passed down the distaff side of the family, from Linda's great-grandmother to her grandmother to her mother. It used to sit in pride of place on the mantelshelf in the living room, and her mother devotedly used to keep it wound up and, twice a year, give it a thorough polish to bring up the gleam of the brass. It was, perhaps, the most elegant thing the family owned, certainly the object with the most sentimental value . . . until the day Linda's father saw to it that Linda never got to inherit it.

The moment she came across the picture of the reproduction clock in the Days catalogue, Linda understood that she had been offered a second chance to possess something which she had been deprived of by an act of cheap, casual malice while she was still a child. It was almost as if the clock had been waiting in the catalogue's pages for her to discover it, and as soon as she laid eyes on it she knew it had to be hers. She had no choice in the matter. And though she has earmarked several other items for purchase today, even if she buys nothing else, she is determined that she will not leave Days without the clock, for her, and the tie, for Gordon.

It is 7.37 according to the digital timer on the oven. In a few minutes she will go back upstairs and wake Gordon, but for now she is going to enjoy her tea, the peace and quiet, and the sweet tingle of anticipation in her belly.

Today, she is confident, is going to be the greatest day of her life.

4

The Seven Wonders of the Ancient World: the Egyptian pyramids, the Hanging Gardens of Babylon, the Temple of Artemis at Ephesus, the statue of Zeus by Phidias at Olympia, the Mausoleum at Halicarnassus, the Colossus of Rhodes, and the lighthouse on the island of Pharos at Alexandria

7.37 a.m.
'Days Plaza North-West. Days Plaza North-West.'

Frank clambers to his feet, folds and pockets his newspaper, and makes his way down the carriage with his empty coffee cup in one hand, his body angled against the train's deceleration.

Out on the platform he meticulously disposes of the cup in a litter bin. No one else has disembarked except him. It is too early for shoppers and too early for most employees. On the other side of the platform a pair of janitors are waiting for the train going the opposite way. The backs of their green overalls are emblazoned with Days logos the size of dinner plates. They talk quietly and sombrely together. As Frank trots down the stairs to the ticket hall he recognises a Days night watchman slogging up the other way. If the night watchman is as tired as he looks, it has been a long night indeed.

Exiting the station on to Days Plaza, Frank is hit full in the face by a powerful gust of wind that momentarily staggers him. The store generates its own microclimate, its two-and-a-half-kilometre flanks funnelling the air currents that swirl around it into long sheeting vortices that collide at each corner and explode outwards, spiralling across the plaza in all directions, making the ornamental shrubberies shudder and the fountains' plumes bend sideways and overshoot their bowls.

Frank squares his jaw, lowers his head like a bull, and sets off across the plaza. His coat tails whip and flap about his legs and his hair is threshed this way and that. The gusts may not be cold but they are insistent and mean. The plaza's trees have grown up sickly and stunted as a result of their constant bullying.

There are train stations at all four corners of Days Plaza and a bus route runs around its circumference, with a single stop midway along each edge. This means that the shopper arriving by public transport has to walk at least half a kilometre to reach the store. The shopper travelling by taxi or private car is better served. Taxi-only approach roads lead up to turning circles outside the store's four entrances, while beneath the plaza lie seven storeys of subterranean car park with lifts that emerge in the entrance halls. The logic behind such an arrangement is faultless, if you have the mind of a retailer. Shoppers who know they are going to have a carry their goods home by hand will ration their purchases, concentrating on smaller, lighter and generally less expensive goods. The inconvenient location of the train stations and bus stops encourages them to use cars and taxis instead. Cars and taxis have plenty of room inside to store purchases. And car parks are, of course, an additional source of revenue.

Frank walks alongside the approach road to Days with his eyes averted, not just to shield them from the stinging particles of grit that are being tossed about by the wind but so that he won't have to look at the building. Even so, he can sense it looming ahead of him, a mountain made of brick. The plaza seems to slope down towards it, as though the weight of the world's first and (reputedly) foremost gigastore has warped the surrounding surface of the planet, although it is possible that this is simply some architectural conceit intended to make your footsteps quicken the closer you come to the store.

As Frank nears the north-western corner of Days, he at last dares to look up at the building that has dominated his life for thirty-three years. Its perspectives are dizzying, but what always strikes him is not so much the gigastore's size as the quantity of bricks used in its construction. There must be billions of them, and each was laid by hand, each individually trowelled with mortar and positioned by a workman who patiently pieced together his segment of the puzzle, making his unacknowledged contribution to the enormity of the whole. Time, wind and weather have pitted and pocked the bricks' surfaces, and the mortar that binds them is crumbling, but Days still stands, the dream of one man, the handiwork of thousands.

Window-shoppers are huddled, as always, one deep, occasionally two deep, beneath the huge display windows, long straggling lines of human beings running unbroken except at the loading bays, which are located midway along each edge of the building. Most of them are awake now.

Some are picking at pieces of sandwich and morsels of pie that they have hoarded overnight. (Each evening, charity workers come and distribute food, water and soup among the window-shoppers, a practice the Days administration tolerates without condoning.) Others are going through their personal exercise routines, flexing the night's stiffness out of their joints. A few have taken to the shrubberies to relieve themselves, and the rest are staking out their patches, unfurling moth-eaten blankets in front of their favourite windows and weighing down the corners with bulging, tattered Days carrier bags. Nearer to nine o'clock, unless the sky clouds over and it looks like rain, more window-shoppers – ones who have homes – will arrive, but by then the best places will have been taken. These other window-shoppers bring picnics, chairs, tables, families, friends with them to watch the displays, but they are not hardcore, all-weather devotees like those who spend their entire lives in the vicinity of Days, who eat and sleep in the gigastore's shadow. Tradition has it that window-shoppers are former customers who for one reason or other have been banned from the store, but this has never conclusively been proved.

At present, each window is draped inside with a pair of heavy green velvet curtains which sport the black and white halves of the Days logo on either side of their adjoining hems.

As Frank arrives at the corner of the building, a few of the window-shoppers look up, nod to him, and look away again. They recognise him not by his face – few people remember Frank's face – but by his demeanour. They recognise him as one of their own, one of the overlooked, the disregarded, the discounted.

He closes his nose to the smell the wind wafts his way, the reek of unwashed clothing and bodies.

A pair of guards wearing quilted jackets and fur-lined caps with Days logos on the ear-flaps are stationed at the top of the shallow flight of steps that leads up to the North-West Entrance. Hopping up the steps, Frank greets them both, showing them his Iridium. One of the guards takes the card and peers at it, at the same time adjusting the weight of the rifle strapped to his shoulder. There is no need for a visual check on the card, but he examines both sides of it just the same, several times, until, satisfied that it doesn't *look* like a fake (as if a skilful forgery would be detectable to the human eye), he turns and swipes it through the slot of the lock unit set into the frame of the pair of doors behind him. He punches in a seven-digit code on the lock unit keypad, and seven bolts within the doors shoot back in quick succession from bottom to top, their ascending clanks like notes in a rising scale. The handle on the left-hand door is a black semicircle, on the right-hand door a white semicircle. Their verticals meet flush when the doors are closed. Grasping the left-hand handle, the guard hauls back on it.

Frank nods his thanks, takes back his card, and steps through the open doorway. The door is closed behind him, and the bolts slide to in reverse order, descending the scale.

5

Seven Names of God: the seven Judaic names for the Divinity – El,
Elohim, Adonia, YHWH, Ehyeh-Asher-Ehyeh, Shaddai, and Zeba'ot

8.00 a.m.

Immediately north of the glass dome on top of Days lies a flat-roofed,
one-storey penthouse complex. At the southern end is a heptagonal
room joined to the rest of the complex by one of its seven points.
Within the heptagonal room resides the store's brain: the Boardroom.

Inside the Boardroom, a circular table seven metres in diameter sits
at the centre of a spread of lush dollar-green carpet. One half of the
table is ash, the other half ebony, and situated at one end of the join
between the two halves, recessed snugly into the wood, are a computer
terminal and a telephone.

Seven chairs are positioned equidistantly around the table. Each is
different and reflects the character and disposition of the person who
regularly occupies it. One is an ornate gilded throne; another is a
wing-backed armchair comfortably upholstered with padded vermil-
ion leather; a third is designed along Art Nouveau lines with a narrow
seat and a straight back composed of staggered rectangles in the
manner of a Frank Lloyd Wright window; and so on.

At eight o'clock, the venetian blinds that cover the triptych of
windows at the Boardroom's southern end rise automatically, furling
upwards to reveal an unhindered view of the base of the rotating
dome. Currently the dome's clear half fills the windows, although a
crescent-shaped sliver of its dark half is visible in one corner and will
encroach more and more on the clear portion as the day wears on.

Opposite lie four oak-panelled walls, completing the heptagon. On
one there hangs a gilt-framed, lifesize portrait of none other than the
founder of Days, Septimus Day himself. Septimus long ago passed
through life's great checkout, but still he glares imperiously down on
the Boardroom and all that takes place within it with his good right eye
glittering, its patched partner menacing. Anyone who knew Old Man

Day thinks the artist has captured his likeness very well indeed. Chillingly well.

Set into the adjacent wall at chest height is a brass panel sporting a hinged knife switch of the kind Victor Frankenstein throws in old horror movies in order to animate his Creature, except that this one is seven times as large and requires a ceramic handle the size of a baseball bat to operate it. At present the switch stands upright in the Off position with the detached handle clipped next to it on the panel.

Each of the two remaining oak-panelled walls carries a bank of sixteen monitors arranged in a four-by-four grid. Their screens show computer-generated composites of the Days logo set against a dollar-green background.

A balding, prim-looking man in a butler's livery of shirtsleeves and a horizontally pinstriped waistcoat opens the pair of large doors that bridge the apex of the angle formed by the two monitor-bearing walls. Turning around, he grasps the handle of a serving trolley the size of a hospital gurney and hauls it backwards into the Boardroom. Seven heavy silver salvers press the trolley's wheels deep into the carpet, making it an effort to pull.

Reaching the centre of the room, the manservant leaves the trolley and goes round the table moving each chair one place clockwise, setting its feet in the indentations left by the previous chair. Then he returns to the trolley and repeats the journey, depositing a salver on the table in front of each seat. This second circuit of the table completed, he guides the trolley out of the room. He returns a minute later with another trolley, this one bearing a silver teapot, a bone-china teapot, three stainless steel coffee pots (one of which contains hot chocolate), a tall glass jug of orange juice, a bottle of gin, a bottle of tonic water, lemon slices on a dish, and an ice-bucket carved from a solid chunk of malachite, plus assorted cups, saucers and tumblers. Once again he circumnavigates the table, placing the appropriate beverages in front of the appropriate chairs. If he experiences a twinge of disapproval as he sets the gin, tonic, lemon and ice before the gilded throne, he hides it well behind the pinched, impassive mask of a family retainer of long standing who has learned over the years not to betray a hint of emotion either in or out of the presence of his employers.

The manservant, whose name is Perch, pauses to take out a gold fob watch. He flips up the lid, nods approvingly at the time, returns the watch to his waistcoat pocket, and wheels the second trolley out of the Boardroom.

A short corridor takes him past the head of a spiral staircase and along to the kitchen. He parks the trolley, goes over a couple of the finer points of the lunchtime menu with the chef, then makes his way on long, soft-stalking legs into an adjoining chamber which he has come to consider as his office, although it is also a repository for all the silverware – the cutlery, snuff boxes, cuspidors and humidors – which it is his duty to polish to brilliance once a month. He seats himself at a small oaken desk on the blotter of which rests an intercom fashioned as a replica of an antique black Bakelite telephone, complete with rotary dial, plaited brown flex and clawed brass cradle. He lifts the receiver and dials 1.

The line chirrups a few times, then there is a click of connection.

'Master Mungo,' says the old retainer.

'Morning, Perch,' comes the reply. There is the sound of wind and lapping water. Mungo is out by the rooftop pool.

'Good morning to you, sir. Breakfast is served.'

'Another couple of lengths and I'll be along.'

'Very good, sir.'

Perch taps on the cradle and dials 2.

'Master Chas.'

A young woman answers. 'Chas is in the shower.'

'Who is this?'

'This is Bliss. Who are *you*?'

'Madam, you should not be using Master Chas's intercom.'

'Chas told me to pick it up,' the girl replies tartly.

'Then would you kindly inform Master Chas, madam, that breakfast is served.'

'Okey-dokey. Will do.'

'Thank you.'

'No trouble. 'Bye.'

Perch taps the cradle again and dials 3.

'Master Wensley.'

A sleep-furred voice responds. 'God, is that the time already, Perch? I'll be up there as quick as I can. Keep my devilled kidneys warm, will you? There's a good fellow.'

Perch dials 4.

'Master Thurston.'

'Already here, Perch.'

'My apologies. I didn't hear you come up the stairs.'

'That's all right. These eggs are tasty.'

'I'm most gratified, sir.'

'Pass my compliments on to the catering staff.'

'That I will, sir. I'm sure they will be most gratified, too.'

Perch dials 5.

'Master Frederick.'

'How's it going, Perch?'

'Well, sir.'

'Papers arrived yet?'

'I shall check, sir. If they have come, I shall have them waiting for you at your position.'

'Great stuff. See you in a mo.'

Perch dials 6.

'Master Sato.'

'Perch.'

'Breakfast is served.'

'Of course. Thank you.'

'Thank *you*, sir.'

Perch taps the cradle, hesitates, then, drawing on all his reserves of self-control (and they are deep), dials 7.

The line chirrups for the best part of two minutes and no one picks up. Master Sonny is either deliberately ignoring the ringing of his portable intercom or incapable of hearing it. Perch confidently suspects the latter. In fact, he would not be surprised if Master Sonny were presently lying on the floor of his bathroom, curled around the pedestal of a vomit-spattered lavatory, comatose. It would not be the first time Perch has gone downstairs to wake him and found him in such a position.

Replacing the receiver, Perch permits himself the merest twitch of a smile. The prospect of rousing Master Sonny from his alcohol-induced stupor fills him with no small pleasure.

Perhaps the glass-of-cold-water-in-the-face method again . . .

6

Seventh Heaven: a state of serene, transcendent bliss

8.01 a.m.
The quiet half-hour.

Over the sea-green marble floor of the entrance hall Frank goes, over the smooth opal-and-onyx cobbles of the Days logo mosaic, past banks of lifts waiting with their doors open, past conga-lines of wire shopping trolleys, past parked rows of motorised shopping carts, beneath an unlit chandelier like a waterfall captured in glass, towards the parade of arches that afford access to the store proper.

He is trying to work out how many times he has crossed this hall and at the same time trying to remember when he started trampling the jewelled logo beneath his feet instead of skirting it respectfully as most people do. The answer to the first question runs into so many thousands that he swiftly and incredulously abandons the calculation. The answer to the second is easier: he started walking over the logo instead of around it the day he realised that he could, that there was no specific rule against doing so, that all that kept people off the circle of precious stones was their belief in the sanctity of wealth – a belief he had ceased to share, or, more accurately, realised had never been part of his personal credo.

This was around the time when he first started to notice that he had lost his reflection. The loss was so gradual, in fact, it was only in retrospect that he realised that it had occurred at all. Every day he would look in the mirror and a little bit more of himself would be absent, and every day he would dismiss this as a trick of the light or the mind – to acknowledge it as an empirical fact would have been to entertain madness. Eventually, however, the truth was impossible to deny. He was forgetting what he looked like and who he was. He was slipping away, slowly, in increments.

The day that he became aware of this was the same day that he dared to set foot on the jewelled mosaic, and also the same day that the idea

34

of leaving Days first stirred in the furthest reaches of his mind. He can almost pin down the genesis of his decision to quit to the moment he first rested his right foot on the tip of the opal semicircle and was not fried to a crisp by a lightning bolt from Mammon's fingertip.

Arriving at the arches, Frank halts, takes out his wallet, and yet again unsheathes his Iridium. Each arch is fitted with a set of vertical stainless steel bars two centimetres thick that slot snugly into the lintel. The uprights between the arches have terminals mounted on them at waist level. The terminals are conical, with oval screens and chrome shells. Each invites Frank in large green letters to insert his card into its slot. He does so with the one nearest to him, and the screen swiftly bitmaps a Days logo, then runs a green message across it:

> CARD INCORRECTLY INSERTED
> PLEASE TRY AGAIN

Frank removes the ejected card, flips it over so that its logo is facing up, and reinserts it, tutting at his own carelessness.

A new message appears:

> HUBBLE FRANCIS J.
> EMPLOYEE #1807-93N
> ACCOUNT STATUS: IRIDIUM
> CARD NO.: 579 216 347 1592

This is erased and replaced with:

> LOG-ON TIME: 8.03 A.M.
> HAVE A GOOD DAY'S WORK, MR HUBBLE

The card is ejected again, and the stainless steel bars of the arch to the left of the terminal retract upwards with a sharp pneumatic burp. He passes through, returning the card to his wallet. He knows metal detectors are scanning him, but as he has nothing metallic on him larger than his house keys and his fillings, alarms do not whoop. The bars descend again smoothly and swiftly like mercury rushing down transparent pipes.

The quiet half-hour.

As far as Frank is concerned the time between now and 8.30 is sacred.

The store is still, its overhead lights at half-power. The night watch-men have gone off duty and the shop assistants have not yet arrived. Days is neither closed nor open but somewhere in between, in a semi-lit limbo of transition. Neither one thing nor the other, neither darkened and empty nor bright and bustling, the place is perhaps at its most honest. Everything it has to offer is laid bare beneath the dimmed bulbs. Nothing is hidden.

If you enter Days by the North-West Entrance, the first department you find yourself in is Cosmetics. As Frank begins to cross the department, he is aware of making a mental note of his impressions, recording what he is seeing as though he is a human video-camera. Frank the man is at one remove from Frank the creature of habit, who would normally stroll through the quiet half-hour in a meditative state, letting his thoughts flow and free-associate. He is observing himself like an anthropologist studying a primitive tribesman. What is he doing now? He is passing between a display of skin-care products in pastel-coloured packaging and a range of lipstick testers racked in individual cubbyholes like miniature missiles in silos. What is he thinking? He is thinking how large this room is – like all the departments in Days, a little over 200 metres long on each side – and yet how cramped it feels, and how the counters, laden to above eye-level, form a honeycomb maze in which it only takes a moment to lose all sense of direction. How does he feel? He is remembering his first day at Days and the awe that filled him as he stepped through one of the arches with his card still in his hand – back then it was a Platinum – to find himself actually on the floor of the world's first and (he was thrilled to think) foremost gigastore. He still feels a trace of that awe now but it is no more than a sedimentary deposit, like limescale, that would be more trouble than it is worth to scrub away. Mostly he just feels a kind of silent emptiness.

All of which he dutifully files away for the benefit of the Frank Hubble of the future, for the man he is going to be as of tomorrow, the secret wanderer adrift in the immensity of America.

From Cosmetics, he has the choice of going either south through the Perfumery or east through Leather Goods. A pungent miasma of 10,000 different musks hangs perpetually over the Perfumery, strong enough to make your eyes water. The combined stench of hectares of cured cowhide in Leather Goods is marginally less stomach-turning, so Frank goes east, then jinks south into the Bakery. Deliveries of fresh bread have not yet arrived but the yeasty aroma of yesterday's batch still lingers in the air. Chilled cabinets loaded with pastries, pies, croissants and bagels hum with full-bellied delight.

The next department is the Global Delicatessen. The Global Delicatessen is divided into subsections, each of which sells the specialities of a different country's cuisine from a counter decked out in stereotypically traditional style. For example, chapatis, samosas and bhajis can be found within a scale-model Taj Mahal made of painted chipboard, while pastas of every imaginable shape and colour are stored in jars in a mock-up of a room from a Florentine palazzo, complete with peeling stucco walls and exposed brickwork. An ersatz Bavarian market square offers sauerkraut and dozens of varieties of bratwurst, a *faux* French village square with boxed orange-trees and a *bar-tabac* backdrop has stalls where browsers may sample escargots, bouillabaisse and onion soup before buying, and trestle tables in a pseudo Greek fishing village groan with hummus, baklava, cabanos sausage and a wide assortment of olives – black, green, stuffed, dried. And so on. At opening time, each subsection will be staffed by shop assistants decked out in the appropriate national costume.

To the east lies the malodorous hell that is the Fromagerie, but Frank steers well clear of the connecting passageway and continues south through the Global Delicatessen to the Ice Cream Parlour. The air in the Ice Cream Parlour is chilled by over three hundred glass-lidded freeze cabinets. They contain tubs of ice cream that run the gamut of flavours from the traditional (vanilla, chocolate, strawberry) to the unlikely (rhubarb crumble with custard, spearmint'n'saveloy, lox and cream cheese, tapioca with a hint of violet), most of which are also available as frozen yoghurts, sorbets and granitas. Frank draws his overcoat tightly about himself and bustles through, his exhalations wisping behind him like a gossamer scarf.

One more department lies between him and the building's heart. The Confectionery Department is a sweet-toothed child's vision of heaven and an honest dentist's vision of hell. Candy canes reach to the ceiling, jar upon jar of foil-wrapped toffees and fudges line the walls, and pyramids of handmade truffles wait on refrigerated shelves to be selected, boxed and weighed. Fistfuls of lollipops sit on countertops like gaudy bunches of flowers, plaited lengths of liquorice wind around the cash registers like electrical cables, and sticks of Days-brand rock – half white, half black, with the name of the store running all the way through in lime green – glisten in their cellophane wrappers. Pear drops, acid drops and cough drops are available by the half-kilo. The polychromatic kaleidoscope of allsorts, jelly beans and dolly mixtures on display would give a chameleon a heart attack. There are butterscotch rectangles, nougat triangles and lumps of marzipan in every shape under the sun. There are gobstoppers, chews and mints from mild to infernal. And there is chocolate – chocolate of every shade from pitch black to milk white, with a hundred grades of brown in between. Bitter, sweet, bittersweet, studded with nuts, raisins, nuts *and* raisins, from cubes as small as dice to slabs as large as tombstones . . . There is so much sugar in the air, just inhaling could send you into a diabetic coma.

Beyond Confectionery, Frank arrives at his destination, the goal of his south-eastward trek through the store. It is the hoop that encircles the Menagerie. Each floor has one, a broad, annular esplanade that offers shoppers somewhere to sit and rest between purchases, and also provides a shortcut from one corner of the store to the other. Furnished with pine benches and potted plants, mainly philodendra and succulents, and floored with white marble, the hoops would appear to be oases of calm and repose amid the relentless, hectic sell-sell-sell of the departments. Restaurants and cafeterias reinforce this impression. It should be noted, however, that the benches are few and far between, that the service in the restaurants is swift and perfunctory, and that the snacks served in the cafeterias are, to put it mildly, inedible.

The Red Floor hoop is deserted. The entire atrium, all the way up to the great glass dome, is silent except for the rustle of foliage, a faint trickle of running water, and the occasional animal-cry, all from the Menagerie.

Frank crosses over to the parapet that runs around the hoop's inner edge, rests his forearms on the guardrail, and leans out. Craning his neck until his windpipe stands proud like a bent arm, his Adam's apple its elbow, he peers up at the dome some hundred and twenty metres above him.

The dome's gyration, like the wheeling of the stars across the sky, is too slow for the human eye to detect. Frank knows that its revolutions are cunningly geared so that, whatever the season, the unsmoked half is always aligned with the sun, but he has never been able to fathom why Old Man Day opted for this arrangement when a static and completely clear dome would have been far cheaper to construct and would do the job of illuminating the atrium just as well, if not better. Yes, the bicoloured dome acts like a giant logo, stamping the imprimature of Days on the entire building, and yes, as a technological achievement it is deserving of admiration, but as far as Frank is concerned all the dome's twenty-four-hour rotation does is serve as an unwelcome reminder of the incremental, inexorable passing of each day. And, according to the dome, every day is divided perfectly into equinoctial halves, twelve hours of light, twelve hours of darkness. According to the dome, every day is the same.

Frank lowers his head and looks across to the rising tiers of floor half a kilometre away, then down through the gauze of monofilament mesh and the gridwork of irrigation pipes to the Menagerie.

The Menagerie's canopy, which begins about five metres below where Frank is standing, is an undulating vista of palms with here and there a fern pushing up sharply between the fringed fronds. Bushy epiphytes cling to the trees' trunks, and in clearings Frank can make out orchids and bamboos clustering around their roots. The manmade tropical forest gives off a humid, steamy aroma, its jungle jade flecked with flickering leaf-shadows.

Over to the west, a macaque shrieks in the treetops. Something else closer to Frank replies with a series of stuttering laughs – *yak-yak-yak* – that develops into a full-throated whooping. The macaque offers its territorial argument again, and the whooping creatures falls into submissive silence. There is a flash of whirring scarlet between the leaves: a parrot darting from one branch to another. Something small like a rabbit skitters through the undergrowth. A big electric-blue butterfly comes bumbling up to the net, flaps stupidly against it for a while, then swirls back down into the green. A thousand other insects softly sing and trill, a high-pitched glee club that will, once the store opens, be swamped by the din of voices and footsteps. Frank half-closes his eyes and lets the Menagerie's soothing susurration fill his ears. This he *will* miss, no doubt about it. On many a morning, the prospect of these few brief ruminative moments spent gazing down on the Menagerie's canopy before the madness of the day begins has been the only reason he has been able to find to drag himself out of bed.

The Menagerie is neither zoo nor conservation project. It is, quite simply, an elaborate cage. Animals are shipped in from around the world on demand and stored in the Menagerie temporarily until their purchasers can make arrangements to have them picked up. The store's policy on selling wildlife displays a refreshing lack of zoological prejudice. It does not matter if an animal is on the endangered species list or as common as dandruff, if a customer desires it and has the wherewithal to pay for it, it can be his.

Nothing stays in the Menagerie for long. The macaque, for instance, will be gone by tomorrow. Later today, trained sales assistants will venture into the manmade jungle clad in protective gear and, toting tranquilliser-dart rifles, close in on the little monkey, put it to sleep, and present it in a cage to its new owner, an industrialist who wants to give his daughter an unusual pet as a gift for her thirteenth birthday. The Menagerie's only permanent residents are the insects, who form an integral part of its ecosystem. But since they breed quickly and are cheap to replace, they too are for sale.

In short, the Menagerie is just another department, like any in the store. Yet to Frank, who has spent his entire life as a city dweller, the Menagerie's lush green abundance is intoxicatingly alien, an exotic symphony of sight and sound and scent. Charged with secret life, the Menagerie is a city of Nature, where the bustle of industry goes on invisibly, and territory is claimed, and transients come and go, a daily round of business that carries on seemingly regardless of the store that encloses it.

Of course this autonomy is an illusion. The Menagerie is as dependent on Days to support it as Days is on the world outside. Without regular irrigation and climate control, the vegetation would die. Without the vegetation, the insects would die. Without the insects and vegetation, the smaller mammals would die. Without the smaller mammals, the reptiles and larger mammals would have nothing to hunt and eat while they waited to be recaptured and sent to their new homes; they would have to be fed directly by the sales assistants, and that would contradict the ethic behind the Menagerie. Old Man Day planted a jungle at the heart of his store for a reason: to symbolise the commerce of Nature, to show that preying and feeding on others is an accepted part of the natural order, perhaps even to justify the very foundation of Days. The Menagerie is a manifesto on a grand scale, a point lavishly made – and Frank knows this, and yet still it is more than metaphor to him. Somehow, with a gorgeous green eloquence, it speaks of truths that are not so easily interpreted. With the sighs of its flora and cries of its fauna it addresses a part of the soul not concerned with gaining and acquiring. After all these years, Frank still does not understand what the Menagerie is trying to say, but like a nursing infant who responds to the tone of his mother's voice, if not the sense of her words, he loves to listen all the same.

Through his serenely half-closed eyes Frank glimpses a white shape moving amid the blur of green. He inclines his head and focuses.

A white tiger has come stalking into a clearing fifteen metres below him and twenty metres away. A white tig*ress*, to be exact. She was captured in the dwindling Rewa forest of India only last week and is soon to be transferred to the private collection of a French rock star at a cost somewhere in the region of a million album sales.

A beautiful creature – her pelt spectrally pale between its black flashes, her eyes a light, lambent blue, her tail gently curved, uptilted and coat-hanger stiff – she walks with an unhurried grace on sinewy legs across the clearing to one of the several streams that meander through the Menagerie, pumped directly from the city's ring main. At its edge she stops, bends her head, and begins lapping languorously at the water with her thick pink tongue, pausing every so often to lick stray droplets from her whiskers and chin.

Frank watches her, transfixed. With her markings and colouring she is like some beast out of mythology, a ghost tiger whose ancestors doubtless inspired many a tall tale around the jungle campfire. Even the sight of her mundanely drinking water, her eyes slitted in contentment, sends chills up his spine. He wonders what it would be like to be standing down there beside her, to inhale her tiger smell and run his fingers over her glossy fur and feel the warmth and muscle of the living animal beneath.

Abruptly, the tigress breaks off from her drinking, lifts her head, and sniffs the air. Her pink nostrils gape and contract rapidly, opening and closing like a pair of tiny mouths, as her head bobs higher and higher, tracing the path of the scent, until, finally, she fixes her gaze on its source: Frank.

She stares at him without blinking. He stares back. She looks puzzled, and takes a few more deep, flaring sniffs. Her eyes narrow to azure almonds. Frank does not move.

The moment of contact stretches on, and on, and on.

8.16 a.m.
Meanwhile, up in the Boardroom, Thurston Day greets his older

brother Mungo and his younger brother Sato as they enter the room together. Neither is surprised to see Thurston already in his seat (a typist's chair with smooth-running castors and a fully adjustable, spine-sparing backrest). Thurston is usually first into the Boardroom even when it isn't his day of chairmanship, punctuality and punctiliousness being the principle character traits of Septimus Day's fourth son.

Thurston asks Mungo how his swim was, and the oldest Day brother runs a hand through his still-damp hair and replies that it was very pleasant indeed. A crisp morning, steam rising from the surface of the pool, twenty lengths instead of the usual fifteen. Thurston then asks Sato if he slept well, and Sato, folding his body like a praying mantis's forelegs into the tall, slender, Frank Lloyd Wright chair, thanks his brother for his kind enquiry and is delighted to be able to inform today's chairman that he enjoyed a very restful night's sleep indeed.

Satisfied, Thurston turns his attention back to the terminal at his elbow, which is displaying today's sales figures at the Unified Ginza Consortium in Tokyo, correct as of U.G.C. closing time, eight o'clock this morning.

Sato's movements are nimble and delicate as he pours himself a cup of jasmine tea from the bone china pot in front of him then removes the lid of the salver beside it to reveal a peeled hardboiled egg, a bowl of coleslaw, a plain roll, and a bowl of bean curd and fried seaweed. Of all the brothers, he is the one who has embraced the eastern side of their mixed Caucasian/Asiatic heritage. Mungo's breakfast is considerably heartier and more occidental. Along with a litre of orange juice in the glass jug, Perch has served him a rare rump steak, scrambled eggs, hash browns, four rashers of bacon, a pile of granary toast ten centimetres high (each slice lathered in crunchy peanut butter), a vanilla-flavoured protein shake, and, if Mungo is still hungry after all that, a bowl of muesli. Not surprisingly, Mungo is a robust figure. Swimming has broadened his shoulders to the width of the average doorway and lunchtime games of tennis and evening workouts in the brothers' private gym have toned his waist and legs. He exudes health from every pore of his taut, unpimpled skin.

Thurston, by comparison with his fitness-fanatic sibling, looks hunched, meek and anaemic. While he sports the brown eyes, glossy dark hair and olive-tinged complexion common to all the sons of Septimus Day, his jaw is narrow and his cheeks are hollow and his wrists are so thin that Mungo could encircle them both at once with his thumb and forefinger. Thurston wears small round spectacles and favours high collars and thin, plain ties. But he is not as timid as he appears. When it comes to business matters, none of the Day brothers can match Thurston for aggression or ruthlessness. Thurston closing a deal is like a hawk swooping on its prey. Equally, if the wholesale cost of coffee beans, say, rises a couple of per cent, Thurston will be the first to suggest that Days hikes up the retail price twice that amount. Conscience is a weakness in any businessman, and Thurston cannot abide weakness.

Sato, though ascetic in his tastes, favouring that which is elegant yet simple, shares his brothers' passion for increased profits and their love of the wealth generated by the massive store beneath them. For Sato, however, it is not what money can buy that attracts him. Someone with his income could own anything they wanted, but Sato prefers his life to be as uncluttered with possessions as possible. Rather, it is money in the abstract that he finds enthralling. The principle of money. The theory of it. Sato lives for the accumulated sales total at the end of the week, which is also, by happy coincidence, his day of chairmanship. Come Saturday evening, as he sits in front of the terminal watching takings from every department float up on the screen, Sato is in his personal nirvana. Even if he cross-references the weekly total against those of the other gigastores and finds that once again the store's figures have fallen well short of those achieved by its international rivals, a league table habitually headed by the Great Souq in Abu Dhabi and Blumberg's, N.Y., he is never annoyed or envious, merely fascinated by the divergent differences. Money is merely numbers to Sato, and numbers obey the laws of mathematics, and the laws of mathematics constitute a system as elegant and as simple as you could wish for.

As Sato takes the first few nibbles of his seaweed and bean curd, using the chopsticks provided by Perch, and Mungo launches ferociously into his feast with fork and serrated knife, Fred arrives, clutching an armful of newspapers taken from Perch, whom he happened to intercept at the top of the spiral staircase. There is nothing Fred likes more than his morning papers (three tabloids, two broadsheets, and a couple of internationals). Like his brothers, he seldom leaves the premises. The Boardroom, the roof with its amenities – swimming pool, tennis court, jogging track, paved garden – and the Violet Floor where each brother has a private apartment, constitute the limits of their existence, and while they do venture down on to the shop floor occasionally and off the premises *very* occasionally, they prefer to stay within those limits. It is safer that way.

Fred's morning papers are his lifeline to the outside world, a tube through which he can breathe air from outside and so avoid being suffocated by his circumstances. Undoubtedly he is happy with his life and would not swap being a co-owner of Days for anything, but without his newspapers and, in the evenings, his cable television, the cloistered existence he and his brothers lead would surely drive him nuts.

Fred bids his three siblings good morning and takes his seat between Thurston and Sato, dumping the pile of newspapers on the table in front of him. His chair suggests a perhaps unconscious desire for freedom. It is a folding canvas chair of the type traditionally used by explorers and movie directors. Fred's longish hair, stubbled chin and gaudy Aztec-patterned shirt reflect the same desire. His breakfast, however, is pure childhood comfort food: pre-sugared corn flakes, hot chocolate and toast with butter and strawberry jam.

Fred opens one of his tabloids and is just starting to peruse the gossip columns when Wensley waddles in. Wensley has dressed hastily in his anxiety to eat his breakfast before it goes cold. One shirt-flap dangles beneath his voluminous belly, and he is walking on stockinged feet, clasping his shoes to his chest. He is breathing hard from mounting the spiral staircase.

Barely acknowledging his brothers' greetings, Wensley crosses to the table and plumps himself down in the wing-backed chair. Its vermilion-upholstered padding sighs beneath his weight. He plucks the lid off his salver, snatches up his knife and fork, and starts urgently scooping mouthfuls of devilled kidney between his pillowy, liver-coloured lips, losing several morsels to the bushy goatee that surrounds them. In addition to the kidneys, Wensley's meal consists of four soft-boiled eggs, kedgeree, a mound of fried potatoes drenched in ketchup and brown sauce, a pile of pancakes with maple syrup, and two hunks of white bread smeared with dripping, plus a jug of cream and twenty grammes of refined sugar for his coffee.

Mungo can seldom resist ribbing his less health-conscious younger brother. 'Enough cholesterol there for you, Wensley?'

Wensley barely pauses from his eating to reply, 'I'll work it off.'

'Work it off? How? You've never taken a stroke of exercise in your life.'

'Nervous energy,' says Wensley, patting his mouth with a linen napkin.

'No one's *that* nervous,' says Mungo with a grin.

'Are you genuinely worried about my well-being,' retorts Wensley, 'or is the source of your concern the fact that, were I no longer here, we would no longer be Seven?'

'A bit of both, to be honest.'

'Ah, fraternal love and self-interest. For a son of Septimus Day the two are one and the same.' Wensley pops one of the soft-boiled eggs into his mouth whole, shell and all. His cheeks bulge, there is a muffled crunch, and then he swallows the egg in one go with a huge, unhealthy-sounding gulp. 'Am I not correct?'

Mungo has to laugh. 'Point well made, Wensley. Point well made.'

Sixth to arrive for breakfast is Chas, the second eldest and by far the best-looking of the brothers. In Chas the genes of Septimus Day and his wife, Hiroko, commingled to create the most aesthetically pleasing product they could, endowing him with lustrous eyes, a cleft chin, a square jaw, hair that no matter how it is brushed, always seems to fall the right way, cheekbones a male model would kill for, an excellent physique that unlike Mungo's does not require intensive maintenance, sharp dress sense, and a firm grasp of the social graces. Chas is generally thought of as the 'face' of the Days administration. He it is who goes to meet wholesalers personally when meeting wholesalers personally is absolutely unavoidable, and he it is who is most often called upon to mollify a disgruntled distributor via video conference or telephone, and head down to the shop floor when a problem needs sorting out. What Chas lacks in business acumen he more than makes up for in charm. When the facts won't swing an argument the Day brothers' way, Chas's silver tongue usually will.

Chas offers his brothers a smile that displays twin rows of mint-white teeth so perfectly shaped and arranged they seem to have been plotted with a ruler and set square. He pats Mungo affectionately on the shoulder as he moves around the table to his place. He sits down in an antique desk-chair that looks like one half of a love-seat, its curved back fitted with hand-tooled spokes. His firm, shapely buttocks come to rest on a maroon velvet cushion trimmed with gold braid and gold corner tassels. His breakfast is half a cantaloupe melon, french toast with bacon, and tea.

Fred slyly comments that Chas is looking a little peaky this morning. He is not. As usual, Chas is looking magnificent. But he takes a yawn and remarks that he did have a somewhat 'interrupted' night.

'I'll bet,' leers Fred. 'And is this "interruption" still with us?'

'I sent her downstairs with a spree card.'

Thurston is quick to enquire whether Chas put a spending cap on the spree card.

'A grand,' is the nonchalant reply.

'And I trust, Chas,' Thurston continues, 'that that was not the only precaution you took.'

'Give me some credit, Thurston,' says Chas, with a calculated measure of irritation.

'Forgive my concern, but you know as well as I do that our rivals would not hesitate to cast aspersions on our reputation if the opportunity – in the form of a paternity suit, for example – presented itself.'

'You think I want that any more than you?'

'I'm merely saying that your behaviour does expose us to a certain level of risk. Honest competition we can contend with, rumour we can ignore, but the whiff of scandal tends to cling.'

Mungo, seeing Chas bristle, intervenes. 'Your women come from the Pleasure Department, don't they, Chas?'

Chas nods.

'Well, there you are then. They're under contract to us. If one of them were to get pregnant – and this is just a general statement, I'm not saying Chas would be responsible – but if she did get pregnant and she decided to sue us, she wouldn't have a legal leg to stand on. She'd be in breach of Clause Six of her contract, the one about "fitness to work". We, in fact, could sue *her*, if we felt like it.'

'See?' says Chas to Thurston.

Thurston concedes gracefully. 'My sincerest apologies.'

'Accepted.'

It's a small squall, and the climate in the Boardroom quickly calms again. Fred helps lighten the atmosphere by reading aloud a gossip-column snippet about an opposition-party spokesman who was spotted yesterday shopping at Days with a woman who is neither his wife nor his secretary nor his official mistress. They were spied in the Lingerie Department making free with the politician's Iridium card.

'I *said* it was him, didn't I?' Fred crows, gesturing in the direction of the monitors. 'Didn't I? I *told* you.'

'Perhaps we should elevate him to Palladium,' says Sato. 'He seems to be a very good customer.'

'The more Palladium politicians we have in both camps, the better,'

Wensley remarks through a mouthful of fried potato. 'From a tax-break point of view.'

'I'll make a note of it,' says Thurston, and turns to tap a short reminder into the terminal. 'Although we really ought not to be discussing business outside opening hours.'

'Well, excuse *me*,' says Fred, and immerses himself again in his newspaper, wiggling his eyebrows humorously for the benefit of anyone caring to look.

The breakfast-time conversation continues in fits and starts, counterpointed by the click of cutlery on crockery and the tap of keyboard keys and the peel of newsprint pages. Meanwhile, Old Man Day glares balefully down at his sons from the portrait, his good eye glittering. All six brothers studiously avoid looking at or mentioning the empty seventh chair, the mock throne, in front of which sit an untouched salver and all the ingredients for a good gin and tonic.

The ice cubes in the malachite bucket have started to melt.

8.28 a.m.

For five minutes Frank has been watching the clearing which the white tigress has now vacated, hoping she will re-emerge from the trees to look at him again, but at last he accepts that she has gone. And it is time he should be going, too. The quiet half-hour is almost over. Distant voices are coming faintly from all floors, drifting across the cathedral vastness of the atrium. Sales assistants are arriving, filtering in through the four main entrances and spreading out through the store to take up their posts by the counters and displays. He ought to be heading downstairs.

But still he keeps gazing down into the clearing, a gibbous striped afterimage of the tigress hovering before his eyes. Not that he believes in such things, but he can't help thinking she may have been an omen of some sort. An omen of his new life, perhaps. The tigress is soon going to be elsewhere, out of Days, as is he. Freed from captivity. But no. She is simply being transferred from one kind of captivity to another. He is not. So, not such a good omen after all. But then, since he doesn't believe in such things, what does it matter?

He stays by the parapet until the last possible moment. When a yawning restaurant chef saunters into the hoop, Frank silently turns and makes his way to the nearest staff lift.

7

Chapter 7: a provision of the U.S. federal Bankruptcy Act for the relief of insolvent debtors and their creditors

8.30 a.m.

'Taxi's here, Gordon!'

Gordon Trivett comes trotting down the stairs, buttoning one shirt-cuff, and muttering, 'Why'd it have to be on time?'

Linda is holding his coat for him in the hallway. She herself is all set to go. She has on her best blouse and skirt, over which she is wearing a cheap plastic mackintosh which has been taped up in several places where the seams have split. These homespun repairs are symptomatic of the make-do-and-mend ethic that the Trivetts adhered to during the time they spent saving up for their Days Silver. Today, that long, arduous, and sometimes seemingly endless period of belt-tightening is over, and Gordon and Linda can at last reap the rewards of their patience and self-denial.

Gordon, typically, has failed to grasp the wonder of the moment.

'Where are my keys?' he says, fishing frantically around in his pockets.

'Gordon, don't worry, I have mine,' Linda says, holding up her set to prove it. 'Now, are you ready?'

'I'd be readier if the taxi hadn't turned up on time. Whoever heard of a taxi turning up when it's supposed to?'

'The taxi turned up on time because the driver knows where we're going and wants to impress us by being punctual. No doubt he thinks we're big tippers.'

'Now, have we got everything?' Gordon grabs his coat from his wife and whisks open the front door.

'I have my keys, my handbag . . .'

'What about the card? Where's the card?'

She blinks at him. 'What card?'

Gordon's eyes bulge behind his spectacles. 'The *card*, Linda! The Days card!'

'I'm just winding you up, Gordon. Here it is.' Linda produces their Silver from her handbag and shows it to him. Satisfied, Gordon turns and sets off down the garden path to the street.

'*Someone's* Mr Grumpy this morning,' Linda says to herself under her breath, and she thinks she knows the reason. Gordon is anxious about taking the day off, scared that the branch manager will somehow, against all the odds, find out that he isn't suffering from the 'flu, and consequently not just deny him the promotion he is hoping for but fire him. She understands his fears, although she has no sympathy with it. She knows that if it weren't for his anxiety, he would never have dreamed of speaking to her the way he just did.

He really should have more faith, though. Her performance on the phone to the branch manager's secretary just now was a superb piece of dissembling. She played the concerned wife to the hilt, assuring the secretary that Gordon was mad keen to go to work but that she was refusing to let him leave the bedroom. She described his symptoms – the racking coughs, the streaming eyes, the dribbling nose – in avid detail. She even pretended to copy down some homespun cold remedy the secretary gave her involving whisky, honey and fresh lemons. For that, Gordon shouldn't be snapping at her; he should be grateful to her. But she forgives him anyway. Today being the day it is, the greatest day of her life, she cannot bring herself to hold a grudge.

She closes the front door behind her, making sure the latch clicks to, then locks the two mortices and sets off after her husband down the straight strip of concrete that bisects the front lawn. She notes that the roses beside the path are withering and will have to be deadheaded soon, and that the privet hedge which separates their property from that of the Winslows, the family occupying the other half of the semi-detached, needs trimming again. It hasn't quite been established whether the hedge is the Winslows' responsibility or hers and Gordon's, but she has taken its upkeep upon herself because the Winslows, frankly, don't have the first clue how to look after a home. Their half of the semi is a mess. They have let the garden grow wild and weed-strewn, the hulk of a broken-down car is rusting by the kerbside out front, and the house itself is a shambles: the brickwork needs repointing, the roof retiling, the curtains washing.

The Winslows have been dogged by a run of bad luck recently. Mr Winslow lost his job on the assembly line at the washing machine factory, his daughter's application to work in the Leisurewear

Department at Days was rejected, and his wife has been forced to swap her full-time position at the local supermarket for a part-time one in order to care for her old and ailing mother. But Linda has only to look at *her* half of the house, with its neat front garden and sparkling white paintwork, and remember how little money she and Gordon have had to spare these past few years, to know that she is correct in her opinion that poverty is no excuse for untidiness. She feels sorry for the Winslows, but these are tough times and the only way to survive them is by being ruthless, both with yourself and with others. Often during her and Gordon's five-year struggle to earn their Silver Linda came close to calling the whole scheme off, unable to foresee a time when their deprivations would be at an end, but since despair was just another luxury they couldn't afford, she never succumbed to it. It was important, too, for her not to let her standards slip, so she taught herself the basics of home decoration, both internal and external, in order that the house would never *look* as though its occupants were in straitened circumstances. She also picked up the rudiments of plumbing and electrical wiring from books in the library, and thus saved on several hefty repair bills.

As for her sideline in hairdressing, after leaving school Linda spent a year as a trainee as a beauty salon, working at slave wages in the anticipation of a full-time job that, in the event, never materialised. Realising that Gordon's salary alone would not be enough to secure them a Silver, she put the skills she acquired at the salon to use, first on friends and then on friends' friends, building a client base by word of mouth. Right from the start she was undercutting the prices of any professional coiffeur by at least a quarter, which certainly contributed to her success, and that and the fact that she could do housecalls made her particularly popular among shut-ins and the elderly. It wasn't long before she had established a thriving, though not especially remunerative, little business that helped tide her and Gordon over through the five lean years and added to their growing Days nest-egg.

All in all, Linda feels she has every right to be proud of herself and disappointed in her next-door neighbours, who have allowed life to get the better of them. If only they would try a little harder, if only they would not wear their defeat so openly, a Days card could be theirs as well – though not, she suspects, a Silver.

Gordon is ensconced in the back seat of the idling taxi, drumming his fingers on his knee. Linda deliberately takes her time over swinging the garden gate shut and ambling across the pavement to climb in beside him. Not only does she not like to be hurried, but she wants as many of the neighbours as possible to see her leave. She knows for a fact that Bella, three houses away, is peering out from her kitchen window. Although Linda can't actually see Bella pinching apart two slats of the venetian blind, she has an instinct for these things. Likewise, five doors down on the opposite side of the street, Margie is watching from behind the net curtains in her living room. Linda has glimpsed her silhouette through the curtains' lacy folds. Others, she is convinced, have their eyes on her. Everyone in the street must know where she and Gordon are going today.

The taxi's interior reeks of an awful air-freshener, a vanilla scent so noxious that the first thing Linda does after closing the door is wind the window all the way down. The driver is a gaunt man with lank hair, sunken eyes and a shaggy moustache. He glances at Linda in the rearview mirror, gives a tiny nod as if he has come to some sort of conclusion about her (although the gesture could simply be a hello), and indicates to pull out.

The taxi grumbles down the street. Linda puts her face to the open window not only so that she can breathe air which hasn't been 'freshened' but so that people will be able to see her more clearly. She is so thrilled she can barely think straight. Days! They are on their way to Days! In all her thirty-one years Linda can't recall feeling this excited before. Even on her wedding day, although she is sure she was happy, she was too nervous and plagued by doubts to enjoy the occasion to its fullest. Now, unlike then, she is filled with the blissful certainty that this is what she really wants.

Of course it's what she wants! Ever since Linda was small, her ambition has been to have an account at Days. Her mother used to laugh at her when she would state, with absolute, unshakeable conviction, that one day she would walk through the doors of the world's first and (unquestionably) foremost gigastore with a card with her name on it in her hand. 'Unless you win the lottery or marry a millionaire,' her mother would reply with a laugh, 'the only way *you'll* ever see the inside of Days is wearing a sales assistant's uniform.' But then that was the kind of woman her mother was. Linda's father was a cold, distant brute of a man who kept his wife in her place with constant venomous criticism, and her mother meekly accepted being treated that way because she was scared to believe that life could offer her more, since that would mean admitting she had settled for less. Linda grew up determined that she would not end up like her mother, and glory be and hallelujah, she hasn't. Today is the proof of that.

As the taxi reaches the end of the street, Linda catches sight of Pat coming out of the tobacconist's on the corner. Pat has a Days lottery ticket in her hand and is stalwartly filling in her 'lucky' numbers once again. Linda calls to her, and Pat glances up and waves. Her smile is uncertain. It seems she needs a moment to recall where Linda and Gordon might be heading in a taxi on a Thursday morning, despite the fact that for the past week Linda has talked about little other than their trip to Days. Linda returns the wave, turning the back of her hand towards Pat and languidly rotating it from the wrist in what she thinks is a funny imitation of royalty. Pat appears not to get the joke, because her smile disappears and is replaced by a frown. Linda will have to explain to her later the satirical intention behind the wave. She doesn't want Pat getting the wrong idea and spreading it about that Linda Trivett has become all la-di-dah since getting her Silver.

The driver turns right, giving a wide berth to a sack of rubbish that has rolled off the pavement into the road and split open like a dead man's belly, and aims the taxi for the heart of the city. The meter mounted on the dashboard busily clocks up the tariff. Gordon starts to fidget. He takes off his spectacles, polishes the lenses with a hand-kerchief and puts them on again. He fondles his lower lip. He traces abstract designs on his trouser leg with one fingernail. He plays with the card, slipping it in and out of its velvet sheath, in and out. Linda, meanwhile, watches the city pass by. The boarded-up shops. The pubs, doing a brisk trade even at this early hour. The cafés haunted by aimless souls trying to make one cup of tea last the whole morning. The beggars waiting at traffic lights, holding cardboard signs that say things like 'Homeless – Will Work For Food' and 'Mother Of Six, No Welfare'. The school-age kids congregating around benches in threadbare parks to drink and smoke. A man who clearly ought to be in an institution shouting at himself as he stalks the gutters. People who, unlike Linda, have given up hope, who lack the energy and the resolve – the dynamism, that's a good word for it – the *dynamism* to improve their lot. The sight of them both angers and saddens her.

The taxi driver breaks into her reverie. 'So, Days then, is it, missus?' he says, eyeing her in the rearview mirror. When he knows that he has got her attention, he twists around in his seat to look at her directly.

'Don't tell me. I can guess just by looking at people.' He turns back to watch the road. 'Silver, right?'

Linda suspects that the driver has seen the card in Gordon's hands but gives him the benefit of the doubt. 'Absolutely right. Well done.'

'I can always tell. Got a knack for it. I bet this is your first time, too.'

'How did you know?'

The driver snaps a quick grin round at her. 'I'm right about that too?' He shakes his head. 'I *am* on form **today**.'

'We must look eager to get there.'

'It's not that, missus. It's more that you both look ... well, "innocent" is the word that springs to mind. Fresh-faced. Like troops who haven't gone into combat yet.'

'What an extraordinary thing to say.'

'But it's true. You can always tell regular Days customers. They have this look about them, sort of wary and jaded.'

'I'm sure we won't end up looking like that. Don't you agree, Gordon?'

Gordon grunts in the affirmative.

'Oh, you say that now,' says the taxi driver, 'but people have had some pretty nasty experiences at Days. Experiences that have, you might say, dampened their enthusiasm for shopping there.'

'I've heard rumours.'

'Oh, they're not – '

The taxi driver breaks off because a dust-caked van has pulled out from a parking space about thirty metres ahead. Spluttering with outrage, the taxi driver accelerates until his front bumper is less than a metre behind the van's tail-lights, then hammers repeatedly on the horn, cursing.

Linda notices that in the skin of dust which coats the van's rear doors someone has drawn a Days logo, etched a large X over it, and written beneath, in finger-thick capitals:

DAYS
DIES!

Just jealous, she thinks.

The van turns off at the next junction, its driver taking one hand off the steering wheel to stroke the air in a slow, masturbatory salute. The taxi driver growls, 'Arsehole,' then says to the Trivetts, 'Did you see that? Did you see the way he pulled out *right* in front of me? I nearly went *straight* into him.'

Gordon declines to comment, and Linda imperturbably resumes the conversation she and the driver were having before this incident. 'You were saying they're not rumours.'

'What aren't rumours?'

'The rumours about Days.'

'The rumours about people getting killed?'

'Those rumours.'

'Oh, they're not rumours. They're the truth.'

'I know they're supposed to have some basis in the truth, but don't you think that these things have been blown up out of all proportion by the media? It can't possibly be as bad as people say.'

'You obviously haven't been reading the papers lately, have you, love? Seventeen shoppers crushed to death in the run-up to last Christmas, another eight during the January sales – that seems pretty bad to me. And those are just the *accidental* deaths.'

'But people still go there to shop.'

'Course they do. It's Days, isn't it? And then there are the lightning sales . . .'

'Gordon and I are going to steer well clear of the lightning sales,' says Linda. 'Aren't we, Gordon?'

'Seems like a good idea,' murmurs Gordon.

'A very good idea,' says the taxi driver. 'If you can.'

'We will.'

'And then, of course, there are the people who run foul of in-store security.'

'You mean shoplifters.'

'Exactly. Did you know, last year a total of thirteen shoplifters were shot dead by Days Security?'

'Because they ran.'

'Wouldn't you? If you were faced with a choice between losing your account for ever and trying to get away, wouldn't you run?'

'I wouldn't shoplift in the first place,' Linda states frostily.

'OK. All right. The point I'm trying to make here is that, even for honest customers like yourselves, Days is a dangerous place.'

'We've signed the disclaimer form,' says Linda. 'We're aware of the risks.' There, that neatly and tidily sums up her case. The taxi driver is referring to all the things that can happen to Days customers who are not careful or do not follow the rules. (Typically, like anyone who hasn't earned an account there, he can see only the store's bad side.) Days isn't to blame for the deaths that occur on the premises; it's the shoppers who are at fault. If you don't know how to behave while you're there, and if you lack the self-control not to take anything you can't pay for, then you thoroughly deserve the consequences.

This Linda thinks but does not say, believing it to be self-evident. Instead, she leans back, folds her arms across her chest, and scans the skyline ahead for a glimpse of the gigastore.

The taxi driver mulls some thoughts over for a while before opening his mouth again. 'It's still a dangerous place. If I were you, I'd be taking some kind of protection in with me.'

'What are you talking about, protection?' The taxi driver seems to be determined to ruin Linda's rosy mood, so the snappish edge in her voice can be forgiven.

'Protection,' he says. 'Self-defence. In case you run into a lunatic.'

'Lunatics don't shop at Days.'

'You'd be surprised.'

'But that's the whole point of the place. Only a certain, for want of a better word, *class* of person can shop there.'

'I wouldn't say class, missus. I'd say type. The type that loves to buy things. The type that *lives* to buy things. The type that goes bananas the moment a lightning sale is announced over the tannoy. The type that'll fly right off the handle if you happen to pick up the last item in stock of something they want. The type that'll bite your fingers off if you refuse to let go of it. *That's* the type of person that shops at Days, and that's the type you've got to watch out for.'

'I've never heard such nonsense,' says Linda. She looks at her husband. 'Have you?'

Gordon shrugs. 'I've heard that people can get a little strange in there.'

'Too right,' says the taxi driver.

'Well, we'll simply avoid anyone we don't like the look of.'

'Right. See, love, I'm not trying to put you off going or anything. I'm just offering some friendly advice.'

'Thank you,' Linda replies curtly. Still, the taxi driver has piqued her curiosity. 'Out of interest, when you said "protection", what exactly did you mean? If you mean a gun, then that's absurd. Out of the question.'

'Couldn't agree with you more, missus. You'd never get it past the metal detectors, for one thing. No, I'm referring to something that isn't going to kill anyone, right, but'll see off whoever's hassling you, should that happen, God forbid.'

'And what would that be?'

Breaking into a broad grin, the taxi driver reaches across the passenger seat and opens the glove compartment. Inside are several small, shiny cylinders that resemble lipstick cases, black with gold caps, bound together with an elastic band.

'Got these off a mate of mine who used to be in the police force. Undercover policewomen carry them in their handbags. Pepper spray. Derived from those, what are they called? Jallypeeno peppers. Did I say that right?'

'Jalapeño,' says Linda, stressing the aspirate 'j'.

'Yeah, that's the one. You know how nasty it is when you're cutting one of *them* up and you make the mistake of rubbing your eyes? Well, this is ten times worse. One squirt in the face and – voom! – your potential rapist, mugger, bargain-hunter, whatever, isn't bothering you any more.' He closes the glove compartment and returns his attention to the road. 'They're made of plastic, so you'll get them through security no problem.'

'Are they legal?' asks Linda.

'Well, if the police can carry them, I reckon technically they must be. You interested?'

'You're asking me if I want one?'

'I'm suggesting you might need one.'

Linda turns to her husband.

'Don't look at me,' says Gordon, waving her away. 'If you think you ought to get one, then get one.'

'I don't think I *ought* to get one, but I think it might be wise to have one handy.'

'It's up to you.'

'Just in case.'

'It's up to you.'

'I'll probably never use it, but I'd feel safer if I was carrying it.'

'You do what you have to, Linda.'

'Can I use our Days Silver?' Linda asks the taxi driver.

'I'll add it to the fare,' the driver says, reaching for the glove compartment again. 'And look.' He points ahead with one finger of the hand still on the steering wheel. 'We're almost there.'

And so they are. Above the rooftops, gliding towards them like a vast, strange galleon under full sail, there it is – a block of dried-blood brick whose dimensions would humble even the most arrogant of men. Linda has seen it before, of course, many times, but until now it has always been closed to her, an impenetrable gulag, a great blank space she has filled in with dreams and imaginings and expectations and longings. Until now, it has been Wonderland. Today, Linda is going to slip down the rabbit-hole.

Days!

8

Ancient Rome: built on seven hills – the Aventine, the Caelian, the Capitoline, the Esquiline, the Palatine, the Quirinal and the Viminal

8.32 a.m.
The Basement is a network of tunnels – broad corridors branching off into narrower corridors which in turn branch off into even narrower corridors, lit at infrequent intervals by ceiling-mounted striplights of low wattage. Ducts and pipes, the building's veins, run parallel overhead, and at each intersection the walls are marked with a colour-coded system of arrows, because it is all too easy to get lost down here, where every surface is painted battleship grey, except the floors, which are carpeted in a worn green cord with a repeating motif of Days logos. When one stretch of corridor looks much like another, even employees of long standing sometimes have to consult the arrows to find their bearings.

Frank, though, is so familiar with the layout of every floor of Days that he doesn't even glance around as he steps out of the lift, simply turns and heads unerringly in the right direction.

On the way, he falls in beside a pair of Eye screen-jockeys, one skinny, one blimp-big, both with blue-tinged cathode tans. Matching his pace to theirs, he eavesdrops on their conversation. They are discussing the football match last night. Apparently the national side lost at home to a scratch team from a remote Micronesian atoll, but the screen-jockeys console themselves with the fact that at least it was only a five–nil defeat. Given the national side's current form, it could have been a lot worse.

Not being a follower of football or any other sport, Frank rapidly loses any interest he might have had in the screen-jockeys' conversation, and drops back a few paces, only to find that he is walking alongside a fellow Ghost. He recognises the other man as a Ghost not so much by his face as by the way he sidles down the corridor, hunch-shouldered and close to the wall.

As is always the case when two Ghosts unexpectedly cross paths, there is a *frisson* of distant familiarity between them, as though they are a pair of violin strings tuned to the exact same pitch: when one is plucked, the other vibrates in sympathy. For each, it is like meeting an identical twin he didn't know he had. In this instance, as is customary, neither offers the other the slightest acknowledgement, and Frank slows to an amble, allowing his co-worker to get ahead.

Reaching a door marked 'Tactical Security', Frank stops and waits until the other man has gone through before stepping forward to do the same. He detects the presence of another Ghost behind him, a woman this time, and does her the courtesy of not holding the door open for her, so that she won't feel obliged to make eye contact and thank him.

Tactical Security is one of several self-contained facilities within the Basement labyrinth, with its own cafeteria, cloakrooms, and locker rooms. Frank shares a locker room with twenty other Ghosts, most of whom are present when he enters. They are men and women of nondescript appearance, indeterminate age, dressed smartly but far from showily. The women wear the minimum of make-up and all the men look as if, like Frank, they trim their hair themselves. Few of the women wear any jewellery, and those that do restrict themselves to plain gold ear-studs and simple finger-rings. There isn't a wedding band in sight. The Ghosts avoid looking at each other, exchange no conversation, just quietly, imperturbably get ready for work. Frank, too.

He springs his locker open with a swipe of his Iridium, removes his overcoat and drapes it over the hanger inside, then shrugs off his jacket and hooks it over the corner of the door. Taking out his shoulder-holster, an infinity symbol of canvas webbing and soft leather, he puts it on and adjusts the buckles until the straps sit comfortably around his chest and the sagging planes of his shoulder-blades.

He reaches into the locker again and removes a gleaming stainless steel .45-calibre automatic pistol from a velvet-lined case. He prefers the lightweight version of the regulation store-issue handgun because it doesn't drag down on the holster like the heavier guns do. A lighter gun means a harder recoil, but that seems a fair price to pay in exchange for greater ease of carrying, given that he seldom actually fires the thing.

Drawing back the slide, he checks that the chamber is empty, even though he never leaves a round in the chamber unless he is about to fire the gun – the habit of checking is as much an act of ceremony as it is a safety procedure. Then he lets the slide snap back into place. He cleans the gun religiously once a month, so the slide action is oil-smooth.

On a shelf at eye-level inside the locker there is a rack holding three clips of thirteen bullets, each with its black teflon tip grooved as though a tiny cog-wheel has been removed, and each with the Days logo stamped into its brass shell casing. Two of the clips Frank slots into the holster's double off-side ammo pouch under his right armpit; the third he thrusts into the grip of the gun, ramming it home with the heel of his palm. He uses his Iridium to take off the gun's safety, running the card's magnetic strip through a centimetre-deep groove in the underside of the barrel. A green LED next to the trigger guard winks alight as the decocking lever disengages. He runs the card through the groove again, the light goes out, and the decocking lever snicks back into place. He holsters the gun beneath his left armpit and puts his card away.

Next, he takes out his Eye-link and, having unravelled the fragile-looking tangle of surgical-pink wires and components, slots the fitted audio pick-up into his right ear then leads the attached wire back over the ear and down behind the lobe. At the other end of the wire is a wafer-thin short-wave receiver/transmitter which he pins inside his shirt collar. Running from this is another wire that ends in a tiny mircophone, slender and curved like a fingernail, which he clips into place behind the top button of his shirt, tightening the knot of his tie so that the microphone presses snugly against his throat.

The only piece of equipment left in the locker is his Sphinx. He unplugs the slim black box from its recharging unit, switches it on, and as soon as the Days logo scrolls up on the screen, flicks the power button back to off and slides the Sphinx into his trouser pocket.

Ready. Another ritual over and done with for the last time.

It is 8.43, and the morning briefing is imminent. Frank accompanies the other Ghosts as they drift out of the locker room, joining the rustling flow of bodies moving down the passageway which leads past the self-service cafeteria to the briefing room. One by one, without a word, eyes averted, the Ghosts glide through the briefing-room doors to take their places on the plastic chairs which are arranged in ten rows of ten, facing the podium at the far end. Sensibly they fill up the rows from the middle outwards, so that no one will have to step over another person's legs, thus minimising the risk of accidental physical contact. They aren't bothered whom they sit next to. Among Ghosts there are no friends, no favourites. All are equal in their lack of individuality.

Seated, the Ghosts adopt postures of nonchalance or self-absorption. Some gaze in fascination at the ceiling, as though they see the work of Michelangelo up there rather than grey-painted plaster, while others gnaw at their cuticles or scratch repeatedly at nonexistent itches.

The last Ghosts enter, filling up all but a few of the chairs, and the briefing room whispers with the sifting-sand hiss that is the sound of almost a hundred pairs of lungs softly filling and emptying.

At 8.45 precisely Donald Bloom, the head of Tactical Security, appears. He eases the doors shut behind him and strolls the length of the room to the podium. He is a short man, amiably portly, with close-cropped hair that, apart from a tuft that clings indomitably to the top of the forehead, is confined to the sides and back of his scalp. He sports a white carnation in his buttonhole which he buys fresh every morning from a flower stall on his way to work, and he is carrying a clipboard with a sheet of computer printout attached to it. A folded handkerchief pokes out from the breast pocket of his houndstooth-pattern tweed jacket.

The Ghosts focus their attention on Mr Bloom as he climbs on to the podium. Those at the rear lean forward in their seats in order to hear him better.

Mr Bloom begins the briefing with the traditional *bon mot*.

'Another day, another debt.'

There are smiles, smirks. Some shoulders twitch in amusement. Traditions, no matter how time-worn, how trite, are respected here.

Mr Bloom consults his clipboard.

'Right. Nothing much out of the ordinary going on today. Expect lightning sales at 10.00 in Dolls, 10.45 in Farm Machinery, 12.00 in Ties, 2.00 in Third World Musical Instruments, 3.00 in Religious Paraphernalia, 4.00 in the Funeral Parlour – I can't see that one being particularly popular, but you never know – 4.15 in Perennial Christmas, and 4.45 in Trusses and Supports.

'Next, those bogus spree cards we saw so many of last year are back.

Technically this is Strategic Security's problem, not ours, but if you see a customer using a spree card you might want to run a check on it. All spree cards issued since Monday have been tagged with new security codes which your Sphinxes have been reformatted to recognise, and everyone who has bought a spree card or won one in the lottery in the past six months has been contacted and asked to return it to us to be replaced, so anyone who isn't using an up-to-date card probably isn't on the level. Use your judgement, and don't be afraid to err on the side of caution.

'Same goes for bogus ID badges. The police tell me they've just busted a forgery ring, but they haven't yet established how long the forgers have been operating and how many of the fake badges, if any, have been sold. So keep an eye out for any employees who don't look like employees. I'm aware that in some cases the badge is the only thing that tells you that an employee works here. You're going to have to trust your instincts on this one.

'The good news is: arrests were up last month. Well done. The bad news is: shrinkage also went up. One's immediate instinct, of course, is to blame shop-floor employees, and I fear a certain amount of pilfering does go on under the counter, despite the fact that we're all account-holders here. I know it's a cliché, but some people don't seem to appreciate that stealing from the store is stealing from themselves.

'However, I have another theory about the shrinkage problem, and like it or not I'm going to share it with you. My theory is that bargain-hunters have learned to take advantage of the confusion of a lightning sale to slip items into their pockets or bags, which is why it's all the more important that Ghosts be on hand during a sale to monitor the crowd. Remember, no matter how hard we try to make it for people to boost from us, they'll always find a way. We are up against mankind's greatest virtue and greatest vice: ingenuity.

'Lastly, I have it on good authority that the Books/Computers dispute is finally, *finally* coming up before the brothers today for arbitration. I know. Sighs of relief all round. It's dragged on for, what, getting on for a year now?'

'A year and a half,' someone says.

'A year and a half, thank you. Well, the wheels of administration may turn slowly around here, but turn they do, so with any luck we can look forward to a swift resolution to that disagreeable little contretemps.'

Mr Bloom glances down the list on his clipboard, making sure he hasn't missed anything. 'Oh yes, Mr Greenaway's greatly deserved holiday began this morning, so I'm going to be minding the Strategic side of things until he comes back. Lucky me. I feel like I've been put in charge of the gorilla cage at the zoo.'

A ripple of laughter.

Mr Bloom consults his clipboard one last time. 'And that really *is* it, ladies and gentlemen. Have a good day out there.' He concludes with the Ghosts' motto: 'Be Silent, Vigilant, Persistent, Intransigent. The Customer Is Not Always Right.'

The Ghosts intone the words along with him, a sibilant echo. Then they rise from their seats and begin filing out, shuffling in lines towards the exit, taking care not to touch one another. Mr Bloom steps down from the podium and makes for the doors too, moving slowly so that the Ghosts can assimilate him into their flow.

He is halfway to his office when he senses someone walking behind him at the very limit of his peripheral vision, in what the driver of a car would call the blind-spot. Knowing better than to stop and address the Ghost, Mr Bloom keeps going. It isn't until he is actually sitting down behind the functional, Formica-topped desk in his cramped, windowless office that he looks up to see who has followed him in.

'Frank,' says Mr Bloom, both pleased and puzzled, and indicates that Frank should take a seat in the chair on the opposite side of the desk.

'No,' says Frank. 'Thank you, I'm fine. I can't stop for long. I'm here because I wanted to say – '

But Frank isn't sure how to put it. He scratches the crown of his head and hums to himself.

'Go on, sit down,' Mr Bloom insists, but Frank shakes his head emphatically.

'I have to be out on the floor in a moment.'

Mr Bloom glances at his watch. 'It's 8.49, Frank. It surely can't take more than eleven minutes to talk about whatever you want to talk about and, even if it does, I feel certain that the store will be able to manage without you for a brief while at the beginning of the least busy hour of the day.'

'Yes, well, it might, Donald.' Frank thinks of his superior as 'Mr Bloom' and refers to him as such behind his back, but to his face it is always 'Donald'. 'Look, I'll tell you what, can we do this a bit later? I mean, you're busy right now.'

'Well, Greenaway's lot *are* due for their pep-talk in a moment, then I've got to oversee a practice at the firing range, then I've got to brief a new bunch of sales assistants on the basics of security. But I'm never too busy to talk to you, Frank. What is it?'

Frank wants to tell him, but something prevents him, and he thinks it might be fear but he also thinks it might be guilt. He has known Donald Bloom for all of his thirty-three years at Days. There is a bond between them – he wouldn't call it friendship, because the concept has as much meaning for him as the concept of air does for a goldfish in a bowl, but certainly they have developed a mutual respect over thirty-three years, and sometimes Frank has found himself thinking about Mr Bloom when Mr Bloom isn't present, thinking it would be nice if they could perhaps go to a pub together after work and sit and have a drink and a chat, talk about things that have nothing to do with Days or shoplifters or Ghosts, the sort of things people normally talk about, whatever *they* are. He has never plucked up the courage to suggest the idea to Mr Bloom, and anyway by closing time he is usually too exhausted to want to do anything except head straight home and go to bed, but the fact remains that he and Mr Bloom have a long history of acquaintance, and for some reason Frank feels sure that Mr Bloom is going to be upset by his decision to resign, and he is reluctant to deliver the blow.

The surge of bravado that carried him all the way into Mr Bloom's office has lost momentum, receded, leaving him high and dry – hesitant, confused, embarrassed.

Mr Bloom, with a patient smile, is still waiting for him to say something.

His nerve cracking completely, Frank gets up to leave.

Mr Bloom sighs. 'All right, then, Frank. Have it your way. The door's always open. OK?'

He gives one last enquiring look at the doorway through which Frank has just exited hastily.

Strange behaviour, he thinks. Frank has always been one of the more level-headed Tactical Security operatives, not to mention one of the best. The constant lurking, the constant suspicion of others – has it finally got to him?

No, Mr Bloom tells himself. He might expect that of any other Ghost, but not Frank. Never Frank.

9

The Seventh Son of a Seventh Son: traditionally regarded as gifted or lucky

8.51 a.m.

Sonny's bed has not been slept in. Perch would have been surprised if it had, but hope springs eternal. He tries the bathroom, and there he finds Septimus Day's youngest son not, as expected, curled around the lavatory pedestal but stretched out in the bath, one leg hooked over the side, his head resting awkwardly against the taps. Dried vomit stains encrust the lavatory ring, but Sonny appears to have had the presence of mind to flush his spewings away before crawling, fully dressed, into the tub and passing out. Perch mentally applauds the young master's self-control.

He bends down and rifles Sonny's pockets until he finds his portable intercom. Flipping it open, he keys 4.

'Master Thurston?'

'Perch.'

'I rather fear that Master Sonny is not in a fit state to participate in the opening ceremony this morning.'

A short silence. Then a sigh. 'All right, Perch. Try and get him up and presentable as soon as you can.'

'I shall endeavour to do my best, sir.'

Perch breaks the connection and sets the intercom down on the lid of the cistern. A trace – just the faintest, remotest scintilla – of contempt can be discerned in his voice as he says, 'Very well, Master Sonny. Let's be having you.'

He reaches up and makes minute adjustments to the angle of the shower head like an artilleryman sighting his target, until at last he is satisfied that the rosette is aiming directly down at Sonny's face. Then he grasps the handle of the cold tap beside Sonny's cheek, pauses a moment, savouring the sweet anticipation . . . and turns the water full on.

8.54 a.m.

'The Afterthought isn't going to be able to make it,' Thurston informs his brothers.

'Now there's a surprise,' says Wensley.

'Maybe we should have a blow-up Sonny doll made,' says Fred. 'It could sit there in his chair and say nothing, and that way everybody would be happy.'

'Sonny is blood,' Mungo admonishes Fred. 'Never forget that.'

'What Sonny is, is a pain in the arse,' Fred replies, unabashed. 'He needed what the rest of us got from Dad when we were growing up.' He aims a respectful if wary nod towards the portrait of Old Man Day. 'Discipline. If Sonny had been indulged a little less when he was a boy and beaten a little more, he might not have turned into the unspeakable *über*-brat he is now.'

'I did the best I could with him,' says Mungo. 'If anyone is to take the blame for the way he is today, it's me.'

'Don't be too hard on yourself,' says Thurston. 'We all had to be a father to Sonny in one way or another.'

'For all Sonny's flaws,' says Chas diplomatically, 'we must accept him and love him for who he is. He is a son of Septimus Day. He is our brother.'

'Don't keep reminding us,' says Fred, rolling his eyes.

'I think I could tolerate his behaviour,' says Sato, 'if only he pulled his weight around here.'

'That he is one of the Seven is enough,' says Chas.

'I'm with Chas there,' says Wensley. 'Sonny's an obnoxious so-and-so, but we can't do without him.'

'In every rose-bed a nettle grows,' Sato murmurs with a hint of genuine bitterness. 'In every Eden a serpent hisses.'

'It's five to,' says Thurston, rapping the table with his knuckles. 'We should get started.'

The brothers set down their cutlery and push aside their breakfast plates. Wensley wolfs down one last bite of bread and dripping, chewing furiously and swallowing hard. Fred closes the tabloid he is reading and lays it tidily on top of the pile of newspapers. Chas, on instinct, runs his fingers through his hair and discreetly huffs into a cupped hand to check that his breath passes muster.

Silence descends on the Boardroom.

Thurston speaks. 'Welcome, my brothers, to another day of custom and commerce, of margins and mark-ups, of retail and revenue, of sales and success, of profit and plenty.'

He makes a fist of his left hand, then extends the thumb and forefinger to form a stooping L, across which he places his right index and middle fingers. His brothers, with ostentatious and not entirely convincing solemnity, copy the gesture.

'We are the sons of Septimus Day,' Thurston continues. 'We are the Seven whose duty it is to manage the store founded by our father and to uphold his philosophy, that if it can be sold, it will be bought, and if it can be bought, it will be sold. That is our task, and we are glad of it.'

Now he locks his right forefinger around his left thumb to form an S, bringing his right thumb up and his left middle finger down until they overlap, bisecting the S vertically. His brothers, as before, emulate him. Chas yawns.

'Each of us was born, or induced to be born, on the day whose name he bears, and each raised in the knowledge that an equal seventh share of the responsibility of running the store and the rewards resulting thereof would be his. Each of us is a seventh part of a greater whole and, Mammon willing, long may it remain so.'

Fred rolls his eyes at Wensley. Wensley responds with a broad smirk. Mungo glares at them both, but it is clear that he, too, finds this opening ritual, which their father instituted and insisted be maintained after his death, somewhat absurd.

Thurston's hands move again. He points the thumb and forefinger of his left hand upwards at an angle to each other, so that they make a Y-shape with his wrist, and just beneath the webbed stretch of skin where they join he lays his right index and middle fingers horizontally. His brothers follow suit.

'We make the symbols of Sterling and Dollar and Yen,' intones Thurston, 'three ordinary letters ennobled, raised to a state of grace by that which they represent, to remind us that money transfigures all.'

He forms an O with his left thumb and forefinger, and lays his right index and middle fingers vertically over it. His brothers do the same.

'We make the symbol of Days to remind us of the source of our wealth.'

As one, the brothers lift away their two right fingers, leaving just the Os.

'And we make an empty circle to remind us that without Days we are nothing.'

There follows a moment of silence which is intended for sober contemplation but which, in the event, most of the brothers use to scratch an itch or grab another bite of breakfast.

'Now,' says Thurston, 'the clock ticks towards opening time once again and, as chairman for the day, the day that bears my name, I would ask you, my brothers, to join me at the switch.'

All six brothers rise to their feet and walk with measured tread to the brass panel mounted on the Boardroom wall. Septimus's good eye seems to follow them as they cross the room. The white dot of reflected light the artist put in his cruel black pupil glistens as though the eye is alive.

Thurston unclips the ceramic handle from its rest and, lifting it up with some effort, screws it into the fitting on the crossbar of the knife switch. Each brother then reaches out with his right hand to grasp the handle, which is exactly long enough to accommodate seven male fists. Mungo fills the space for the seventh with his left hand.

'I will pull for two,' he says.

Thurston extends his left wrist from his sleeve to consult his watch. Less than a minute to go till nine. The second hand sweeps inexorably round. The brothers stand there patiently, clustered together, their arms radiating from the switch like ribbons from a maypole.

'Fifteen seconds,' says Thurston.

Beneath their feet the store waits, like a dead thing about to be reanimated.

'Ten seconds,' says Thurston.

And it seems that the knife switch's contacts, through which all the power in the store flows, are crackling in their eagerness to be connected.

'Five,' says Thurston. 'On my mark. Four.'

And the brothers can feel a vibration through the soles of their shoes, a low bass drone like the humming of a million bees.

'Three.'

And each fancies he can hear a stunned hush as of a thousand breaths being held.

'Two. One. And *pull*!'

It takes the combined strength of all six of them, with Mungo performing the work of two, to haul the switch down from its upright position. The brothers grunt and gasp as they lever it through horizontal on its squealing hinges, and push and keep pushing until its two brass prongs are nearly touching the contact clips. One more shove, with all the effort they can muster, and the switch slides home.

They let go at once. The lights in the Boardroom dim, then brighten again.

'My brothers,' says Thurston, shaking out his aching right arm, 'we are open for business.'

10

9.00 a.m.

In all 666 departments, the lights go from half strength to full, bathing the counters and displays of merchandise in brilliance.

At each of the four corner entrances the bolts in the doors shoot back and a handful of waiting shoppers swarm forward. The guards, for whom opening time means night shift's end, hold the doors open for them and usher them through, a courtesy that largely goes unremarked. The guards then head indoors themselves.

In the hallways, the lifts to the car parks are summoned down.

Escalators on every floor, frozen in place, start to crawl.

Outside, the window-shoppers, who have been growing increasingly agitated and excited as nine o'clock has neared, sigh with one voice as the curtains in the windows part.

The green LEDs on the closed-circuit cameras that scan every square centimetre of the shop floor come alight. Signals flash along the cables threaded through the spaces between the walls, a fibre-optic web whose thousands of strands radiate throughout the store. All the cables originate in the Eye, a long, low bunker in the Basement where several dozen half-shell clusters of black-and-white monitors occupy all the available wallspace, each cluster attended by a screen-jockey in a wheeled chair. The only light in the chamber comes from the monitors and the screens of the terminals affixed to the chairs' arms: flickering, sickly, blue-grey. The screen-jockeys begin speaking into their headset microphones, at the same time unwrapping Days-brand chocolate bars and popping the ringpulls on cans of Days-brand soft drink.

The two banks of monitors in the Boardroom also come on. Fuzzy bands of static jump down their screens simultaneously, then stabilise and resolve to show different corners of different departments. The images start to change, switching at random between feeds, one after another at seven-second intervals, a hypnotically shifting televisual collage.

Sales assistants take their places, adopting practised expressions of mild, polite interest. Floor-walkers stand ready to greet the first influx of customers. Promotional reps tense, poised to pounce with their samples and testers.

Oblivious to all this activity, the creatures in the Menagerie continue to go about their business, secretly beneath the jungle's green canopy.

11

The Seven Joys of Mary: namely the Annunciation, the Visitation, the Nativity, the adoration of the Magi, the presentation in the temple, the finding of the lost child, and the Assumption

9.03 a.m.
The taxi pulls up to the turning circle outside the South-East Entrance, and Linda, imagining a carriage arriving at a stately home, hears the crackle of gravel beneath iron-banded wheels rather than the thrum of tyre-tread on tarmac. As the taxi comes to a halt at the foot of the steps, she extends the Silver to the driver between two fingers, flourishing it beside his left ear. He takes the card and stuffs it into the meter with the air of one who has handled Palladiums and even Rhodiums in his time and for whom a mere Silver holds no mystique. Gordon butts open the door and swings his legs out. Standing up, he straightens a crick out of his spine and turns to look at the window-shoppers, who are already in thrall to the displays.

The taxi driver, tapping keys on the meter, tots up the cost of the fare, plus the pepper spray, plus tax, plus tip, and announces the total, the steepness of which surprises Linda. Reminding herself, however, that she is the co-holder of a Days Silver account, she adopts a serene smile and signs the authorisation slip without a murmur. The taxi driver hands her back the card and wishes her a safe day's shopping, laying emphasis on the word 'safe'. She thanks him and climbs out into a gust of wind that sways her with its unexpected force. The taxi pulls away.

Bowing her head, Linda mounts the steps, clutching the Silver in both hands. At the top, she divests herself of her taped-up plastic mackintosh and folds it into a neat square package which she stuffs into her handbag. The wind knifes through her blouse, stippling her flesh with gooseflesh and making her shiver. Looking round to see what has happened to Gordon, she finds him still staring at the window-shoppers. She trots back down, calling his name.

Gordon does not respond.

'Gordon,' she urges. 'Come on.'

But Gordon is mesmerised. Whether by the sight of clumps of ragged, hunched, wind-blown human beings sitting or squatting or reclining before the one-storey-high windows along the edge of the building, or by the displays themselves, Linda cannot tell, but as she reaches his side, she finds her eye drawn to the window immediately to the left of the South-East Entrance, and all at once her eagerness to enter the store melts away, to be replaced by rapt, acquiescent fascination.

A window display can attract a crowd anything up to a hundred strong. Some are more popular than others, but even the least well attended regularly draw audiences of two or three dozen. The window-shoppers have a tendency to drift from one to the next as the whim takes them, but certain displays have devoted followers who stay with them from opening time to closing time. There is no rhyme or reason why one display should command greater loyalty than another, since they are all essentially alike. But then, popularity is as much a product of the herd instinct as it is of superior quality.

The display Linda is watching isn't among the best attended but boasts a respectable number of fans. The window-frame forms the proscenium arch to a set dressed to look like the interior of a typical suburban home, comprising a well-appointed living-room-cum-dining-room and, at the top of a flight of stairs, a recessed upper-level master bedroom with bathroom en suite. Through the ground-floor windows can be seen a backdrop diorama of a garden with a neatly mown lawn ending in flower beds and a fence. The interior of the house is decorated in no particular style, unless an abundant, disorganised profusion of furnishings, ornaments and gadgets can be called style. The rooms are crammed with knick-knacks, bric-à-brac, baubles, trinkets and high-tech appliances, in the midst of which a family of four – father, mother, teenage daughter, young son – are eating breakfast.

The four living mannequins, who bear scant familial resemblance to one another, are talking animatedly over their meal. Their conversation is relayed to the window-shoppers through loudspeakers mounted on either side of the window and angled towards the audience. Every utensil they use and every item of clothing they wear has a price tag dangling from it, and the family are careful to refer to the cost and the quality of any product they come into contact with. As Linda watches, the actress playing the mother gets up and goes to the sideboard. There, she slices some oranges in half, first holding up the cutting board so that everyone can have a good look at it (and its price tag), then making a great show of the sharpness of the knife, running the ball of her thumb along the blade and pretending to give herself an accidental nick. Laughing, she sucks at the imaginary wound. Her stage family laugh along with her.

When she finishes cutting the oranges, which she assures her family are the freshest and finest on offer anywhere, she holds up a Days-brand electric orange squeezer, showing off its attractive, ergonomic styling and its easy-to-disassemble, easy-to-clean components. In fact, she liked the squeezer so much she bought two, one in white, one in beige. Her family are equally admiring of both. Son demands to be allowed to squeeze the oranges, and excitedly scampers up to the sideboard and starts turning the orange halves to juice. Mother looks on proudly, saying, 'See, it's so straightforward and safe, even a child can use it.'

Meanwhile, Father is complimenting Daughter on her hairdo. She shows him how easy it is to put your hair up in a chignon with a loop device which she just happens to have with her at the breakfast table and which is available exclusively from the Styling Salon Department at Days. Father is fascinated by the simple yet cunning implement. He strokes his thinning crown and says that he would do something similar with *his* hair, if only he had enough. Daughter finds the joke unbelievably hilarious, giggling and slapping her father's forearm in an oh-you! way.

Linda wonders if she might not buy that loop device. She will, if nothing else, visit the Styling Salon Department and bring herself up to date on the latest tools of the trade.

Mother and Son, returning to the table with a jug of delicious, freshly squeezed orange juice, give the other two members of the family looks of amused confusion, which sends Father and Daughter into paroxysms of conspiratorial glee.

Then an elderly neighbour comes in by the front door, stage right, clutching a bottle of pills which she simply *has* to tell the family about. She reminds them of her *terrible* back pains, bending double, clapping a hand to her lower lumbar region and wincing. It used to feel as though someone was stabbing knitting needles into her spine. Mother shakes her head compassionately as she recalls what miseries the poor dear suffered. But then Elderly Neighbour's face brightens. She taps the lid of the bottle of pills and says that after just five days on these she noticed a significant improvement. Mother can scarcely believe it. 'Just five days and you noticed a significant improvement?' Elderly Neighbour nods enthusiastically. She straightens her back. 'See? The pain is all gone.'

The family – and the window-shoppers – gaze at the bottle of pills as though it contains water from Lourdes. Elderly Neighbour holds it up with the label and Days logo showing, so that no one watching can be under any misapprehension as to where these miracle-working analgesics can be purchased.

Linda finally manages to tear her gaze away from the scene, only to find her attention roving to the other displays, each of which is equally absorbing in its own way. Families, couples, flat-sharing friends, holidaymakers at a tropical resort, women at a beauty parlour, workers in an office, fitness enthusiasts in a gym, schoolchildren in a classroom, swimsuit-clad sunbathers basking on a narrow strip of sand and bronzed by a battery of arc-lights, thespians all, theatrically sing the praises of the items of merchandise that surround them in a cornucopic clutter.

Up until at least the age of eight, Linda used to think that the people in the displays lived there all the time. Never mind that her mother insisted that they were just actors and actresses, Linda remained firmly convinced that when the people inside the windows walked off-stage they carried on being who they were on another hidden part of the set – a belief which survived long after the truth about Santa Claus and the Tooth Fairy was out.

Remembering this childhood misapprehension now, she feels both affection for the naive creature she was and amazement that, given her upbringing, she had any illusions left at all by the time she was eight. But then Days has always been a magical place for Linda. Every Advent, she and her mother would make the pilgrimage here to see the Christmas displays. On cold December afternoons, wrapped up in so many layers of clothing that she could hardly move her limbs, she would hold her mother's hand tight as they strolled from one window to the next. It was impossible for them to circumnavigate the building completely, ten kilometres being much too far for a child to walk in a single afternoon, but every year, as Linda grew taller and stronger, they would cover a little more of the distance than previously, and as they walked they would stop at any window that caught their eye and gaze in at a wintry outdoors set with leafless trees and drifts of fake snow or a cosy, firelit interior scene where the living mannequins would be busy decorating the hearth or wrapping gifts or singing carols, scenes of domestic harmony utterly unlike the sullen Christmases at Linda's house, with her father stomping and grumbling like Ebeneezer Scrooge for the entire festive season and moaning at Linda's mother whenever she tentatively broached the subject of having relatives over for lunch on Christmas Day or getting Linda the bicycle they had been promising her year after year, calling her a sentimental old cow or a swindling bitch.

Those trips to Days are among the few happy memories Linda has of her childhood. Her mother, no doubt because she was free of her husband's debilitating influence, would talk and laugh with a brightness and lightness in her voice Linda never heard at any other time of the year and, as the two of them rode the bus home afterwards through the deep-blue dark, they would discuss which window was the best and how this year's displays compared with last year's and what might have been in the windows they were unable to reach and what novelties they might look forward to seeing next year. And those were the only times that Linda could reassert her claim that one day she would have an account at Days and receive nothing from her mother in reply but a slow, sweet and, in retrospect, sad smile.

'Gordon,' Linda says softly, and her husband starts and blinks, unaccustomed to hearing his name spoken with such tenderness. 'Let's go in, shall we?'

She slips her hand into his and tugs him toward the steps. She wishes her mother was alive to see her now, her mother who never had faith in anyone because she was never allowed to have faith in herself. She wishes her mother could see how believing in yourself makes anything possible.

They mount the steps and pass through the entrance doors. The hallway makes Linda gasp. Photographs she has seen have not prepared her for the real thing. Bustling with customers. The lifts disgorging new arrivals. The lofty ceiling. The sea-green marble floor. The chandelier. The mosaic of precious stones, too beautiful to pass by. The Trivetts pause at its perimeter, and Linda gazes down in awe at the twin semicircles of opal and onyx.

'Wish I'd brought a hammer and chisel with me,' says Gordon.

Linda tells her husband not to be vulgar. That's precisely the sort of thing a Days customer *doesn't* say.

A woman approaches them. Her jacket and skirt are matching dollar green, and around her neck she wears a silk scarf with tiny Days logos printed on it, pinned at her throat with a cloisonné Days-logo brooch. Her hair, Linda notes, is hennaed. It doesn't match her dark eyebrows, and anyway, no one's hair is naturally that red. A skilful job, none the less, and the way the woman wears it scraped back offsets the roundness of her face, giving her the appropriate air of authority and efficiency. The ID badge attached to her breast pocket says that her name is Kimberly-Anne. Below her name is her employee barcode.

'Lovely, isn't it?' says Kimberly-Anne, gesturing at the jewel mosaic. If her smile were any brighter you would need sunglasses to look at it.

Linda nods.

'Is this your first visit to Days?'

'It is,' says Linda. She is too entranced by the floor mosaic to be annoyed that her and Gordon's inexperience is apparently so obvious to everyone.

'Then let me tell you a little bit about finding your way around the store. First of all, you'll need this.' Kimberly-Anne hands them a booklet from the small stack in her hand. 'It contains maps to all six floors, showing every department and indicating where the cloakrooms, lifts, escalators and restaurants are. Usually we advise newcomers to plan out a route beforehand so that they can visit all the departments they need to with less risk of getting lost, but you look like intelligent people, you probably won't have to do that.'

Linda graciously thanks her for the compliment.

'The next thing you have to consider is something to put your purchases in. We have a range of options available. Would you care to accompany me?'

Before either of the Trivetts can answer, Kimberly-Anne is striding off in the direction of the motorised carts and shopping trolleys. Linda turns to Gordon, he shrugs, and they follow her.

Kimberly-Anne leads them to one of the motorised carts, an electric buggy that seats two, with a large cubic volume of open boot space at the rear. She waves her hands over it like a conjuror's assistant demonstrating the apparatus for the next trick.

'A cart is the most comfortable and convenient way of getting around Days,' she says, 'and is complimentary to all Osmium and Rhodium customers.'

'That's not us,' says Linda, flattered by the implicit assumption that she and Gordon look like the sort of people who could hold one of the two highest accounts.

'Then for a small hire-charge – '

'We don't need one,' says Gordon. He looks at his wife. 'Well, we don't.'

Kimberly-Anne indicates the phalanxes of gleaming wire trolleys. 'Then how about a trolley instead? Every wheel guaranteed to turn without wobbling or sticking at speeds not in excess of seven kilometres per hour, i.e. a brisk walking pace, and complimentary to all Palladium and Iridium customers.'

'That's not us either,' Linda admits, a touch ruefully. 'But it might be a good idea to hire one.'

'Linda,' says Gordon under his breath, 'we haven't been here five minutes, you've already made a large dent in our account, and now you want to make a larger one. I thought you said we were going to be careful.'

Linda vaguely recalls saying something to that effect, once, before their application was accepted. 'Fair enough, the taxi was an extravagance,' she replies, 'but a shopping trolley is a necessity.'

'It'll only encourage us to buy more than we can afford.'

To appease her husband, Linda relents. 'How about one of those?' she asked Kimberly-Anne, pointing to some tall stacks of wire handbaskets.

'Of course,' says Kimberly-Anne. 'Free to anyone with a Platinum or Gold account.'

'Platinum or Gold?'

'That's right.'

'Not Silver.'

Kimberly-Anne's smile loses a degree of candlepower. 'Not Silver, no. Silver account-holders may hire a handbasket for – '

'You mean we have to pay to use a basket?' exclaims Gordon.

Kimberly-Anne flinches but quickly recovers her composure and her smile, although the latter is perceptibly dimmer now.

'Silver and Aluminium account-holders *are* expected to pay a nominal charge in return for the use of any of the available carrying devices,' she says.

'It won't kill us to hire a basket, Gordon,' Linda insists. 'We can afford it.'

'That's not the point. They shouldn't be charging us for something that should by rights be free. That's extortion. Daylight robbery.'

'Gordon, the Day brothers don't run Days for the fun of it. This isn't a charitable concern. This is a business, and the purpose of a business is to turn a profit. Isn't that so, Kimberly-Anne?'

Kimberly-Anne nods warily, not certain if it is wise to agree with one customer at the expense of another, even when the other customer is obviously in the wrong.

'There's a difference between turning a profit and ripping people off,' grumbles Gordon. 'Come on. We'll do without.'

He is heading for the arches before Linda can stop him. She apologises to Kimberly-Anne, whose smile has by now been reduced to a feeble one-amp flicker, and hurries after her husband.

Catching up with him, she hisses, 'You embarrassed me awfully back there, Gordon.'

Gordon does not reply, merely strides purposefully up to an arch and waits for her to join him there with their card.

An obliging guard shows Linda how to insert the Silver into the wall-mounted terminal and gain admittance. Linda is so annoyed with Gordon that neither the sight of their names appearing on the terminal screen (confirmation that they belong here) nor the sight of the bars retracting to let them through thrills her. Luckily, her anger also means that she forgets about the pepper spray in her handbag and is thus spared the anxiety she would otherwise have felt over smuggling it through the metal detectors.

Then they are on the shop floor.

12

Covetousness: another of the Seven Deadly Sins

9.05 a.m.

Still smarting over his cowardly behaviour in Mr Bloom's office, Frank takes a lift from the Basement to the Red Floor, then rides a double-helix strand of escalators, zigzagging up through the levels. As one escalator after another lifts him higher and higher, a vague, dismal dread settles in his stomach. The prospect of the day ahead, with its tedium, its irritations and its unpredictable dangers, is a gloomy one, scarcely alleviated by the knowledge that for him it is going to be the last of its kind. His thoughts start to clot like bad milk, and he literally has to shake his head to disperse them. Eight hours, he tells himself. Less, counting breaks. Less than eight hours of this life to go, and then he is a free man. He can grit his teeth and endure the job for another eight hours, can't he?

On a whim he gets off at the Blue Floor. There is never any pattern to Frank's working day once the store opens except the timing of his breaks, which are staggered with those of his fellow Ghosts so that at least eighty per cent of the Tactical Security workforce is out on the shop floor at any given moment. He travels at random, letting impulse and the ebb and flow of events direct him. The difference between the hours leading up to opening time and the hours after is the same as the difference between waking thought and dreaming – a matter of control. Frank surrenders himself to the random.

Finding himself in Taxidermy, he wanders through to Dolls, from there to Classic Toys, and from there to Collectable Miniatures, staying with a knot of customers, then latching on to a lone browser, then hovering for a while beside an open cabinet of temptingly pocketable hand-painted thimbles.

He keeps an eye on customers carrying large shoulder-bags, customers with rolled-up newspapers clutched under their arms, customers with long coats on, customers pushing prams with blanket-swaddled toddlers on board. They could all be perfectly innocent. They could all be as guilty as sin. His job is to hope for the former but always suspect the latter.

He watches a customer engage a sales assistant in conversation, and immediately he starts looking around for an accomplice. It is an old pro trick. While one shoplifter diverts the sales assistant's attention, his partner makes the boost. In this instance, however, it seems that the customer is on his own, and is genuinely interested in some Meissen figurines.

Then a pair of Burlingtons swan past, and Frank moves off silently in their wake.

The Burlingtons are a cult of spoilt teenage boys who parade their parents' wealth like a badge of honour, wearing the glaringly expensive designer trainers, the crisp white socks, the tight black trousers, and the gold-moiré blouson jackets that are the unofficial uniform of their rich-kid tribe. These two, it transpires, are on the hunt for rare baseball cards, and Frank dogs them so closely that he could, if he wanted to, raise his hand and stroke the fuzz of their close-shaved hair, half of which has been dyed black, half bleached blond.

The Burlingtons lead him into Showbusiness Souvenirs, where he detaches himself from them in order to circulate among the displays of stage costumes, old props, production stills, foyer cards, autographed publicity shots of long-faded stars, and crumbling movie and concert posters preserved behind clear perspex.

The centrepiece of Showbusiness Souvenirs is a locked, reinforced-glass case that holds, among other things, a pair of incontinence pants soiled by an internationally renowned rock'n'roll star during his drug-sodden twilight years; the polyp removed from a former US president's lower intestine; the skull of a universally despised yet unfathomably successful blue-collar comedian; the steering wheel from the car fatally crashed by a screen legend; a blunted bullet retrieved from a dictator's shattered head by a souvenir-seeking soldier at the climax of a successful *coup d'état*; the stub of the last cigar ever smoked by an unusually long-lived revolutionary leader; a specimen of blood extracted post mortem from the body of a notoriously bibulous politician and decanted into a phial disrespectfully labelled '100% Proof'; a preserving jar containing the aborted foetus of the love-child begotten by an actress and a prominent member of the clergy; a razor-thin cross-section of a famous theoretical physicist's brain sandwiched between two plates of glass; and a framed arrangement of pubic-hair clippings from various porn-film artistes. All of the above items are accompanied by certificates testifying to their authenticity.

A ponytailed man in a navy blue suit is loitering beside this cabinet of curiosities, and at the sight of him Frank's nape hairs start to prickle, as they did at the sight of the girl on the train.

There is nothing intrinsically suspicious about what the ponytailed man is doing. Plenty of people linger over the collection, gazing at the rare and expensive mortal mementoes with disgust or fascination or a ghoulish combination of the two. And he isn't exhibiting any of the tics and mannerisms that usually prefigure an act of store-theft. His casual air seems genuine. He isn't aiming surreptitious glances at the sales assistants or other customers, one of the 'flagging' signs Frank was trained to recognise. His breathing is controlled and steady. But Frank doesn't always go by visual clues alone.

Frank would be surprised if over the course of his thirty-three-year career he *hadn't* developed an instinct about shoplifters. In the same way that older deep-sea fishermen can somehow sense where the big shoals are going to be and experienced palaeontologists sometimes seem to know that a patch of ground will yield fossils even before the first spade has struck soil, Frank can identify a potential shoplifter almost without looking. It is as if thieving thoughts send out ripples in the air like a stone cast into a pond, subtle fluctuations which he has become attuned to and which set alarm bells ringing in his subconscious. It is not the most reliable of talents, and has been known to mislead him, but as a rough guide it is right far more frequently than it is wrong.

The closer he gets to the ponytailed man, the deeper his conviction grows that the man is planning to steal something. Possibly not from this department, and certainly not from the case in front of him, not unless he is carrying a sledgehammer or a set of skeleton keys, but soon, very soon. The man is pausing here to prepare himself mentally, turning his intentions over and over in his head. Outwardly he betrays not the slightest sign of anxiety or anticipation. A professional.

When the ponytailed man finally moves away from the glass case, Frank falls in behind him and follows him like a silent second shadow.

They proceed out of Showbusiness Souvenirs in tandem, the suspect unsuspecting of his pursuer. Their course takes them away from the centre of the building, and the further from the atrium they go, the less frequented, less splendid, and less brightly illuminated the departments become. Soon they arrive at the dim and dusty perimeter departments known as the Peripheries.

A kind of commercial vortex holds sway on the floors of Days: the closer you get to the centre of the building, the more popular the departments become. The most heavily in-demand departments with the fattest profit margins are clustered around the hoops, while, at the opposite end of the retail scale, the departments that constitute the Peripheries are consigned to the far-flung edges by the slightness of their sales figures. The only exception to this rule is the Red Floor, which, being the one floor every customer has no choice but to visit, consists of nothing but in-demand departments.

Conditions in the Peripheries are commensurate with their lowly status. You might expect them to enjoy windows and a view to compensate for their remoteness and for the fact that they are accessible from only three adjacent departments – in the case of those at the corners of the building, only two – instead of the usual four, but though the Peripheries possess exterior walls, the exterior walls are solid. No windows on the shop floor of Days means no outside world to distract the customers within from their shopping. The only natural light to be found anywhere in the store enters via the clear half of the dome, a semicircular gift of sunshine to nourish the chlorophyll of the Menagerie.

The Peripheries specialise in commodities that are obscure, exotic, inessential, or just plain arcane. Some of the items on offer are of great value, but buyers are far and few between, hence trade is always slow and sales figures always low.

Quiet, intense, obsessive men and women, all experts in their particular fields, staff the counters here, and so absorbed are they in their daily round of cataloguing recondite items of stock and rearranging merchandise according to abstruse personal systems that they barely notice when the ponytailed man passes. When Frank ghosts by a few paces behind, his rubber-soled shoes padding softly on the carpeted floor, they fail to notice at all.

Through Used Cardboard, through Occult Paraphernalia, through

Vinyl & 8-Track, through Beer Bottles, the quiet, leisurely chase continues. If the ponytailed man pauses for a moment to inspect some piece of merchandise, Frank pauses to inspect a piece of merchandise, too. If the ponytailed man slackens or quickens his pace, Frank slackens or quickens his. If the ponytailed man scratches his earlobe or purses his lips, Frank finds himelf reflexively copying the action. He becomes the ponytailed man's doppelgänger, matching him move for move, gesture for gesture, in split-second-delayed symmetry.

At one point, in Nazi Memorabilia, the ponytailed man glances behind him, and catches sight of a man dressed as smartly as you would expect a Days customer to be dressed, a man intently inspecting a display of Luftwaffe uniform insignia, a man in every respect unremarkable, unmemorable. A second after he has glimpsed Frank's face, the ponytailed man has forgotten it. When, a department later, he happens to look over his shoulder and catch sight of Frank again, he doesn't even register that this is the very same person he saw before.

On they go, shadower and shadowee, possible perpetrator and Ghost, until they reach Cigars & Matchbooks.

As the ponytailed man passes through the connecting passageway to this particular department, there is an all but imperceptible stiffening of his spine, and Frank knows in his gut that this is where the suspect is going to make his play.

He utters a subvocal cough to activate his Eye-link.

'Eye,' says a male screen-jockey.

'Hubble.'

'Mr Hubble! What can I do for you?'

The connection is so clear that Frank can hear other voices in the background, keyboards rattling, the trundle of chair-wheels across linoleum, a muted but urgent warble of activity underpinned by the cicada whine emitted by hundreds of heated cathode-ray tubes – the ambient hubbub of the Eye leaking through into his ear.

'I'm on Blue, trailing a possible into Cigars & Matchbooks.'

'Cigars & Matchbooks? Cor, strike a light, guv!' The screen-jockey giggles at his own joke. Eye employees and their tiresome sense of humour are aspects of the job Frank will definitely feel no nostalgia for in his retirement.

'He's a white male. About a metre eighty. Medium build, I'd say seventy-five to eighty kilos. Early thirties. Suit, tie. Ponytail. Two small hoops in right earlobe.'

'Hang on,' A ferocious tapping of keys. 'Cigars & Matchbooks, Cigars & Matchbooks . . . OK, got him. Corporate non-conformist type.'

'If you say so. I think he's a professional. I don't recognise the face, but that doesn't mean a thing.'

'Early bird, isn't he?'

'The early bird catches the worm unawares. Or so he hopes.'

'Nice one, Mr Hubble. That was almost funny.'

'Eye, please just get on with what you're supposed to be doing.'

'Actually,' says the screen-jockey with a school-playground inflection, 'I've already triangulated him.'

A quick upward glance confirms this. The security camera above Frank's head is locked on to the ponytailed man, following his every movement. In another corner of the ceiling a second camera also has a fix on him. Swivelling on their armatures, the two cameras track his progress like a pair of accusing fingers.

'I can't see you yet, Mr Hubble,' the screen-jockey adds.

'I'm about ten metres behind.'

'Oh yes. It's so easy to miss you lot. Want me to start recording?'

'Yes, I do.'

'Okey-doo. Smile and say cheese.'

'Please,' says Frank, striving to inject a note of impatience into his ventriloqual drone.

'Sor-ee,' says the screen-jockey, and mutters to a colleague, off-mic but loud enough for Frank to hear, 'I've got old Hubble Bubble, Toil and Trouble.'

His colleague offers a sympathetic groan.

Frank says nothing, and two seconds later the short-wave automatically cuts the connection in order to conserve its tiny lithium cell.

The Cigars portion of Cigars & Matchbooks resembles the smoking room of a gentleman's club, with magazine-strewn coffee tables and green-shaded lamps, dark-framed etchings on the walls and bookcases lined with old volumes of the kind bought by the metre. Lounging on the buttoned-leather furniture, their feet resting on footstools, customers – predominantly male – make their selections from humidors held open for them by liveried sales assistants. Some, unable to wait until they get home to sample their purchases, have lit up and are sitting back contentedly puffing out plumes of smoke, idly leafing through a periodical or admiring the shine on their toecaps.

The Matchbooks portion, which once boasted the floorspace of an entire Violet Periphery department to itself, now occupies a partitioned-off area roughly the tenth of the size it used to enjoy. When the Day brothers took over the Violet Floor for themselves, Matchbooks was merged with – though perhaps the correct phrase should be absorbed by – Cigars, and in order to adapt to its reduced circumstances, most of its existing stock was sold off and its staff whittled down to one. It could have been worse. Those displaced Violet departments for which a natural lodging could not be found on a lower floor, which constituted the majority, were simply closed down and deleted from existence.

The smells of cigar smoke, cardboard and sulphur mingle and tingle in Frank's nostrils as he trails the ponytailed man towards the burnished mahogany rolltop desk that serves as Matchbooks' sales counter. Along the way the ponytailed man pauses to admire several of the matchbooks mounted in clear vinyl wallets on the partition walls. He's a cool one all right; so relaxed and confident Frank could almost believe that this is one of the occasions when his instinct has let him down.

Except the man's eyes are unfocused. He doesn't look at the matchbooks he is supposed to be examining, only goes through the motions of looking, his thoughts elsewhere. Another giveaway sign, obvious if you have been trained to recognise it.

At last he approaches the mahogany desk. The sole remaining Matchbooks sales assistant is a man whose white hair and sallow, wrinkled features put him somewhere in the same age bracket as Frank. The name on his ID badge is Moyle, and at present his attention is absorbed by the matchbook he is examining through the jeweller's loupe screwed into his right eye-socket. The ponytailed man ahems to attract his attention. He ahems again, and this time Moyle notices. He looks up, the loupe dropping expertly into a waiting cupped hand.

'Sir,' he says. 'How may I help you?'

'I'm looking for a birthday present for a friend of mine. He's into matchbooks.'

'Well, you've certainly come to the right place. What did you have in mind?'

'I'm entirely in your hands.'

'Avid collector is he, this friend of yours?'

'Oh yes, very.'

'Then I suggest the easiest thing to do would be for you to name a price range, and I can tell you what we have that fits the bill.'

The ponytailed man mentions a figure that causes Moyle to raise his chin and purse his lips in a silent whistle.

'A most generous birthday present, sir. A close friend of yours, I take it?'

'Very close.'

'Well then, let's see what we've got, shall we?' Moyle turns to the baize-covered board behind him to which are pinned several dozen more of those vinyl wallets containing matchbooks of various colours and sizes – prime specimens all. He plucks three down.

'This is no less than a Purple Pineapple Club matchbook,' he begins, holding the first wallet up delicately by the corner for the ponytailed man to view its contents at close quarters. 'As your friend will no doubt be able to tell you, the Purple Pineapple Club was shut down three days before it was due to open when the principal member of the backing consortium filed for bankruptcy and took his own life. Fifty specimen promotional matchbooks were printed up, but only about half that number are believed to be currently in circulation. Note the use of purple metallic ink for the logo and the cheerful cartoon illustration.'

'All of your matchbooks have had the matches removed,' the ponytailed man observed.

'Oh, sir, one never leaves the matches attached. Oh no.'

'Why not?'

'For one thing, the phosphorus discolours the card. Mainly, though, it's because matchbooks are better stored and displayed flat.'

'I didn't know that. All right, how much?'

Moyle picks up a scanning wand from the desk and runs its winking red tip over the barcode sticker attached to the back of the vinyl wallet. The price appears on the readout of the credit register linked to the scanning wand by a coil of flex. He draws the ponytailed man's attention to the figure.

'I see,' says the ponytailed man. 'Anything slightly more expensive?'

'More expensive,' says Moyle, with poorly disguised eagerness. 'Well, there's this one.' He picks up another of the wallets. 'A special edition released to coincide with the official coming-out of a member of the royal family. Note the coat-of-arms motif featuring a pink crown and an entwined pair of human bodies. Rampant, as a heraldry expert might say. The story behind this one goes that the royal in question got cold feet at the last minute, hence the public proclamation of his sexual proclivities was never made, but a small number of the special edition matchbooks were pocketed by an equerry and thence made their way into the hands of private collectors. Naturally the palace press office denied there ever was going to be a coming-out announcement of any description and implied that the matchbooks must have been issued by an anti-royalist faction in order to discredit the royal family.'

'Like they need discrediting.'

'As you say, sir. Regardless, palace-authorised or not, a tiny quantity of these matchbooks exist, and the story attached lends them a certain novelty, don't you think?'

'I don't suppose there's any way of guaranteeing its provenance?'

'None at all, I'm afraid, sir. That's the trouble with what we call curio matchbooks.'

'Pity. My friend's a stickler for provenance.'

'All the best phillumenists are.'

Frank, hovering close by, observing all this unnoticed, makes a quick check of the security cameras. Every one he can see is trained on the ponytailed man. Good.

'Eye?'

'Still here, Mr Hubble.'

'Is there a guard on standby?'

'I've alerted one. He's two departments away. Name of Miller.'

'Well done.'

'You see? We're not all incompetent idiots down here.'

'I wish I could believe that.'

There is a spurt of sarcastic laughter. 'You're on form this morning, Mr Hubble!'

Thinking thunderclouds, Frank returns his attention to the scene being played out at the counter.

'What about that one?' says the ponytailed man, pointing to the third matchbook Moyle has selected.

'Ah, this one. The Raj Tandoori, an upscale Indian restaurant. First printing. Lovely design but, as you can see, there was a typographical error. "The Rat Tandoori." Unfortunate oversight or malicious printer's prank? Who can say? Either way, the restaurateur felt, understandably, that the association of rodent and food might not encourage repeat custom and ordered a new batch printed up and the originals pulped. A few, however, survived. Much sought-after. Almost unique. But there is some slight damage to the striking pad, as you may have noticed, and the cover hinge has a tiny split in it.'

'May I take it out and have a look anyway?'

'Certainly. Just be careful with it, I beg of you.'

'Of course.'

The ponytailed man slips the matchbook out of its wallet and looks it over. Moyle watches with a concern that is not wholly proprietorial, which is almost that of a parent for a child, his hands poised to catch the matchbook should it happen to drop, but the customer seems to know how to handle precious artefacts such as this, holding it by the corners only, touching it with his fingertips alone, treating it with the kind of awed respect usually accorded a venerable, crumbling religious relic.

Satisfied that the man isn't about to damage the matchbook, Moyle turns back to the baize-covered board. Tapping a thumb against his lips and humming, he casts an eye over the stock, then reaches up decisively and unpins two more wallets, which he lays in front of his customer just as the ponytailed man is resealing the 'Rat Tandoori' matchbook into its wallet.

'Interested?' Moyle enquires.

'Not in that one, no.'

'Any particular reason why, might I ask?'

'My friend has a penchant for the immaculate.'

'For a mint-condition "Rat Tandoori" original you're looking at a price considerably higher than the admittedly handsome sum you mentioned, sir, but I could try to track down one in slightly better health if you like. One's bound to turn up at an auction sooner or later.'

'Bound to,' agrees the ponytailed man. 'But in that case I'd rather buy it myself and avoid your outrageous mark-up.'

'Then I'm afraid neither of these will suit you,' says Moyle, puzzled by his customer's sudden bluntness.

'They both look a bit tatty,' the ponytailed man agrees, glancing briefly at the new offerings.

'Remember, we're dealing with ephemera here,' Moyle points out. 'The appeal of matchbooks as collector's items is their very lack of durability. I'm sure that's the way your friend feels about them.'

'I'm beginning to think I'd be better off spending my money on something else for my friend,' the ponytailed man says. 'Thanks for your time anyway, but no sale.' He turns to go.

Moyle's shrug doesn't adequately hide his obvious dismay.

`'Eye?'`

`'Yup.'`

`'Get Miller to intercept. He's heading back out of the Peripheries into Oriental Weaponry.'`

`'He boosted? I didn't see a thing.'`

`'Let's hope one of the cameras did.'`

Cunning devil, thinks Frank as he dogs the ponytailed man out of the department.

9.19 a.m.

The ponytailed man has stopped to admire a pair of *katana* in beautiful black-lacquered scabbards when a hand grabs his upper arm, fingers digging into his biceps with a polite but insistent pressure.

'Excuse me, sir.'

The ponytailed man looks round into a crinkled, saturnine face into which are embedded a pair of eyes the colour of rainy twilight. He fails to recognise a man he has seen at least twice already in the last quarter of an hour.

'Tactical Security,' says Frank. 'Would you mind if I had a word?'

The ponytailed man immediately starts looking for an exit, and in doing so catches sight of a security guard ambling towards them. The guard is over two metres tall and as broad at the waist as he is at the shoulders, packed densely into his nylon dollar-green uniform like minced meat into a sausage skin.

The ponytailed man tenses. With a weary inward sigh Frank realises he is going to make a run for it.

'Please, sir. It'll be so much better for everyone if you stay put.'

Miller, the guard, is still ten metres away when the ponytailed man wrenches his arm out of Frank's grasp and makes his bid for freedom. Miller moves to intercept him, and the man blindly dashes right, running headlong into a rice-paper screen on which has been mounted an array of *shuriken*. The screen folds around him and collapses, and the ponytailed man collapses with it. Throwing stars fly off in all directions, spinning like large steel snowflakes.

Miller rushes forward, but the ponytailed man scrambles to his feet, snarling and brandishing one of the *shuriken* like a knife.

'Get away! Get away from me!'

Shrugging, Miller raises his hands and backs off a few paces.

'False arrest!' the ponytailed man shouts. 'I haven't done anything! False arrest!'

A small crowd of spectators swiftly gathers.

'I haven't stolen anything!' The man gesticulates frantically with the throwing star.

Frank is by Miller's side. 'Can you take him?' he asks.

'Course I can,' Miller growls. 'When I was inside, I used to kick seven shades of shit out of blokes like him all the time. Just for fun.'

'What about the throwing star?'

'He doesn't know what he's doing with it. You get 'im on disk?'

'Eye?'

'I'm searching, I'm searching. Hang on. Yeah, there it is. Shit. That was *fast*.'

Frank nods to Miller, and the guard breaks into a huge, humourless grin.

He moves swiftly for a man of his bulk. Three brisk strides, and he is inside the arc of the ponytailed man's arm. Before the man can bring his weapon around, Miller's hand flashes out, encloses the fist holding the *shuriken*, and squeezes. The ponytailed man shrieks as the star's points pierce his palm. He falls to his knees, and Miller twists his arm behind his back, still squeezing. Blood streaks the ponytailed man's wrist and smears the back of his jacket. He tries to writhe his way out of the hold Miller has him in, but the guard only tightens his grip on the *shuriken*-wielding hand, forcing the throwing star's points further into the flesh of the ponytailed man's palm until they grind bone. The man bends double, snivelling with the pain, unable to think about anything except the pain, the riveting, sickening pain.

Frank has his Sphinx out. He hunkers down beside the agonised shoplifter and recites the Booster's Blessing.

'For the record, sir,' he says, 'at 9.18 a.m. you were spotted removing an item from the Cigars & Matchbooks Department without having purchased it and with no obvious intent to purchase it. For this offence, the penalty is immediate expulsion from the premises and the irrevocable cancellation of all account facilities. If you wish to take the matter to court, you may do so. Bear in mind, however, that we have the following evidence on disk.'

Frank holds the Sphinx's screen up before the man's face and the Eye duly transmits the recording of the theft.

It was a skilful piece of sleight of hand, one no doubt practised countless times until it was honed to perfection. While Moyle's back was turned, the ponytailed man whipped out a duplicate of the 'Rat Tandoori' matchbook from his pocket, simultaneously palming the original into a slit cut in the lining of his jacket. It was the duplicate he was reinserting into the vinyl wallet when Moyle turned back to the counter, and were it not for Frank the substitution would most likely have gone unnoticed until the day a genuine matchbook aficionado with money to burn chose to add that particular rarity to his collection.

The crime is replayed on the Sphinx's screen in two short clips from two different angles. The first clip shows the fake matchbook coming out but not the real one going in. The second leaves little room for doubt, although, even when slowed to half-speed, the exchange seems to take place in the blink of an eye. Much as he hates to, Frank has to admire the shoplifter's dexterity. Just as he thought: a professional.

'Do you understand what I'm showing you?'

Frank isn't certain the ponytailed man was looking, but when he repeats the question, the man nods and says yes.

'Good. Now, I need to see your card.'

'Come on, you, on your feet,' says Miller, hoisting the ponytailed man upright. 'Get your card out. Slowly. No tricks.'

His face is livid and streaked with tears but the ponytailed man's eyes are still defiant as he reaches into his inside pocket with his uninjured hand and produces a Silver.

'Cheap sod,' mutters Miller. 'Couldn't score better than that?'

'Fuck off,' says the ponytailed man, without too much enthusiasm.

Having extracted the *shuriken* from the ponytailed man's palm, the guard proceeds to handcuff him. Frank, meanwhile, runs the card through his Sphinx. Central Accounts has no record of the card being reported as stolen, but when the account-holder's picture appears on the Sphinx's screen it doesn't take Frank long to deduce that the man standing in front of him is not Alphonse Ng, aged sixty-two, a jowly, pugnacious-looking Korean.

'How much did you pay this man Ng?' he asks the shoplifter.

'I don't know what you're talking about.'

'And how long did he agree to wait before reporting it missing? A week? Two weeks?'

The man does not answer.

'OK, fine. We'll have a word with Mr Ng, see what he says.'

But Frank and the shoplifter both know what Mr Ng is going to say. He is going to say either that he lost the card or that it was stolen from him, and he will express delight at having it back, and he will swear to look after it more carefully in the future, and nothing further will be done about the matter. The store's policy is always to reunite cards with their owners, whatever the circumstances, no questions asked. To do otherwise would not make commercial sense.

'Now,' Frank tells the ponytailed man, 'the guard is going to take you downstairs for processing and eviction. If at any time you attempt to resist him or to escape, he is within his rights to subdue you using any means necessary, up to and including lethal force. Do you understand this, sir?'

The shoplifter gives a short, weary nod.

'Very good. Don't come back.'

Yet even as he utters those last three words, Frank knows it is useless. The shoplifter will be back just as soon as his hand heals, if not sooner. The ponytail will be gone, as will the earrings and the blue suit, and he will be disguised – as a Burlington, perhaps, or a foreign diplomat, or a priest (it has happened) – with yet another black-market card in his pocket and yet another legerdemain tactic for obtaining goods without payment. If only the Days administration didn't cling to their belief that permanent banishment from the store is suitable punishment for any crime committed on the premises and didn't refuse to prosecute shoplifters through the courts, professionals like this one wouldn't exist and Frank wouldn't feel as if he is trying to bale out a leaky boat with a sieve. As it is, all he can do is make the arrests, have the thieves thrown out, and catch them at it again the next time. The most he can hope for is that one person in the now-dispersing crowd of onlookers, just one, having seen how shoplifters are treated when they are caught, will think twice before succumbing to the temptation in the future. It's a slim hope, but what is the alternative?

None of this, of course, will matter after today, and that is why Frank is calmer than he might have been as he pulls back the flap of the shoplifter's jacket and fishes out the purloined matchbook from the slit in the lining. It gladdens him to think that tomorrow he will no longer have to be stoically playing his part in this cyclical exercise in futility; that tomorrow he will be free.

9.25 a.m.
'Oh my,' says Moyle. 'Oh dear.' He holds up the two matchbooks side by side for comparison, switching them over, switching them over again. 'That's a skilful piece of forgery, that is, and no mistake. He must have had it made up from the picture in the catalogue. A perfect copy right down to the split in the cover hinge. You can see why I was fooled, can't you?'

'Yes, I can,' says Frank, 'but what I can't see is why you turned your back on him. That was negligent in the extreme.'

'He seemed legitimate.'

'They *all* seem legitimate, Mr Moyle.'

'True. And you know, now that I think about it, the way he suddenly changed his mind about buying a matchbook *was* rather odd, wasn't it? It was as if he couldn't wait to get out of here.'

'He couldn't.'

'Well, you've got him, that's the main thing,' Moyle says. 'You've caught him and I get my "Rat Tandoori" original back. All's well that ends well, eh?' He raises his eyebrows hopefully.

'It'll have to go down in my report that you turned your back on him.'

Moyle nods slowly to himself, digesting this information. 'Yes, I thought as much. That's the sort of mistake that can cost a chap his job, isn't it?'

'I'm sure it won't come to that. A few retirement credits docked. A slap on the wrist.'

Moyle gives a resigned laugh. 'That I can live with, I suppose. The main thing is that you recovered the matchbook, for which I and all other *genuine* phillumenists thank you, Mr Hubble, from the bottom of our hearts.'

'Just doing my job.'

Moyle carefully slots the genuine matchbook into its wallet and tosses the replica contemptuously into the waste-paper basket.

'It must seem rather odd to you, my interest in these little cardboard trifles,' he says with a self-deprecating smile. 'Most people find it incomprehensible. My former wife, for one. Though that surely says more about her than it does me.'

'I must admit the fascination is rather lost on me.'

'You obviously don't have the soul of a collector.'

'I do accumulate objects. Possessions. By accident, mostly.'

'And then, without realising it, you find your possessions have come to possess you?' It is more of a statement than a query.

'I try to keep things in perspective.'

'Then you aren't a collector,' says Moyle. 'A collector's perspective is entirely skewed. He sees only that which obsesses him. Everything else is relegated to the background. I speak from experience.' He sighs the resigned sigh of a man too set in his ways to change. 'But I mustn't keep you. I know your job prohibits you from fraternising at length with other employees. Thank you again, Mr Hubble. I am in your debt, and if there is any way I can repay the favour, I will. I mean it. If I ever have the chance to do something for you, I'll do it. Anything you need, anything at all.'

'Just keep a closer watch on your stock,' says Frank.

13

9.26 a.m.

Up in the Boardroom, Thurston has been rattling through the day's admin with characteristic efficiency, typing notes and e-memos into the terminal at the same time as he talks.

Currently he and his brothers are discussing a fire which broke out at one of the Days depositories the previous week. Thurston can reveal that an exhaustive internal investigation has traced the culprit: a sacked forklift operator nursing a grudge. However, since the fire was discovered and extinguished by a night watchman before it could do much damage, and the destroyed stock was insured anyway, the brothers vote as one not to prosecute the arsonist – a decision which has nothing to do with magnanimity and everything to do with the brothers' aversion to dealing with the courts of the land. Days, they like to think, is a nation within a nation, a law unto itself, and resorting to common legal procedures would tarnish, and perhaps diminish, the store's scrupulously cultivated aura of sovereignty.

Next on the agenda is the possibility of a new and even lower grade of account. This idea has been put forward by Fred, who, as he is only too keen to remind everyone, was responsible for initiating the Aluminium scheme that rescued them during that bad spell a couple of years back when the monthly figures dropped into the red for the first time ever. Now, with sales falling again – though still healthy enough, Fred hastens to add – it might be a good idea to allow another stratum of the population in through the doors of Days.

Wensley wants to know what Fred would call the new grade. Tin? Lead? Rusty Iron?

Fred thinks Copper has a nice ring to it.

Thurston wonders whether an account which will be available to just about anybody might not fatally compromise the exclusivity that Days relies upon to attract and keep its clientele. Why not, he says, if the store is going to go *that* downmarket, simply throw the doors wide open and let the whole world in?

Mungo concurs. For all the extra income that another grade of account will bring in, wealthier customers and regulars of some years' standing might decide that the world's first and (naturally) foremost gigastore has let its standards slip a shade too far and transfer their custom to another gigastore in protest – the EuroMart in Brussels springs to mind as a likely candidate, confusingly laid-out and ill-organised though it is. Besides, the effort it takes to become an account-holder is precisely what makes Days so alluring to so many. You don't value highly what you haven't had to struggle for.

Fred concedes the point and in the ensuing show of hands votes against his own proposal, which is defeated six to none.

Thurston then lists the latest appeals that have been made to the brothers for charitable donations. Each is voted on in turn. Human rights campaigns are summarily dismissed. The countries that supply the store with the cheapest raw materials and manufactured goods tend, by uncanny coincidence, to be those whose governments most loosely interpret the meaning of the term 'democracy', and the brothers are reluctant to be seen to be censuring the dictatorships and military juntas that help fatten their profit margins. Animal rights groups, conservationists, and disarmament lobbyists are also deemed too politically sensitive. Which leaves societies for the disabled, arts funding and a scheme for providing inner-city children with two-week holidays in the countryside as the least controversial recipients of tax-deductible gifts from Days, and at the same time the most likely to enhance the store's prestige.

Thurston mentions in passing that the cost of maintaining Days Scholarships in Retail Studies at the nation's two oldest universities is due to increase as a consequence of fresh government education cuts, and that they should give serious consideration to scrapping at least one of the endowments. Since all the brothers attended one of the universities and not the other, their natural inclination is to favour their alma mater at the expense of its rival. However, as Sato slyly points out, since the other university can't boast the Day brothers among its distinguished alumni, it, surely, is more deserving of their beneficence. The vote is split, three to three, and since Sonny is not on hand to cast a deciding vote, Thurston resolves that both scholarships will remain in place for the time being.

Then there are the numerous requests for television and newspaper interviews to be dealt with. These the reclusive brothers turn down without exception, but it is always a pleasure to read the letters from editors and producers forwarded to them by the Public Relations people in the Basement. They find the tone of the letters – a syrupy cocktail of flattery and extreme unctuousness – amusing.

Likewise, it is customary for invitations to attend this or that prestigious dinner or art gallery opening or film première to be read out by the day's chairman, and then equally customary for them to be consigned with lofty disdain to the rejection pile. The brothers take great pleasure in confounding all efforts to popularise and demystify them. There is always speculation, of course. Almost daily the electronic and print media run stories attributing bizarre illnesses, manias, and eccentricities to the sons of Septimus Day, and at Thurston's request Fred, the brothers' self-elected media monitor, reads aloud a list of the latest, gleaned from the tabloids and the TV gossip shows.

1) Sato has taken to walking naked around the Violet Floor all day long;

2) Wensley's weight has ballooned to two hundred kilos;

3) Thurston has contracted a wasting disease;

4) Thurston is going blind in his left eye (a story headlined, 'Their Father's Disfigurement Is A Curse!');

5) Fred is dependent on barbiturates and can't sleep a night unless he is sharing a bed with Mungo;

6) Mungo has so overdeveloped the muscles in his arms and thighs that he can no longer straighten his limbs fully;

7) Chas has had plastic surgery to correct a minor defect in the cleft in his chin; and

8) Sonny has cleaned up his act and has subscribed to a phone-in alcoholics support group – anonymously, of course.

If only (the brothers wish) that last story had any basis in the truth. As for the other fictions, they laugh them off. Let the world believe what it wants to believe about them. Let it ridicule them, turn them into cartoon figures. Nothing anyone can say can affect them. Over a hundred metres above the ground in their self-contained Violet Floor eyrie, insulated from the sweat, fuss and filth of the city, why should they care what people think of them? As long as customers keep coming to Days, what difference can a few tall tales make?

Further points of business are raised and tackled, and then Thurston comes to the matter of a territorial dispute between two departments.

'This one's been pending for quite a while,' he says. 'I came across it yesterday evening while going through the files in preparation for this morning. Something we've all been overlooking.'

'Probably with good reason,' mutters Fred.

'The e-memo comes from both sections of Security,' Thurston continues. 'E-memos plural, actually. The first reads, "The Heads of Strategic and Tactical Security would be grateful if the administration would investigate the present hostilities between the Books Department and the Computers Department and deliver a binding judgement to resolve the situation."' He taps keys, reading selections from the texts of the subsequent e-memos. ' "The ongoing 'state of siege' that exists between Books and Computers shows no signs of improving and every indication of impending deterioration." "Numerous customers have been caught in the 'crossfire' of acts of aggression and intimidation . . ." "Possibility of fatalities arising as a consequence of the state of mutual intimidation . . ." "Violence and sabotage . . ."' He looks around at his brothers. 'Has anyone heard anything about this before?'

Heads are shaken.

'Apparently it's been going on for well over a year, ever since we authorised Computers to expand into floorspace occupied by Books.'

'A sensible decision,' says Sato. 'Computers has a larger turnover of product and therefore demands a greater amount of display area. Books has been consistently running at a loss, so it seemed logical that it should surrender floorspace to its immediate neighbour. We told Computers to annex a strip of floorspace one metre wide and ten long. Ten square metres of Books.'

'And the Bookworms don't like it,' says Wensley. 'Well, we made our decision. They're just going to have to learn to live with it.'

'The trouble is,' says Thurston, 'they haven't. In a series of what the memos call "guerrilla raids", the Bookworms have system-atically been throwing out whatever merchandise the Computers

Department employees set out in this ten-metre strip and replacing it with their own merchandise. And the Computers employees – '

'Technoids, I believe they call themselves,' Chas offers helpfully, keen to show off his knowledge of shop-floor jargon.

'The Technoids,' says Thurston, using the nickname with some distaste, 'haven't been taking it lying down. Fights have been breaking out and sales assistants on both sides have been getting hurt.' He pulls up another e-memo on the terminal: '"Three sales assistants had to be hospitalised today as a result of a skirmish on the strip of floorspace between Books and Computers, the latest and bloodiest episode in this rapidly escalating conflict. This matter now demands the administration's most urgent attention."'

Sato winces. 'Sick-leave. Sick-pay.'

'Worse,' says Mungo, 'stock has been damaged. Why didn't anyone draw our attention to this sooner?'

'As I said, it was on the file,' says Thurston. 'Security has put in a total of seventeen e-memos, but the first was filed under Employee Disputes and all the subsequent memos were automatically routed the same way.'

That explains it. Every once in a while a head of department will single out one of his subordinates for a hard time or a floor-walker will be accused of claiming others' commissions as his own, but the arguments almost always resolve themselves by the time the reports reach the Boardroom, and so the brothers have taken to ignoring Employee Dispute e-memos. Why bother?

'But still we should have noticed,' says Chas, 'because Employee Dispute e-memos usually come from Personnel and these ones came from Security.'

There are murmurs of agreement.

'So it's an oversight,' says Wensley, shrugging. 'It's not too late to rectify it.'

'Quite,' says Sato. 'But in the light of our apparent inefficiency, instead of issuing our decision electronically it would be more politic if one of us actually went down there and dealt with the matter in person. The personal touch may make all the difference.'

'And we all know who that someone's going to be,' says Chas, with feigned rancour. As though he never has any choice in the matter.

'Oh, Chas,' says Fred, clasping his hands together beseechingly. 'Please. None of us wants to go down there, and you're the best at dealing with, you know, *ordinary* people. Oh, please say you'll do it for us. Please. I'll get down on my hands and knees and kiss your patent leather slip-ons if I have to. Anything. Just say you'll go.'

'Chas, would you mind?' says Thurston. 'It's simply a question of getting the heads of both departments together and giving them a good talking-to.'

'Threaten them with their jobs if you have to,' says Mungo. 'That's what I'd do.'

'Just get them to stop damaging our property,' says Wensley.

Chas is about to raise his hands in surrender and agree to do as his brothers ask, at the same time declining Fred's generous offer for fear that his brother's lips will ruin the shine on his shoes, when one of the Boardroom doors is flung open.

A moment later a head appears round the other door, followed by a body. The hair on the head shows signs of having recently been towelled dry, while the body is clad in wrinkled jeans and a checked shirt that has been buttoned incorrectly.

The new arrival comes tottering into the Boardroom, a hand clamped to one side of his forehead as though to keep his brains from spilling out through a fissure in his cranium. He shuffles across the floor, each step seeming to cost him a world of effort, until he reaches the table. There he stops, steadying himself against its edge, and, swaying slightly, stares around at the faces of the six brothers, who look back at him with expressions ranging from mild concern to thinly veiled contempt. He takes his hand from his forehead and examines the palm as though genuinely expecting to find it smeared with grey matter. Then he returns his gaze to the brothers.

His brothers.

'Morning, all,' he says, then lets out a short, abrupt laugh, as though he has cracked the funniest joke of all time.

'Good morning, Sonny,' says Thurston, icily. 'We were wondering where you'd got to.'

14

Benten: one of the Shichi Fukijin, the seven Japanese gods of luck, and the only female among them, she brings good fortune in matters pertaining to wealth, feminine beauty, and the fine arts

9.58 a.m.

A glance at a wall clock reminds Frank that a lightning sale is about to take place.

Having memorised the order of the day's sales while Mr Bloom was running through them during the morning briefing, he doesn't have to check his Sphinx for the location. First on the list is Dolls. Four departments away, and therefore close enough for him to feel obliged to attend.

Since collaring the shoplifter, Frank has been wandering the Blue Floor, mulling over his conversation with Moyle. Moyle is right about him not having the soul of a collector. But how to account for the objects and gadgets that cram his apartment? All the artworks and items of furniture he has accumulated over the years almost without being aware of it, all the possessions purchased on a whim, all the *things* he has surrounded himself with and barely notices – what absence in him do these fill?

The root of the problem lies, he thinks, in his time at the Academy. In his Ghost training.

Frank was eighteen and fresh out of school, a young man with high hopes and low self-esteem, when he applied for a job at Days. He had no idea what aptitude he might have for working at the store. His exam results had been good, but they alone would not guarantee him employment even as a sales assistant, and anything higher than a sales assistant – anything at the administrative level, for instance – was barred to all but university graduates with good degrees. He filled in the relevant forms and sent them off simply because that was what everyone else was doing and, while he waited for the response to his application to come through, he found work as a night porter in a medium-grade hotel, a nice, unobtrusive job that gave him plenty of time to read, think and generally be by himself.

Months went by, and every once in a while he would ring Days Personnel to enquire whether his application had even been received. More often than not he listened to a recorded message informing him that all the lines were busy. On those rare occasions when he got through to a human being, he was assured that job applications were being processed as fast as humanly possible and that his would doubtless be got round to eventually.

He was beginning to lose hope, and considering reapplying, when the reply came. Inside a fat brown envelope watermarked with Days logos was a vast questionnaire dozens of pages long that covered over a thousand topics, some as innocuous as Frank's favourite foodstuffs, television programmes and newspapers, others as prurient as his religious inclinations, his sexual feelings (if any) for children under the age of consent, and his relationship with his parents (which was almost nonexistent, seeing as his father had passed away several years ago and his mother was surviving on state benefit and a diet of prescription tranquillisers). The questionnaire took hours to fill in, but he persevered, suspecting that it was intended as a kind of first hurdle for prospective employees, there to winnow out the half-hearted.

He sent it back, and expected to have to wait several months more before learning if he had earned an interview or not. The form letter accompanying the questionnaire had warned him that interviews were being booked as far as two years in advance. He resigned himself to a long wait, and continued working nights at the hotel.

But the response from Days was surprisingly swift. Barely weeks passed before a letter arrived asking him if he could come in for an interview that autumn.

The interview, in a chamber in Personnel in the Basement, lasted three hours. Senior Personnel administrators went over many of the same topics that had been covered by the questionnaire, interrogating Frank closely in order to ascertain whether he had been telling the truth or not.

He was an only child?

That was correct, he told them.

Good. And his father?

Died when Frank was eleven.

He rated family and friends low on a scale of 'things important to him'. Why was that?

Because he found people in general troubling and intrusive.

Good, good. And did he have trouble getting served in shops?

Sometimes, yes.

Did people sometimes barge in front of him in queues without apologising?

That had happened, yes.

Did he often find himself standing alone in the corner at parties?

He didn't get invited to too many parties.

And so it went for three long, gruelling hours, and at the end of it Frank was sent to sit out in the hallway while the Personnel administrators conferred. He slumped on a chair, feeling like a wrung-out dish rag. Some time later, he wasn't sure how long, he was invited to come back in, and was told that his personality profile was ideally suited to Tactical Security.

Embarrassed by his ignorance, he asked what Tactical Security meant, exactly, please.

Store detection, he was told. Would he consider training to become a Ghost?

Not entirely sure that he wanted to spend the rest of his life as a store detective, and a little hazy about what the job entailed, Frank was nevertheless not so stupid as to turn the opportunity down, reasoning that if things didn't work out he could always go back to night portering or, since it appeared that he had a bent for law enforcement, apply to join the police force. He told the administrators yes, went home and told his mother what had happened (she, predictably, was underwhelmed), went to the hotel and handed in his notice (the manager there was considerably more impressed and encouraging), and almost immediately embarked on the year-long course of Ghost Training.

The first six months of Ghost Training took place at the Academy, a fenced-in compound on the outskirts of the city, situated in one corner of the spacious grounds of the mansion owned by Septimus Day. There, at the hands of a team of instructors made up of former Ghosts, Frank was taught the basics of self-defence, use of sidearms, and the technique of guttural ventriloquism known as subvocalisation. He learned how to recognise the flagging signs that identify a shoplifter and was instructed in the methods the more inventive professional boosters employ, such as carrying a box with a false side for slipping stolen goods into, or pushing a hand through a slit in a coat pocket in order to pillage shelves under cover of the coat flap.

Once he had mastered those skills, he was initiated into the mysteries of congruity – the art of blending into the background, of appearing just like anyone else and therefore like no one. In this his natural drabness helped him greatly. Since childhood Frank had always been one of those people who are overlooked, whose face no one remembers, whose name slips out of people's memories and lodges on the tip of their tongue where they can't find it. He was, not to put too fine a point on it, a nobody, and naturally this was an attribute he had always considered a drawback, but his Ghost Training showed him that it could also be a virtue. He was taught to cultivate a bland, abstracted air and never let his face show what he was thinking; to avoid making sudden, erratic gestures which might mark him out as an individual; in short, to damp down what little spark of personality he possessed until it was no more than a infinitesimal wink of light, dimmer than the farthest star. By the end of the six months he had refined his innate innocuousness to such a degree that he could, if he wanted to, walk through a crowded room and pass entirely unnoticed.

Halfway through his training his mother died. He was given time off to organise the funeral, which he did in an efficient but perfunctory manner. At the ceremony itself, in the company of a handful of estranged relatives and his mother's semi-estranged friends, he felt some sadness, but not much. Perhaps this was a by-product of his training, perhaps not. For a long time there had been a distance between him and his mother, a drug-chilled void. Death only made that distance slightly more remote. In many ways losing her came as a relief. It shaved further complications from his personality, helping to strip away the emotional ties that stood between him and full Ghosthood.

On average, only a tenth of the trainees at the Academy develop congruity sufficiently to go on to become fully fledged Ghosts. The rest are advised to seek an alternative career. Frank was singled out by his instructors as being an exceptionally apt pupil. Without much difficulty he graduated to the second part of the course: six months of practical experience on the shop floor.

Donald Bloom, who himself had been a Ghost for only a little over a year, showed Frank the ropes. Under Mr Bloom's affable tutelage he learned the ins and outs of the store, tramping the floors (all seven of them, because this was back in the days before the brothers commandeered the Violet Floor for themselves), going over and over the same ground until he had the location of all 777 departments securely locked away in his memory. At the same time he further refined the skills he had acquired at the Academy. Side by side with Mr Bloom he drifted behind customers and lurked where he was least likely to be seen but where *he* could see as much as he needed. The two of them loitered without intent, lingered without langour. It was Mr Bloom who helped Frank make his first official collar, and that was a moment of achievement whose sweetness Frank will never forget.

By the time the year of Ghost Training was up, the metamorphosis was complete. Frank had becoming a living cypher. A professional nonentity. Congruous. A Ghost.

And in return for effecting that transformation, Days offered him a gun, a Platinum account with the performance-related possibility of promotion to Iridium, and a job for life.

It is hard to believe now that he could have thought this a fair trade, but then how many sane twenty-year-olds would turn down the offer of a generous salary linked to a secure career?

In short, Days made him who and what he is today. Days took a shy, introverted young man and stripped him of any last vestige of personality he might have had. His Ghost Training hollowed him out like a rotten tooth, and since then the only means he has found of filling the emptiness inside him is by buying expensive things that he has little time or desire to enjoy.

And the worst of it is, all this was done with his consent. He has no one to blame for how he is but himself. Days merely capitalised on a natural asset, and he willingly allowed the exploitation.

At least the imminent sale gives him something to think about other than himself. With his intimate knowledge of the store it doesn't take him long to work out the quickest route to Dolls, and off he goes. East through Private Surveillance, filled with all manner of bugs, phone taps, body wires and miniaturised recording devices – a therapeutic playpen for paranoiacs. North through Oriental Weaponry, where sales assistants dressed in black ninja garb have almost finished resurrecting the folding screen of *shuriken*. North again through Military Surplus, the department for the professional mercenary and for anyone who can't get through the night without a camouflage hot-water bottle cover. And once more north, this time through Classic Toys.

He arrives at the passageway connecting Classic Toys to Dolls just as a phrase of seven notes chimes out over the store's PA system, followed by a female voice announcing the lightning sale in the stern yet seductive tones of a dominatrix.

'Attention, customers. For the next five minutes there will be a fifteen per cent reduction on all items in Dolls. I repeat, for the next five minutes only, all items in Dolls will be marked down by fifteen per cent. Dolls is located in the north-eastern quadrant of the Blue Floor and may be reached using the banks of lifts designated B and C. This offer will be extended to you for five minutes only. Any purchases made after that period will retail at full price. Thank you for your attention.'

The hush that descends on the store for the duration of the announcement is absolute. Then, as the seven-note phrase is repeated, shoppers begin to move. They drop whatever they are doing, and hoisting up their handbaskets or swinging their trolleys around or stamping down on the go pedals of their motorised carts and spinning the steering wheels, they make for Dolls. Never mind that few of these people, if any, had the urge to buy a doll until now, and never mind that a fifteen per cent discount hardly amounts to the offer of a lifetime, a lightning sale is a lightning sale, and it summons bargain-hungry customers like an aid convoy summons the starving.

To those awaiting them in Dolls, the sound of their approach starts out as a distant whisper that shivers through the air like the wind before a storm. The expressions on the faces of the thousands of pieces of merchandise in Dolls remains unchanged but the expressions on the faces of the sales assistants and guards become apprehensive as the whisper increases in volume, deepening to a rumble like far off thunder in the hills, the noise of wheels on carpet and of hundreds of pairs of feet beating the floor.

The sound grows and grows, exploding to a crescendo as the first customers spill into the department. They rush in by all four entrances and swiftly fan out among the displays, plucking items off the shelves and scrutinising price-tags, their mouths wide open in avaricious rictus grins.

Frank has to leap smartly aside as a motorised cart comes hurtling past him through the passageway, missing him by a whisker. The driver is a hunched, withered old woman, ninety if she's a day, with brown, broken teeth, a jet-black pompadour wig perched on her head, crimson lipstick smeared roughly in the vicinity of her mouth, and a manic gleam in her eye that would perturb a psychopath. Frank recognises Clothilda Westheimer, the multimillionaire heiress.

Waving a walking stick in the air like a cavalryman's sabre and tooting on the cart's horn at anyone careless enough to get in her way, Clothilda Westheimer careers around the aisles until she almost collides with a florrid-faced, heavy-set man who is examining a box containing a lifelike plastic replica of a six-month-old baby. Brakes whine, the cart grinds to a halt, and Clothilda Westheimer screams at the man to move, using language that would make a sailor blush. The man's startled response is to hold up the baby in front of him as if its production-line innocence will somehow ward off this cursing, haranguing crone, but Clothilda Westheimer merely snatches the box out of his grasp and aims her cart for the nearest cash register.

A regular customer since the day the store opened, Clothilda Westheimer buys all her groceries at Days, and also buys extravagant gifts which, having no one else to lavish them on – she has disowned her relatives and has remained unmarried, despite the attentions of a stream of suitors – she lavishes on herself. She has an unmatched eye for a bargain and, as she has just proved, an unequalled skill at getting what she wants.

And on they come, flooding in by the dozen, more customers and yet more, barging, shouldering, elbowing one another out of the way, seizing merchandise off the shelves like a rabble of looters. All pretence of civility disappears, the rules of etiquette are abandoned, as they battle for bargains, dive into the displays, emerge with their prizes, and then join the crowd around the cash registers, there to brandish cards of all hues from dull grey Aluminium to pink-tinged Rhodium. Knowing they only have a limited time in which to secure a purchase and grimly determined not to leave the department without the doll they didn't know they wanted so desperately until now, the customers clamour for the sales assistants' attention and squeal like frustrated infants when other, less deserving individuals are given precedence.

Keeping to the shifting perimeter of the crowd, careful to stay out of reach of jabbing elbows and butting shoulders, Frank watches for suspicious behaviour, but all he sees is a collection of well-dressed, well-heeled men and women behaving like ravening animals. He sees two middle-aged men in lounge suits tussling over a purple-haired troll, each insisting, with mounting indignation, that *he* saw it first. He sees a rosy-cheeked porcelain Bo Peep, one of a collector's series based on characters from nursery rhymes, being used as a club by its prospective owner to batter a path through the heaving throng. He sees a small boy clasping a khaki-clad action figure to his chest and bawling raucously while his mother tries to force both him and herself through the crush of bodies to the cash registers. At one point the top half of the largest of a nest of Russian dolls pops clear of the mêlée and goes rolling across the carpet to fetch up at Frank's feet, its painted babushka face gazing up at him plaintively, as if begging him to intercede in the madness.

Disagreements degenerate into arguments. Queue-jumpers are dragged back by the scruff of the neck. A rough kind of frontier justice holds sway.

And all the while the harassed, wand-wielding sales assistants process the purchases as fast as is humanly possible (but nowhere near fast enough to satisfy the baying, demanding mob), and the overhead cameras, under manual control from the Eye, wheel and nod, viewing the activity below with a lofty, lazy curiosity.

A glance at his watch tells Frank that the sale has less than a minute to run, but the frenzy shows no sign of abating. If anything, the customers become more agitated as they sense the seconds slipping away. Pushy latecomers are given short shrift. Competitive jostling gives way to blatant shoving.

Then, at last, the seven-note sequence chimes out again and the female voice, with incisive calmness, pronounces the sale at an end. There is a collective sigh of disappointment from unsuccessful customers as they turn away from the cash registers, disgustedly discarding the dolls that only seconds ago they were frantic to buy. Those who were lucky enough to make a purchase leave the department hugging their booty, boasting to anyone who will listen how much money they saved. Arguments peter out, the antagonists coming to their senses as though awakening from a trance. They blink at one another in confusion, suddenly no longer sure what all the fuss was about. Some even exchange apologies (they don't know what came over them).

Slowly, in dribs and drabs, the crowd departs, leaving behind a litter of débris, dolls of all shapes and sizes lying everywhere, limbs twisted, like corpses in the aftermath of a nerve-gas attack.

The sales assistants, glad it's over, set about tidying up. The guards, shaking their heads in weary disbelief, stroll away.

Frank is just turning to go when a voice buzzes in his ear.

'Mr Hubble?'

'Hubble here.'

'A guard's made an arrest in Optical Supplies. You're in the vicinity. Can you get over there?'

'No problem.'

'Cool.' The screen-jockey breaks the connection.

Optical Supplies: two departments west, one south. Frank sets off, wondering if the rest of the day is going to be this busy and rather hoping it will. At least that way the hours will pass quickly.

10.07 a.m.

The guard is a young, petite, wiry-looking woman with dark eyes offset in a slight cast. Her black hair is pinned up at the back of her head in a tight bun. Frank knows her face, and her ID badge reminds him that her name is Gould.

He introduces himself – 'Hubble, Tactical' – and casts a cursory glance at the arrestee, who is sitting in a chair with her back to the wall, slumped and gazing abjectly at her hands in her lap as if they are the ones who have committed the crime, independently of her. She is – to judge by the fine striations that star her mouth and radiate like lines of magnetic polarity from the outer corners of her eyes to her temples – in her early fifties, and she is dressed in a pair of dark slacks and a maroon mohair jersey with a gold-and-diamanté brooch fastened at her collarbone. Her hair is a rich, dark-chocolate brown shot through with streaks of silver. Although some effort has been made to organise it, it looks matted and unkempt. Her slacks are rumpled and in need of pressing. In fact, the overall image she presents is a curious blend of customer and baglady, but despite this it occurs to Frank – a thought beamed down from an alien planet – that she is far from unattractive. In the right clothes, the right situation (which this abundantly is not), she could be quite striking. There is no ring on the fourth finger of her left hand, an absence Frank notes because it is a store detective's task to be alert to such details and not for any other reason.

'What did she take?' he asks Gould, drawing out his Sphinx.

'Just this.' Gould holds up a bottle of contact lens solution. 'Between you and me . . .' She moves closer to Frank for a confidential whisper. Frank recoils a fraction, but Gould does not appear to notice. 'She's one of the clumsiest shoplifters I've ever seen. I mean, she might as well have walked in carrying a placard saying, "I Am Here To Steal Something." Even without my training I would have known she wasn't kosher the moment I clapped eyes on her. She was trembling so badly I thought she had some kind of condition, you know, Parkinson's or something, but then when she spotted me, she jumped like a scalded cat, turned away, you know, like this.' Gould ducks her head to one side, hunching her shoulders and raising a hand to shield her face. An exaggeration, surely, and looking over at the arrestee again, Frank is pleased to see that the woman is still contemplating her hands and has not witnessed Gould's tactless impersonation.

'So I kept an eye on her,' Gould continues, 'and sure enough, not two minutes later she boosted. Her hands were shaking so much she could hardly get the thing into her pocket. It'd be laughable if it wasn't so pathetic,' she concludes with a grim twist of her mouth.

'Did you get her card off her?'

'She says she doesn't have one. Says she lost it.'

'Then how did she get in?'

'I have no idea. We'll find out downstairs, but I need you to make the arrest formal before I can take her down.'

'Of course.'

Frank goes over to the shoplifter. As he draws near he catches a strong scent of perfume emanating from her. Several different perfumes, in fact, a mingling of musks intended to disguise the smell of bodily secretions but, like a white sheet draped over a patch of wet mud, not wholly effective.

His nose and forehead wrinkle simultaneously.

At his approach the woman raises her head, and he sees that her eyes are inflamed, their whites crazed with capillaries, their lashes slick with moisture, all of which add to her general look of haggardness and disarray. The rest of her well-shaped face, though, is serene, resigned, perhaps even hopeful.

'Do I know you?' she asks, blinking rapidly and rubbing one eye.

'I don't think so.'

'I'm sure I recognise your face.'

It is possible she may have glimpsed him before somewhere on the shop floor, but she won't have remembered his face. No one does. That's the whole point.

He shakes his head. 'Not likely.'

'Oh. And I'm usually so good with faces. Have you come to throw me out?'

'That's not my job.' For some reason Frank finds himself unable to resist the inclination to speak gently to this woman.'I'm here to arrest you.'

'I thought I'd already been arrested.'

'Procedure.'

'What about her?' She points to Gould.

'As soon as I'm done with you, the guard will assume responsibility for your processing and eviction.'

'I know what you are,' the woman says slowly. 'You're a Ghost.'

'I'm with Tactical Security, yes.'

'Does anybody call you a store detective these days?'

'Sometimes. That, at any rate, is how I prefer to think of myself.'

'You prefer "store detective" to "Ghost"?'

'Most definitely.'

'How interesting,' the woman says, nodding to herself. Frank has the impression that she thinks she is at a cocktail party, making small talk. Consequently her next question catches him off-guard. 'Have you ever shot a shoplifter?'

He hesitates before deciding that he has nothing to lose by telling her the truth. 'A few times.'

'How many times?'

Frank frowns. 'Five, perhaps six. Back when I was starting out.

'And did you kill any of them?'

'I shoot to wound.'

'But it's not always possible to aim accurately, not in the heat of the moment.'

'No, it isn't.'

'So have you killed anyone by accident?'

'Not me,' he says. 'But it has happened.'

'And would you shoot me?' The woman fixes her bloodshot gaze on Frank, giving him such a searching look that for a worrying moment he fears she can actually see into him, see into his soul.

'If you resisted arrest or ran,' he answered eventually, 'it would be my duty to bring you down using any means at my disposal.'

112

'Would the fact that I'm a woman make any difference?'

Thinking of Clothilda Westheimer at the sale, Frank replies, 'None at all.'

'How interesting,' she says again.

Frank holds up a hand, pausing the conversation to subvocalise to the Eye. `Did you get a clip of the woman in Optical Supplies?'

`Certainly did. I was following her all the way. Subtle she was not.'

`All right.' He clears his throat and addresses the shoplifter formally. The Booster's Blessing. 'Madam, I regret that it is my duty to inform you that at 10.03 a.m. – 10.03?' He looks to Gould for confirmation.

The guard nods. 'Thereabouts.'

'Well, is it or isn't it 10.03?'

'Precisely?' Gould retorts coolly. 'I don't know. I was looking at *her*, not my watch.'

'We'll say 10.03 for now, but the time is subject to amendment.' Testily, Frank returns his attention to the shoplifter. 'At 10.03 a.m. you were spotted removing an item from the Optical Supplies Department without having purchased it and with no obvious intent to purchase it. For this offence – '

'I needed it.'

'I'm sure you did, madam.'

'My contact lenses were hurting, and I'd lost my card. I'd never have taken it otherwise.'

'For this offence, the penalty is immediate expulsion from the premises and the irrevocable cancellation of all account facilities. If you wish to take the matter to court, you may do so.'

'I don't.'

'Bear in mind, however, that we have the following evidence on disk.'

He presses the play key on his Sphinx, and he and the woman watch the clip of the theft on the screen. Gould was right: the woman is no natural born shoplifter. Trying to act casually while at the same time trembling like a palsy victim, she spends far too long inspecting the plastic bottles on the revolving rack in front of her before reaching out to take one, and as she does so she makes the elementary mistake of darting a glance over each shoulder – the quintessential flagging sign.

She tries three times to slip the bottle into the pocket of her slacks, becoming visibly more flustered with each attempt, until in the end she actually looks down in order to guide the stolen article into its hiding place. By this time Gould has appeared on-camera, coming up behind her. The clip ends with Gould taking hold of her arm.

'Do you understand what I'm showing you, madam?'

'Yes. Yes, I do.' The woman peers up at the ceiling. 'You know, I've often watched those little cameras following people around. I suppose I should have realised that they've also been following *me*. Perhaps I did realise but preferred not to think about it. It's quite disconcerting to think that someone is watching us all the time, seeing everything we do, don't you agree? I'm not a religious person, but that's how I'd feel if I were. That God has His eyes on me every second of the day, like those cameras, and that He's just waiting for me to slip up.' She returns her gaze to Frank. 'And what does that make you, I wonder, Mr Store Detective, if those cameras are God's eyes? You whose job is to hover at our shoulders and not be seen? You who force us by the threat of your presence to listen to our consciences?' Her tone shifts from ruminative to sly. 'An angel, perhaps?'

'Hardly.' Frank allows a small measure of irony to lift the word. 'I'm nowhere near pure enough.'

'Oh, angels don't need to be pure. They just need to be there.'

'Then that's us,' he said, humouring her. 'That's store detectives. Always there, always at your shoulder.'

'But not mine,' the shoplifter points out with a sorrowful little smile. 'Not any more. I broke the rules, didn't I? I'm not coming back.'

Neither am I, thinks Frank. Which makes them a pair, of sorts. The sinner and the disaffected angel, both denied a place in Mammon's heaven, one because she has strayed from the straight and narrow, the other because he can no longer bear the notion of staying.

'Well, let's get it over with, then,' says the shoplifter, rising stiffly to her feet. 'Mr Store Detective? You've been polite and considerate. Thank you.' The woman extends a hand. 'My name is Mrs Shukhov. Carmen Shukhov.'

The gesture utterly flummoxes Frank, who only touches people when he has to, when he has no choice, for instance when collaring a shoplifter. This woman, this Mrs Shukhov, wants him to take her hand in his? Their bodies to make contact, skin against skin? Absurd. It's bad enough that she has got him conjuring up abstract similarities between them. Now he has to form a physical bridge with her? Out of the question.

He bows instead, just a tiny forward tip of the head.

Realising she has stumbled over an unseen boundary, Mrs Shukhov embarrassedly withdraws the proffered hand. She tries to apologise, and is almost relieved when Gould takes her by the elbow and leads her away from Frank and her *faux pas*.

As the guard and the shoplifter leave the department, Mrs Shukhov makes a doomed attempt to pat her unruly hair into shape, and again Frank is puzzled by her air of neglected elegance. It looks as if she has been wearing the same clothes for at least a couple of days, and in that time hasn't been near a make-up case or a bath. None of which would mean anything if she didn't come across as the kind of woman for whom appearance and personal hygiene matter. And then there is the question of how she got in without a card, unless she is lying about losing it. And why risk your Days account over a bottle of contact lens solution, for heaven's sake?

All very perplexing, but let them sort it out in Processing. Ultimately, it's not Frank's problem.

15

Heptarchy: government by seven persons

10.07 a.m.

By now the rightmost of the Boardroom's triptych of south-facing windows is almost entirely taken up by the dome's dark side. A dazzling reflection of the cloudless sky whitens the surface area of clear glass that still predominates, a convex mirror of the convex heavens, while scratches and flaws in the ever-encroaching segment of smoked glass refract the light into needle-thin rainbows.

Inside the Boardroom there is a strained silence as six of Septimus Day's sons look on while the seventh painstakingly mixes himself a gin and tonic.

Sonny, the tip of his tongue lodged in one corner of his mouth, is concentrating as hard on the task at hand as if he were constructing a scale model of a Gothic cathedral out of matchsticks. He has succeeded in pouring a generous measure of gin and a top-up of tonic into the glass without spilling too much of either, but now he finds himself having to grapple with the slippery problem of how to get half-melted cubes of ice out of the malachite bucket with only a pair of silver ice tongs to help him.

The way Sonny handles the tongs, you could be forgiven for thinking that they were not a tool designed expressly for the purpose of retrieving ice cubes from an open container. He operates them as though hampered by an invisible pair of gardening gloves, and whenever he does manage to secure one of the deliquescing lozenges of frozen water between the tongs' clawed tips, it invariably escapes and goes skidding across the tabletop (and more often than not over the edge of the table and on to the carpet) before he can transfer it to the glass.

For his audience it is the worst kind of slapstick, teeth-grindingly aggravating to watch. Each brother has the urge to go over, snatch the tongs out of Sonny's hands and, as if he were an invalid, do the job for him. Anything to bring the whole pitiful performance to an end.

Sonny saves them the trouble. Losing patience, he abandons the tongs, reaches into the bucket, and plucks out a fistful of ice to toss into his drink. A slice of lemon follows. Then, carefully sliding the brim-full glass towards him, he brings his nose to the surface and inhales, revelling in the tangle of tangy aromas – juniper, quinine, lemon. Puckering his lips into a funnel, he sucks up a mouthful.

'Fabulous!' he croaks, slapping the arm of his throne, and takes another long, noisy slurp, and another.

Having drained two centimetres of liquid by this means, he feels he can safely pick up the glass. He polishes the drink off in two swift swallows.

His hands are steadier, his movements more fluent and less grimly precise, as he pours himself a follow-up. Gulping it down, he feels the pulsing, nauseating rage of his hangover begin to dim as the alcohol spreads its glacial tendrils through his bloodstream. The hot iron bands cinching his eyeballs slacken their pressure, and his brain begins to feel less like a dozen kilogrammes of molten magma and more like an organ capable of reason and deduction. To his observers, the outward signs of this inward regeneration are the pinkish glow that dawns in his pallid cheeks and the substantial improvement in his physical co-ordination.

Confidently Sonny reaches out to pour himself a third drink. This one winds up being nine parts gin to one part tonic, a tongue-blistering ratio that, when swallowed, sends a wave of regurgitative heat burning back up his throat. He sucks in air. 'Whoa! Ooh! Ah!'

Eventually the inside of his mouth cools, and a big fat grin butters itself across his face.

'Well,' he says, beaming blearily around the table, 'here we all are again. Another day of custom and commerce and profit and plenty and all that shit. What have I missed?'

'Only everything,' says Sato tonelessly.

'Perhaps a quick recap of the morning's admin would refresh all of our memories,' says Mungo to Thurston.

Thurston sighs, twists his lips into a Möbius strip, then punches his minutes of the day's meeting back up on to the screen and scrolls quickly through them, reading each heading aloud. He concludes by saying, 'We've voted decisions on all of those,' and sits back in his typist's chair, folding his arms.

'Actually, not all,' says Mungo. 'That interdepartmental dispute . . .'

'We came to a decision on that.' Thurston eyes his eldest brother cautiously.

'But we didn't actually vote on it and, now that Sonny's here, it's only right that his opinion be sought and his vote counted. So, Thurston, run through the details of the dispute again, and if Sonny or anyone else feels like adding any comments, fine. If not, let's just vote on it and call the meeting to an end.'

'Thanks, Mungo,' says Sonny. 'I knew I could count on you.'

Thurston, with a surly grimace, leans over the terminal again, calls up the history of the disagreement between Books and Computers, and summarises it in a few terse sentences. Sonny, meanwhile, takes the opportunity to mix himself a fourth drink. The food on the silver salver in front of him – grilled bacon, eggs and tomatoes, a round of toast with butter and marmalade – goes untouched. Sonny rarely feels up to eating anything until after midday, by which time he has relaxed his stomach with a soothing lining of liquor. Nevertheless, at Mungo's insistence Perch serves Sonny a solid breakfast every morning as well as a liquid one, in the hope that one day the former will suggest itself as an appetising alternative to the latter.

'And so,' Thurston concludes, 'we decided that Chas should go down and sort it out.'

'Good idea,' says Sonny, without looking up. 'A few silken words from the Sultan of Smooth and they'll be rolling over on to their backs, begging to have their bellies tickled.'

'You have a better suggestion?' says Chas, a crease of annoyance unbalancing the enviable symmetry of his features.

'I do, but what chance does it have of getting a fair hearing?'

'Not much,' Chas admits.

'There you go. No point in opening my mouth. But then *that's* hardly news, is it? For all the influence I have around here, I might as well be a janitor.'

'It's not our fault you don't get a day of chairmanship,' says Wensley in what he hopes is a placatory tone. 'It's just how Dad arranged it. We may think that his obsession with the number seven was perhaps a little misguided, a little *anal*, but there's nothing we can do about it. What's ordained cannot be unordained.'

'Yes, it can,' says Sonny. 'We could open on Sundays, for one thing. That would put me on an equal footing with the rest of you.'

The response is as immediate as it is inevitable. Sonny would have

118

expected little else of his brothers. He knows what each is going to say almost before he has said it.

'Out of the question,' Thurston snaps.

'Think of the expense,' says Sato. 'We'd have to put employees on shifts and we'd have to pay them overtime rates. That would never do.'

'And we wouldn't want to offend our Christian customers,' adds Chas.

'And what about the living mannequins?' says Fred. 'They deserve a day of rest as much as anyone.'

'*We* need a day of rest,' says Wensley.

'Besides,' says Chas, 'Dad specifically decreed that the store would never open on a Sunday. "Sunday," he said, "is the keystone of the week." Remember? "Its purpose is to hold the other six in place, and for that reason it must be kept distinct from the rest."'

'How predictable, how absolutely fucking predictable.' Sonny looks imperiously from his gilded throne at each of his brothers in turn. 'And how absolutely fucking hypocritical, too. I can think of at least two conditions Dad laid down when he handed the store over to us that you've overridden since he died.'

'Introducing the Aluminium was a sound commercial move,' Fred asserts. 'And a necessary one. Dad would have approved.'

'But he said there should never be more than seven grades of account.'

'And as for taking over this floor for ourselves, we needed to,' Wensley says. 'We couldn't go on living out *there*.' The sweep of his arm indicates the unseen city beyond the Boardroom's walls. 'Out among the *customers*, for heaven's sake.'

'But he said the store should always occupy all seven floors of the building.'

'If you count the Basement as part of the shop floor, then it still does,' says Sato.

'I see,' says Sonny. 'So it's all right to bend Dad's rules when it suits us but not when it doesn't. Not, for instance, if it means that *Sonny* might actually have some responsibility.'

The hush that falls around the table – each brother expecting another to respond – implicitly acknowledges the truth of what Sonny has just said.

'We realise that Dad's conditions were unfair,' says Mungo, aware that he is arriving a little too late with this piece of conciliation, 'and we fully intend to give you some responsibility, Sonny, but only when you prove you're worthy of it.'

'I *am* worthy of it.'

'Maybe, but you haven't yet *shown* us that you are.'

'It's a vicious circle. How can I show you if you won't give me the opportunity?'

'If you turned up for work in the mornings on time, smartly dressed and sober,' says Thurston, 'that would be a start.'

'What difference would it make?' The words are prettified with a laugh, but not enough to disguise the despair in them. 'You'd still ignore anything I had to say.'

'We might not,' says Mungo. 'Didn't you say you had a suggestion about the dispute?'

'You'll only laugh when you hear it,' says Sonny sullenly.

'We won't.'

'You will.'

'We won't. I swear. We all swear.' Spoken so solemnly by Mungo that no one else at the table dares demur.

'All right then. You asked for it. Hang on a second.' Sonny takes a courage-instilling gulp of gin and tonic, and says, 'Send me instead of Chas.'

His brothers break out into hoots of derision.

'I knew it!' Sonny's face sags with dismay. 'I knew you wouldn't take the idea seriously. You're nothing but a bunch of bare-faced fucking liars, the lot of you.'

'I'm sorry,' says Mungo, shaking his head, grinning. 'If I'd known you were about to crack a joke, I wouldn't have promised not to laugh.'

'It *wasn't* a joke. I mean it. Let me go down and talk to the heads of the departments. All I have to do is let them know that we stand by our decision about the area of floorspace and that if they don't like it, they can bugger off.'

'I doubt an approach like that would do much to resolve the situation,' says Chas. 'The job calls for tact, diplomacy, subtlety, empathy, a certain delicacy of touch. Hardly your strong suits, Sonny.'

'Yeah,' says Fred, 'sending *you* would be like sending an axe-murderer to perform brain surgery.'

But Sonny is determined to be heard out. 'Look, how can I possibly screw up? They'll listen to whatever I have to say to them, and they'll do whatever I tell them to do. I'm a Day brother. I'm their boss.'

'Yeah, right,' snorts Fred.

'He does have a point there,' Mungo admits, nodding slowly.

'He does?'

'One of us going down to visit them in person will make it clear we're serious. What difference will it make which one of us it is? As far as they're concerned each of us carries the authority of all seven, and they'll be too awed to do anything but go along with whatever Sonny says.'

'Don't do this, Mungo.'

'Don't do what, Thurston?'

'Don't take his side. It's not profitable.'

Mungo turns to face his youngest sibling, commanding his full attention. 'Sonny, if we do confer this responsibility on you, and I'm not saying we're going to, but if we do, you have to be prepared to give us something in return.'

'What sort of something?'

'An assurance.'

'I'm not sure I follow you.'

'If, perhaps,' Mungo says, 'you were to leave that drink in front of you unfinished, and we had Perch come in and take away the gin bottle . . .'

'You mean jump on the wagon?' Sonny says, in the same tone of voice he might use to say, 'You mean jump off a cliff?'

'For this morning, to begin with. At least until after you've been downstairs. I think the employees will respond more favourably if you're not falling-down drunk when you address them, and more to the point your head will be clearer and so will your judgement.'

'Wouldn't you say I was drunk now?' Sonny gestures at the level of gin in the bottle, which is several centimetres lower than it was when he arrived.

'For someone with your capacity, Sonny, it takes three and a half G and T's just to reach minimum operating efficiency.'

Sonny nods. 'True. That's true.'

'And if you prove that you can stay sober, or as sober as you need to be, when we ask you to, then maybe we'll give you other things to do,' says Thurston, tumbling to Mungo's scheme and quietly impressed. 'Work will be your incentive to clean up your act.'

'I see,' says Sonny. 'You're offering me a deal.'

'Correct,' says Mungo. 'Which indicates that I respect you as a son of Septimus Day.'

'So let me get this straight. If I don't drink the rest of this bottle, you'll let me go down and deliver an arbitration.'

'That's about the size of it.'

'I can't believe this. This is a practical joke, isn't it? I'm going to go downstairs and find you've made this whole Books/Computers thing up.'

'I wish we had.'

'So you'll really let me do it?'

'As long as you keep your side of the bargain.'

'No problem.'

'So that's a promise?'

'It is.'

'Then you can go.'

Sonny lets out a whoop. 'Wow! This is great! This is fantastic! What can I say? Thanks, brothers. Thanks a lot.'

'You're welcome,' says Chas.

'If,' Mungo adds, 'no one has any objections.'

He sees Sato bite his lip.

'Well?'

'I think we're making a mistake,' says Sato after a moment.

'That's a reservation, not an objection.'

'I'm aware of that, but given the mood currently prevailing around this table, to make any sort of protest will seem churlish and lacking in public spirit, so it'll be better for all of us if I hold my peace.'

'And does anyone else have anything further to add on the subject?'

No one does.

'We have to vote on it,' says Thurston.

Sonny's hand shoots up to the full extent of his arm. 'And the rest of you,' he cajoles. 'Come on.'

Five other hands are raised one after another. Sato's comes last, slowly and reluctantly joining its fellows in the air.

'Carried unanimously,' says Mungo.

'Who'd have thought it?' says Fred with a whistle. 'We just agreed to let Sonny do some work.'

'Wonders will never cease,' says Wensley.

'Right, I'm off down to my apartment to get ready,' says Sonny, excitedly shunting back his throne and rising to his feet. 'Have to look my best for the staff, eh?'

Chas offers to come down with him and give him a few fashion pointers, but Sonny replies that he will be fine. 'I can still remember a thing or two about turning myself out well, from back in the dim and distant past.'

'Thurston,' says Mungo, 'send an e-memo down to both departments warning them Sonny's coming.'

'Tell them to roll out the red carpet,' says Sonny as he skips away from the table.

'And contact Strategic Security and have four guards waiting for Sonny on the Yellow Floor at, oh, let's say eleven thirty.'

'Very well.'

'Got that, Sonny? Eleven thirty.'

Sonny is at the door. 'Yup, half eleven, no problem.'

A moment after he leaves the Boardroom, Sonny pops his head back through the doorway. The look of earnest gratitude on his face is touching to behold.

'You won't regret this,' he tells his brothers, brow knotted in sincerity. 'I swear you won't.'

'You'd damn well better hope we don't,' says Thurston, under his breath.

16

House of Marriage: in astrology, the seventh house

.

10.16 a.m.
Oh Mum, I wish you could be here to see this with me. It's so much more wonderful than either of us could ever have imagined.

That was Linda's first thought as she passed through the arch and emerged into Silks. The shiny drapes and swathes of material swooping down in all directions and hollowing into aisles brought to mind a vast, labyrinthine sheik's tent and, as she stared around, Linda's irritation with Gordon instantly abated, to be replaced by a serene, almost hypnotic sense of contentment.

An hour and eight departments later, she still feels as if she is floating rather than walking. Nothing is entirely real, eveything brighter and more colourful than usual, yet at the same time vague and somehow insubstantial. Half convinced that the entire store and all the merchandise and people in it are concocted from smoke, she is scared to touch anything in case it shimmers and vanishes and the illusion is spoiled, and so she touches nothing, merely looks. And what her vision reports, her memory hoards.

Persian and Armenian rugs hanging in leaved rows like the pages of a gigantic illuminated manuscript. Bolts of curtain material and upholstery fabric stacked in ziggurats whose peaks brush the fourteen-metre-high ceiling. A seemingly unending chain of kitchen showrooms, each opening on to the next like the different-coloured chambers in the Edgar Allen Poe story. Wallpapers – chintz, flock, screenprinted, anaglypta, plain. And the constant, courteous attention of the sales assistants and floor-walkers. 'May I help you, madam?' 'See something you like, madam?' 'Would madam like to look at . . .?' 'Would madam care to try . . .?'

Madam! In all her life Linda can't recall being referred to as madam before, except by her father when he was in one of his moods and everything he said was laced with snarling sarcasm. *These* madams are sincere and deferential; likewise the sirs that come Gordon's way. It seems that Days staff genuinely find it a pleasure to serve customers, and it doesn't matter that she graciously turns down their offers of help, because they sound not one jot less polite as they apologise for troubling her and wish her a very pleasant day's shopping.

She could spent the rest of her life here. The sheer abundance of worldly goods on display, the respect she is automatically accorded, and the sense of being on an (almost) equal footing with the wealthiest and most powerful people in the land, make the world outside the store seem cheap and hard and coarse by comparison. There is a refinement to Days and a feeling of order that is not to be found elsewhere in the city. Some part of Linda has understood all along that she belongs in here rather than out there, and she feels she has found her haven, and knows the exhilaration of a bird when it finally alights at the end of a long, arduous migration.

Even when the lightning sale was announced at ten, Linda was pleasantly surprised to discover that there was nothing mindless or aggressive about the way several of the shoppers in the immediate vicinity turned and bolted for the nearest lift or escalator. They didn't, as she had been conditioned by rumour and hearsay to expect, behave like a rabble. Rather, they mobilised themselves with military efficiency, as if they existed in a state of perpetual readiness for moments like these. That impressed her, and she looked forward to a time when she, too, would be familiar enough with the layout of the store and confident enough of her place here to make such well-judged and well-informed decisions. That, surely, would be soon.

She is beginning to think that she was a fool to listen to the taxi driver and buy his pepper spray. Judging from her experiences so far, Days isn't a dangerous place at all. She has seldom felt safer or more at home.

If there is a fly in the ointment, it is a small one, but an irksome one none the less: her husband.

It is nothing Gordon has said over the past hour that has annoyed her. Rather, it is the fact that he hasn't said *anything*, in spite of her best attempts to engage him in conversation. She has asked for his opinion on various kinds of shelving, on a spice rack, on a tortoiseshell photograph frame, all things to do with the house, the living space he shares with her, all things he ought to be interested in, and what has she received in return? At best, monosyllables; at worst, grunts. He has been traipsing after her from department to department like an old, footsore dog on a leash. Any enthusiasm he might have had an hour ago has definitely waned, while she is as brisk and as eager as ever. Proof (as if she needed it) that men do not have the stamina for serious shopping.

Finally, when she can bear Gordon's sullen, uncommunicative presence no longer, Linda comes to a halt at the entrance to the Lighting Department. Squinting against the blaze from several thousand lamps and lanterns, she can just make out sales assistants equipped with tinted goggles drifting to and fro within, ministering to the merchandise, replacing expended bulbs with spares from bandoliers strapped across their chests. Haloed by brightness, the sales assistants are etiolated, angelic figures.

She turns to her husband. 'Gordon, what would you say to going our separate ways for a while?'

The question takes him aback.

'It only makes sense,' she goes on. 'After all, you don't want to be tagging along behind me all day. There must be departments you want to explore by yourself.'

'No, this is fine.'

'Your voice rises an octave when you lie, Gordon, did you know that?'

'It does not,' Gordon protests squeakily.

'Go on, I know you're dying to head off on your own. It's ten twenty now. Let's meet up again at a quarter to one, here.' That should give her enough time to buy the tie she picked out for him from the catalogue, and then she can present it to him over lunch.

Gordon, with a great and not wholly convincing show of reluctance, gives in. 'So which one of us gets to hang on to the card?'

'I do, of course.'

'Is that wise?'

Linda thinks he might be teasing her, but he isn't teasing her. His eyes are narrow and serious behind his spectacles.

'Gordon, I'd hate to think that you don't trust me with our Days Silver.'

'I do trust you,' he says, too quickly.

'But still you think it'll be safer if you hold on to it instead of me.'

'That's not what I said.'

'That's what you implied.'

126

'I'm sorry if that's how it sounded. What I meant was, since the account is held jointly in both our names, every purchase made with the card ought to be agreed on by both of us. Don't you think?'

'Whatever happened to man and wife being one body, one flesh?'

'Come on, that's just a metaphor.'

'I don't know about you, Gordon, but when I took my marriage vows, I meant every word of them sincerely.'

'You're not being rational, Linda.'

'And you're not being fair. This is just as much my card as yours.' She waves the Silver in front of his nose. 'Either one of us on our own couldn't have earned it. Together, we did. This card represents the fact that we are greater than the sum of our individual parts. It shows what two people can achieve if they pool their resources and work as one.'

'The majority of those resources coming from my salary.'

'I'm not just talking about the money, I'm talking about the sacrifices we made *together*, the hardships we endured *together*. And anyway, I've done my bit. What with the upkeep of the house and shopping thriftily and coming up with money-saving scheme after money-saving scheme, not to mention my hairdressing, I'm at least an equal partner in our Days account.'

'Well, let's not get into that now,' says Gordon. 'What concerns me, Linda, is that we don't run up a debt we can't pay off. I see people at the bank every day who've got themselves into all sorts of difficulties over credit cards or Days accounts.'

'And they've come to you for help, which you give them in the form of a loan, on which, of course, the bank charges interest.' Linda grins venomously. 'Or have I got it wrong, Gordon? Have banks started giving money away free?'

'Better to owe money to a reputable bank than to some dodgy character who'll break your legs if you don't pay up,' Gordon replies, unflustered. 'But that has no bearing on the point I'm making. The point I'm making is, people wouldn't be tempted to borrow money if borrowing money wasn't looked on as an acceptable alternative – no, as *preferable* – to doing without what you can't afford. It takes strength of character to say no and wait rather than say yes and have immediately, and it's that lack of strength of character in all of us that gets exploited time and time again.'

'We did without for five years,' Linda asserts firmly. 'We've earned the right to our Silver.'

'But let's be careful with it, eh? That's all I'm getting at. Let's not go mad.'

'Have I gone mad yet, Gordon? Have I? So far I haven't bought one item from this store. I've looked around, I've seen dozens of things I'd like to own, things that would look nice in our home, but what have I bought? Nothing. Not a thing.'

'And I admire your restraint. For most people the limit on a credit account is a goal rather than a boundary, something to race for rather than keep as far away as possible from.'

'You of all people, Gordon, should know that I have more self-control than "most people".'

'Linda, please. I'm not criticising you. I'm just sounding a note of caution.'

'But don't you see, that's all I've heard all morning!' She clutches the air in exasperation. 'People warning me, people trying to sow doubts. It seems like no one except me believes I know what I'm doing. This is *my* day, Gordon. This is the day I've been dreaming about all my life. All my life!' She can feel her face growing hot as her voice rises, but she is unable to do anything about either. Shoppers are turning and looking in her direction. She strives to ignore their scrutiny. 'I've suffered and struggled and compromised just to get to the place I'm in now, and I won't have you, I won't have *anyone*, ruining this for me. This is *my* moment of glory. Please have the good grace to let me savour it. You can caution me all you want when we get back home tonight.'

Gordon has more to say on this subject but deems it wise to save it for later. He simply nods. 'All right, Linda. All right. Let's have it your way. We'll split up, and you can hang on to the card. I trust you.'

'Do you? Do you really?'

'Do I have a choice?'

Linda beams at him in vindication. '*That's* more like it, Gordon.'

17

Seventh-Inning Stretch: a traditional pause during a baseball game, after the first half of the seventh inning

10.30 a.m.
It is time for Frank's mid-morning break and, on cue, his bladder starts to exert a mild, insistent pressure against his lower abdominal wall. Not painful, but not to be ignored either.

From years of repetition, Frank's body has synchronised its urges with the dictates of his daily timetable. He wakes moments before his alarm clock tells him to wake, he starts to feel hungry just when his schedule permits him to eat, and his bladder has learned to regulate the incoming flow of liquid so that it reaches capacity just when it is convenient for him to drain it. Indeed, his physiological functions dovetail so immaculately with the pattern of his working days that on Sunday, when in theory he ought to be free to do as he pleases, he ingests and eliminates at exactly the same times as during the rest of the week. Some might cite this as a demonstration of mankind's evolutionary talent for adapting to circumstances, but Frank knows better. To him it implies that inside every human brain sits a mainspring regulating the turn of the cogs that govern the body's rhythms. People run on clockwork, and if they are forced to go through the same routine day after day, their rhythms become rigidly attuned to the work-metronome – so much so that, sometimes, they find they literally cannot live without it. Frank knows of numerous retired or sacked employees who have gone mad or dropped dead shortly after their last day at Days, unable to cope with being liberated from the strict tick-tocking of a timetable. Time suddenly slackens its grip on them, and their mainsprings whirl and spool out.

By leaving today he may be able to prevent suffering the same fate himself. If he stays any longer, it may be too late.

'This is Frank Hubble,' he subvocalises to the Eye. 'I'm clocking off for half an hour.'

'OK, Mr Hubble,' says a screen-jockey, a girl this time. Frank hears the rattle of a keyboard. 'Enjoy your coffee break.'

Polite, cheerful – she can't have been on the job more than a week. It won't be long before poor diet, stress and overexposure to the ion-charged atmosphere generated by myriad TV screens have turned her into a short-tempered, facetious pest like her colleagues.

Finding a staff lift, Frank summons it with a swipe of his Iridium, and on his way down studies his smeary reflection in the steel doors. This blurred other Frank appears and disappears and reappears over and over as his concentration waxes and wanes, until finally he stops bothering to look for it, and it vanishes altogether.

I am there, he tells himself, *I am there, I am there, I am.* But the words ring hollow when the evidence of his eyes tells him the truth.

He longs for the day when he will once more be able to glance into a reflecting surface and see himself there without having to make a conscious effort, and suddenly his resolve to seek out Mr Bloom and tender his resignation burgeons again.

But first, having arrived in the Basement, he heads for Tactical Security, and there, in the gents' cloakroom, he assumes the position at a urinal and braces himself for his regularly scheduled relief.

10.33 a.m.

Years ago, the Tactical Security cafeteria had a buffet counter manned by serving staff, but they found it a disagreeable place to work. The Ghosts – as cold a bunch of fish as you could ever hope to meet – treated them as though they were beings from another dimension, barely talking to them beyond the basic courtesies of 'Please' and 'Thank you' and never able to look them in the eye, until after a while some of the staff actually started to believe that the Ghosts' behaviour was normal and that it was they themselves, with their friendly, outgoing attitude, who had something wrong with them.

Automation was infinitely preferable for all concerned, and was introduced shortly after Frank started at Days. The food is of an inferior quality, tending towards the prepackaged and the microwaveable, the preservative-laced and the just-add-water instant, but the Ghosts find the dispensing machines a great deal more amenable than real people. The machines do not try to strike up a rapport, do not jabber pointlessly about the weather or politics, and do not take umbrage when their conversational overtures are rejected. The machines dole out food and drink at the touch of a button, without fuss, with comforting predictability, and thanks to them and to plastic cutlery, paper napkins, and cardboard plates and cups, the need for human staff in the Tactical Security cafeteria has been all but done away. There remains a skeleton staff of two: the janitor who comes in after closing time to empty the bins and mop up, and the technician who comes in once a week to restock and service the machines.

Withdrawing a near-scalding cup of coffee from the delivery chute of the hot-beverage dispenser, Frank scans the cafeteria for an unoccupied table. He manages to reach one and set the coffee down before its heat, efficiently conducted by the polystyrene cup, starts to blister his fingertips.

He will go and see Mr Bloom once he has finished the coffee. The coffee is a delaying tactic, he knows that, but a few moments to clear his head before tendering his resignation won't go amiss.

He has barely had a chance to take more than a few sips when Mr Bloom strolls into the cafeteria.

Nonchalantly the head of Tactical Security fetches himself a cup of milky tea and a jam doughnut, and chooses an empty table. Mr Bloom seldom eats in the cafeteria, and it can't be coincidence that he has chosen to be here at a time when Frank is likely to be here too.

Frank contemplates slipping quietly out of the room, but he realises that would be childish. Besides, Mr Bloom's attempt to pin him down – if that is what it is – may be an abuse of their thirty-three years of acquaintance, but it is a miscalculation rather than an act of malice.

With a sigh, Frank takes a last swig of the by now merely piping-hot coffee, gets up, and strides heavily over to Mr Bloom's table. A part of him cannot believe what he is about to do, and begs him not to put himself through this ordeal. Why this compulsion to make his resignation official? Why not just slip away without telling a soul?

Because that would not be proper. Because he owes Mr Bloom, if no one else, an explanation. And because to sneak away furtively is the action of a thief, and thieves are a breed Frank has dedicated half a lifetime to thwarting.

'Donald?'

'Frank.' There is little surprise in Mr Bloom's eyes.

Frank can almost hear the grinding of neck bones as the Ghosts around him surreptitiously strain to listen.

'Could we have that chat now?'

'Of course. My office?'

'Of course.'

10.39 a.m.

For the first time Frank notices the homely touches in the office as he sits facing Mr Bloom across his desk. The small framed photograph of a young girl (Mr Bloom has mentioned a niece in the past). The paperback novels sandwiched on a shelf between bulky file boxes – Joyce, Solzhenitsyn, Woolf. The yellowed, frail clipping from a financial newspaper tacked to one corner of the year planner on the wall, an amusing ambiguity in its headline: 'Spring Figures Prove That Days Has Not Lost Its Bloom.' The yellow smiley-face sticker pasted over the Days logo on the desktop terminal. Tiny, personal additions it would never occur to Frank to make were this bland subterranean cell his own.

Mr Bloom is waiting for him to speak. He has been waiting a full three minutes, patiently eating the jam doughnut and licking the sugar granules off his fingers, sipping his tea. Frank's silence is about to cross the line dividing hesitation from rudeness.

He admits defeat. 'I don't know where to begin.'

'Begin at the beginning,' says Mr Bloom.

'That's the trouble. I'm not sure where the beginning is. Things just seem to have . . . *accumulated*. I thought I was happy in my job, now it seems I'm not.'

'Ah.' Mr Bloom's eyebrows lift, parallel wavy furrows bunching across his brow all the way up to his tenacious foretuft. 'And is there any particular aspect of the job that you're not happy with, or is it nothing you can put a finger on?'

'It's . . . me, I suppose. The job is the job. It doesn't change, so I must have changed.' Why is he making this difficult for himself? He should just come right out with it, American-style. *I quit.* That's all he needs to say, those two little words. Why this pussyfooting about? Why the absurd desire to break it gently? What difference will it mean to Mr Bloom, one less Ghost, one less responsibility?

'Changed in what way?'

'It's hard to say.'

'Frank, I appreciate that this can't be much fun for you, so take your

132

time, and when you feel ready, tell me what's on your mind. I don't need to remind you that nothing you say will go beyond these four walls, so feel free to have a go at the customers, the brothers, a co-worker, a sales assistant with offensive halitosis, me, anyone you want.'

'This has nothing to do with anyone else. This is just *me*.'

Mr Bloom regards Frank placidly. 'Yes, I know. I was just trying to get you to crack a smile. Silly me.'

'Donald, why did *you* leave the job?'

'I thought we were here to talk about you.'

'It might help.'

'Really? Well, if you say so. Why did I give up the Ghost? Mainly because I couldn't hack it any more. I wasn't making as many collars as I used to. Customers were noticing me. I was losing my touch.'

'Losing touch?' Frank asks carefully, pretending to have misheard.

'No, losing *my* touch,' says Mr Bloom, flashing a look of curiosity across the desk. 'I was offered the promotion at just the right time. I didn't accept it because I wanted to, I accepted it because I had to. I had no choice. There was no way they could keep me on as a Ghost, so it was either this or retirement, and I wasn't ready for the pipe and slippers just then. I'm still not. And the Academy wasn't an option. How could I be expected to train people to become Ghosts if I didn't have the talent for it myself any more? Is any of this relevant to your problem?'

'Not really.'

'I didn't think so. *You* still have the knack for it, Frank. Your arrest record is as high as ever. You're one of the best, I might even say *the* best and, Lord, I'd give my eye-teeth to be out on the shop floor like you, still plugging away, still getting the old tingle when you spot a likely one. Granted, it can be godawful at times, it can get as boring as hell, and there are days when your feet feel like two lumps of lead and your legs have knives in place of bones, and there are departments you hate going into but feel obliged to go into anyway, and you get sick of looking at customers' faces day in, day out, those empty, eager faces – you'd think they'd have enough of what they wanted, but it's never enough, and even the fat ones look hungry, don't they? And the screen-jockeys, God, the screen-jockeys! Imps of the perverse, sent to torment us. But Frank – isn't it all worth it the moment you make a good, clean collar? When you catch a real smooth operator red-handed, and you know the sticky-fingered bastard is *yours*, he's not getting away from you, he's a done deal? Isn't any amount of crap worth the wonderful feeling of utter conviction you get as you lay your hand on his shoulder and show him what he did on your Sphinx and recite the Booster's Blessing? Those few minutes of pure, sweet clarity of purpose are a Ghost's reward for all the hours of fuss and tedium and aggravation. Don't you agree?'

Frank is about to reply when two things happen. First, seven notes ring out over the loudspeaker mounted outside the door, the echoes bouncing down the corridor, and the announcement of a lightning sale in Farm Machinery commences.

'Attention, customers.'

Almost simultaneously, the Eye whispers in Frank's ear.

'Mr Hubble?' It is the same girl he spoke to quarter of an hour ago. 'I'm sorry to interrupt you on your break, but they want you over in Processing.'

'What?'

'It's a shoplifter you collared. Wants to talk to you. Insists on it.'

'I have something else on at the moment.'

'Frank?'

'Farm Machinery is located in the south-eastern quadrant of the Red Floor and may be reached using the banks of lifts designated I, J and K.'

'Processing think it'll help if you go over there.'

'Frank?'

'Excuse me, Dona – ' 'Excuse me, Donald, I'm talking to the Eye.' 'Eye, this is highly irregular.'

'I know, Mr Hubble, and I wouldn't have dreamed of bothering you, but Processing says the shoplifter won't talk to anyone until you get there.'

'Talk? What about?'

'I'm sorry, they didn't tell me.'

'Well, the timing stinks.' *But actually*, Frank thinks, *it could have been a lot worse.*

'What can I say? I'm sorry.'

'Hubble out.' 'Donald, I have to go.'

'What's up?'

'I'm not sure.'

'Well, can't it wait? Can't someone else deal with it?'

'Apparently not.'

Mr Bloom keeps his suspicions to himself. It wouldn't be out of character for a Ghost to fake an emergency appointment in order to get out of a situation that was in danger of becoming uncomfortably personal. 'All right. Look, we obviously have a lot more to talk about. Let's meet for lunch.'

'Donald, I don't – '

'One o'clock, at the Italian restaurant on the Green Floor hoop.'

'I don't think that's such a good place for a talk.'

'Frank, no one'll pay any attention to you. Or to me, if I really don't want them to.'

'Well . . .' Frank is at the door.

'It's a date, then. One sharp. Promise me you'll be there.'

Embarrassed at the eagerness with which he has seized his chance to escape, Frank can hardly refuse.

'I usually eat lunch at quarter to one,' he says.

'Quarter to it is, then.'

18

Sze: the seventh hexagram of the *I-Ching*, usually interpreted as meaning the need for discipline and for the leadership of a superior general with age and experience on his side

10.42 a.m.

Over dinner, Septimus Day was fond of lecturing his sons in the art of retailing, which was also, as far as he was concerned, the art of life. In lieu of proper conversation, the founder of the world's first and (for the best part of his lifetime) foremost gigastore would spend the duration of the meal holding forth on any topic that entered his head and contriving to draw from it lessons that applied to the store, in much the same way that a priest in his sermon draws lessons from everyday events and applies them to his religion. Always Septimus's homilies ended in epigrammatic maxims, of which he had dozens, his equivalent of Biblical quotations.

In Septimus's later years, the audience for these lectures consisted for the most part of just Sonny and Mungo. With the other five brothers away at boarding school or university, Mungo having graduated *summa cum laude* in the same year that Sonny graduated from nappies to a potty, the three of them would eat their evening meals in the sepulchral, candlelit cavernousness of the family mansion's dining room, scrupulously waited on by Perch. Regardless of the empty places at table, the old man would pontificate as usual, bestowing only the occasional glance on his oldest and youngest sons, as though Mungo and Sonny were just two of many present.

Sonny grew up watching his father physically and mentally decline. He never knew a time when Septimus was not in poor health and, as he saw the shine in his father's remaining eye grow daily duller and observed the increasing fragility of the old man's hands and thought processes, he wished in his child's heart that there was something he could do, some gesture he could make to reassure Septimus that all was well, that there was no need for this quiet sadness that seemed to be eating him from the inside out. A simple hug might have helped, but displays of affection, especially those of the spontaneous variety, were out of the question in the Day household. Septimus Day was training the men who would assume control of his business after he died, not raising a family.

As Sonny turned five, six, seven, the dinnertime lectures grew ever more discursive and rambling. Sometimes, in the depths of a long and convoluted sentence, the old man would give a start, as though he had been asleep and someone had just shouted in his ear. He would stop talking, blink around, then resume the lecture on a completely different tack. Other times, he would get himself stuck in a loop, repeating a sentence over and over as though unable to stress its meaning enough or with a sufficient variety of emphases. And even the prepubescent Sonny could tell that it was a good thing that Mungo had assumed the burden of running the store. Their father was clearly no longer up to it.

If the lectures taught Sonny nothing else, they taught him patience. He learned how to sit through them in respectful silence, and he learned how to tune out the sound of his father's voice until almost nothing the old man said penetrated. Still, many of Septimus's maxims did somehow – perhaps through sheer repetition – lodge in his brain, and there have stuck fast.

For example: 'Other people exist to be subjugated to your will. Will is all. With will, anything can be achieved. Dreams can be forced into existence, a vast building can be raised out of a wasteland, wealth can be generated. Lack of experience and lack of expertise are no obstacle as long as you have will.'

And: 'Numbers have power. Numbers are the engines with which one can assault the stronghold of Fate, scale its ramparts and loot its treasures. And there is no number quite as significant as the number seven. I myself am the youngest of seven brothers, and I have sired seven sons for the express purpose of ensuring the continuation of my success. The number seven is a charm that has many meanings, great power, and should never be broken.'

And: 'Customers are sheep and expect to be treated like sheep. Treat them like royalty, and though they will remain sheep, they'll be less likely to complain when you fleece them.'

And: 'A contract improperly worded deserves to be broken. If one party fails to specify down to the finest detail what is required, the other party has the right, if not the duty, to take advantage of such carelessness. *Caveat emptor!*'

The lectures were frequently punctuated with that phrase, '*Caveat emptor!*', usually accompanied by a loud, cutlery-rattling thump on the tabletop. It was Septimus's amen.

Other than watch his father totter off into the grounds of the estate for long walks, his white head bowed in melancholy contemplation, Sonny's memories of the old man consist almost entirely of those dinnertime discourses. This is hardly surprising since, evening meals apart, there was little contact between Septimus Day and any of his sons.

Sonny was eight years old when the old man succumbed to an inoperable liver cancer.

At the funeral, in front of a battery of news cameras from around the world, he surprised himself by crying.

As he stands in his walk-in wardrobe now, gazing at a long row of suits on hangers, he is thinking not how sorry he is that he hardly knew his father but how proud the old man would be of him today, were he alive. Sonny has taken the first step on the road to acceptance by his brothers. Until today they have merely tolerated his presence in the Boardroom, making it clear that they consider him superfluous to requirements and that he is there only to make up numbers. His exclusion from their six-man enclave has been a source of some bitterness and not a little misery. Many a night Sonny has lain awake in bed seething at the unfairness of it all. To be born a son of Septimus Day, to inherit a seventh part of total control of the world's first and (sinking sales be damned) foremost gigastore, and yet never to be fully his brothers' equal, has seemed the cruellest and most unjust punishment ever visited on a human being. But today – by the electric tingle all over his skin Sonny knows this to be true – today a corner has been turned. Today everything has begun to change. And the catalyst for that change was none other than Sonny himself. Certainly Mungo did his bit but, reviewing what occurred in the Boardroom a few minutes ago, Sonny is convinced that he himself was at least ninety-nine per cent responsible for the shift in his brothers' previously intransigent stance. He coaxed them. He persuaded them. He sub-jugated them to his will.

As Sonny examines the dozens of tailor-made suits in front of him, each ordered from the Gentlemen's Outfitters Department on a whim, few ever worn, he feels a tune well up in his chest. He starts to hum as he lifts suit after suit off the rail, holding each up by the hook of its hanger and rating its suitability for the job ahead.

A three-piece in mustard-yellow flannel? Too garish.

A chessboard-chequered two-piece with lapels whose pointed tips rise clear of the shoulderpads? Too gangsterish.

A double-breasted jacket and a pair of pleated trousers stitched together from blackcurrant-purple cotton? Not bad, except for the embroidered gold Days logos adorning the cuffs and pockets, which make the suit look like some sort of bizarre military dress-uniform.

This one in silver lamé? Sonny can't bring himself to look twice at that particular monstrosity, and tosses it aside. What on earth could have been going through his mind when he ordered it? He must have been drunk. But then it's pretty safe to say that anything Sonny has done since achieving his majority has been done drunk.

His humming evolves into a warbling whistle.

What he is looking for is an outfit that will combine seriousness with approachability. A look that will say, 'Here I am. Respect me but don't fear me.' Surprisingly, given the range of suits available, finding one that fits those criteria is proving quite a challenge. Still he rummages on, content that the right suit will present itself soon enough.

Downstairs. Sonny hasn't been downstairs, on the shop floor itself, in quite a while. A couple of years, at least. Two years spent living cloistered above the store, confined to one floor and the roof, cut off from human contact, his only company his brothers, Perch, and the flitting, furtive menials who are under permanent instruction to vacate a room immediately should he or his brothers enter. It's a peculiar way to live, if you think about it, but it seems to agree with him, with all of them. When you consider the alternative, a home somewhere out there in the teeming city, rubbing shoulders with the rest of the world, it actually seems quite a desirable lifestyle, if somewhat monastic.

He wonders if the store will look and feel any different from the way he remembers, and suspects that things will have stayed pretty much the same. Days is like a granite mountain, through sheer size resisting everything but the most incremental changes. The depart ments will be the same, the sales assistants will be the same, the customers will be the same . . .

Abruptly, the whistled tune dies on Sonny's lips. He remembers only too clearly the last time he was downstairs. It was the day he returned from his final term at university, and instead of using the private lift from the car park to the Violet Floor he decided to ride the escalators up to the Indigo and take the lift from there. It was meant to be a kind of triumphal homecoming procession, and with his entourage of security guards Sonny certainly felt the part of the heroic soldier returning from some distant conflict, until he became conscious of the stares of the customers he passed. Dozens of pairs of strangers' eyes turning, being brought to bear on him.

He dismisses the memory with a shudder. He is older now, wiser and, anyway, it's only to be expected that a son of Septimus Day should be an object of curiosity.

Except there seemed to be more than curiosity in the customers' stares. They were looking at him as if they knew everything there was to know about him and hated what they saw.

He would say that his imagination was conspiring to play tricks on him had he not also seen that same look in his brothers' eyes from time to time. Occasionally, he would see it in his father's eye, too. Every now and then at the dinner table he would catch the old man watching him very carefully. His schoolmates, too, had it in certain lights. And his fellow undergraduates. A look with actual weight, exerting a tangible pressure on the object of scrutiny.

A look of accusation. A look of resentment.

At that, a subtle scratching begins in Sonny's head.

The scratching sound is made by a creature which Sonny imagines has claws like a rat's, claws that carry all kinds of festering infections beneath their white crescent sharpness. He knows that it does not pay to listen to that creature's soft, insinuating scurry, or to let it come too near with its talons. He refocuses his attention on the task at hand.

A fiery ginger camel-hair number? Uh-uh. Nope.

A baggy green-and-orange woollen tartan jacket with matching trousers? Only if he has a pair of clown shoes and a squirting buttonhole flower to go with it.

He delves on through the racks, trying not to think about the purpose for which he is searching out a suit, trying to think only of the positive aspects of the responsibility that has been thrust upon him, the fact that it shows that his brothers are prepared to take him seriously at last.

But the creature, having emerged from its lair, will not be sent back there so easily. In wainscot whispers it reminds Sonny of the mother's love he never knew, and of the envy he used to feel when other boys at school were picked up for exeats by their parents – both parents, both smiling, a hand-shaking father, an embracing mother – while he had to make do with a hired chauffeur-cum-bodyguard, grim and vigilant. It speaks to him of the basic right granted to almost every other living thing but denied him, and it hisses the sibilant name of the one to blame for his deprivation.

'No.' Sonny has to dredge the word up out of himself. The sky-blue silk suit he is holding trembles. He clenches his eyelids shut and presses his forehead against the edge of a shelf bearing folded pullovers, a narrow line of pain. His upper teeth slide out to gnaw his lower lip.

Everything that moments ago was rosy and delightful crumbles away. His enthusiasm for the task ahead is gone with a pop, like a floating soap bubble jabbed by a killjoy's fingertip. He attempts to recover the mood of optimism – the feeling of near-invulnerability – that had him waltzing out of the Boardroom and down the spiral staircase and along the corridors of the Violet Floor to his apartment, but it is ruined beyond repair, and the act of trying to recapture it only damages it further.

And now the creature – an emotion Sonny cannot give a name, a patchwork beast of doubt and guilt and paranoia – is scuttling and snuffling around yet more busily.

What if the task his brothers have set him is a hopeless one? What if the dispute proves impossible to arbitrate? What if they *intend* for him to fail? After all, if he fails, that will justify once and for all their lack of faith in him. No longer will they have to hunt around for excuses to deny him equal status. A disaster downstairs will give them all the proof they need that he is unreliable. It will be an example they can trot out whenever he campaigns for a fair crack of the whip in the future. 'But Sonny,' they will say, 'look what happened the last time we gave you something to do. Look what a mess you made of *that*.'

The suit slips from Sonny's fingers, billowing to the floor, forming a slinky, rumpled puddle of sky blue.

There is a way to get rid of the nagging creature, banish it back to its lair. A guaranteed method. Tried and tested.

But he made a deal with his brothers.

He imagines them laughing at him right now, their faces around the table: Sato tittering, Fred chortling, Thurston chuckling almost sound-lessly, Wensley hurrh-hurrhing throatily, Chas gently snickering, Mungo guffawing with authoritative gusto. Laughing at him because they never really expected him to keep his half of the bargain. Laughing because he was a fool to try.

And he pictures customers and employees staring at him as if he is half god, half madman. Whispers passing behind cupped hands: 'Do you see that? That's Sonny Day. The Afterthought. If it hadn't been for *him* . . .'

He must have been mad to agree to go downstairs sober, with all his nerve endings exposed, raw to the world, without the extra lucidity and calmness that a drink or two brings.

No, the conditions Mungo laid down were completely unreason-able, and Mungo knew it. His brothers want him to screw up the arbitration, that's all there is to it. They have deliberately put him in an impossible situation. If he isn't drunk, he won't have the courage to go downstairs, and if he goes downstairs drunk, he will have reneged on the deal. Damned if he does, damned if he doesn't.

The creature in his head is hopping from foot to foot with all the glee of a crow that has alighted on fresh carrion. Its talons tick-tack on the inside of Sonny's skull, a sound like sinuses cracking.

He could silence it in seconds. All he has to do is go to the bar in the liv-ing room, pour himself a measure of something (anything), pour himself another, and keep on pouring. In no time the creature will be gone.

Which is exactly what the creature wants. It crawls out from its lair with the sole purpose of tormenting him into drinking it back into submission. Allowing the creature into his head means it has one kind of weakness to feast on, exorcising it with booze offers it another kind. The creature doesn't care. Either way, it gets its fill of frailty. *His* frailty.

But he made a deal, and what kind of Day brother is he if he can't make a deal and stick to it? What kind of son of Septimus Day?

At that precise moment, the old man's opinion on the subject of deals comes zinging to the forefront of Sonny's thoughts.

'A contract improperly worded deserves to be broken.'

And he can see again, as if it were only yesterday, his father seated at the head of the dining tabale, bent nearly double over his plate with didactic fervour, spearing his point home with a thrust of his fork in the air.

'If one party fails to specify down to the finest detail what is required, the other party has the right, if not the duty, to take advantage of such carelessness.'

And then the thump of fist on rosewood, making everything on the table jump, and the familiar oath:

'*Caveat emptor!*'

All very well and fine, sound advice, but with his brothers there was no written contract, just a simple verbal agreement.

'If, perhaps, you leave that drink in front of you unfinished,' Mungo said, 'and we had Perch come in and take away the gin bottle . . .'

Even when Sonny clarified the conditions, the deal sounded no less watertight. 'All I have to do is not drink the rest of this bottle.' No room for manouevring there.

Or is there?

'All I have to do is not drink the rest of this bottle.'

Of *this* bottle.

No one said anything about any other bottle.

'Sonny,' Sonny Day says to himself, 'you are a genius.' He raises his forehead from the shelf and opens his eyes. 'A grade-A, certified genius.'

The creature is rubbing its grubby paws together, obscenely gratified.

Sonny turns and stumbles out of the wardrobe, out of the bedroom. Down a broad corridor wanly illuminated by skylights he hurries, until he reaches a large chamber that used to be the Wickerwork Department before it was absorbed into Handicrafts on the Blue Floor, and which now serves as his living room. The decor is entirely of Sonny's choosing. Cream-coloured shagpile carpet covers the floor like an ankle-deep layer of milk froth. Chairs and sofas upholstered in white suede, marshmallow-plump, are arranged around a sheared slab of basalt a metre thick and three metres square that serves as a coffee table, its polished surface strewn with magazines, handheld electronic puzzles, and gimmicky executive toys. A state-of-the-art home entertainment system takes up virtually one entire wall, stacks of matt-black units clustered around a television set the size of a chest of drawers. A parade of picture windows offers a widescreen view of the city most ordinary citizens would give all they owned to have – roads busy with twinkling traffic, sun-warmed buildings basking shoulder to shoulder. Kept at bay by Days Plaza, at this remove the city actually looks like a pleasant place to live.

One corner of the living room is taken up by the bar, a dipsomaniac's dream built of glass bricks and mirrors, with stainless steel stools and rack upon rack of bottles inverted over optics. Sonny heads for it like a homing missile. Grabbing a tumbler, he hesitates, momentarily bewildered by the choice before him. Every type of spirit is represented by several brands. Which should he have? He selects one at random, thinking, *What differences does it make? Booze is booze.* A shot of cinnamon-spiced vodka glugs into the glass. The optic bubbles greasily. What the hell, make it a double. He chugs it down at a swallow.

The rest of this bottle.

Idiots. They thought they had him on a hook, but he has outsmarted them, has found a way to wriggle off. He tosses another six measures of the vodka down his gullet in quick succession, toasting his brothers one after another with furious sarcasm. The result is as swift as it is magnificent. A warm, rising tide of confidence engulfs him from belly to brow.

Oh yes, this is better. Much, much better.

The old man would definitely be proud of him, there's no doubt about it.

There's no doubt about anything at all.

19

Commit the Seventh: break the Seventh Commandment,
i.e. commit adultery

10.51 a.m.
Frank has sent innumerable shoplifters down to Processing, but he has
never actually had cause to go there himself. There's a first time for
everything, he supposes. Even on your last day at work.

As he makes his way through the Byzantine twists and turns of the
Basement corridors, it strikes him as fitting that a shoplifter's last few
minutes on the premises should be spent down here. How better to
drive home to the criminal the full consequences of his crime than by
leading him out of the bright, bustling departments, filled with people
and opulence, down to a functional, stuffy layer of grey duct-lined
corridors and confined spaces sandwiched between the seven storeys
of the store and the seven levels of underground car park? For in this
drab limbo, this dimly lit interzone, the shoplifter is granted a
foretaste of what he can expect from the life that awaits him, a life
without Days: a monotonous tangle of dead ends and drudgery.

Processing turns out to be a plain, rectangular chamber, one side of
which is partitioned off into a row of glass-fronted soundproofed
interview booths. Three shoplifters waiting their turn to be processed
sit on wooden benches facing away from the booths – their fates, so to
speak, behind them, sealed. They are paired off with the security
guards who escorted them down and who will remain with them, a
constant hip-joined presence, right up until the moment of eviction.
They make for ludicrously mismatched couples – stiff-spined guards,
slumped shoplifters. One of the shoplifters is quietly sobbing.
Another, clearly a troublemaker, sits hunched forward with his hands
manacled behind his back. There is a bruise below his right eye,
swollen and puffy, pale yellow turning to black. 'I was going to pay for
it,' he keeps telling the guard, over and over, as if honesty can be
earned by insistence. 'I was going to pay for it. I was going to pay for it.'

Obtrusive to no one, Frank glides past the booth windows. Through one of the large double-glazed panes he spies a familiar profile, but he continues to the end of the row before turning back, mildly vexed. For some reason he was expecting it to be the arrogant ponytailed professional who summoned him here, not sore-eyed, dishevelled Mrs Shukhov.

He taps on the door to the booth in which Mrs Shukhov is sitting. Also inside are the guard Gould and a short, trim, sandy-haired man in a Days dollar-green suit, the employee in charge of Mrs Shukhov's processing. All three look up. Mrs Shukhov smiles, but Frank ignores her. The processor rises from his desk and steps out of the booth for a quiet word.

'You're Frank Hubble?' he asks in frowsty Celtic tones. The name on his ID is Morrison, and if his tie were any more tightly knotted, it would be strangling him.

Frank says, 'I hope you appreciate what an imposition this is.'

'I do, but she was being difficult. She *had* to have you here.'

'Any idea why?'

'If I didn't know better' – Morrison flashes a narrow-toothed grin – 'I'd say the lady's taken a shine to you.'

'Ridiculous,' Frank snorts, and bats open the door and strides into the booth, Morrison in his wake.

'Mr Hubble.' Mrs Shukhov half rises from her seat to greet him.

Frank scowls at her, and she hunches contritely, crumpling in on herself like a withering flower. 'I've put you out, haven't I? How rude of me. Please, go back to whatever it was you were doing. I've obviously dragged you away from something important. Go on. I apologise for having disturbed you.'

'I'm here now,' he says, and shrinks back to allow Morrison to squeeze past him to reach the desk, making himself small so that there is no danger of even their clothes touching. There isn't room for a fourth chair in the booth, so Frank does what he can with the meagre area of floorspace available to him between the edge of the desk and Gould's knees. He sets his shoulderblades against the wall, squares his feet on the carpet, and folds his arms across his chest, feeling the butt of his gun pressing into his left triceps, and he tries not to think how close he is to three other human beings, close enough to be breathing in their exhalations, claustrophobically close. Four people crammed into a few cubic metres of air, a miasma of scents, personal spaces overlapping. Stifling.

'I feel such a fool,' Mrs Shukhov confides to Gould.

'All right then,' says Morrison, seating himself at his desk. He brisks his palms together. 'No more time-wasting, Mrs Shukhov, eh?'

'Yes, of course,' says Mrs Shukhov. 'I really am very sorry. About everything.'

'Fine. Now, for Mr Hubble's benefit, I'm going to recap what little information I've managed to glean so far. The lady here, Mrs Carmen Andrea Shukhov, née Jenkins, is, or I should say was, the proud holder of a Platinum account. On Tuesday last, she happened to mislay her card, and for reasons she is just about to reveal to us did not report it missing and request a replacement, as you or I might have done, but chose instead to embark – with, I might add, a singular lack of success – on a career of five-fingered discounting. A decision made all the more curious by the fact that her account is in an acceptably healthy condition. No outstanding debts, and still some way below its limit.' Morrison gestures at the lists of dates and figures scrolling up the screen of his terminal, a record of every transaction carried out with Mrs Shukhov's Platinum since its issue. With a single keystroke, he pulls up a second list. 'Same goes for her bank account, which receives a handsome credit on the first of each month from an offshore account held in the name of a Mr G. Shukhov. Housekeeping, I take it, Mrs Shukhov?'

'Actually, maintenance.'

'You and Mr Shukhov are no longer together.'

'Not for over a decade. After the divorce, Grigor remained in Moscow, I came back home. We met and married while I was working out there. We had a few good years together. We lived in a gorgeous apartment in a converted mansion on Tverskaya, and Grigor looked after me well, and promised to continue to look after me even after the marriage fell apart. He was always generous with his money. The problem was, I wasn't the only woman who benefited from his generosity.' The bitterness is buried so deeply in her voice as to be almost undetectable.

Mrs Shukhov goes on to explain that a condition of the divorce settlement was that her entitlement to the money depended on her not holding down a paying job of any description. The result was that she came to rely on the monthly payments, a decision she regrets now but which at the time seemed eminently sensible. If the alternative to living on a nice monthly stipend for no effort is working full-time for

147

less money, probably a great deal less, who but a lunatic would opt for the latter?

'Then last month the payments suddenly stopped, and that, basically, left me up the creek without the proverbial paddle. No source of income and no prospect of being able to find a source of income in the immediate future.'

'Ah,' says Morrison, referring again to the screen. 'Yes, they did stop, didn't they? Why was that, Mrs Shukhov?'

'Because Grigor himself stopped.'

There is a moment of uncertain silence.

'Dead,' she clarifies. 'A heart attack. Sudden, massive, instantly fatal. Brought on, no doubt, by one of those gymnastic floozies he was so fond of, or by a glass too many of vodka, most likely a combination of the two.'

'My condolences,' says Gould sincerely.

Mrs Shukhov waves the sympathy away with a flap of her hand. 'No need. Grigor and I hadn't had any contact, apart from through our lawyers, for years. I mourned his loss long before he died. To me he was already a memory.'

'Even so.'

'An old wound. Besides, I'm currently too busy being angry with him to be sad. Leaving me high and dry like that, without a penny to my name! Silly, I know, but that's how I feel about it. How *dare* he not make provision for me in case of his death. Although, if I'm to be honest with myself, it's as much my fault as his. I ought to have known he'd leave no assets, no capital, nothing. That's the kind of man Grigor was. His philosophy was live for today and let tomorrow take care of itself. That's what charmed me so much when I first met him – his lack of worry, his pleasure in whatever was in front of him wherever he might be, his delight in the moment. I was working at Novi GUM at the time, taking groups of foreign customers around, mainly tourists from Western Europe. It was a stressful job, and Grigor was so carefree. The perfect antidote.'

Morrison can't resist an opportunity to trot out the old joke about Russia's only gigastore. 'Novi GUM – they changed the name, they rebuilt the store, but there still isn't anything on the shelves.'

'Not true, Mr Morrison, not true,' says Mrs Shukhov. 'Yes, the place was hopelessly disorganised when I was there, definitely. A shambles compared to most other gigastores, and you couldn't buy anything

148

you wanted, not like here. But that was part of its attraction, that uniquely Russian atmosphere of amiable chaos. Like the country itself, a huge old bumbling institution that somehow, almost in spite of itself, muddles through. At the very least Novi GUM, in my day, was full of surprises. How many gigastores can you say that about?'

Certainly not this one, thinks Frank, a man neck-deep in the mire of routine.

'Every day there was a chance you could round a corner and come across something that wasn't there the night before,' Mrs Shukhov goes on. 'Sometimes, without warning, whole departments would swap around. Whichever department needed extra floorspace got extra floorspace, that was how it worked. A strangely democratic game of musical chairs, which made my job more difficult but also kept me from getting bored and falling into a rut. What was available depended on what the management could get hold of, you see. One day the store might take delivery of ten thousand pairs of chopsticks, the next it might be a hundred gross of ping-pong balls, the next several tonnes of tinned baby food. There was never any rhyme or reason to it, but people bought the stuff because the feeling was, "Well, you never know when chopsticks or ping-pong balls or baby food might come in handy." Which, I suppose, only goes to prove old Septimus Day's point about whatever can be sold will be bought and vice versa. One morning, I remember, they cleared out the Hall of Samovars and wheeled in this huge woolly mammoth which someone had chiselled out of the Siberian ice. It had been stuffed and mounted on a car chassis. On a car chassis, can you believe it!' She chuckles at the recollection, shaking her head. 'A day later it was gone and the samovars were back. Somebody bought it, some museum I expect. I don't know who else but museum curators would have a use for a stuffed woolly mammoth on wheels, do you?'

'I've heard Novi GUM is run much more efficiently these days,' says Gould.

'Since the mafia took it over? Probably. Grigor always used to say that the whole of Russia would move over to a black market economy eventually, and he was right. He used that to his advantage, naturally. He was in the fur trade, and there fur isn't a luxury, it's a necessity, so he did well for himself. And for me. This is all somewhat off the point, isn't it?'

Morrison has to agree. 'Somewhat.'

'What you really want to know is why I didn't report the loss of my card.'

'Well, I think you've explained that already, in so many words. You didn't report it because you were concerned that, since your ex-husband's alimony payments had ceased, Days wouldn't issue you with a replacement.'

'Concerned? Terrified, more like. And without my Platinum how would I live? More to the point, who would I be?'

'And you were right. Not only would the store have refused to replace the card until a suitable level of income had been re-established, but even if you hadn't lost it, your account would automatically have been suspended as soon as its limit was reached. But there's still one thing that puzzles me.' Morrison glances at his terminal. 'The last transaction carried out on the card took place the day before yesterday, the day you say you lost it, Tuesday. You bought, let me see, a Russian phrasebook.'

'And I was going to buy a one-way plane ticket to Moscow next. I still have friends back there, and under the circumstances it seemed like the best place for me to be.'

'You weren't by any chance planning on doing a bunk?' Gould asks, raising an eyebrow.

Mrs Shukhov confesses that she was.

'You'd never have got away with it,' Morrison states with authority. 'Days would have caught up with you. In fact, there's every chance you would have been stopped at the airport before you could leave the country. Nothing, Mrs Shukhov, but nothing, comes between Days and a debt.'

Frank knows the truth of this. There is a clause in the disclaimer form which states that should a customer die owing more on his account than can be recovered from immediately accessible funds, the store is entitled to scoop the remainder from his estate, plus any legal expenses incurred during this process, the store's needs taking precedence over those of the relicts named in the deceased customer's will. Not even death is an escape from Days.

'Well,' says Mrs Shukhov with a light shrug, 'you can't blame a girl for trying.'

'But back to the point,' says Morrison. 'You say you lost the card two days ago.'

'And rotten luck it was too. I can't for the life of me think what happened to it.'

'So tell me – how did you get in this morning?'

And at that Mrs Shukhov gives a broad, clever grin, and suddenly Frank thinks he has the answer. It is an unlikely answer, to be sure, but one that fits all the facts.

'She's been hiding out inside Days,' he says.

Mrs Shukhov blesses him with a gracious, approving nod. 'How astute of you, Mr Hubble.'

'But surely . . .' Morrison grapples with the concept and comes off worst. 'No, there has to be some other explanation.'

'That's why she needed the contact lens solution,' says Frank, 'and why she looks and smells the way she does.'

'Blunt,' Gould mutters to Mrs Shukhov.

'Let's be kind and call it pointed,' Mrs Shukhov mutters back.

'No, it's ridiculous,' Morrison insists. 'How could she? The night watchmen . . . The Eye . . .' He swings his head from side to side as though trying to evade a persistent fly.

'Believe me, Mr Morrison, it wasn't easy,' says Mrs Shukhov, 'but you'd be surprised what you can do when you have no fear of the consequences.'

And she explains.

As soon as she noticed her card was missing, she realised that whether it had been handed in by some honest person or pocketed by some unscrupulous person, it didn't matter; either way, she wasn't going to see it again. She retraced her steps anyway, hoping against hope that she would come across it lying on the floor somewhere, peeking out from under a counter perhaps. She spent the whole afternoon looking for it, in a state of silent, panicked disbelief.

Then suddenly it was closing time, and she knew that if she walked out of the store that evening she was never going to be allowed back in again. And at that moment she stopped and said to herself, 'So why not stay?'

At first she found it hard to believe that she could have come up with such an idea but the more she thought about it the more deliciously audacious, and at the same thoroughly sensible, it seemed. After all, if she got caught, what was the worst that could happen to her? She would be thrown out and forbidden to return. So what had she got to lose?

She didn't know whether she would have the courage to pull it off, but she decided it would be a shame not to try, so she asked herself where would be the best place to spend a night in Days, and the answer that came to her was both logical and childlike in its simplicity. Where would anyone spend a night in Days but in the Beds Department on the Orange Floor?

So, while other customers were making their way to the exits, Mrs Shukhov made her way to Beds. There, she loitered in one of the show bedrooms, waited until she was sure that all the sales assistants were looking in the other direction, then knelt down and crawled beneath a four-poster with a long counterpane that went all the way down to the floor. Huddled beneath the bedsprings, curled up on the carpeted floor, she heard everyone leave, the store close, silence fall. Soon, in spite of everything, she was asleep.

At this point Gould cannot help breaking into a smile, although she does her best to hide it by lowering her head and putting her hand to her mouth. Morrison, meanwhile, scratches one cheek sceptically. Frank just says one word: 'Uncomfortable.'

'You don't know the half of it, Mr Hubble,' says Mrs Shukhov. 'At about four in the morning I woke up bursting for a pee, but I didn't dare creep out and go and look for a Ladies, not with all those guards with torches roving around, and I'm too well brought up to go on the spot, so for five long hours I had to lie there with my legs crossed and my teeth gritted. Nine o'clock couldn't come soon enough, let me tell you. Even then, I decided to put off emerging for another quarter of an hour, because I'm sure it would have raised a few eyebrows among the sales assistants in Beds if someone were to miraculously appear in their department only seconds after opening time.'

'No one saw you crawl out?' says Gould.

'I was very cautious. Also very lucky.'

'*Very* lucky,' says Morrison. 'What happened then?'

Then Mrs Shukhov beat a path to the nearest Ladies, did her business, washed as best she could in the basin, smartened herself up, and went out and spent the whole day wandering around the store.

Once she had settled into the idea of being a stowaway of sorts, it was fun. She tested out various perfumes, partly to cover up the fact that she had slept in her clothes and hadn't had a bath, but also because it amused her. A nice salesgirl in Cosmetics did her make-up for free, and shortly after that, while looking at casserole dishes in Kitchenware, she was propositioned by a young female customer – the first time something like *that* has happened to her, and very flattering, although not her thing at all. She browsed, she meandered, she tried on shoes and hats, and when she got hungry she headed for the food departments and filled up on free samples, picking and moving on, a little bit of this, a little bit of that, until her stomach stopped growling. In short, she did everything that she could have done as a legitimate account-holder except make a purchase, and no one was the least suspicious because as long as she looked and behaved like a customer as far as everyone was concerned she *was* a customer.

Mrs Shukhov pauses for a moment to collect her thoughts, and in that moment Frank notices how self-possessed she has become during the telling of her tale. Something radiates out from her towards her audience of three, in particular (Frank feels) towards him. He can only suppose it is her confidence, drawn to his lack of that same quality like a current sucked along a wire from the positive to the negative terminal of a battery. It gives her a regal air, lending her attractive looks a deeper, truer beauty. He listens with a more attentive ear.

It was an exciting day (Mrs Shukhov continues), though tiring, too. At one point in the afternoon she sat down in a plush leather recliner to rest her feet for a moment, and the next thing she knew a sales assistant was shaking her and telling her to wake up. She had been out for half an hour, but the fellow was very kind about it and told her that people were dropping off in his chairs all the time.

'Do you know, I think on my travels I took in every single department there is,' Mrs Shukhov proudly tells them, 'including the Peripheries, and I've never dreamed of visiting the Peripheries before. For me there's never been much call for departments like Single Socks or Buttons & Shoelaces or Used Cardboard. All that walking! My legs are *still* stiff.' She rubs her calves emphatically. 'Although Mr Hubble here probably thinks nothing of covering such distances.'

Frank, not knowing how to respond, inspects the uppers of his shoes and says nothing.

'Shall we hurry this along?' says Morrison. 'I think Mr Hubble wants to get back to work.'

'There isn't much more to add,' says Mrs Shukhov, with just a hint of a pout. 'When closing time came round again, I went back to Beds, making sure I'd emptied by bladder thoroughly first, and I did the same as the night before, crawled under that four-poster while no one was looking. After the sales assistants had gone home I raised the counterpane a chink to let in some light and brushed up on my

Russian with the help of my new phrasebook – I used to be fluent, you know – till I fell asleep. I slept pretty well, except that I was woken up at about two in the morning by somebody with a vacuum cleaner. Fortunately for me, whoever it was didn't do their job properly and vacuum under the beds, otherwise I might have been in trouble. I went back to sleep again, woke about six, and as I was lying there waiting for opening time, it occurred to me that if I had a mind to it and was careful, I might be able to keep it up indefinitely, this game of living secretly inside Days. There was nothing to stop me, or so I thought.

'It turned out that there was one thing. I hadn't taken my contact lenses out in almost forty-eight hours, and they were starting to dry out and become painful. I'm blind as a bat without them, so I knew that if I was going to continue as a stowaway I had to get hold of some contact lens solution. I mulled the problem over while eating breakfast on the hoof in the Bakery and the Global Delicatessen – how to get hold of a bottle of contact lens solution without my Days card – and in the end I came to the conclusion that there was only one way. You know the outcome of that, and, well, here I am. A convicted shoplifter. My little escapade at an end.

'To be honest with you,' she adds, 'I'm relieved. Despite what I said just now, even if I had got away with my crime, realistically I doubt the game of stowaway could have gone on for longer than about a week. Sooner or later one of the sales assistants in the food departments was bound to think it strange, the same woman coming along and stuffing her face with samples day after day, and there's only so much a lady of a certain age can do with one set of clothes and a cloakroom basin before her appearance degenerates to a level unbecoming of a Days customer. But you know, apart from the shoplifting bit, which I hated, I enjoyed it. It was a thrill. For a decade my life has been too easy. I needed a challenge, and the past couple of days have been, if nothing else, certainly that. And if the chance ever arose, I'd do it again, like a shot.'

She stops talking, clears her throat, smiles.

'Well, that's a pretty tale you've spun for us, Mrs Shukhov,' says Morrison. His face hardens. 'Now how about the truth?'

'That *is* the truth,' says Mrs Shukhov firmly, with just a hint of a pout. 'Why would I make something like that up?'

'Oh, you'd be surprised the nonsense some shoplifters come up with in the hope that I'll be lenient with them and let them off with a warning,' says Morrison. 'Yours, I admit, is definitely not the run-of-the-mill hard-luck yarn I'm used to hearing. Starving children, dying grandmothers, sisters with leukaemia, that's the usual standard of sob-story I get. Yours at least has the virtue of originality. Not that that makes it any more credible.'

'But – '

'Now look, Mrs Shukhov, I've been fair with you. I've played along. I dragged Mr Hubble away from his break because you asked me to. I've been as co-operative as can be. The least you can do is co-operate back.'

'I *am* co-operating! I haven't denied that I shoplifted, have I? In fact, I admitted it, and I'll admit it again if you want me to. I shoplifted! There you have it. A confession. Throw me out and banish me for ever.' A fuschia spot of indignation blooms on each of Mrs Shukhov's cheeks. 'For God's sake, what could I possibly hope to gain by lying? I only told you what I told you just now because . . . well, partly because I'm quite pleased with myself, I'm not ashamed to admit it, but also because I thought you and a senior member of the security staff might be interested to hear about certain loopholes in your apparently not-so-infallible security system. But honestly, if I'd known you were going to react like such a pompous ass, I'd have kept my mouth shut.'

'If you want my opinion,' Frank says, pointedly glancing at his watch (the time is three minutes past eleven, and his break is very definitely over), 'her story sounds plausible enough.'

'*Thank* you, Mr Hubble.' Mrs Shukhov lets her hands fall into her lap and fixes Morrison with a defiant glare.

'And I think you, Morrison,' Frank continues, 'ought to make out a detailed report concerning Mrs Shukhov's activities, with her help, and then file it to the heads of both divisions of security. That's what I think.'

His soft tones carry a deceptive weight, like a feather landing with the force of a cannonball. Morrison blusters, because he has to in order to save face, but inevitably relents. 'Well, if you really think it's necessary . . .'

'I do. I also want you to get Accounts to flag her card, in case someone tries to use it.'

'Of course.' Morrison recovers some of his composure. 'I was going to do that anyway.'

And then Frank does a strange thing. An impulsive thing. The words are out of his mouth before he can stop them. 'And have the Eye contact me if the card is used.'

Morrison eyes him curiously. 'What for?'

'If someone has appropriated Mrs Shukhov's card, I want to personally supervise their apprehension.'

That sounds good, but it isn't standard operating procedure, and Morrison's doubtful look says he knows it. There is no reason why Frank has to be present for that particular arrest. Any other Security operative could do the job just as well.

So why did he just say what he said? Even Frank isn't quite sure, and he is alarmed by the rashness of the action, quite out of character. He supposes he did it because, regardless that Mrs Shukhov is a shoplifter, he admires her. He admires her nerve, stowing away in the store like that. Desperate she might have been, but it was still a plucky thing to do. He feels sorry for her, too, and who can begrudge him a small act of decency towards a woman who has earned both his admiration and his compassion? Besides, given that he has just half a day left at Days, chances are he will not be here when the card is used, if it is used.

Realising this considerably reduces his alarm.

'Well, I'll do as you request,' says Morrison, making a note on his computer, 'although I'd like to go on record here as saying that it is somewhat irregular.'

'I think it's a very nice gesture,' says Gould.

'So do I,' says Mrs Shukhov. 'It's reassuring to know that Mr Hubble himself will be personally responsible for recovering my card.'

Frank pretends to ignore the meaningful look that passes between the two women.

'Am I needed for anything further?' he says to Morrison.

'Not that I can think of.'

'Then, if you'll all excuse me, I should have been back at work well over five minutes ago.'

He bolts for the door, but cannot avoid taking one last glance at Mrs Shukhov. Her bloodshot gaze, strangely serene, holds his.

'Grigor would have liked you, Mr Hubble,' she tells him quietly. 'He liked everybody, but you he would have singled out for special attention. He called people like you "compass needles wavering from north".'

'And that means . . .?' says Frank, poised in the doorway.

'You think about it,' says Mrs Shukhov.

On the way back upstairs he does think about it.

A compass needle has no choice but to point to magnetic north. It may waver on its axis as if attempting to point elsewhere, but in the end it will always fix itself in that direction. Was Mrs Shukhov implying that his fight against the path his life has taken is in vain?

He doesn't know. He wishes he knew. Maybe she is wrong. He hopes so.

20

The Seven Sacred Books: the seven major works of religion – the Christian Bible, the Scandinavian Eddas, the Chinese *Five Kings*, the Muhammadan Koran, the Hindu Three Vedas, the Buddhist *Tri Pitikes*, and the Persian *Zendavesta*

11.06 a.m.
Miss Dalloway sneers at the boxes of software that have been placed just inside one of the entrances to her department.

It is a familiar tactic. First, a few innocuous items of computer paraphernalia appear – an exploratory foray. Then, if the incursion is not swiftly nipped in the bud, a display stand follows. Then, suddenly, as if by magic, there is a computer there too, gleaming with keyboard and monitor and hard drive. Sometimes, if the Technoids are feeling especially bold, a complete workstation – desk, chair, computer, printer with stand – is wheeled covertly into her department, to occupy space which rightly belongs to hardbacks and paperbacks, novels and works of reference, coffee-table books and discounted titles.

A familiar tactic indeed, wearying in its predictability, and ordinarily Miss Dalloway would go up to the group of Technoids who are slouching and grinning in the connecting passageway between her department and theirs, a no man's land, and she would shout at them, perhaps pick up their merchandise and hurl it at them, send them running. Ordinarily this is what she would do, but this morning she is content just to sneer, refusing to be provoked. For the moment at least, she is going to turn a blind eye to their deeds.

The Technoids, crackling in their tight white polyester shirts, their breast pockets bristling with ballpoint pens, jeer at her anyway.

'What's wrong, Miss Dalloway? Aren't you going to swear and throw stuff?'

'Maybe she's finally getting the message. That's *our* floorspace.'

'Careful, lads. She may set one of her darling Bookworm boys on us.'

'Ooh, a Bookworm! I'm scared!'

'Why, what'll he do? Read us some poetry and *bore* us to death?'

Their goading, however, is confounded by her apparent indifference, and lacks conviction. If nothing else Miss Dalloway is usually good for a tirade of baroque threats, but today she just isn't rising to the bait, and that confuses and disappoints the Technoids. Consequently they resort to a time-honoured ritual for baiting Books Department employees: chanting the words 'Dead wood' over and over.

'Dead wood. Dead wood. Dead wood. Dead wood.' The chant gathering speed. 'Dead wood, dead wood, dead wood, dead wood.' Growing in volume, until soon it resembles the rhythmic whoop of apes. 'Dead wood dead wood dead wood dead wood!'

But today not even this elicits a response from Miss Dalloway. Instead, the head of Books merely turns on her heel and strides away and, as she disappears from view between two tall bookcases, the Technoids fall silent and look at one another as if to say, 'What do you suppose has got into *her* then?'

As the bookcases rise around her, enfolding her like a pair of embracing arms, Miss Dalloway feels shoulders that she didn't realise were taut slacken and hands that she didn't realise were fists unclench. The bookcases, old guardians, are a comforting presence – bulwarks, fortifications. A huge weight of wood (no plastic here, nothing so ephemeral), they bear the eternal verities of the printed page ranked cover to cover, forming dense walls of words, and around their bases books litter the floor in unruly stacks; on their shelves, books hide behind books; on the steps of their wheeled ladders, books balance precariously. The sweet clove smell of ageing paper wafts over Miss Dalloway as she moves through her realm, and gradually the Technoids' insults are soothed away, though not forgotten. Nothing the Technoids do is ever forgotten.

She threads her way among the bookcases, a tall woman, narrow and bony. She walks with a birdlike precision, picking her way around piles of merchandise and browsing customers with long ostrich unfoldings of her tweed-trouser-clad legs. Everything about her, from her flat chest to her tight mouth, says iron and impenetrabilty; her flinty eyes and bunned black hair, iron and impenetrability. She is forty-five years old, looks fifty-five, feels sixty-five. She is not a woman you would want to have as an enemy, nor one you would much like to have as a friend – her passions are too intense, too internalised, too focused, to make her easy company. But she is, for all that, a worthy head of Books.

She reaches the heart of the department, the information counter, where a dozen young men are waiting for her. Her faithful subordinates. Her darlings. As one they raise their faces towards her, like chicks in the nest when the mother bird returns with a worm. Glad as the sight of them makes her, Miss Dalloway purses her lips tighter still, crushing any possibility of a smile.

'What do you want us to do, Miss Dalloway?' one of the young men asks, a gloomy-looking lad with a bulging forehead like a cumulonimbus cloud. 'Do you want us to go and sort them out?' It is evident from the way he poses the question that he doesn't relish the prospect of a physical altercation but is none the less ready to carry out whatever orders his head of department gives.

'That won't be necessary, Edgar. Not yet.'

'I could set up a dumpbin there,' offers another – poor, plump Oscar, who, as a result of a run-in with the Technoids a couple of weeks ago, is wearing a cast on his forearm. It started out as name-calling across the connecting passageway, escalated to pushing and shoving, and climaxed in a brawl, with Oscar in the thick of it. Poor, brave boy.

'Thank you, Oscar,' says Miss Dalloway, 'but for now we're going to sit tight and wait. Master Sonny will be down within the hour, and whichever way he resolves the matter will govern our next move. "Our patience will achieve more than our force" – for now.'

'What chance do you think we have of getting that floorspace back, I mean legitimately?' asks another of the Bookworms.

'I can't say, Mervyn. The best we can hope for is that Master Sonny hears the strength of our argument and judges fairly.'

It isn't much comfort to her dear worried darlings, but Miss Dalloway herself isn't convinced that the arbitration will go their way and, much as she would like to, she cannot project an optimism she doesn't feel. Her misgivings are many, but principal among them is the concern that although she has right on her side (about that she *is* convinced), she isn't going to put her case across as charismatically as Mr Armitage, head of Computers, will put his. She has never had much skill as a diplomat, largely because she has never had to be much of a saleswoman. She is firmly of the belief that books should be bought on their own merits, without hype or pressure tactics, and so hard sell is anathema to her and her department, whereas in Computers hard sell is all customers get from the moment they cross the threshold. And so Miss Dalloway fears that, the rightness of her cause notwithstanding, Mr Armitage's polished, coaxing, genial style will prove more appealing to Master Sonny than any fervent, impassioned pleading on her part.

She wishes her uncertainty and anxiety were not so transparent to her darlings, she wishes she could spare them worry, but she can't, so instead she orders them back to work. Work is the eternal balm for the troubled mind.

'Mervyn, some of the titles in the Mystery section have got out of alphabetical order. Salman, the Bargains table needs tidying up. Oscar, there's a customer over there who looks like he needs serving. Colin, you and Edgar set out that delivery of atlases in the Travel section. The rest of you all have things to do. Off you go and do them. Come on, chop-chop!'

She claps her hands, and they scatter obediently. They would die for her. They would.

Miss Dalloway retires to her desk, which is tucked away in a corner of the department more book-strewn than most, and which is sheltered on one side by piles of hardbacks which rise to form a teetering, haphazardly stacked crescent three metres high. The desk is an antique cherrywood monster with scroll feet and deep drawers. On it sits the only computer Miss Dalloway will permit in her department. If it was up to her she would do without the machine – nothing wrong with pen, paper and typewriter, in her view – but she is obliged to use the computer in order to submit inventories and accounts, carry out stock-taking, and send and receive internal memoranda. It's a handy enough tool in its way, but Miss Dalloway cannot for the life of her understand the mystique, the hysteria, that seems to surround anything even remotely computer-related. All this talk of cutting-edge technology when there exists already a piece of technology so honed, so refined over the ages, so wholly suited to its task, that it can only be described as perfect.

A book.

As a source of easily retrievable information, portable, needing no peripheral support systems, instantly accessible to anyone on the planet old enough to read and turn a page, a book is without peer. A book does not come with an instruction manual. A book is not subject to constant software upgrades. A book is not technologically outmoded after five years. A book will never 'go wrong' and have to be repaired by a trained (and expensive) technician. A book cannot be accidentally erased at the touch of a button or have its contents corrupted by magnetic fields. Is it possible to think of any object on this earth more – horrible term – *user-friendly* than a book?

Dead wood. The Technoids' chant echoes dully, hurtfully through her head.

That, alas, is how the majority of people, not just Technoids, regard books: not simply as artefacts made of pulped tree but as obsolete things, redundant, in need of paring away. Dead wood. It's cruel, and no less so for being true. More and more these days people are deriving their entertainment and education from electronic media, the theatre of the screen replacing the theatre of the mind as the principle arena of the imagination. That, she supposes, is understandable, in that it requires less effort to look passively at visual images than to synthesise one's own mental images from the printed word. Yet how much more intense and indelible in the memory than a computer graphic is the mental picture evoked by a skilled writer's prose! Take the pleasure of being led through a good story well told and compare it with the multiple choices and countless frustrating U-turns, reiterations, and dead ends of the average computer game or 'interactive' (whatever *that's* supposed to mean) CD-Rom – no contest. By simple virtue of the fact that it takes place on a machine, digital entertainment is cold and clinical, lacking tactility, lacking *humanity*, whereas a book is a warm, vibrant thing that shows its age in the wear and tear of usage and bears the stamp of its reader in fingerprints and spine creases and dog-ears. On a winter's night, beside a blazing log fire, with a glass of wine or a mug of hot chocolate to hand, which would you rather snuggle up with – a computer or a book? A construct of plastic and silicon and wires that displays committee-assembled collages of text and image premasticated into easy-to-swallow chunks, or the carefully crafted thoughts of a single author beamed almost directly from mind to mind through the medium of words?

Oh, Miss Dalloway knows in her heart of hearts that it is wrong to single out computers (and Computers) as the source of her department's woes when there are dozens of other factors contributing to the decline in popularity of the printed word, but it is better to have an enemy that is concrete, visible, and conveniently close-to-hand than to rail vainly against the growing indifference of the entire world. And so, for better or worse, she has chosen Computers (and computers) as her enemy. Or rather, her enemy was chosen for her by a callous, thoughtless decision made eighteen months ago in the Boardroom of Days.

And that is another reason why she does not feel confident that the imminent arbitration will go her way. The Day brothers run their store electronically, dispensing their edicts and e-memos from on high, and none of them has, to her knowledge, ever expressed a particular fondness for the literary arts, unless you count Master Fred's love of newspapers, which Miss Dalloway does not. (Newspapers, in her view, can barely be described as *literate*, let alone literary.) The Day brothers were the ones who handed over part of her department to Mr Armitage and his Technoids. How can she expect them to be on her side?

With a weary sigh, Miss Dalloway switches on her computer and waits for it to boot up. (You don't have to wait for a book to boot up.) She has achieved the minimum level of computer literacy necessary to operate the machine, no more, so her fingers are not confident on the keyboard as she calls up the e-memo that arrived half an hour ago from the Boardroom.

```
From: the Boardroom                          Time: 10.28
To: Rebecca Dalloway, Books

The MANAGEMENT's attention has been drawn to the various
uncontractual deeds perpetrated by members of your de-
partment, arising as a result of strained relations with
an adjacent department.

The MANAGEMENT is keen to resolve the situation as
quickly as possible, and to this end will be sending down
a representative to hear the grievances of both depart-
ment heads and deliver a binding judgement.

Once MASTER SONNY's judgement has been delivered, both
departments are to abide by his decision. Any further
violations of employee behaviour protocols as stipu-
lated in Clause 17 sections a) to f) of the employer/
employee contract will result in the immediate dis-
missal of the staff members involved and their head of
department.
```

MASTER SONNY will arrive between 11.30 and 11.40 this morning.

cc. Roland Armitage, Computers

She studies the e-memo carefully in the hope of finding something new in its wording, some hitherto unnoticed hint of bias that will reassure her that everything is not as dark as it looks. Nothing about it offers a clue to the mood prevailing in the Boardroom, although, given that Security has been advising the brothers about the dispute since it began, the phrase 'keen to resolve the situation as quickly as possible' wins a small, mirthless smile from her each time her eyes pass over it. Having shown absolutely no interest in the acts of vandalism and violence going on in their store for so many months, for the brothers suddenly to send down one of their number at such short notice smacks of irritation. It is as though they have been hoping the problem would go away of its own accord but, as it hasn't, have finally decided that enough is enough. That, again, does not bode well. Exasperation and clear-eyed impartiality seldom go hand in hand.

The fact that it is Master Sonny and not Master Chas who is coming down gives Miss Dalloway further cause to frown. A visit from Master Chas to the shop floor is a rarity, from Master Sonny unheard of. Everyone knows about Master Sonny's drinking habit, his dissolute lifestyle. Is this a mark of how seriously the brothers are taking the dispute, that they are sending down the youngest, least experienced, and least reliable of them? But then why should that be a surprise? It has often occurred to Miss Dalloway that the sons of Septimus Day don't have the faintest idea what they are doing, and that it is in spite of them, and not thanks to them, that the store continues to turn over a profit at all.

Things were not like this in Mr Septimus's day, an era Miss Dalloway is not alone in recalling with fondness. The founder of Days might have been a hard, fearful man, but at least you knew where you were with him. *He* was not prone to issuing decrees wilfully. *He* did not go around allocating portions of one department to another for no worthwhile reason. He was a man whose very ruthlessness meant he could be trusted.

Miss Dalloway well recalls how every day Mr Septimus would tour the premises, striding through departments with perhaps a valued customer or a cherished supplier in tow but more often than not on his own, unafraid, wearing his aura of authority like an invisible suit of armour, pausing now and then to chide a sales assistant for sloppy dressing, or listen to a query from a head of department, or receive the compliments of a passing (and patently awestruck) shopper.

Was that when things began to go wrong for Days, when Mr Septimus, in the wake of his wife's death, gave up his public appearances in the store, withdrew to his mansion, and handed over the reins of management to his sons? Was that when the rot set in, when the proprietor no longer appeared accessible, and therefore accountable, to staff or customers? Or is it simply that Mr Septimus's seven sons cannot hope to maintain the high standard he set? It would seem inevitable that the clarity of one man's unique vision should be diffused when his sons try to take his place, as when a single beam of white light, refracted, breaks up into a blurred spectrum of colours, losing its sharpness and its power to illuminate.

Miss Dalloway switches off the computer and reaches for the well-thumbed paperback edition of Sun Tzu's *The Art of War* which is lying on the desktop. The book has become her Bible since the dispute began. Opening it, she extracts a Days card she has been both concealing inside it and using as a bookmark.

The card is a Platinum, and the name on it reads MRS C A SHUKHOV.

Malcolm – like all her darlings, a good, honest boy – handed the card in to her on Tuesday afternoon, saying it had been left behind on the counter accidentally by its owner, a rather distracted-looking woman who had used it to buy a Russian phrasebook. Miss Dalloway's first instinct was that of any honourable employee: she would contact Accounts and inform them about the lost card.

Then it occurred to her that a God-given opportunity had just fallen into her lap.

She glances over her shoulder. The haphazard stack of books which seems to have accumulated arbitrarily over the past few weeks around her desk is tall enough to hide her from the security camera that is positioned to include her desk in its viewing sweep. It is unlikely that her department is scanned very thoroughly anyway, since shrinkage has never been much of a problem in Books. Nevertheless, the privacy afforded by this screen of hardbacks (which her Bookworms built to her specifications, carefully and conscientiously adding to it day after day) has been useful in masking from the Eye some industrious activity of the kind that the Day brothers, were they to learn of it, would doubtless consider extremely 'uncontractual'.

Within the books, in a small, hollowed-out cavity specially created for its concealment, lies the fruit of her industry.

Waiting.

Almost complete.

Whatever happens this morning, whether Master Sonny decides in favour of her department or Computers, Miss Dalloway has an appropriate response. Should things go her way, she will organise a celebration for herself and her Bookworms, and in that event the purloined card will not, after all, be necessary, since she will use her own card to buy wine and paper hats. Should things not go her way, however, then she will put her primary plan into effect, and for that plan to succeed Mrs Shukhov's Platinum account is going to be vital.

Flexibility, adaptability, readiness. As Sun Tzu says:

As water varies its flow according to the fall of the land, so an army varies its methods of gaining victory according to the enemy.

Thus an army does not have fixed strategic advantages or an invariable position.

Miss Dalloway is prepared for every contingency and, while she prays that she will not have to resort to her primary plan, she knows that if it comes to it she will not hesitate, not for an instant.

If justice does not prevail, there will come a reckoning.

Oh, such a reckoning.

21

Seven Senses: according to *Ecclesiasticus* there are two further senses in addition to the standard five: understanding and speech

11.25 a.m.

A fungus has formed over his senses, furring his vision and hearing and touch, a fog of fine penicillin strands spun between him and reality. His brain twirls like a coracle loose of its moorings. Trying to stand, he sits back heavily.

The sofa beneath him is a cloud. The world spins erratically, stopping and starting, a broken centrifuge. The weight of gravity shifts and shifts: one moment he feels light as anything, the next a bowling ball rolls down the alley of his spine and rams into his pelvis. Trying to stand up, he sits back heavily.

There is a dampness in his lap as though he has pissed himself. His glass is empty, the crotch of his jeans cold and clinging. How *did* that happen? Ah yes. He recalls. A momentary lapse of concentration. His fingers fumbled. A waste, such a waste of good alcohol. But it doesn't matter, there is plenty more where that came from. Over there at the bar, a plethora of bottles. Over there. If only he could stand up, he could go and fetch himself a refill. If only he could stand up . . .

He tries, and sits back heavily.

He giggles, loud and hard. If his brothers could see him now, how they would despise him, how high-and-mightily disapproving they would be.

'Well, fuck 'em,' Sonny snarls, his eyebrows knotting. Then he giggles, louder and harder.

Raising his head, he peers around his apartment, dislocated, not belonging. The planet's spin is still juddering and irregular. He has to steady himself with his hands on the sofa cushions in order to stay sitting upright. The building is at sea, a gigantic galleon tossed on a mountainous swell, with Sonny in its crow's nest, grogged to the gills, the ship's sway even worse for him than for those down below. Pitch and yaw, pitch and yaw.

He really ought to be standing up. Isn't there something he has to be doing?

There *is* something, although what precisely it is has escaped him for the moment. He is sure it will come back if he doesn't rack his brains for it. A thought on the cusp of memory should not be chased down. Like a sheep on a clifftop, it will panic and run over the edge if you try. Leave it alone and it'll come home.

Chirrup-chirrup.

What was that? He must be hallucinating. He could have sworn he heard a cricket.

Chirrup-chirrup.

The sound is coming from beneath his right buttock. He's sitting on the little bugger! Not that the cricket seems to mind, chirruping away merrily like that.

Chirrup-chirrup.

Sonny lolls over to his left, raising his backside like a rugby player about to unlease a fart. He peers underneath. Nothing there.

Chirrup-chirrup.

It's coming from his back pocket of his jeans.

Where he keeps his portable intercom.

Ah, of course. He knew what was really making the noise all along. A cricket? Just his little joke with himself. Ha ha ha.

He attempts to insert his fingers into the pocket in order to extract the slim intercom unit, but his fingers exhibit all the dexterity of uncooked sausages. Prodding rubberily, torso half twisted over, he grunts in frustration and gives up. Trying another tactic, he presses down on the base of the pocket and succeeds in squirting the intercom out of its denim pouch like some hard fruit from its skin.

Chirrup-chirrup.

He unfolds the mouthpiece, and after a few misses manages to hit the receive button.

'Sonny?'

Thurston.

Instinctively Sonny knows he has to sound sober. It's important.

His tongue feels as though it is swathed in peanut butter, but he manages to curl it around a single word: 'Yes?'

Was that the right answer?

'Sonny, is everything all right?' Suspicious.

'Of course. Why shouldn't it be?'

'It's just that you took so long picking up.'

A ripple of panic. He remembers now why he has to appear sober. Because he is meant to *be* sober. Because he has to go down to the shop floor soon. Because he promised his brothers he wouldn't drink beforehand. Oh shit. Shit shit shit. What if Thurston guesses? If Thurston guesses he has been drinking, that'll be it, his chance blown.

It is an effort to force out one innocent little lie.

'My intercom was in my other trousers.'

And then there is a long whisper of white noise, static fluttering in the connection, the aural equivalent of a piece of lint caught in the lens of a movie projector.

And then Thurston says, 'No. Never mind. Not even you would be that stupid.'

Relief flows out through, it seems, Sonny's every orifice, his every pore, lightening him by evaporation.

'The security guards are waiting for you down on Yellow. You're ready, aren't you?'

'Yes,' Sonny replies, glancing down at his shirt and damp-crotched jeans. 'Absolutely.'

'Now, if there are any problems, if you run into any difficulties at all, for God's sake call me. Remember, all you're down there to do is deliver a message.'

'Deliver a message, yes.'

'Chas wants to say something. Hold on.'

'Sonny? Listen. If the heads of department start to get shirty, back out and leave. Don't stand there arguing with them. It's unseemly. I doubt they're going to give you any grief, you being who you are, but you never know. When feelings are running high, people sometimes forget their place. Just don't let them rattle you. Be calm, unflappable. You're right, they're wrong. Got that?'

'I'm right, they're wrong.'

'OK, I'm handing you back to Thurston. Oh no, hang on, Mungo wants a word.'

'Sonny?' Mungo's deep, resonant voice, the bass pipes of a church organ. 'We're counting on you. I have faith in you. You're going to do fine.'

Sonny is filled with so much love for his eldest brother that he almost bursts into tears.

'I'll do my best, Mungo.'

'That's all we ask.'

Distantly, from across the Boardroom table, Fred can be heard, 'Give 'em hell, Sonny-boy!'

'Off you go then. The guards are waiting.'

''Bye, Mungo. 'Bye.'

Sonny clasps the intercom shut and presses it to his chest. He must get moving. Urgency injects adrenalin into his bloodstream, bringing a surge of clear-headedness, brief but sufficient to enable him to resist the plush seducing suck of the sofa and the wobble of the world's wild whirling. He clambers triumphantly to his feet.

Upright, he staggers, his brain flushing empty of blood. The apartment rises to a tremendous peak then swoops down, down, down into a trough. For an instant Sonny thinks he is about to faint. Then everything calms, settles, evens, levels out.

Half walking, half lurching, Sonny sets off for his bedroom.

11.28 a.m.

'I hate to say this,' says Thurston, taking his intercom from Mungo and laying it in front of him on the table, 'but I can't help feeling we've made a terrible mistake.'

'You worry to much,' says Fred.

'Why don't we follow him with the Eye?' says Sato. 'At least that way we'll have some idea what he gets up to.'

'I'll get them to patch the feed through,' says Thurston. 'Good idea, Sato.'

If the portrait of Old Man Day on the wall could speak, it would probably say that nothing that has happened in the Boardroom today has been a good idea.

11.29 a.m.

Suits hurtle out of the walk-in wardrobe one after another like canaries from a cage.

Inside, Sonny is frantically rifling through his extensive collection of formal wear, hauling each outfit off the racks in turn and giving it a

170

cursory once-over before flinging it over his shoulder to join the other rejects in a lavish, polychromatic jumble on the floor.

What to wear? What to wear?

Earlier, when it seemed he had all the time in the world, he couldn't make up his mind which of his suits was suitable. Now that he is in a hurry, not to mention drunk, it's as hard, if not harder, to decide. He knows he ought just to grab a suit, any suit, it doesn't matter which one, and throw it on, but this is his one-time-only chance to make an impression and he wants to look absolutely right. If only there wasn't such a wide range, if only so many of the damned things weren't so garish and unwearable . . .

The tangled heap in the wardrobe doorway continues to grow layer by layer, discard by discard, and then, abruptly, is no longer added to.

Sonny has made his choice.

11.41 a.m.
Between them, Jorgenson, Kofi, Goring and Wallace, the four security guards waiting in the Yellow Floor hoop outside the doors to the brothers' private lift, have a combined previous work experience of fifteen years in the armed services, six years in the police force, and eight and a half years in a variety of correctional centres, either as warders or inmates. They are four stone giants, weathered but not worn, seemingly impervious to pain and emotion, and so it is impossible to tell if they are at all excited to have been detailed as escorts to one of the seven human beings in whose hands rests control of the world's first and (oh, what the hell, give it the benefit of the doubt) foremost gigastore. In fact, to look at them, you might think that accompanying a Day brother around the store was an everyday occurrence on a par with picking a shred of meat from between two back teeth.

Prepared for anything, the guards stand with their arms wrapped across their chests, their legs spread slightly apart, and their heads cocked to one side, the classic pose of paid thugs the world over. Not a word is exchanged between Jorgenson and Kofi and Goring and Wallace as they wait for Master Sonny to descend. His lateness is not commented on, not even by a covert glance at wristwatch or wall clock. The guards merely stand and wait as they have been told to do, just as mountains were told to stand and wait by God.

Shoppers mill past, some wondering why these four guards are stationed before a set of lift doors marked 'PRIVATE – NOT FOR CUSTOMER USE,' but none so bold as to approach and enquire. Likewise, even the most geographically bewildered customer in the store would take one look at these four and go and find someone else to ask for directions.

When they hear the lift finally begin to descend from the Violet Floor, the four, as one, unfold their arms and unbutton their hip-belt holsters. Ready for anything.

There is no floor indicator above the doors to the brothers' private lift, and so the guards have no idea that Master Sonny has arrived until the lift-car heaves to a halt and the doors roll open.

Jorgenson, on whom was conferred the task of rounding up the three of his colleagues for this detail, and who therefore considers himself in charge, swivels on his heels, puffs out his chest, and snaps a salute at his employer.

Sonny, after a moment's swaying hesitation, raggedly returns the salute.

'Good morning, sir,' Jorgenson says without so much as a flicker of his unsurprisable eyes.

'Good morning,' Sonny replies brightly, like a child. He slaps his fingers to his forehead again, then, taking a liking to this saluting lark, turns and repeats the action three more times to Kofi, Goring and Wallace in turn. He bids them all good morning, and they wish him the same back.

Sonny is wearing the blackcurrant-purple suit he previously rejected, the one with the embroidered gold Days logos at the shoulders, cuffs, and pockets. Second thoughts, and a large quantity of cinnamon-spiced vodka, have convinced him that the hue and the logos work in the suit's favour rather than against it. The jolliness of the one and the vaguely military aspect of the other together create the desired balance between approachability and authority. He has put on a saffron shirt and a lilac tie, and his feet are the meat filling to a pair of pie-like light-brown cross-stitched loafers. His flushed, perspiration-sheened face rounds out the ensemble perfectly.

'Shall we be on our way then?' he enquires, and the guards fall quickly into position, Jorgenson and Kofi in the lead, Goring and Wallace behind, four corners of a square of which Sonny is the central point.

There isn't a smirk to be seen on the guards' faces as they march towards Books and Computers.

22

The Seven Years' War: the war in which England and Prussia defeated Austria, Russia, Sweden, Saxony, and France (1756–63)

11.46 a.m.
On one side of the connecting passageway between Books and Computers, Miss Dalloway waits, along with three of her Bookworms, Oscar, Salman and Kurt. Opposite them, a couple of metres and an ideological gulf away, stand Mr Armitage and three Technoids. Originally Mr Armitage brought along more of his staff to accompany him but, seeing that Miss Dalloway had confined herself to a retinue of just three, he dismissed the rest. The courtesy has not been remarked upon, has in fact been studiously ignored.

The air between the two four-person factions is cat's-cradled with antagonistic stares. Silence holds sway.

11.48 a.m.
Everybody is looking at him. Of course. Who wouldn't stop and look at a man being escorted by four security guards? A few of the shoppers recognise him, most don't. Recent photographs of the Day brothers are hard to come by, but the family features are definitely there for all to see. The nose, the Oriental colouring – unmistakable.

But the stares have no weight. That is what's important to Sonny as the guards steer him anticlockwise around the Yellow Floor hoop towards the entrance to Computers. No one is peering at him with that intense light of knowledge in their eyes that says that they are privy to his secrets. None of them are using that look that seems to claim ownership of his soul, as if the public have some kind of proprietorial right over public figures. Perhaps it is because they can't see into him properly through his gauze of inebriation, or perhaps it is because *he* can't make *them* out properly. Either way, it makes no difference. The effect is the same. He is protected. So let them look.

11.49 a.m.

There is a shimmer of commotion from the opposite entrance of Computers. A whisper races across the department like an electric current. *He is coming. Master Sonny is coming.*

And Miss Dalloway thinks, *How typical that he should choose a path that takes him through Computers.* She is aware that Computers, being one of those sales-favoured departments that abuts on to a hoop, lies directly between her department and the brothers' private lift; it would be absurd for him to come any other way, and yet . . . *How typical.*

There is a bustle of noise between the high-stacked racks of computer paraphernalia and peripherals, the mouse mats and manuals, the dust-covers and disk drives. Master Sonny is not yet in view but the hissed news of his approach breaks before him like a bow wave. Mr Armitage switches on a smile in readiness. That is the first thing Master Sonny will see as he reaches the connecting passageway: Mr Armitage's studied smile. Miss Dalloway grits her teeth and puts it out of her mind. Nothing matters except stating her case. The truth. Justice.

And here he is. Not as tall as she expected, although the four guards surrounding him would make a dwarf of anyone. Not as assured in his bearing as his father. An incipient puffiness around the jawline which, given time and no change in his habits, will develop into jowls. Eyes averted, watching the floor, or perhaps the boots of the guards in front. And that outfit! The outfit has to be some kind of joke, doesn't it? It chills Miss Dalloway to think that Master Sonny might consider what he is wearing appropriate attire for a serious businessman. A catwalk model at one of the more eccentric fashion shows might be able to pull off a get-up like that, but one of the joint owners of the world's first and (formerly) foremost gigastore? No. Never.

Here he is, and Mr Armitage is stepping forward, hand outstretched, seizing the initiative.

'Sir, a great honour. Roland Armitage, Computers. A great honour indeed. We're so grateful you could make it down here. It'll be good to have this misunderstanding straightened out once and for all.'

The leading pair of guards move apart, leaving Sonny standing, perplexed, staring at Mr Armitage's proffered hand. Then, as if suddenly remembering what to do in such circumstances, he reaches out and clasps it.

After a few forthright pumps of Sonny's arm, Mr Armitage disengages, turns, and begins introducing the Technoids present by name. Greeting their employer, they writhe humbly.

As for Miss Dalloway, she is so furious over Mr Armitage's remark about a 'misunderstanding' she can barely think straight. Was he simply trying to annoy her or does he sincerely believe that her committed resistance to eighteen months of attempted annexation has stemmed from nothing more than a *misunderstanding*? But it quickly dawns on her that standing there seething will get her nowhere, and so, with a resolute snort and a shake of her head, she steps forward into the connecting passageway.

Technically nowhere on the shop floor is out of bounds to Miss Dalloway, but since the dispute began she has struck the Computers Department off her personal map, refusing to acknowledge its existence, even if that has meant having to make time-consuming detours to avoid it. Now, crossing the threshold to that department, she feels like a soldier venturing behind enemy lines.

Behind her, the three Bookworms hesitate. Miss Dalloway has forbidden them to enter Computers territory. Should they continue to obey that order, or does showing support for their head of department take precedence? They decide to follow her, and cross no man's land in a nervous gaggle.

Pushing her way past the trio of Technoids, Miss Dalloway thrusts herself between Mr Armitage and Sonny. Mr Armitage has been telling Sonny how useful the extra display space has proved in enticing shoppers into Computers. He is halfway through suggesting that the department's other entrances might benefit from a similar arrangement when she interrupts him.

'Rebecca Dalloway.'

Sonny's head snaps round. His eyes and his attention seem to follow a couple of seconds behind.

'And you are?'

'Rebecca Dalloway,' she repeats patiently.

'No, I mean, what do you do?'

'Head of Books.'

'Oh. OK. Right.'

'I'd like you to know, Master Sonny, before anything else is said, that as a loyal employee of some twenty-five years' standing I have nothing but the utmost respect for the way you and your brothers manage

Days, and I would never dream of calling your undoubted competence into question.'

'Easy does it with the flattery, Miss Dalloway,' Mr Armitage mutters, too low for Sonny to hear. 'A paintbrush rather than a trowel.'

That's rich coming from the arch sycophant himself, but Miss Dalloway refuses to be waylaid. 'Nor is it for me to argue with any decision made on economic grounds. After all, we're all working together for the common good of the store, aren't we?' Here she attempts an ingratiating smile. It is not a pretty sight, as she would be the first to admit, but desperate times call for desperate measures. 'However, I think you'll agree, when you see for yourself the size of the area of floorspace involved, that the negligible increase it brings to the Computers Department's sales figures scarcely warrants the time and effort Mr Armitage and his staff spend setting out their stock there.'

That's good, she thinks. *Appeal to his need for cost-effectiveness. There, surely, lies the Day brothers' Achilles heel.*

'But, Miss Dalloway,' says Mr Armitage, butting in before Sonny has been able to stir himself to reply, 'by the same token, if the area of floorspace is so small, it scarcely warrants the time and effort *your* department devotes to trying to keep *my* department out. Perhaps you'd be better off channelling the energy you put into thwarting us into drumming up custom and improving your department's dismal sales figures.'

'My sales figures might not be so "dismal", Mr Armitage, were I allowed to keep all the floorspace I'm entitled to.'

'Hear, hear,' says Oscar, and he is echoed by Salman and Kurt.

The encouragement stiffens Miss Dalloway from head to toe like a leather scabbard when the sword is sheathed. 'And as my staff will testify,' she continues, 'our attention to our duties as Days employees has inevitably been compromised by the Computers Department's repeated acts of aggression and intimidation. How can we be expected to concentrate on our customers and merchandise under a constant barrage of threats and harassment?'

'If by threats and harassment you mean laying claim to what is rightfully ours, then my staff and I stand guilty as charged,' says Mr Armitage. 'We have threatened, we have harassed. But we wouldn't have had to resort to such drastic action if you and your Bookworms, Miss Dalloway, hadn't been so obstinate from the start. Not just obstinate, downright rebellious.'

'Rebellious!'

'The e-memo granting my department the extra floorspace came, did it not, from the Boardroom. Is that not so, Master Sonny? From the very highest authority in Days. And so resisting the order contained in that e-memo would seem to me an act of insubordination at the very least, if not open rebellion.'

'Don't exaggerate.' Miss Dalloway can feel her cheeks reddening. She knew this would happen. Mr Armitage is twisting her argument around, trying to make it look like *she* is the one in the wrong. She turns to Sonny. 'He's exaggerating, sir. He wants you to believe that by opposing him I have somehow been opposing *you*. That certainly is not the case. As I told you just now, I am a loyal employee of some twenty-five years' standing. It's hardly likely that I'm going to turn against the people who have employed me for a quarter of a century, now, am I?'

'Aren't you?' Mr Armitage gives a tiny, knowing tweak of his eyebrows.

'Of course not.'

'But if I'm carrying out the brothers' orders and you oppose me, by definition that means you must be opposing the brothers.'

'A equals B and B equals C, therefore A must equal C. If only the world ran according to your simple, logical patterns, Mr Armitage.' Miss Dalloway moves a step closer to Master Sonny, narrowing, she hopes, not just the physical distance between them. She catches a whiff of his breath, and suddenly the reason for his bleary indifference becomes clear. She is appalled, but she knows she mustn't allow anything to deter her. 'If you could only have seen, sir, how eagerly Computers leapt on the new floorspace, without so much as a syllable of apology in my direction, not one gramme of remorse, only the arrogant, gloating assumption that I was going to let them have whatever they wanted. If you could only have seen that, I think you would have agreed with me that they didn't deserve it.'

'Ah, so now it's down to what we deserved as opposed to what we've been granted,' says Mr Armitage. 'It's about our *attitude*, which you, in your infinite wisdom, have judged inappropriate.'

'Inappropriate, insensitive, insulting . . .'

'Would it have made a difference if we'd approached you with a bunch of flowers and a box of chocolates and asked, pretty please, Miss Dalloway, would you let us have the ten square metres of your department the Day brothers have already said are ours? Would you have given them up without a murmur then? I doubt it.'

'I might at least have thought about it.'

'Thought about it and then gone ahead and done exactly the same.' Mr Armitage shrugs extravagantly at Sonny. 'It's no use, sir. There's no point discussing this. We aren't going to get anywhere until Miss Dalloway realises that an order from you and your brothers isn't just something she can ignore if she doesn't like it. We all understand about wounded pride, but there are times when you have to admit defeat and accept the inevitable. Take it – if I can use the phrase with reference to a lady – like a man.'

'A man wouldn't take the way I've been treated half as well as I have,' says Miss Dalloway. 'My sex has a long history of bearing up nobly in the face of injustice and oppression. It's about time they changed the phrase to "take it like a woman".'

'However you wish to put it, then. Bite the bullet. Concede gracefully. Bow under pressure. Go with the flow.'

'This particular flow I would rather resist.'

'The willow that bends with the breeze survives.'

Miss Dalloway cannot suppress a burst of contemptuous laughter. 'Where did you dig up that fatuous little epigram, Mr Armitage? From some self-improvement manual for ambitious executives?'

There. Is that a twitch she sees? A tiny wrinkling in Mr Armitage's oh-so-smooth-and-placid surface? Has she finally succeeded in getting to him?

If so, he recovers his composure swiftly and with consummate skill. 'It's a wise person, Miss Dalloway, who knows how to handle change.'

'It's a wiser person who knows how to distinguish good change from bad. Not everything new is improved, Mr Armitage. That may be the reigning philosophy in the world of computers where a piece of equipment is obsolete almost from the moment it hits the shelves, but in most other walks of life the new does not automatically oust the old, at least not without a Stalin or a Mao or a Pol Pot in charge. In most walks of life change is an extension of tradition. It happens naturally. It isn't forced on you like a software upgrade or a faster processing chip; you don't *have* to have it if you don't want it.'

'When you talk about tradition, Miss Dalloway, the image that comes into my head is of a bunch of cobwebby old books mouldering in a pile on a table, unbought and unread.'

'But some traditions survive because they *work*. For example, when Mr Septimus divided Days into seven hundred and seventy-seven departments and allotted each department exactly the same amount of floorspace irrespective of its profit potential or the dimensions of the merchandise it would stock or the number of staff members required to sell that merchandise, he did so for a purpose, to show, in effect, that he regarded every department as the equal of its neighbour, no one department less worthy of his attention than any other.'

'But you can't compare one of the Indigo Floor Peripheries, where they're lucky if they make a sale a day, with, say, Jewellery. That's preposterous.'

'Let me finish, Mr Armitage. To Mr Septimus – to your father, Master Sonny – each department was as important as the next. Obviously in financial terms you can't compare Jewellery with Single Socks, only a fool would, but the fact that there *is* a Jewellery Department ensures that a department like Single Socks – which is a godsend to anyone who has ever lost a sock in the laundry and doesn't want to spring for a brand new pair – can continue to exist. Days was designed to be in equilibrium, every part in harmony with every other part.'

'If that's so, then how come all those departments disappeared or got merged when the brothers took over Violet for themselves?' says Mr Armitage. 'Why would the brothers disturb this precious equilibrium of yours if it was one of the main reasons the store was raking in money?'

Miss Dalloway chooses her words carefully. 'Perhaps the brothers were not entirely aware of the significance of what they were doing.' She watches Sonny for an adverse reaction, but nothing in his glazed demeanour suggests that she has offended him or, indeed, that he has taken on board anything she has been saying for the past few minutes.

'There she goes again!' Mr Armitage throws his hands in the air despairingly. 'Questioning your decisions, Master Sonny, casting doubt on your managerial wisdom. How can you let her get away with this?'

'You make it sound as if disputing store policy is a form of heresy.'

'Isn't it?'

'Only an idiot or a fanatic goes along with everything his superiors say and do.' Miss Dalloway knows she isn't helping her argument any by saying this, but nevertheless she feels it has to be said.

'Really, Miss Dalloway,' Mr Armitage replies, 'I think you must be confusing me with someone you've invented. You want to paint me as some sort of grasping, rapacious ogre because that's how you need to think of me, whereas all I am – and you know this in your heart of hearts – is a head of department who follows instructions.'

'Master Sonny, sir,' says Miss Dalloway, 'you've heard from Mr Armitage's own lips that he and his staff have harassed and threatened my staff and me. You've seen how contemptuous he is of my department. It's clear that he's simply using a Boardroom edict as an excuse to further his own ends and expand his little empire. Natural justice would demand that you rescind your original decision. It wouldn't be admitting a mistake, it would merely be making a *better* decision.'

'Sir, there's a principle at stake here. If you let her get her way, you'll be sending a message to every head of department, every member of staff, that they can do however they feel, and to hell with discipline or the corporate structure.'

'Sir, the principle at stake here is the right of every department to manage itself as best it can, according to its needs.'

'Sir, that's of no benefit to the store.'

'Sir, on the contrary, it is.'

'Sir? Hello?'

'Sir?'

'Sir?'

11.56 a.m.

Throughout the foregoing exchange, Sonny's head has been bobbing to and fro, now to listen to Mr Armitage, now Miss Dalloway. The alternating currents of their dialogue have switched him this way and that until he is no longer sure what has been said by whom. Here and there a random phrase has snagged in his brain, but for the most part it has all been so much gibberish, a melange of words thrown together for no obvious reason except perhaps to confuse him, somehow made all the more incomprehensible by the occasional flashes of sense. He feels like a radio tuned between two stations, receiving intermittent bursts of signal from one or the other amid a surf of white noise.

The faces of the two people talking are no help. The man looks honest enough, the kind of chap you can trust, but the woman – all those forward jabs of her sharp nose – has the air of someone who has never been wrong about anything in her life. Is it possible they can both be right? Is this a problem without a solution, like one of those Zen thingies about trees falling in forests and one hand clapping?

Thurston's words flit into his head: 'All you're down there to do is deliver a message.' The trouble is, Sonny has only the dimmest recollection now of what that message is. But unless he wants to stand here all day listening to these two yammer at him, he is going to have to say something to keep them happy.

They're saying, 'Sir?' to him. 'Sir? Sir?' They want him to speak.

Very well.

11.57 a.m.
'One of you's right, one of you's wrong.'

'True.'

'Yes, sir.'

'Well, at least both of you agree on that. I don't suppose there's any chance you'll agree on anything else, is there?'

Miss Dalloway and Mr Armitage exchange glances.

'No, sir,' they say in unison.

'Thought not. Well . . .' Sonny delves into a pocket of his blackcurrant-purple jacket. 'What we used to do at university when we'd lost track of whose round it was . . .' The pocket is empty. He tries another. 'Is we'd flip a card.' That pocket, too, is empty, as is the next he tries. 'Usually it was my card we'd flip.' He digs into both trouser pockets. 'Everyone liked it when I brought out my card.' Finally he tries his breast pocket. 'It gave them a thrill. Ah, here it is.'

He produces his Osmium. Tar-black and gleaming, it is an object so rarely glimpsed on the shop floor, so mythical, that even those lucky enough to have seen one before cannot take their eyes off it and follow its every movement, mesmerised, as Sonny waves it for emphasis.

'So I'm going to do the same now. I'm going to flip this, and if it lands with the logo side facing up then *you*' – he points the card at Mr Armitage – 'get to keep the floorspace, and if it lands with the side with the magnetic strip and my signature on it facing up then *you*' – now he aims the card at Miss Dalloway – 'get to keep the floorspace. OK? Got that? Logo, you. Magnetic strip, you. Couldn't be simpler, could it? Or fairer. All right. Ready, everyone? Here goes.'

Sonny makes a fist of his right hand, cocks the thumb, and balances the Osmium carefully across the middle joint. Mr Armitage calmly folds his arms, letting it be known that he isn't too much bothered which way the card falls or, for that matter, that the dispute is being resolved by the flip of a card. Clearly, if this method of arbitration is good enough for a Day brother, it's good enough for him.

Miss Dalloway, on the other hand, can scarcely believe what she is seeing. She would like to think that Master Sonny is simply teasing them, that in a moment he is going to wink and put the card away and say, 'Just kidding,' and then deliver a reasoned and well-considered assessment of the situation . . . but no, it seems that he means it, he is really going to go through with this, her fate really does rest on the spiralling trajectory of a piece of plastic.

And what can she do about it? Can she snatch the card off him and tell him not to be so ridiculous? Can she grab him by the scruff of the neck and shake him until he sobers up and starts behaving like an intelligent adult and not like an inebriate lout in a college bar? Of course she can't. All she can do is reach behind and grope for the hands of her darling boys, and from the three sweaty palms that grip her thin dry fingers draw strength and succour.

The Osmium topples from Sonny's none-too-steady fist and tumbles to the floor.

It lands with its logo downwards, the brown magnetic strip and the white oblong containing Sonny's scrawled signature facing up, plain as day.

Miss Dalloway's heart gives a little leap. She has won!

'That doesn't count.' Sonny stoops and retrieves the card from the carpet. 'That was an accident. Doesn't count.'

Hope crouches down again in Miss Dalloway's breast, swaying back and forth on its hunkers.

'All right.' Sonny perches the card on the two knuckles of his thumb once more. It seems that not only has the Computers Department gone quiet but that a hush has descended over the entire store. It is as if the outcome of more than a mere dispute over a strip of floorspace depends on which way up Sonny Day's Osmium lands, as if the very future of Days revolves around this moment, this cocked thumb, this poised wafer of black plastic.

Everyone is concentrating on the card: Miss Dalloway, Mr Armitage, the Bookworms, the Technoids, the small crowd of intrigued customers that has gathered over the past few minutes. Even the guards – who are meant to be looking elsewhere, scanning for potential threats to their employer – are squinting sidelong at the Osmium and at the man holding the Osmium.

And Miss Dalloway, no great believer in God, none the less prays. She prays that, though the rest of the world seems to have lost its head, there still exists a pocket of sanity wherein things turn out as they are meant to. She prays that, though justice has been reduced to a fifty-fifty lottery, there is still some hope that right will prevail. She prays that Samuel Butler was not mistaken when he wrote that 'Justice, though she's painted blind,/Is to the weaker side inclin'd.' But above all she prays that, when Master Sonny flicks the Osmium into the air, it will exactly reproduce the pirouette it performed just now, executing the exact same number of turns, and land the same way up.

Sonny locks his thumbnail beneath the pad at the tip of his forefinger. Flexing tendons dimple the heel of his thumb.

Nothing happens, and for one awful instant Miss Dalloway believes that time has ground to a halt. Master Sonny will never flip the card. She will remain trapped in this ecstasy of fear and trepidation for ever.

Then the sprung thumb is released and the card is launched, an oblong black projectile spinning upwards from Sonny's fist on the rising curve of a parabola, end over end over end over end, light planing across its two rectangular faces in turn, end over end, reaching its zenith in front of Sonny's nose, then beginning its descent, describing an arc that mirrors the curve of its ascent, still gracefully whirling around its own axis like a drum majorette's baton, with Miss Dalloway willing it to fall logo side down, willing the very air molecules through which it is passing to strike it leniently as it begins the long drop to the logo-patterned carpet of the Computers Department, willing it to land favourably on enemy ground. And down it goes, this thin, fragile thing that, were the wealth it represents realised as a block of precious metal, would need a dozen strong men to lift it – down it goes, turning and turning, down and down and down, until one rounded corner strikes the carpet's green furze and it bounces, comes down on another corner, twirls like a ballerina, slumps on to one edge, then flops flat.

Miss Dalloway can't bring herself to look.

'Oscar? Which way up is it, Oscar?'

Oscar's silence is all the answer she needs.

She lowers her gaze to the Osmium, and there they are – the grainy and smooth semicircles of the card's Days logo, the right half sanded to a pale grey sheen, the left as shiny as fresh creosote on a roadway.

11.58 a.m.
'What's he doing?' says Wensley. 'I can't make out what he's doing.'

'It's clearer on the other camera,' says Mungo. 'Slightly.' He points across the table to the second four-by-four bank of monitors, which shows the same scene at a different angle: Sonny addressing the heads of Books and Computers, flashing his Osmium at them. Both images, expanded to fit sixteen screens, are blurry and ill-defined. The card is a vaguely rectangular black blob, Sonny's suit a man-shaped mass of dark grey, and the employees' faces ovals of white, their features dark smudges.

'What's he got his card out for?' Fred asks.

'A badge of authority,' Thurston suggests.

'You can't argue with an Osmium,' says Chas, nodding.

'Especially one which has the surname Day on it,' Sato adds.

'Whoops! Dropped it!' says Fred, chuckling. 'You're going to have to learn to keep a tighter grip on your money, Sonny. There, pick it up, that's a good boy. No! Fumbled again!'

'Was that a fumble?' says Thurston with a frown. 'Looked to me more like he flipped it.'

'It was a fumble,' says Mungo with a confidence he does not entirely feel. 'See, he's picking it up again and putting it away. He just wanted them to see that he means business.'

'I wish the angle were better,' says Sato. Sonny has his back to both cameras.

'These are the best feeds the Eye could give us,' says Thurston. 'We'd have a better view if he wasn't so close to the entrance. The deeper you go into a department, the more cameras there are.'

'This is good enough,' says Mungo. 'We can tell he isn't doing anything stupid. He's listened to the heads of department, and now he's telling them what we think.'

The dark side of the great dome now occupies fully half of the Boardroom's triptych of windows. Septimus Day continues to glower impotently down from his portrait. The brothers begin to relax. It seems that Sonny has pulled it off, that their fears were unfounded.

Perhaps, after all, they can work together, all seven of them, as their father wanted them to.

Mungo reminds Chas that they are due for their daily tennis game and, as the two of them leave the Boardroom to go down to their apartments to get changed, Mungo feels that the respect his brothers hold him in has been immeasurably enhanced by the bravery of his decisions this morning.

It is a good feeling.

11.59 a.m.
'Well,' says Sonny, stowing away his Osmium, 'I have to go now. I'm sure my brothers must have other work for me to do. Congratulations to the winners, commiserations to the losers. Goodbye to you all.'

The guards fall in place around Sonny, and off they go, a phalanx of five.

'Wisely made?' splutters Miss Dalloway, finally finding her voice after a full minute of stunned inarticulacy. 'It wasn't even a *decision*. It was the absolute antithesis of a decision. It was a travesty. "Judgement drunk, and brib'd to lose his way,/Winks hard, and talks of darkness at noon-day." Sir? Master Sonny, sir?'

She makes to pursue her employer, but Mr Armitage restrains her with a firm hand.

'Miss Dalloway,' he says, 'accept it, you've lost. Deal with it.'

The head of Books has never been so tempted to punch someone. Instead, she growls and brushes Mr Armitage's hand away as though it is a tarantula that has dropped on to her shoulder.

'This isn't over,' she tells him. 'This is far from over.' And with an imperious toss of her head, she strides off into the connecting passageway.

Her darlings cluster around her as she storms back into Books.

'What now, Miss Dalloway?' asks Kurt.

'We have to let them have the floorspace, don't we?' says Oscar.

'We don't have a choice,' says Salman. 'Master Sonny – '

'Damn Master Sonny!' Miss Dalloway snaps. 'Damn him, damn his brothers, damn the whole sorry lot of them! If they think they can get away with treating a loyal employee like this, they've got another think coming.'

'But we've lost.'

'Lost, Oscar? *Lost*? On the contrary. In the words of John Paul Jones' – Miss Dalloway is incandescent with righteous rage; her fury is awesome in its purity – ' "I have not yet begun to fight." '

It is midday.

23

Seventh Avenue: a street in New York City, part of which is
nicknamed 'Fashion Avenue' – also known as the 'garment centre'

12.00 p.m.
Midday finds Linda Trivett in Ties on the Blue Floor, rummaging
through her handbag for her shopping list. She needs to find the
catalogue serial number of the tie she wants to buy for Gordon,
because the department has turned out to be too full of merchandise
for her to track it down unaided. There are ties everywhere. Ties
dangling like jungle lianas from wires suspended across the ceiling.
Ties hanging on rotating stands. Ties knotted around the necks of
torso mannequins. Ties snugly rolled in presentation boxes. Ties
interleaved on the walls head to tail, like long, thin segments of a huge
silky quilt. Ties snaking around pillars in candystripe swirls. A
wilderness of ties, in which Linda has about as much chance of
locating the one she wants as she does of locating a specific grain of
sand in the desert.

Still, it is fun to look, and she has been looking for over quarter of an
hour, roaming the aisles, running her fingers over the merchandise,
admiring. Yes, letting Gordon go off on his own is the best thing she
could have done. She would never have had this luxury to browse
(and, of course, the tie would not be a surprise) were he still tagging
along behind her. Without him she can wander where she wants and
linger as long as she likes over any items that happen to catch her eye,
free from the insistent, nagging pressure of his impatience. She misses
him, really she does. She would love to be able to spend the entire day
with him, because the taste of triumph is that much sweeter when
shared with another, but she acknowledges that the temporary
separation is for the best, and she suspects that, in the future, marital
harmony will be best maintained if she and Gordon visit Days apart
rather than together.

Wherever he is, she hopes he is safe and enjoying himself.

At last she unearths the slip of paper containing the serial numbers of the tie, the cherub carriage clock, and the other items on her shopping list. She approaches a nearby sales assistant.

'Excuse me, please. I'm looking for a particular – ' She stops mid-sentence.

'A particular what, Madam?'

Linda smiles. 'Never mind. I've just found it.'

'Isn't that always the way, madam?' says the sales assistant. 'The moment the plumber arrives, the tap stops dripping.'

Linda laughs, thanks him, and goes over to the rack she spotted where, among others, hangs the coin-motif tie.

'Attention, customers.'

She glances up. How exciting. Another lightning sale. There was one an hour and a quarter ago in Farm Machinery, and although a swift examination of the leaflet map showed Linda that she was four floors up and on the opposite side of the building from that department, she was tempted to make a dash for it all the same. Seeing other shoppers spin on their heels and head off, she felt a tug, an instinctive pull. *I could go too*, she thought. *I am part of the pack, I could run with them.* Fortunately she retained sufficient presence of mind to realise that her small, well-tended plot of garden at home was unlikely to be improved by the deployment of heavyweight agricultural equipment. Had the sale been in another department – any other department – she might well have gone.

She listens attentively.

'For the next five minutes there will be a twenty per cent reduction on all items in Ties. I repeat, for the next five minutes only, all items in Ties will be marked down by twenty per cent. Ties is located in the south-eastern quadrant of the Blue Floor and may be reached using the banks of lifts designated G, H and I. This offer will be extended to you for five minutes only. Any purchases made after that period will retail at full price. Thank you for your attention.'

Linda looks around to see which way other shoppers are going to move. She will join them this time. Race with them, hunt down that bargain. Yes.

The faces she sees are taut and anxious.

Then she hears the sales assistant she just talked to whisper under his breath, 'Oh shit.'

Then it dawns on her.

The announcement said Ties.

Here. The sale is *here*.

The emotion that wells up in Linda Trivett then is too pure and blinding to sully with a name. It surges through her in a great white wave, clarifying her thoughts, sharpening her senses, purging her of uncertainty. She knows what she has to do but, more than that, she knows that this is what she was *born* to do. Never has she felt such an undiluted sense of purpose before. It races through her veins, as cold and clear as a subterranean stream. Deep in her being she is suddenly connected with all that is and all that was and all that is meant to be.

Trembling in the throes of epiphany, she snatches the coin-motif tie from the rack and casts about for the nearest sales counter. The announcement said twenty per cent off. A whole fifth. Other shoppers are grabbing merchandise, seizing ties by the handfuls. She can hear a faint rumbling from afar. Twenty per cent. Quickly, thoughtlessly, she turns and plucks another three ties from the rack. One has a squadron of blue pigs with wings embroidered on it, another is printed with close-typed rows of random binary-code sequences that form a sort of variegated polka-dot pattern, while the third is a duplicate of the tie with the coin motif already in her hands. Well, after all, Gordon always wears a tie to work. He can never have too many. She looks around again for a sales counter, and in doing so catches sight of the first bargain-hunters as they come stampeding in through the nearest connecting passageway.

In they charge, like the Mongol Horde sweeping across a plain, wielding Days cards instead of scimitars and their gaping mouths silent where the troops of Ghenghis Khan would be screaming battle-cries, but their eyes just as wild, their intent just as clear. And Linda with her fistful of ties doesn't step cowering out of their way but holds herself steady, erect, ready to meet them. These are *her* ties, and no one shall have them except her.

The customers in the vanguard of the charge reach her, and unresisting she lets their impetus carry her along. She has glimpses of teeth and well-coiffed hair, whites of the eye and flashing jewellery, clutching fingers and bulky shoulderpads, and suddenly a fist flails out of nowhere and catches her a glancing blow to the cheekbone, and someone stamps with elephant force on her foot, but still she rides along with the mob, struggling to keep herself upright and planting an elbow in someone's ribs and a knee in someone else's thigh, while the air around her head resounds with the whipcrack of ties being snatched from stands.

A shove from behind sends her stumbling forwards, her teeth clacking painfully on her tongue, the ties nearly spilling from her grasp. She wheels around to find a woman with a shoddily home-bleached frizz of hair waving a chrome-coloured card at her and yelling, 'Those are mine! I have a Palladium! Those are *my* ties!'

'No, they're not, they're mine,' Linda replies calmly, 'and the last person I'd give them up to is a stingy little bitch with an inch of root showing and abominable split ends.'

The bottle-blonde roars like a lioness and makes a grab for the ties. Linda's response is as swift as it is savage. Stepping back, she swipes the woman's legs out from under her with a scything kick – a physical feat which she would never have been able to pull off under normal circumstances but which, in the heat of the moment, she executes with perfect and ferocious accuracy.

As the bottle-blonde goes down she makes an ineffectual grab for Linda's blouse, but Linda leaps nimbly aside, batting her hands away.

'Bitch!' the bottle-blonde wails, prone on the floor.

'Slut!' Linda yells back, as the flow of bargain-hunters sweeps her away once more.

Like a swimmer in a crowd-torrent Linda is borne thunderously along, until suddenly, dead ahead, through a gap in the seethe of customers, she sees a sales counter, and she heaves herself towards it, at the same time groping for the clasp of her handbag with her free hand. How long has it been since the sale was announced? How many minutes? One? A thousand? Buffeted left and right, Linda propels herself up to the sales counter, at the same time fumbling her card out. She squeezes in sideways between two other customers and thrusts the ties into the face of the sales assistant, a young man barely out of his teens who, according to his ID badge, is a first-year trainee.

'These!' she cries. 'Now!'

'He was about to serve *me*,' one of her neighbours asserts crossly. 'Isn't that right?'

The sales assistant blinks in uncertainty. He is terrified, close to tears. Who can blame him, all these red, raging faces surrounding him, bellowing at him?

'*I* was next,' someone else insists.

The sales assistant gyrates plaintively from one customer to another. Whom should he serve? Whom?

Linda stretches her free hand across the counter, grabs him by the lapel, and yanks him close.

'Serve me or it's your job.'

That galvanises him. He takes the ties and the card off her, which causes the customers on either side to gasp and gripe and grumble and glare their resentment. Linda responds with a serene sneer.

If only they knew this was her first ever lightning sale. Then they would *really* have something to complain about.

And as the sales assistant runs his scanning wand over the four ties one after another and swipes Linda's Silver through the credit register, Linda nurses a warm, spreading glow of contentment.

She beat the other customers fair and square. She has a real talent for this.

24

Dance of the Seven Veils: the erotic dance performed by the title character in Wilde's play *Salome* to entertain Herod before the beheading of John the Baptist

12.00 p.m.

Midday finds Gordon crouched with his back to a mirror. A pair of Iridium cards are being waved to and fro mere millimetres from his face. The rainbow coruscations at play across the cards' surfaces are hypnotically beautiful. Not so beautiful is the smear of blood staining one edge of one of the cards. *His* blood.

The blood comes from a throbbing, burning wound in the palm of Gordon's right hand, and there is more of it, warm and sticky, trickling down his fingers and dripping off the tips. It feels as though his hand has been slashed to the bone, but, much as he would like to, Gordon doesn't dare examine the cut.

The pair of Burlingtons who have cornered him in the dead-end aisle in Mirrors move in closer, snickering. Their Iridiums fan a breeze across Gordon's cheeks as they weave their hypnotic cobra dance around his face. He can see how sharp their edges have been filed, razor-sharp, and thinking of the damage edges so sharp could do to him a dull little whimper escapes his throat.

He didn't even mean to be in this department, that's the awful irony of it. If it hadn't been for the woman in Pleasure. If it hadn't been for Rose . . .

And despite the pain and the paralysing fear of the moment, Gordon feels a faint, residual flush of lust as he recalls his first glimpse of Rose – Rose in the clinging pink nylon gown that sinuously emphasised her curves and contours, flowing over her naked body like cloudy pink water over a riverbed of worn-smooth rocks. He remembers how the dark ovals of her nipples loomed alluringly through the gauzy material, and he remembers the intoxicating perfume of her smile, and the way she boldly took his hand and said, like a teacher to a little boy, 'Come on then, let's see what we can do with you.' Words that sent a shockwave of images – possibilities – through his brain. He remembers it all clearly, even though it seemed to take place a lifetime, and not just a few minutes, ago.

He hadn't meant to set foot in the Pleasure Department either, but the muted red glow emanating from its entrance caught his eye as he was wandering by, and a waft of sweet incense drew him inquisitively in, past an at-attention security guard whose expression, he thinks now, did have something of a knowing smirk about it.

Having no sense of where he was in the store, and without the map to guide him, Gordon was at first unable to fathom what could possibly be sold in this department. In front of him a pair of long bare partition walls reached all the way to the opposite entrance, with bead-curtained doorways set into them on either side at regular intervals. Cubicles of some sort. Two similar rows ran off to the right and the left. There seemed to be no sales assistants about, and if it hadn't been for the pungent, aromatic smoke purling from ornate silver censers that hung from the ceiling on silver chains, Gordon might have thought the department had been abandoned or was in the process of being refurbished.

He was about to turn and ask the guard where this was when he became aware of muffled sounds issuing from several of the cubicles. His initial thought was that these were the grunts and gasps of people trying on outfits several sizes too small. It seems ridiculous now, but that is honestly what he first took the sounds to signify – that the cubicles were fitting rooms, and that in each there was a fat person struggling to get into clothing intended for someone thinner. It made a kind of sense. It was only after listening more closely for several moments that Gordon realised that the sounds were coming in pairs, each grunt matched to a reciprocal grunt, each gasp to an answering gasp, a rhythmic, guttural strophe and antistrophe interspersed with random sighs, squeals, and moaned obscenities.

When the penny finally dropped, the quietly rational part of his mind which usually assesses loan risks and calculates interest percentages simply said, *Well, it's a business deal like any other, isn't it? A straightforward exchange of commodities*, even as something unruly and libidinous stirred within him.

He didn't realise the woman was standing by his side until she addressed him, saying, 'Welcome to the Pleasure Department, sir.' The woman in her diaphonous rose-pink gown. The woman who then took his hand and said the words that unleashed a torrent of pent-up fantasies – all the positions he had never attempted with Linda, all the acts he had never dared ask her to perform, all the deeds he had pored sweatily over in novels and magazines but never, in his very limited sexual experience, actually tried. Dazed by the enormity of the horizons suddenly opening up before him, and giddy with the reek of incense, he meekly let the woman lead him down the left-hand row of cubicles and usher him into one. There, as the bead curtain rattled back into place behind him, he took stock of the narrow single bed, the table groaning with all manner of lubricants, prophylactics, and alarmingly-shaped rubber devices, and the credit register mounted on the wall adjoining the next cubicle, which was shuddering with the exertions of the transaction taking place on the other side.

The woman asked him his name, and he told her, and he asked her hers, and she said he could call her whatever he liked, and looking at the colour of her gown he said, 'Rose,' and she said, 'Then Rose I am.'

And then she said, 'Gordon, what kind of account do you have?'

And he said, 'Silver.'

And trying to disguise her pity, Rose said, 'I'll be honest with you, Gordon, there's not a lot I'll do for a Silver.' And he must have looked crestfallen because she then said, 'But we can still have some fun, can't we? If we're imaginative.'

And he said, 'Yes.'

And with that, she removed her gown, just like that, slipping the shoulder-straps off with a shrug, letting it slither down and crumple around her feet, and there she stood, naked and pink in the low red light, her arms outstretched, completely open about her nudity, unlike Linda, who clutches an arm across her breasts whenever Gordon walks in on her while she is taking a bath, and who will only make love with the lights out. And she was trim and firm where a woman should be, voluptuous where a woman should be, majestically so. Quite unlike Linda.

And she said, 'Out with it, then,' and Gordon blindly and obediently began fumbling with his fly, and she said, 'No, not *that*,' and laughed. 'Your card.'

And he said, 'My wife . . .'

And she said, 'Ah, your wife. Seven-year itch, is it?'

And he said, 'No. My, um, my wife has our card.'

And Rose laughed again, coldly this time, and said, 'Then, Gordon, you had better leave, because without your card you don't get anything. And I should warn you that if you try to take something that you can't pay for, I can have a guard here in three seconds flat to arrest you.' She indicated a red emergency button fixed to the wall above the bedhead.

'Arrest me?'

'For taking goods without payment. Shoplifting, Gordon.'

And Gordon nodded numbly, and Rose said, 'Off you go then. Another time, perhaps.'

And she bent to put her gown back on, and Gordon turned and fled. Bursting through the bead curtain and sprinting down the row of cubicles, ashamed and embarrassed and guilty and desperate to get out of the department as quickly as possible, he ran, and for a while it seemed that the row of cubicles would never end and that he would have to keep running for ever, and then suddenly he was in Mirrors, and blushing madly – because everyone must have known where he had just been and what had happened to him there, it must have been written all over his face – he foundered deeper into the department, losing himself amid a dizzying myriad of reflected Gordons, furtive, manic Gordons, flustered, panicked Gordons, until he found himself running towards himself and he realised he had stumbled into a dead end, and skidding to a halt before his likeness he turned, only to be confronted by a pair of gormlessly grinning Burlingtons, and before he could say anything something blurred through the air towards him, and not knowing what it was he instinctively raised a hand to protect himself, and felt his palm scorch . . .

And now he tries to speak again, to ask the Burlingtons what they want from him, why are they doing this to him, why him, but again all that comes out of his mouth is another fear-filled, knock-kneed little whimper, which the taller of the two Burlingtons is quick to mimic, compounding the humiliation. This Burlington, the one who cut Gordon, has a long horselike face and long horselike teeth exaggerated by the tapering inadequacy of his lower jaw. The other has been even less well served by the limited genetic scope of upper-class in-breeding. His forehead is low and his eyes close-set, his protruding lips are rippled like the mouth of a clam, and his skin is so wattled with acne scabs and scars that it looks like burgundy leather. Where his comrade is gangly and tall, this one is short and squat, but their half-black, half-bleached buzzcuts and their matching uniform of gold moiré jacket, black drainpipe trousers, and designer trainers lessen the physical differences between them, making them look, in a strange, scary way, almost like twins.

Gordon scans around desperately for help, but this section of the department is deserted and all he can see is his predicament reflected back at him from a dozen different angles, each image a variation on the same theme: that of two Burlingtons cornering a hunched, white-faced figure whose spectacles are askew and whose breathing is coming in heaving, irregular shudders and the fingers of whose right hand are barber's poles of blood. And it almost seems possible to Gordon that if, in the mirrors, one of the two razor-sharp Iridiums were to suddenly whir through the air and carve a gash in his reflection's throat, it wouldn't be him that would gargle to death on his own blood but an inverted Gordon safely tucked away in looking-glass land. It is a crazy thought, but no crazier than the grotesque insanity of his present situation.

The first Burlington sneers down at Gordon speculatively, saying, 'This is the kind of riffraff they're letting in these days? This is the sort of jumped-up nobody we have to share our store with?' He snorts. 'Pathetic.'

'Pathetic,' his comrade agrees.

'Please,' Gordon says, risking another whimper but managing, at last, to find his voice, or at any rate a pale imitation of same. 'Let me go. I promise I won't report you to anyone, I'll just be quietly on my way. Please.'

'Bit of a nasal twang there,' the taller Burlington remarks, leaning back. 'What do you think, Algy? Something in the service industries? Middle management?'

Algy, clearly selected as a friend and sidekick because he possesses no opinions of his own, merely chuckles and nods.

'Please,' says Gordon. 'I'm just a customer like yourself.'

'Got it now. Banking or insurance. Possibly accountancy, but I'm betting on banking or insurance. That servile note in the voice, that horrible job's-worth whine.'

'I'm the loans manager for a branch of a major national clearing bank,' Gordon intones, neither defiantly nor defensively but because it is the truth.

'And you've saved up all your hard-earned pennies to become a Days account-holder, and – don't tell me – wifey's chipped in by taking on extra work, because it's all about bettering yourselves, isn't it? It's all about clawing your way up the ladder.'

'It was Linda's idea,' Gordon whispers.

'But don't you see, you four-eyed nonentity?' The Burlington clamps a hand around Gordon's throat and shoves his head back against the mirror with a surprisingly resonant clack of skull against glass. He inserts the bloody Iridium beneath the left-hand lens of Gordon's spectacles and skewers the corner into Gordon's eyelid, pricking out a droplet of blood. 'There *is* no ladder. That's just a lie dreamed up to give your insignificant little lives hope and meaning, to make you work your fingers to the bone for your precious Aluminiums and Silvers, but it doesn't make any difference. *It doesn't make any difference.* You're born boring, lower-middle-class drones, and that's all you'll ever be.'

'Er, Rupert?'

'Not now, Algy,' says the taller Burlington, still staring fixedly into Gordon's face. 'I'm busy.'

'Um . . . Rupert, I really think you should let him go.'

Rupert sighs testily. 'What *is* it, Algy? What could be more important than a demonstration of the class system in action?'

He glances up into the mirror behind Gordon's head and his undersized chin plummets.

There is a guard. He is holding Algy by the collar of his jacket. His other hand is resting on the grip of his hip-holstered pistol.

Instantly Rupert lets go of Gordon and steps smartly back, the sharpened card vanishing from view. Gordon staggers and wheezes, one hand flying to his neck to palpate his tender throat.

'Morning,' says Rupert to the guard, from sneering snob to guilty schoolboy in no time flat.

'Afternoon, actually,' says the guard.

'Sorry. Afternoon. My friend and I were just, er . . . just helping this fellow with directions. Appears he's lost. Took a wrong turn some-where.'

'Is that so? How thoughtful of you.'

'We thought so too.'

Gordon tries to force words out through his traumatised trachea but it isn't possible to make sense of the hoarse, moist clucks his throat produces. Luckily, the guard has seen all he needs to see.

'Perhaps it would be better if you left us now, sir,' he tells Gordon, politeness itself. 'The boys and I have some private matters to discuss. I have to demonstrate to them how the class system really works.'

Gordon needs no further prompting.

As he scurries away, he hears Rupert the Burlington say, 'Look, can't we sort this out like rational human beeeEEEYARRGHHH!'

Then there is only the sound of fists smacking flesh, and awful cries.

25

Seven-League Boots: ogre's boots donned by the fairy-tale hero Hop-o'-my-Thumb, enabling him to walk seven leagues (approximately 34 kilometres) at a stride

12.00 p.m.

At the turning point of the day, high noon, after an hour of fruitless wandering without so much as a sniff of a possible perpetrator to break the monotony of department after department after department, Frank has walked himself into a state of dulled lethargy.

Nothing is happening. Around him customers are ambling, browsing, pausing, lingering, staring, discussing, comparing, matching, calculating, considering and acquiring, while sales assistants are smiling, bobbing, bowing, suggesting, hinting, agreeing, detagging, scanning, checking, bagging and returning. Nothing is happening but the give-and-take of commerce, as elemental and eternal as the ebb and neap of the tide, and Frank has nothing to do except plod from one department to another, through the various vectors of Days, his legs carrying him along in a mindless, relentless forward-urge. Every so often he checks in with the Eye. Anything nearby? Anything that requires his presence? Each time the answer comes back the same: nothing. The Eye sounds quieter than usual, its background hubbub subdued, as though down there in that screen-lit Basement chamber they are experiencing their own doldrums.

Frank's trail crosses and recrosses itself as he proceeds through the immensity of Days, covering ground purely for the sake of covering ground, because that is what he is paid to do. He walks neither towards any particular goal nor to put distance between him and anything but simply to rack up the kilometres. There is no finishing line ahead, no Sodom behind, just the journey itself, the act of going. He travels hopefully, never to arrive.

Riding a lift, he is still moving.

Idling by a display, he is still moving.

Standing on an escalator, he is still moving.

Waiting until a traffic jam of shoppers clears so that he can continue down an aisle, he is still moving.

Hovering at the entrance to a fitting room to make sure that customers come out wearing the same clothes they had on going in, he is still moving.

Still moving, moving and still, as though his thirty-three years as a store detective have built up an inner inertia that pushes him on even when stationary. If his legs suddenly stopped working, perhaps deciding that they had had enough, that they had covered several lifetimes' worth of distance, far more than their fair share, and they refused point-blank to go another step – if that happened, he feels that somehow his body would be unable to remain at rest. The accumulated momentum of thirty-three years of day-long walking would propel him onwards for ever, like a space probe sailing effortlessly through the void, endlessly, without entropy, into infinity.

Time slows when nothing is happening, and thoughts spit in all directions from Frank's becalmed brain like sap-sparks from a smouldering log. His head fills with a babble of his own creation, a stream-of-consciousness monologue so loud and inane that he has, in the past, wanted to put his hands over his ears and yell at himself to shut up.

Simply talking to someone else might help relieve the mental pressure, but Ghosts are discouraged from unnecessary communication with other employees while on duty. Ghost Training, in fact, teaches you to have as little contact as possible with your co-workers, for to open your mouth is to draw attention to yourself. As for customers, in the unlikely event that one should mistake you for a fellow shopper and attempt to strike up a conversation, the terser your replies are, the better. The four main attributes of a good Ghost are, as the Ghost's Motto says, silence, vigilance, persistence, and intransigence. The greatest of these is silence. Silence at any price, even at the cost of being driven insane by your brain's unconscious blather.

Sometimes when he passes a fellow Ghost, Frank thinks he can see in the other's face a reflection of the look that must be on his own. Beneath the Ghost's affected impassiveness, in the eyes, he thinks he can discern a barely restrained yearning to uncork a head-full of bottled-up thoughts, preferably in banter, failing that as a scream.

But perhaps he only imagines this. Perhaps it is just something his brain, in its skull-bound isolation, invents while his legs drive him aimlessly through the over-familiar, never-changing storescape. Perhaps, after thirty-three years of pounding the same floors, going over and over the imprints of his own footsteps, wearing the Days-logo carpets thin with his soles, he is simply displacing his pent-up frustrations on to others.

And as he keeps on walking and nothing keeps on happening Frank feels himself veering down once again into the pit of wraiths inside him, into that well of milling, voiceless creatures who writhe heedlessly around one another like a knot of mating snakes. Loud and clear he hears the unspoken summons as they call to him with goldfish-gaping lips and begging eyes, saying in their inarticulacy that this is the place to be, down here in anonymity, down here where there are no individuals, where your name will be Legion, where you can be just one of many, where the configuration of meat and bone that is Frank Hubble will cease to have significance. Withdraw, withdraw. Pull yourself in like a snail into its shell and never come out again.

How easy it would be to answer that call. He knows of other Ghosts who did succumb. There was Falconer a few years back, who came to believe that he was genuinely invisible and arrived for work one morning stark naked, thinking that no one would notice. (He was pensioned off quickly, quietly, without fuss.) There was Eames, who failed to come in two days running, and was found at his flat, sitting in a corner of his bedroom, dressed in his pyjamas and hugging his knees and rocking to and fro, staring vacantly into space, drooling. And then there was Burgess, who went on a killing-spree through the store, shooting four customers dead and wounding another six before security guards brought him down. No one could have predicted that any of these loyal, hard-working Tactical Security employees would all of a sudden, and for no apparent reason, snap the way they did, but they did, and another few months at Days and that is probably what will happen to Frank, too. One morning he will wake up and won't feel the urge to get out of bed or feed himself or clothe himself or go anywhere. It will all be too much effort. They will find him like Eames, lying in bed, catatonic. Down among the wraiths. Down among the wraiths for ever.

That would be his future for sure, were he not going to do something about it today; were he not going to tender his resignation to

Mr Bloom in – a discreet glance at his watch – three quarters of an hour's time.

Three quarters of an hour of slow time. Forty-five oozing minutes. Two thousand seven hundred syrup-seconds measured out in steady footfalls in the protracted somnambulistic dream-random of Nothing Happening at Days.

26

Heptathlon: a seven-event Olympic contest consisting of 100 metres hurdles, shot put, javelin, high jump, long jump, 200 metres sprint, and 800 metres race

12.15 p.m.
A cold, brisk wind snaps across the rooftop, whipping between the huge vents that rise like ships' funnels and warp the air with their hot exhalations, whistling around the blockish lift-heads that poke up at regular intervals, tousling the pollarded trees and potted shrubs of the sunken garden, wrinkling the surface of the swimming pool, and rattling the chainlink fence that encloses the tennis court.

Mungo, on the tennis court, extends his arms upwards, grunting pleasurably at the fluent meshing of his biceps, triceps, deltoids and laterals. Linking his fingers, he swivels his torso from the waist. The wind pricks gooseflesh from his bare legs. It feels good to be out of the Boardroom. Not that Mungo dislikes immersing himself in the day-to-day concerns of the running of the store, far from it. He relishes the daily mental challenge. But out here or down in the gym, where the only exertions he has to make are physical, that is when he is at his happiest.

Chas, at the other end of the court, is leaning louchely on the end of his racquet, one leg crossed over the other. He is dressed in crisp white shorts and a pale pink polo shirt, with a cream woollen jumper slung around his neck, the sleeves knotted. His long fringe is flapping this way and that in the wind. He yawns provocatively, but Mungo, ignoring him, continues with his warm-up routine, crouching down for a hamstring stretch.

The yawn having failed, Chas continues to feign boredom by gazing around, first at the sky, then at the city that crowds beyond the lip of the roof, huddled and brown and inferior all the way to the sun-hazed horizon. After a while he returns his gaze to his eldest brother, to find that he has completed his limbering up and has begun jogging on the spot.

'Ready at last?'

'Ready.'

'About time too. I was beginning to lose all feeling in my toes.'

'Ten a point?' says Mungo, picking up his racquet and unloading a ball from his pocket. Mungo, on account of his seniority, always serves first.

'Let's make it twenty. I'm feeling confident today.'

'Confident or extravagant?'

'I'm a Day. Extravagance is my middle name.'

Mungo steps back to the baseline, bounces the ball a couple of times on the smooth green clay of the court, and winds himself up to unleash a devastating serve. The ball skims the corner of the service box and rockets into the chainlink fence, ricocheting with a loud clattering shimmer.

'Nice one,' says Chas, having made no move to intercept the serve. He crosses to the other side of his baseline. 'Fifteen–love.'

'And twenty down.'

'It's only money.'

Of Mungo's next three serves Chas makes the effort to return only the one that is delivered virtually to the head of his racquet. Mungo counters the half-hearted return easily, volleying the ball into the opposite corner from where Chas is standing.

As they change ends, Mungo remarks, 'I see you've decided to take it easy today.'

'Lulling you into a false sense of security, big bro.'

Chas's serves are deceptively languid, the ball leaving his slow-rising racquet at lightning speed even though its only propulsion is a tiny, last-minute flick of the wrist. Mungo lunges to make the returns, pounding across the clay. The rallies are lengthy, the ball traversing the net seven, eight, and on one occasion eleven, times. Chas wins. Mungo aces the next game, but by now he is huffing heavily and his heart is beating hard, while Chas hasn't even begun to perspire.

They meet at the net.

'Do you know what I think about sometimes when I'm up here?' says Chas. Chas has a tendency to draw out the intervals between games so as to spread out the minimum amount of physical effort over the maximum period of time. It is a habit Mungo tolerates only because none of his other brothers will play tennis with him.

'I've no idea,' Mungo replies, thumbing sweat from his eyebrows. 'I only know that the way you play leaves you a great deal of time for thinking.'

'I think of a castle and the village that lies beyond its ramparts. I think of the seven of us as feudal barons taking our tithes from the peasants around us.'

'I knew you should never have read PPE at university.'

'Oh, don't get me wrong, I'm not saying that the arrangement is a bad one. I'm just saying that it's been going on for centuries. We're all of us hostages of history, conforming unconsciously to social archetypes laid down long ago.'

'Whatever gets you through the night, Chas. Your serve.'

The next game goes to deuce. Chas wins the advantage point, and with a backhand of elegant insouciance clinches the game.

'Don't start celebrating yet,' says Mungo. 'You still owe me nearly a hundred.'

Chas puts up a fight for the next game, but Mungo's mighty serve wins through.

As they meet again at the net, Chas says, 'It's a crazy person who would resist you, Mungo.'

Mungo looks at his brother askance. 'I take it you're not just referring to my game.'

Chas nods, pleased that his subtext has been noted. 'You did a brave thing this morning. I mean, you always stand up for Sonny, we've accepted that, and in a perverse way it's quite admirable. But this morning you really stuck your neck out for him. For a while there Thurston and Sato looked fit to shit.'

'It was a gamble, I admit.'

'I'll say. If it had backfired . . .'

'The rest of you would have locked Sonny up in his apartment and thrown away the key.'

'Something like that.'

'It's what Dad would have wanted.'

'Sonny locked up?'

'The integrity of the Seven preserved.'

'At all costs?'

'At all costs. Why else would he have gone to the effort of having seven of us?'

'As I recall, it was our mother who went to the effort. All Dad did was calculate the due dates and bribe doctors to make sure that each of us arrived on the correct day of the week. He was an odd sort, Dad, really, when you think about it.'

'He was a visionary,' says Mungo, as if this excuses everything.

'A visionary with only one eye. What do you call that? A semi-visionary? A monovisionary?'

'That was all part of his vision,' says Mungo. 'Now, are we going to stand here flapping our lips all day or are we going to play tennis?'

'Are you offering me a choice?'

'No.'

'Attaboy. That's the Septimus Day in you talking.'

Mungo breaks Chas's serve and holds his own. Chas, for all that he exploits the vagaries of the wind to make his shots unpredictable, cannot compete with Mungo's dogged determination to reach the ball no matter where it bounces.

'Four–two, two–four,' says Mungo, hurdling the net. 'I hope you've got your card to hand, because by my reckoning you're over a hundred and sixty in the hole.'

'All according to plan, Mungo. I keep this up, and you'll become overconfident and start making mistakes.'

'As if.'

Chas laughs, holding the net down to step over it. 'God, you really are a chip off the old block. The same unswerving conviction in yourself, the same absolute refusal to contemplate the possibility of failure.'

'To contemplate failure is to court failure.'

'Well said, "Septimus". But would you, I wonder, gouge your own eye out in order to prove a point?'

Mungo considered this. 'Probably not, no. I need depth of field so that I can keep trouncing you at tennis.'

'Seriously. Would you ever go that far?'

'Our father was an exceptional human being,' Mungo replies. 'He did what he felt he had to do. He made what he considered the appropriate sacrifice to ensure the success of his venture. If I was in his shoes, gambling millions of other people's money on a project as insanely ambitious as Days, and I thought – no, I firmly believed – that removing my left eye with a pen-knife was going to make the difference between triumph and disaster, who knows, perhaps under those circumstances I'd do it. An offering to Mammon, a few moments of agony in return for a lifetime of success – I don't know. A fair deal? I don't know.'

'But he also did it to prove that it could be done, as a test of will.'

'It was both a test of will *and* a propitiatory sacrifice to the gods of commerce. In Dad's eyes – eye – will and fate were inextricably linked. "Fate isn't what happens to you, it's what you make happen." Isn't that what he used to say? And let's face it, he certainly made this place happen. When he first dreamed up Days, investors were hardly beating a path to his door waving blank cheques at him. He had to browbeat people for every single penny, he had to *force* them into believing in him. And the same goes for fate, or the gods of commerce, or Mammon, or whatever you want to call it. The divine order of things. Dad had to show the universe how determined he was, how far he was prepared to go in order to get his way, and he did, and it worked. Whether I'd be able to convince myself that it would work for me, I'm not sure.'

'Oh, I can picture you doing the same,' says Chas blithely, knowing that there is nothing his older brother likes more than to be compared favourably with their father. 'I can picture you kneeling in the middle of an empty tract of wasteland you've just purchased, looking around at the land that your building is going to occupy, knowing as you do so that this is the very last time you are going to have the use of both eyes. The boarded-up shopping arcade on one side, the row of short-lease charity shops and thrift shops on the other, all to be demolished soon to make way for your dream – the dream set out on the blueprints flapping in the mud around your feet. I can imagine you digging the small, shallow hole that is shortly going to contain a part of you, and then taking the pen-knife out of your pocket, unclipping the largest blade, and bracing yourself as you bring it up to your left eye . . .'

Chas seems to take a gleeful delight in rehearsing the details of their father's act of self-mutilation. Mungo, however, only shudders. 'You may be able to imagine it,' he says. 'I can't. Which suggests that I lack our father's capacity for making sacrifices, and therefore that I'm nothing like him.'

'Sacrifices? What do you call the way you stick up for Sonny if it isn't a sacrifice?'

'Losing the esteem of one's brothers is hardly as painful as losing an eye, Chas, and esteem can always be recovered, whereas an eye can't. Enough of this. We have to be back in the Boardroom for lunch soon. You to serve, again.'

During the next game, perhaps spurred on by the memory of their father, Chas evinces an increased enthusiasm for victory. He uses every trick he knows to make Mungo's life difficult, from high lobs to low backspin grounders. He feints powerful shots that barely trickle over the net and launches volleys across the court masterfully, but somehow Mungo manages to reach every ball, however unreturnable it seems, and snatch it across the net, always recovering in time to respond to the next of Chas's challenges. Throughout the game he grins and pants like a happy dog.

Deuce is reached, and continues interminably. Mungo enters a delicious delirium of effort, grunting explosively with each swing of his racquet, and Chas in his own way becomes engrossed in the game too, frowning like a chess grandmaster as if each exchange of shots is a conundrum he has to solve. Neither of them is aware that they have been joined on the rooftop by a spectator who, slumped against the chainlink fence with his face pressed into the diamond-shaped holes, is following the back-and-forth of the game with a glassy, ill-focused interest.

Mungo finally capitalises on an advantage point and batters the ball home to win the game. Exhausted, he drops his racquet and bends double, bracing his hands on his knees. It is then, looking up from under his red, dripping brow, that he notices the new arrival watching from the sidelines.

Chas spots the spectator at the same time, and says, drolly, 'Ah, the conquering hero returns. Nice outfit, Sonny. I assume you've changed clothes since coming up from the shop floor.'

Sonny doesn't reply. His fingers are clawed into the fence; this appears to be all that is holding him upright. His eyes moon from one brother to the other as though, as far as he is concerned, the game hasn't come to an end.

Mungo straightens up warily. 'Sonny? Is everything all right? How did it go downstairs?'

There is a pause. Then, slowly, Sonny turns his head in Mungo's direction. 'Hm?'

'I said – '

'What's the score, Mungo? Who's winning?'

'Oh Christ,' whispers Chas.

Mungo reaches the fence in a few brisk strides. He lowers his face to Sonny's and inhales once, hard, then leans back, nodding sombrely. Sonny grins sloppily up at him. One of his hands loses its grip and he slips and almost collapses, but manages to secure himself a fresh handhold just in time.

Mungo's words begin as a moan but rise steadily to a roar, 'Oh, you little bastard, you little fucking bastard, you idiot, you fucking idiot, what have you done, what have you done, what in Christ's name have you done? Couldn't even abstain for a couple of hours, could you? A couple of hours, you mindless fuckwit, you stupid little turd! You couldn't even do that one thing, that one tiny thing you were asked to do, without screwing it up! You useless piece of shit, you useless, traitorous piece of shit! Do you know what I'm going to do to you? Do you? I'm going to *kill* you! I'm going to rip your heart out of your chest and fucking *feed* it to you, that's what I'm going to do!'

'Mungo, cool it.'

'No, Chas, I will not "cool it". I will *not* fucking "cool it"! I bend over backwards to help this fly-covered heap of dogshit, I give him another chance, a chance he does *not* deserve, and what do I get? How does he reward me? By spitting in my face!'

Regardless of the fence between them, Mungo makes a furious lunge for Sonny. Likewise regardless of the fence between them, Sonny backpedals hurriedly. Stumbling, he falls squarely on his behind, scraping his hands on the gravel.

'What happened downstairs, Sonny?' says Mungo, shaking the chainlink. 'What did you do? What did you say to the heads of Books and Computers? Did you tell them what we told you to tell them? Or did you just manage to make *us* look ridiculous? What did you do, Sonny? What did you *say*?'

For the first time Sonny is fearful. Mungo's bulging scarlet face looms in his vision like a medieval gargoyle. It would seem to be well within Mungo's power to tear a hole in the fence and reach through the gap to do the same to Sonny.

Chas lays a tentative hand on Mungo's shoulder. 'Mungo, listen.'

Mungo twitches his head, not taking his eyes off Sonny. 'What, Chas?'

'We don't know what went on down there.'

'We don't have to know. Look at him. Pissed out of his skull. And don't tell me he got that way since coming back upstairs. I know Sonny's drinking habits, and these are the results of a good hour's worth we're seeing here. He *must* have gone down there drunk and he *must* have screwed things up.'

'But we don't know that for sure, not yet. And, until we do, our best course is to get him stowed away safely out of sight. Take him down to his apartment and make sure he stays there.'

'Why?'

'Because if the others find out that he went downstairs in this state, there's no telling what'll happen. I mean, look how well *you* reacted, and you're supposed to be his ally.'

Mungo peers down at Sonny, who has by this time lost interest in his brothers and is distractedly picking pieces of grit from his palms. 'Wouldn't it be better just to drag him straight to the Boardroom and show them? Show them what a worthless little prick he is?'

'Possibly, but like I said, I doubt they'll take it well.'

'So what? Why do you all of a sudden care what happens to Sonny?'

Chas hesitates, then says, 'Let's put it this way. I may not completely believe in this Seven business, but that's no reason to put it in jeopardy.'

Mungo lets the implication of his brother's statement sink in. 'Yes. I see. So we keep Sonny's condition hidden from the others, and hope and pray that he did what he was supposed to downstairs.'

'That's about the size of it.'

'All in the name of preserving the integrity of the Seven.'

'Correct.'

Mungo draws in a deep, controlling breath and lets it out again, his shoulders slumping, his anger unbinding. 'You're right, of course. The Seven comes before everything else.' He lets go of the fence and turns in the direction of the tennis court gate. 'But I swear to God, Chas,' he growls, 'if he's done any damage down there, any damage at all, I'll murder him with my bare hands.'

'If it turns out he did, Mungo, you'll have to take a number and join the queue.'

Neither of these statements is an idle boast. Mungo and Chas are the sons of a man who gouged out his own eye with a pen-knife in order to get his own way. That streak of determination, that desire to succeed whatever the cost, is in their genes. Just as Septimus committed violence against himself, so his offspring have the potential to commit violence against *them*selves. It is, you might say, a sin of the father that is ready to be visited upon the sons.

27

7th December 1941: the day the Japanese launched their surprise air attack on the U.S. Naval base at Pearl Harbor, Hawaii, precipitating active U.S. participation in World War II

12.35 p.m.

In her office cubicle Miss Dalloway sits with a Brie-and-cucumber sandwich in one hand and *The Art of War* open on her knee. The book's spine is so well broken that she does not have to hold the pages down with her hand.

She eats the sandwich mechanically and methodically, and when she has finished she licks the tips of her fingers clean one by one. Then she drinks a small bottle of mineral water, and fastidiously disposes of the empty bottle and the sandwich wrapper in the waste-paper basket. Silly, she knows, to be so concerned about tidiness when, if all goes according to plan this afternoon, a litter-free office will be the least of her worries. But old habits, of course, die hard.

She closes *The Art of War* and places it on top of the desk. She has read the book so many times by now that she knows it by heart, but she finds the familiar cadences of the sentences reassuring, the logical precision of Sun Tzu's words comforting and calming.

Taking a key from her trouser pocket, she unlocks one of the desk's drawers and takes out another book, this one a more recent addition to her personal library.

It is a cheaply produced trade paperback printed on thick, coarse paper and published by a small press whose list otherwise consists of conspiracy-theory tracts, UFO-spotting manuals, and how-to guides on the subject of growing and smoking marijuana. The book's front cover mimics a manila dossier, with the title 'rubber- stamped' across it at an angle in blockish, rough-textured characters, as though this is in fact some top-secret government file. No author is credited anywhere, not even in the publishers's indicia.

The book is called *Kitchen-Sink Arsenal* and, like *The Art of War*, it shows the signs of having been well read and well used.

Miss Dalloway sets *Kitchen-Sink Arsenal* down beside *The Art of War* on her desktop and smooths it open, ready, at a certain page. Then, stiffly, she stands up, pressing her knuckles into the small of her back, all of a sudden conscious of a dozen skeletal aches and pains that she could have sworn weren't there before. She feels old. Not just in years. Spiritually. Her soul sick and weary – the legacy of a life of devotion to the ailing and ungenerous master that is literature.

Picking up the Platinum card belonging to Mrs C A Shukhov, she heads out to the information desk.

Oscar and Edgar are on duty. The rest of her darlings are either at lunch or busy elsewhere in the department.

'My boys,' she says.

The two Bookworms melt with delight at the tenderness with which she has addressed them.

'My boys, I have need of you.'

'What can we do for you, Miss Dalloway?' says Oscar. 'Anything you want. Name it.'

Before she can tell them, a customer approaches the desk, wanting to know where he can find books on cassette.

'We don't stock books on cassette here, sir,' Miss Dalloway informs the man. 'You'll find those in the Visual Impairment Department on the Indigo Floor. The only kinds of books we stock in this department are the kind you read.'

'Books on cassette!' Oscar exclaims before the customer is quite out of earshot. 'What a joke!'

'Pretty soon you won't have to bother reading any more,' says Edgar. 'All you'll do is attach an electrode to your head and download a book directly into your brain in a couple of seconds.'

'Edgar, we don't use words like "download" in this department.'

'Sorry, Miss Dalloway.'

'But the sentiment is a noble one, and appreciated. Thank you. Now, as I was saying. The mission. As you will no doubt recall, last Tuesday afternoon I sent a number of you out into the store to buy me certain items. You, Oscar, I asked to get me a can of fuel oil.'

'And you asked *me* to buy you a nine-volt battery,' says Edgar.

'And didn't Malcolm have to get you a camera flashbulb?' says Oscar.

'And it was Colin, I think, you sent for a bag of garden fertiliser.'

'And Mervyn got you a beer keg.'

'Quite,' says Miss Dalloway. 'And I'm sure you all thought it was an eccentric shopping list, but you went out and brought back every item on it all the same, without question, because you're good boys, all of you.'

At the compliment the two Bookworms preen and quiver like stroked cats.

'And now I need one of you to go and buy two more items in order to complete the list.'

'Say no more, Miss Dalloway,' says Oscar. 'Just tell me what they are, and I'll go and get them.'

'Thank you, Oscar,' says Miss Dalloway, 'but, as you will see in a moment, this task is going to require someone who is quick on his feet.' She gently pats the roll of fat that bulges between the base of Oscar's skull and his collar. 'No offence, my darling, but you're hardly built for speed. Not to mention the fact that you have a broken arm . . .'

Oscar puts on a not wholly convincing show of dismay.

'Besides, I have need of you here,' Miss Dalloway adds. 'For moral support.'

'But – '

'"They also serve who only stand and wait," Oscar.'

'Which therefore, by a process of elimination, leaves me,' says the habitually gloomy Edgar, managing to look both pleased and put-upon at once. 'What is it you want me to buy, Miss Dalloway?'

'Before I tell you that, Edgar, I feel it is only fair to warn you that there is going to be an element of risk involved. If, once you learn what I want from you, you change your mind, I will understand perfectly, and I won't think any less of you.'

Edgar reassures his head of department that nothing can be too much trouble, that she can never ask too much of him, that she is in fact doing *him* a favour by sending him out on this mission, risky though it may be. And even though Miss Dalloway knew that that was what his response would be, she is still touched.

'Then listen carefully. I need a roll of insulated copper wire and an alarm clock – the old-fashioned kind, nothing digital, one with a wind-up mechanism and bells on top.'

'I thought you said the mission was going to be dangerous,' says Edgar with a snort. 'I think I can manage to get you some wire and an alarm clock without too much difficulty.'

'Perhaps. However, unlike last time, this time you won't be using your own card. You'll be using this.' And she holds up the purloined Platinum.

'Isn't that the one Malcolm handed in the other day?' says Oscar, squinting.

'That's correct.'

'So shouldn't you have – ?' Oscar catches himself before he can finish a question that might be construed as casting aspersions on his beloved head of department's judgement.

Miss Dalloway finishes the question for him anyway. 'Yes, Oscar, you're right, I should have passed it on to Accounts, and I didn't. A breach of regulations, but then posterity will show that, on balance, I have been a woman more sinned against than sinning.'

'But surely it'll have been reported lost,' says Edgar. 'If I try to use it, Security will come down on me like a tonne of bricks.'

'Which is what lends the mission its element of risk. Knowing that, are you still willing to go?'

'May I enquire why you want me to use that particular card, Miss Dalloway?' says Edgar. 'You must have a reason. You always have a reason for everything you do.'

'True, Edgar, and yes, you may enquire. The answer is simple. I want Days to know what I am up to. I want everyone to know.'

'Um, Miss Dalloway,' says Oscar hesitantly. 'Sorry for asking this, but what *is* it, exactly, that you're up to?'

Miss Dalloway shakes her head. It will be better if she doesn't tell them yet. That way Edgar's pleas of ignorance, should Security catch up with him, will have the added virtue of authenticity. 'When the time comes, all will be revealed. Until then, I must ask you to trust me, and for you, Edgar, to demonstrate that trust by buying the wire and the clock and bringing them safely back here.'

'Does it have something to do with what you were up to yesterday behind the books, at your desk?' says Oscar. 'You know, when you told us not to disturb you for a couple of hours?'

'Oscar!' Miss Dalloway holds up a hand. ' "How poor are they that have not patience." All will be revealed soon enough.'

'Yes, Miss Dalloway. Sorry, Miss Dalloway.'

'I also have need of a trolley,' she tells Edgar, handing Mrs Shukhov's Platinum to him. 'That should be the first thing you obtain, and I suggest you use your own card to hire it. For the wire and the clock, however, you must use the Platinum.'

'And then run like hell,' says Edgar.

'Precisely. Your employee ID badge should give you a certain immunity from suspicion, but still your principal concern is going to be staying ahead of Security. Now that you're aware of the possible consequences of this mission, are you still prepared to go? Speak now or for ever hold your peace.'

Edgar swallows hard and says, 'I'm prepared to go.'

'Then bless you.' She strokes his head. 'I have every confidence in you to succeed.'

'I won't let you down, Miss Dalloway.'

'Well? What are you waiting for?'

'You want me to leave right away?'

'Stand not upon the order of your going, my darling, but go!'

28

The Seven Golden Cities of Cibola: a collection of seven towns, a pueblo of the Zuñi Indians in what is now Zuñi, New Mexico, fabled by Fray Marcos de Niza to be the source of great riches, which prompted Francisco Vásquez de Coronado in 1540 to head an expedition of 1,300 men to conquer them – no riches were found

12.45 p.m.

'Frank,' says Mr Bloom, smiling and gesturing to the chair on the opposite side of the small table. 'I took the liberty of ordering wine.'

'I don't drink during the daytime,' says Frank, sitting down.

'Go on, give the cat a goldfish.' Mr Bloom makes to fill Frank's glass from a wicker-bound bottle of Chianti. 'It's not bad. Not as raw as some of these Italian wines can get.'

Frank clamps a hand firmly over the rim of the glass. 'No. Please.'

'Suit yourself.'

The restaurant is a mock trattoria on the Green Floor hoop, white-painted wrought-iron tables and matching chairs clustered beneath a wooden pergola densely interlaced with vine leaves. Mr Bloom's rank has secured them a table directly next to the parapet. Some twenty metres below their elbows lies the Menagerie, one half of its canopy illuminated by a vast shaft of sunlight that descends almost vertically from the great dome, the rest in smoky shadow. The brightness in the atrium is so intense that several of the diners have resorted to wearing sunglasses.

The atrium resounds to the sound of six floors' worth of activity. Around lunchtime, shoppers gravitate toward the hoops. Many of them have come to Days for the sole purpose of meeting for lunch, since the store provides a dining venue unparalleled in social cachet. Indeed, the first thing Mr Bloom does after refreshing his own glass is draw Frank's attention to the celebrities at neighbouring tables. He indicates the famous model alone, studiously not eating the Caesar salad in front of her; the pair of well-respected actors colluding conspiratorially over some project; and the *enfant terrible* fashion designers in the company of the movie director and the head of the huge PR company (the smell of a major deal being struck at the latter table is pungent even at a distance). Frank obligingly steals a sidelong glance as Mr Bloom points out each famous person, but he only vaguely recognises their faces and, frankly, doesn't care who they are. To him they are merely customers.

'So,' says Mr Bloom, hoisting a menu aloft and flapping it open. As if to compensate for a lifetime of reticence, he has taken to making his post-Ghosthood gestures as grandiose as possible. 'Let's have a look what's on offer today.'

Frank picks up his own menu and runs his eye down the hand-written list of available dishes, but his mind is not on food. 'You order for both of us,' he says, setting the menu aside. He rests an elbow on the table, slots his chin into his cupped hand, and stares across the atrium to the parapet opposite, drumming his fingers against his lower lip.

Mr Bloom catches a waiter's eye – something Frank cannot easily do – and summons him over. He orders minestrone soup, followed by fettuccine puttanesca.

'You don't have a problem with peppers, do you?' he asks Frank.

Frank shakes his head.

The waiter departs.

A silence falls over the table.

'Well,' says Mr Bloom, 'seeing as you're not going to come straight to the point, I will. From our earlier, abortive conversations, I think I can pretty much guess what you have to say to me.'

Frank continues to stare across the atrium. Mr Bloom pauses, then goes on. 'I'm sure this isn't a decision you've reached lightly, Frank, and I'm sure you're quite determined that nothing I can say is going to make you change your mind. So you'll no doubt be relieved to hear that I'm not going to try. All I'm going to say is that Days will miss you. No emotional blackmail here, the honest-to-goodness truth. You are an excellent store detective. It'll be a shame to see you go.'

Again, no reaction from Frank, but Mr Bloom is used to the ways of Ghosts. He knows he is not wasting his breath.

'Is it the use of guns that bothers you?'

A shake of the head so infinitesimal that only another Ghost would spot it.

'Ah. Usually it's the use of guns. It gets to some Ghosts after a while. Got to me. The idea of causing pain and injury to others, and worse than pain and injury. Mostly I could justify it to myself. Shoplifters know the risks they're taking, and if they don't then they deserve what comes to them. But every once in a while . . .' Mr Bloom scratches his foretuft with his little finger. 'When I told you earlier about losing my touch, Frank, I didn't tell you why it happened. I'm not sure if this is the reason, but . . . well, it *seemed* to be the reason at the time. You remember when I shot that kid?'

'I'm sorry, no.'

'No reason why you should. We don't go around boasting about these things, do we? He couldn't have been more than fifteen or sixteen. Skinny as a lizard. He stole a comic, and I nabbed him, but he was a slippery devil, twisted right out of my grasp, leaving me holding the big baggy coat he was wearing. A guard hadn't yet arrived, and I knew the kid would have no trouble outrunning me, so, of course, out came the gun. I shouted a warning. He didn't react. I fired. I was aiming to wing him, but he was so thin, not an ounce of meat on him . . . He was just a kid, but I shot him all the same, without hesitation, because that's what I've been trained to do. The bullet tore out half his ribcage. I still have nightmares about it. I've killed five shoplifters, wounded half a dozen others, and every time I've told myself I was just doing my job. Just doing my job. But when I think about that kid's face and the horrible wheezy gargling he made as he bled to death right there on the carpet, right there at my feet . . . Well, "just doing my job" doesn't begin to cover it, does it?'

For a moment Mr Bloom looks older than he is, the pain of the memory casting a haggard, spectral shadow over his face. His private remorse has been dredged up, at great personal cost, as a bargaining chip – *I've given you this much, now you give me something in return* – but Frank, unskilled in the wheeling and dealing of human relationships, isn't clear how to respond.

'I've never killed anyone,' he says, without turning his head.

Mr Bloom nods slowly. 'I know. In fact, you've hardly ever drawn your gun. The mark of a good Ghost.'

'Usually it takes nothing more than tact and firmness to deal with a shoplifter.'

'There you go. That's what I'm getting at. You were *born* for the job, Frank.'

'That's a good thing?'

'It's not a bad thing for a man to be doing the work that best suits him.'

'To be born to do a job that requires you to have no personality, to blend into the background and be ignored – that's a good thing?'

The bitter edge in Frank's normally mild voice is not lost on Mr Bloom. 'Congruity,' Mr Bloom says carefully, 'need only be an art. It doesn't have to become a personality trait.'

'But what if that's unavoidable?' Frank at long last looks directly at Mr Bloom, bringing the full sad weight of his gravestone-grey gaze to bear on his superior. 'What if it's impossible to prevent the one leaking across into the other, the art becoming the personality trait, the job becoming the man? Remember Falconer? And Eames?'

'They were exceptional cases, Frank.'

'But what does it take to become an exceptional case? How much or how little of a push do you need to go over the edge?'

Just then the minestrone soup arrives, vegetable-packed and steaming, in earthenware bowls with Days logos hand-painted around the inside of the rim. The waiter also brings focaccia bread in a napkin-lined basket. Mr Bloom tucks in immediately. Frank leans back in his chair and resumes his finger-drumming, this time on the lip of the table.

'So what do you intend to do with yourself?' Mr Bloom asks between slurps of soup. 'If you resign?'

'Travel.'

'Where to?'

'America.'

Mr Bloom splutters into his spoon. 'America, Frank? Why in God's name America?'

'Because it's big. You can get lost in it.'

'So is Days big, and people are getting lost here all the time. Honestly, Frank – America? I know it's supposed to be a wonderful place, the land of opportunity and all that, but if it's really so great how come everyone who lives there is seeing a psychiatrist?'

'That's an exaggeration, Donald.'

Mr Bloom dismisses the objection with a wave of his spoon. 'Whichever way you look at it, Frank, Americans are a strange lot.'

That annoys Frank. What does Mr Bloom know about America? What does he know about anywhere that isn't Days?

'America is just a starting point,' he says, working hard to restrain his irritation. 'Ultimately it doesn't bother me where I go, as long as it's somewhere that isn't here. I'm in my early fifties, and I haven't once travelled beyond the outskirts of this city. Isn't that pathetic? I've covered thousands of kilometres in my career, maybe millions, I've walked around the world several times over, and yet all I've seen is this city and the interior of this store.'

'It's not pathetic, Frank. You're a dedicated employee. We all know how hard it is to tear ourselves away from Days. Take me, for instance. I've been meaning to visit my sister and her family in Vancouver for years. I haven't seen my niece since they emigrated. She was fourteen then, she'll be a grown woman now. I'd love to pop over and see them, but I can never seem to find the time. The job always gets in the way. There's always too much unfinished business, too much to be done.'

'But that's precisely what keeps us here, Donald. We keep convincing ourselves that the job needs us and that we need the job and that our loyalty and dedication will eventually be rewarded somehow, I don't know how. But it's an excuse; it's pure cowardice and nothing more. Believe me, I know. For years I thought there was nothing on this earth worth having more than a job at Days, but lately I've come to realise that it can't compensate for what I've lost by working here. I've lost things that normal people take for granted – friends, a social life, a family. I want to start clawing back everything this store has taken from me before it's too late, and I want to start as soon as possible.'

Should he tell Mr Bloom that he has also lost the ability to see his own reflection? Probably not a good idea. He wants to be seen to be leaving for rational, considered reasons. The same goes for the imaginary wraiths who long to claim him as their own. These things must remain his secret.

'Well, fine,' says Mr Bloom. 'Far be it from me to stop you. I assume you have a ticket already booked. Take a holiday then. Jet off to the States. Have a rest. Relax. You deserve the time off. Come to think of it, that's probably the best thing you can do. A change of scenery, a chance to breathe some different air . . .' Mr Bloom nods to himself and spoons more soup into his mouth. He seems to have convinced himself that all Frank wants is to take a break, although he could be hoping that if he believes this misconception to be the truth hard enough, then, by a kind of emotional osmosis, Frank will come to believe it too.

221

'Going away and coming back won't change anything, Donald. I have to leave, full stop. I have to resign. To quit.'

There. He has finally said the word. Finally it has come tripping from his lips. *Quit*. Oddly, though, he feels none of the exhilaration he was expecting to feel. He had hopes that that one small word would carry on its narrow shoulders the whole burden of his concerns, and that in sallying forth from his mouth it would leave him lighter and freer, a purged man. But the anticipated relief is not there; all that's there is just a permanent residual clutter, the dusty, cobwebbed accumulation of a career's worth of unspoken frustrations.

Mr Bloom says nothing, merely goes on drinking his minestrone, while around their table other conversations rattle back and forth, their echoes rolling across the atrium. When his bowl is nearly empty, he grabs a hunk of focaccia bread and uses it to mop up the remnants of the soup. 'So what are you going to do for money? Have you thought about that?'

'Transient jobs. Find work for a little while, save up, move on.'

'Easier said than done.'

'I'll manage.'

'A man your age should be looking forward to a comfortable retirement, Frank, not a life of dishwashing and floor-cleaning and fast-food serving. You really haven't thought this through properly, have you? How about Ghost Training. Did you consider that possibility? You could become a teacher. That wouldn't be so bad, would it?'

'I want to have a life beyond Days.'

'Don't we all, Frank, don't we all?' Mr Bloom's smile is, Frank feels, a touch patronising. 'But, like you say, this place owns us. Everything we have, everything we are, belongs to the store. We may not like it, but that's what we signed on for. And if you want to abandon all that, that's your prerogative, but bear in mind that without Days you'll be nobody.'

'Then what have I got to lose? I already *am* nobody.'

'And you think that leaving will make you somebody?'

'It can't hurt to try.'

'I admire your courage, Frank, but in case you haven't noticed it's a grim old world out there. It's fine if you're rich – it's always been fine if you're rich – but if you're not it's a struggle from start to finish, with no guarantee that the struggling is going to get you anywhere. That's why gigastores have become so important to people. With their rigid rules and their strict hierarchies, they're symbols of permanence. People look on them as refuges from the chaos and undependability of life, and whether, in practice, that's true or not, that's what Days and Blumberg's and the Unified Ginza Consortium and the EuroMart and all of them represent. The rest of the world may be going to hell in a handcart, but the gigastores will always be there.'

'Why would I give up the life of luxury and the security that Days has brought me and throw myself out into a harsh and uncertain world? That's what you find so hard to understand, isn't it? Why fly the gilded cage, unless I've gone mad?'

'Whatever hardships you have to endure in here, Frank, they can't be any worse than what you'll find out there.'

'I'll take my chances.'

The waiter brings the main course and clears away the two bowls of soup, one wiped clean, the other untouched. He returns a moment later with a cheese-grater and some parmesan. Mr Bloom requests that his pasta be sprinkled liberally. The waiter obliges, and then leaves without thinking to offer Frank the same service. Frank is so used to this kind of accidental oversight that he doesn't even notice.

Mr Bloom gets straight to work with a fork. After a few mouthfuls he gestures at Frank's plate and says, 'Aren't you going to eat anything? It's very good.'

'I'm not that hungry.'

Sensing that his eagerness for his food might be considered insensitive, Mr Bloom reluctantly sets down his fork, a bandage of fettuccine wrapped loosely around its tines.

'Listen, Frank. I want you to think this over a bit more. Compare how much you stand to lose with how little you can hope to gain. You spend the rest of the afternoon weighing up what I've said, and then come and see me at closing time. If by then you haven't changed your mind, I'll accept your decision and see if I can't try to negotiate some kind of severance settlement with Accounts. Not a likely prospect, I grant you, Accounts being the tight-fisted bastards they are, but I may be able to swing something. If, however, you *have* changed your mind, then it'll be as if this conversation never happened. Fair enough?'

'I don't see what difference a couple of hours will make.'

'Probably none at all,' Mr Bloom admits, picking up his fork again. 'But you never know. Now, you may have got away with ignoring your minestrone but I will not tolerate a plate of excellent fettuccine puttanesca going to waste. Eat!'

Frank heaves his sagging shoulders and complies. And anyone looking at the two of them, Frank and Mr Bloom, as they sit facing one another, quietly forking pasta into their mouths, would take them for a pair of old friends who have run out of things to say but who still find pleasure in each other's company. But then no one is looking at two drab, ordinary, middle-aged men in a restaurant that is patronised by the famous and the beautiful and the notorious.

29

Seven Years' Bad Luck: according to superstition, the penalty for breaking a mirror, seven years being the length of time the Romans believed it took for life – and thus the ruined image of life – to renew itself

12.48 p.m.

Gordon finds the way to his and Linda's prearranged meeting point more by luck than judgement. Wandering from department to department in a state of shock, his sense of direction, fortunately, does not desert him.

Linda is waiting outside the entrance to the Lighting Department, clutching a small Days bag in one hand. Gordon is three and a half minutes late, and the fact that she refrains from commenting on this would, under any other circumstances, be cause for alarm. When Linda fails to pick up on a fault, it usually means she is already brooding on another pre-existing fault, one far more serious, which she will let him know about only after making him sweat a while wondering what else he has done. At that precise moment, however, Gordon's main concern isn't Linda's scorn; his main concern is getting out of Days as quickly as possible.

'Let's go home, shall we?' are the first words out of his mouth as he draws up to her, shielding his eyes against the golden glare radiating from the connecting passageway.

The same light seems to lend Linda's face a balmy, seraphic glow. 'What happened to your hand, Gordon?'

'It's nothing. So? Home, eh?'

'Let me take a look.'

Reluctantly, Gordon lets her examine his wounded hand.

As soon as he regained his composure after his hasty exit from the Mirrors Department, he found a cloakroom and cleaned up his wounds at the basin. Once he washed the caked blood off his hand under the cold tap, he was surprised to find the cut in his palm both

225

shorter and shallower than it felt. What he imagined to be a deep gash turned out to have barely broken the skin. A lot of blood for very little actual damage. It still hurt like buggery, but not as badly as when he had assumed that the hand was lacerated to the bone.

And it was while he was in the clockroom bandaging the hand with his handkerchief and inspecting the nick in his eyelid in the mirror above the basin that he asked himself whether or not he should tell Linda the truth about his injuries. He had a pretty good idea what she would say if he informed her that he had been assaulted and insulted by a pair of teenagers. 'You mean you just stood there and let them threaten you? Two boys? You didn't fight back? You let them say those things to you and you didn't give back as good as you got?' That is what *she* would have done in his shoes. Nobody, not even a Burlington brandishing a sharpened Days card, abuses Linda Trivett and gets away with it – as many an uncivil shopkeeper and talkative cinemagoer has discovered to their cost. No doubt about it, Linda would have stood her ground, head held high, and given the Burlingtons the tongue-lashing of their lives. She might even have seen them off, browbeating them into retreat. That fierce indomitability of hers is what Gordon loves about her the most, and envies about her the most, and fears about her the most.

And (he decided in the cloakroom) there was another reason why lying would be a good idea. Confessing his cowardly behaviour in Mirrors would be one thing. He could probably live with the shame. But if, even jokingly, he were to mention to Linda about his close encounter in the Pleasure Department, his life would not be worth living. Even though nothing actually happened in that red-lit cubicle, it so nearly did, and Linda would hear the guilt in his voice. She would smell it on him, the way a lioness can smell fear.

So, all things considered, it would be better to forget both those unfortunate episodes, and the easiest way to do that would be to act as if they had never happened, and the easiest way to do *that*, he concluded, was to lie. Drawing a veil over his cowardice in Mirrors would mean he could also draw a veil over his close shave in Pleasure, the lesser omission legitimising the greater. If he could come up with a cover story clever enough, both events would remain secrets he could carry with him to the grave.

So he racked his brain, and came up with a cover story, and it went like this. He was in Mirrors, looking for something to go above the mantelshelf over the fireplace in the lounge. (Yes, that was good. It would show he did care after all about the living space they shared.) And he had a little accident. He tripped on the join between two sections of carpet, stumbled, and put out a hand to break his fall. The hand landed on a small shaving mirror, and the mirror snapped. Hence the cut in his palm. (It would be a good idea to laugh here. Laughing at his own clumsiness would appeal to Linda. Self-deprecation always goes down well with her.) At the same time, extraordinarily enough, a tiny fragment of glass flew up as the mirror broke and hit him in the eye. His glasses would have protected him but – would you believe it? – they had slipped down his nose as he tripped. Luckily for him, the fragment only nicked his eyelid. A few millimetres higher and he might have been left like Septimus Day. Ha ha ha ha ha!

Not the most plausible of explanations, perhaps, but it was the best he could come up with in the time available, and the only way he could think of to account for both wounds. And as he made his way to the rendezvous, he rehearsed the story over and over in his head until he was halfway to believing that it was the truth.

Now, as he nervously allows Linda to untie the handkerchief bandage, he regales her with his fabrication, cunningly placed laughter and all, interrupting himself only once in order to let out an involuntary hiss of pain as her fingers probe the edges of the cut a little too firmly.

She lets go of his hand just as he reaches his conclusion: '. . . A few millimetres higher and I'd have been left like Septimus Day. Ha ha ha ha ha!'

For an agonising moment Linda makes no reply. It would not surprise Gordon to find out that his wife possesses the forensic skills to distinguish between a cut caused by a shaving mirror and any other kind. Then she says, 'You'll live,' and starts refastening the makeshift bandage. 'But we should maybe think about getting hold of some sticking plaster and antiseptic ointment from the Medical Supplies Department.'

'It can wait till we get home.'

She peers at his eyelid. 'And also have a doctor look at your eyelid, just in case.'

'Right.' Finding it hard to believe that Linda has swallowed the story whole, because she is normally a sensitive lie detector, Gordon decides to risk sounding out a further reaction. 'It was incredible bad luck.'

'Broken mirrors usually are,' she replies vaguely. 'Now, shall we go and find ourselves some lunch? According to the map, there are places to eat in the hoops.'

No courtroom-style cross-examination? Not even a quizzically raised eyebrow? Is it possible that he can have got away with it?

No, there is something not right – something decidedly un-Linda – about her lack of suspicion. And as Gordon trots alongside his wife in the direction of the Red Floor hoop, he notices that the lambent serenity in her face, which he assumed to be a reflection of the glow of the Lighting Department, is not fading as they leave that department behind. It is her own expression. The glow is coming from within her. And her gestures aren't as abrupt as usual. She no longer walks in a series of tight, quick steps – her strides are long and graceful. And her voice seems to have lost much of its customary brittleness.

He can't for the life of him fathom what can have brought about this change in her. The Days bag means she has made a purchase, but a mere purchase alone can't explain it. Perhaps the store has a tranquillising effect on certain customers.

They emerge on to the hoop, into the flare of sunlight glancing off white marble flooring. The air, cleaned by the green lungs of the Menagerie, is appreciably fresher and sharper than the dead conditioned air in the departments, and is laced with food smells from the kiosks and cafés.

After they have dutifully spent a few minutes admiring the Menagerie, Gordon asks Linda what she would like to eat, and she surprises him by letting him decide.

The cheapest foodstuff on offer seems to be Chinese noodles, so Gordon tentatively suggests those. Linda says Chinese noodles will be fine, and hands Gordon their card. And so Gordon Trivett makes his first purchase at Days: two helpings of chicken chow mein, plastic chopsticks an optional extra.

They take the cartons of chow mein to the nearest unoccupied bench, and eat sitting side by side, gazing up at the rainbow tiers of the atrium.

'It's like being inside some great big hollow cake,' Gordon murmurs.

He is resigned to Linda telling him what a crass remarks he has just made, but she merely nods.

Very strange.

'So what did you get?' he asks, gesturing at the Days bag.

'See for yourself. A present for you.'

'A present?' Gordon puts his chopsticks down, wipes his fingers on a paper napkin (another optional extra), opens the bag, and peers in.

'There was a lightning sale,' Linda says. 'I was right in the middle of it.'

Gordon reaches into the bag and takes out the four ties, arranging them in a row along his thigh. 'All for me? Why so many?'

'Don't you like them?'

'I like the coin ones.'

'Really?'

'Really.' And he means it, he genuinely does like them, and he is touched that she went to the trouble of buying the ties for him, all of them, even though he, in effect, is the one who is going to be paying for them. 'But did you really need to buy four? And why two with the same pattern?'

'It was a lightning sale, Gordon. You grab what you can get. And they were at twenty per cent off. That means the fourth one was almost free.'

'Almost.'

'I don't think you quite realise what I went through to get those for you. I *fought* for those ties.'

'Fought for them?'

Linda shakes her head sadly. 'I wouldn't expect you to understand. If you haven't been in a lightning sale, you won't know what I'm talking about.' She says this with grave authority, like a hoary, battle-scarred war veteran reminiscing about his time in the trenches.

'From what I've heard about lightning sales, I'm not sure I *want* to be in one.'

'It was an incredible experience, Gordon. I can't really put it into words. It was as though I'd been asleep for years and suddenly an alarm bell rang in my soul and I was awake. I mean truly *awake*.' She becomes animated at the memory. Sparks scintillate in her eyes. 'I'm tingling all over just thinking about it. Look at my arm.' Gordon does. The hairs on her arm are standing on end. 'It was quite scary, actually,' she goes on, 'but thrilling too. There was a lot of noise and confusion. I think I might have hit someone . . . Some of what happened is a bit hazy . . . But I got what I went in there for, that's the main thing.'

'Hit someone? Linda, what *has* come over you?'

'Nothing bad, Gordon, so don't give me that disapproving frown. I just think I've learned, at last, how much I'm capable of. What's the phrase? My full potential. I've discovered my full potential.'

'By hitting someone?'

'Like I said, I wouldn't expect you to understand. You came here with negative expectations. Don't try to deny it, Gordon, you did. You came here convinced you were going to have a rotten time. That's why you were so bad-tempered in the taxi. And what happens? You break a mirror and cut yourself. Whereas I came here firmly convinced that today was going to be the greatest day of my life. And guess what? It is. What does that tell you, Gordon? It tells *me* that we make our own luck in life. It tells me that attitude governs outcome. And that's such a simple lesson, and yet so many people could do with learning it.'

The glow is gone from her face. A hard, imperious expression has taken its place, her facial muscles becoming taut again, as if not designed to stay relaxed for long. The old Linda is back, and Gordon is strangely relieved to see her return. He was finding the somewhat slightly dazed Linda who was letting him make the decisions for both of them not a little unnerving.

'These noodles are horrible,' she says, setting the carton of chow mein aside. 'Why did you make us eat noodles?'

That's more like it. Gordon feels like leaning over and kissing the woman he knows and loves, and envies, and fears. Instead he merely copies her, setting his chow mein aside.

'You're right. The chicken is rubbery.'

Equilibrium restored, order returned to his world, Gordon resolves to keep a very close eye on his wife for the rest of the afternoon. Since it seems that he has no choice but to remain in Days, he would rather spend the time with her than off on his own.

It will be safer that way.

For both of them.

30

> **Hell**: according to Islamic belief, Hell is divided into seven distinct regions, for Muslims, Jews, Christians, Sabaeans (a pagan cult who worshipped Orpheus as a god), Zoroastrians, idolaters, and hypocrites

12.51 p.m.

Mungo and Chas escort Sonny down the flight of access stairs that connects Sonny's apartment to the roof (each brother's apartment has one). At the foot of the stairwell, Mungo uses his knee to nudge open the door to the hallway, and they manhandle Sonny through.

Their entrance startles a cleaning woman. Hurriedly stowing away her spray-polish and dustcloth, she slips past the three of them with a bob of her head and exits by the apartment's main door.

Sonny is slung between his brothers, his arms looped around their necks. He didn't actually need their support for the journey down from the roof but, since they were kind enough to offer it, it would have been rude to refuse. Besides, Mungo was quite insistent that he accompany them in this manner, almost as if he didn't trust Sonny to make it down the stairs unaided. And Mungo is angry with him and, when Mungo is angry with you, it is best just to do as he says.

Recognising his own apartment, Sonny chants, 'Home again, home again, jiggedy-jig,' then adds, 'Drink, anyone?'

'This way,' Mungo says to Chas grimly.

They march Sonny into the living room and dunk him down on one of the marshmallow sofas.

'Bar's over there, help yourselves,' says Sonny, waving in the wrong direction. He slumps over on to his side.

Mungo grabs a fistful of blackcurrant-purple lapel and yanks him upright, splitting the seams.

'Hey, careful of the suit,' says Sonny, inspecting a tear in the underside of his jacket sleeve. With ruffled dignity, he smooths out the creases Mungo has put in his lapels.

Mungo, meanwhile, lowers himself down on to the edge of the basalt-slab coffee table so that he is sitting directly opposite Sonny. Splaying his hands on the hillocks of his bare thighs, he hunkers forward, arms akimbo.

'Look at me.'

Sonny attempts to bring Mungo's face into focus, but it is difficult. Mungo's face is a moving target swaying in every direction, up, down, left, right, back, forth. Hard to get a fix on.

A firework ignites in the left half of Sonny's field of vision, the force of the detonation slamming his head sideways. The pain arrives a second later, swelling the left side of his face like acid seeping into a sponge.

'Ow,' he says, gingerly touching his cheek. 'What did you do that for?'

The pain subsides, to be replaced by tingling numbness. The numbness takes the shape of Mungo's open hand, so clearly defined Sonny thinks he can feel the imprints of individual fingers.

'Now look at me.'

This time Sonny has more success in focusing on his eldest brother's features.

'If you drop your gaze for a moment, I will hit you again. Understood?'

Sonny nods.

'Good. Now tell me a couple of things. First, did you go downstairs dressed the way you are for any other reason than to look an absolute prize idiot?'

Sonny launches into a spirited defence of his choice of outfit, but Mungo silences him by raising a hand, the same hand that slapped him.

'I don't want to listen to any long convoluted explanations. A simple answer: yes or no?'

'Yes. I mean, no. I don't know.'

'The public sees so little of us,' says Chas, 'that we have to make the best impression we can each time. Therefore you looking like an idiot makes us look like idiots, too.'

'Precisely,' says Mungo. 'Which leads me to my next question. We watched you via the Eye talking to the heads of Books and Computers. What did you say to them? The abridged version, if you will.'

'I adjucidated . . . I adjuti– I acudjidated . . .'

'Adjudicated.'

'I adjudicated in favour of Computers.'

'You did? You're quite sure about that?'

'Yes.'

Mungo glances round at Chas. 'Not a complete disaster, then.'

'Did anyone give you any grief, Sonny?'

'Not as far as I recall. They did talk to me for a long time.'

'Yes, we saw that.'

'But I decided by . . .' Sonny thinks it would be better not to mention the means by which he made his decision. 'By how you told me to decide.' Yes, the method is immaterial. The important thing is that, by luck, he arrived at the right result.

'I wouldn't advise lying to me, Sonny,' says Mungo. 'I'm going to check into this later and ask both heads of department for a report, so make sure of your story now. If it doesn't tally with what I find out later . . .'

A sudden dismal chill descends on Sonny, and he debates whether to own up about using his Osmium to settle the dispute. Perhaps if he dresses it up in heroic terms and says he used the card like Alexander the Great used his sword to cut through the . . . cut through the . . . the Something-or-Other Knot. What was it called? The Guardian Knot? That's not it. Something like that, but . . . No good, he can't remember. He doubts Mungo will go for it anyhow. It wasn't very professional of him, he has to admit, though he was under pressure and both heads of department did seem to have a point and he really couldn't think of any other way to choose between them and, besides, it always used to work perfectly well in pubs . . .

He will just have to hope Mungo doesn't find out about it. The heads of department probably won't mention it. They wouldn't dare say anything that would show a Day brother in a bad light, would they? Not if they value their jobs.

'That's my story,' says Sonny, 'and I'm sticking to it.'

'All right.' Mungo draws a deep breath and lets it go as a long sigh. 'Well, youngest brother. It seems you haven't disgraced yourself as badly as I thought. Don't get me wrong, you've let me down – let us all down – by going back on your word and drinking before you went downstairs.'

Sonny feels this isn't the time to mention the loophole he found in their bargain. Mungo would not take it well.

'Moreover,' Mungo continues, 'you've abused the trust of your brothers and tarnished our reputation, and that's something I take a very dim view of. Were Thurston and the others to learn about your behaviour, I'm sure the view they would take would be even dimmer. But I'm going to do you this favour. I'm not going to tell them. Neither is Chas. This is going to remain our secret. And in order for it to remain our secret I need you to stay down here for the rest of the afternoon. Drink, sleep, watch daytime fucking television, I don't care what you do, just as long as you stay out of the Boardroom. Chas and I are going to tell our brothers that we visited you here after our game and found you sober but in a celebratory mood. Got that? You were a good boy, you did as you were told, you didn't touch a drop before you went downstairs, but then afterwards, when you came back here, you decided you were free to indulge, so you did. Therefore, should anyone check up on you this afternoon and find you three sheets to the wind, you will have got that way *after* Chas and I left you. Is that clear?'

Sonny is confused by the tenses Mungo is using but thinks he has the gist of it. He nods.

Mungo says, 'This is the last time I am ever going to do anything like this for you again. From now on you are on your own. You and you alone are going to have to take responsibility for your own fuck-ups. I am washing my hands of you.'

Sonny nods once more.

Mungo's tone and expression soften – a little. 'Sonny, ever since Dad died, I've tried to raise you the way he would have wanted, but it hasn't been easy. For any of us. We're Day brothers, but that doesn't mean we're not human too. We do the best we can but sometimes our best isn't good enough.' He lays his other hand – his non-hitting hand – on Sonny's knee. 'So I'm begging you. For the last time. Clean up your act. Straighten yourself out. We want you to help us run the store. We need you. We need to be Seven.'

The tears catch Sonny by surprise, springing from his eyes in a sharp, burning squirt. He asks himself why he is crying, and realises that he is crying because Mungo loves him and he is unworthy of that love. He is a cockroach, an amoeba, a speck, a useless piece of matter stuck to the bootheel of humanity, and yet his brother still loves him.

'I'm sorry, Mungo,' he says. 'I'm sorry, I'm sorry, I'm sorry. It's all my fault. Everything's my fault. Everything. If it wasn't for me, Dad would still be here, Mum would still be here . . .'

Mungo hears Chas tut softly. *Not this again.*

'Sonny,' Mungo says, 'you know as well as I do that you weren't to blame for that.'

'But if she hadn't had me . . .'

'It was an accident. These things happen.'

'But why did he choose me? Why not her? Why me over her?' These last sentences are hacked out of Sonny in a series of choking coughs. His cheeks are glazed with tears, and his fingers clutch convulsively at his trouser leg. His entire body is racked with shudders, as though his despair is a physical thing, a parasite trying to squirm its way out.

'Dad believed he was doing the right thing,' Mungo says, words of cold comfort he has uttered countless times before. 'He never forgave himself.'

'Or *me*,' Sonny wails. A bulb of yellow mucus droops out of one nostril. He reels it back in with a sniff. The tears continue to pour. 'He never forgave *me*. The way he used to look at me. The way you sometimes look at me. The way *everyone* looks at me.'

'Sonny . . .'

Sonny slumps over on to his side again, bringing his knees up to his chest, burying his face in his hands. 'Everyone knows what I did, and everyone hates me for it,' he sobs through his fingers. 'Why did he let me live, Mungo? Didn't he realise what he was doing? Didn't he realise what he was condemning me to?'

Mungo can't answer that. Truth to tell, he has never found it easy to accept the way their father acted over Sonny's birth.

He recalls taking tea one afternoon with their mother in the mansion drawing room, when she was six months pregnant with Sonny. She was lying propped up against a landslide of cushions on the oak sill of the drawing room's huge bay window, her upper body framed in profile against a diamond-paned vista of the mansion lawns in autumn. He remembers that she looked as regal as ever, for Hiroko Day had come from a Japanese family of good stock and had been brought up to hold herself well whatever the circumstances, but that she also looked tired, drawn, uncomfortable, mother-to-be heavy, and old, much too old. She had been in her late twenties when Mungo was born, and Mungo was now only a few weeks away from his twenty-first birthday.

No one else was around and, in response to a casual enquiry about her health, his mother stroked her swollen belly thoughtfully for a while before replying, 'It would break your father's heart if I didn't have this child.' It was not the answer to the question Mungo had asked but the answer to a question she had been asking herself.

'But why not adopt?'

'Not part of your father's plan, Mungo,' said his mother. 'Not part of the deal he struck with himself when he founded the store. For your father's filial cosmology to be complete all seven of his sons have to be his and my flesh and blood.' She lowered her voice conspiratorially. 'You know, I shouldn't tell you this, but I was secretly hoping for a daughter. Amniocentesis says it's going to be yet another boy, of course. As if I could bear the great Septimus Day anything but the boys he requires. But a daughter . . .' A gentle smile played about her mouth. 'That would have been my little act of rebellion.'

'But it's dangerous, isn't it? I mean, the doctors recommended that you . . .' Mungo was not at ease discussing such matters with her. 'You know.'

'Terminate,' said their mother. 'Oh yes. And your father, grudgingly, accepted that recommendation as wise, and gave me permission to go ahead. But the way he looked at me when he said that, the pain in his eye . . .' She smiled ruefully at her firstborn, and shifted around on the cushions to get comfortable. 'I know how much he wants this child. What else can I do except give him what he wants? Since when has anyone ever refused Septimus Day anything?'

'But the risk involved,' said Mungo. 'A woman of your age . . .'

'No one's forcing me to go through with this pregnancy, Mungo,' said their mother, not sternly. 'No one except myself.'

And Mungo remembers, even more vividly, the night Sonny was born – a Sunday night, of course. When the college porter conveyed to him the news that their mother had gone into labour, Mungo went straight round to Chas's digs, and together they drove the hundred kilometres home through driving rain in Chas's sports convertible, running red lights and breaking speed limits all the way. A police car pulled them over for doing a hundred and eighty k.p.h. on the motorway, but all it took was a flash of their Osmium cards and a promise to the officer that they would arrange a Days account for him, and they were on their way again. The promise was forgotten as soon as the police car's flashing blue lights were out of sight.

They arrived home to find the mansion a flurry of anxious doctors and midwives. It didn't take long to establish that there were complications with the birth. The baby was not coming out the right way. Their mother was haemorrhaging. Their mother was in danger, and the best medical help money could hire was helpless. Either the baby lived or she lived. It was one or the other. It could not be both. Their mother, drugged but lucid, had said she was prepared to sacrifice herself for the child. It was up to their father whether her wish should be granted.

They found the old man pacing the floor of his study. His eye-patch was lying on the desk. It was not the first time Mungo and Chas had seen him without it, but it was still hard to avoid staring at the sealed lids of his left eye, sunken and puckered like the mouth of someone who has resolved never to speak again.

'I don't know what to do,' their father said in a hoarse, haggard whisper. 'The doctor said even if she lives through this, she'll never be able to bear another child. This is my last chance.'

The founder of the world's first and (as if it mattered at that moment) foremost gigastore was foundering, torn between the woman he loved and the child who would, he believed, ensure the future of his store. He looked desolately at his two eldest sons. 'I don't know what to do.'

To this day Mungo still isn't certain which terrified the old man more – the mortal danger his wife was in, or the fact that, after a lifetime of confident, correct decisions, he was, for the first time, paralysed by uncertainty.

'Well, which is more important to you,' he said to the old man, as angrily as he dared, 'Mum or Days?'

Septimus Day could not answer that.

The decision was made eventually. A crisis point was reached, and the obstetrician in charge asked their father which it was to be, the mother or the child.

Gravely the old man told him.

He was never the same again. From that day on, he slipped into a long slow twilight of depression. He withdrew from the world, divested himself of responsibility for running the store, neglected all but the most fundamental of his personal needs (eating, bathing, sleeping), and restricted contact with his sons to those didactic dinnertime monologues in which he rambled through his obsessions as if trying to justify them to himself, reminding himself with his cries of '*Caveat emptor!*' of the price at which he had bought his dream. *He* was the buyer who should have been beware.

Gradually, one by one, the old man unpicked the threads that tethered him to life, until there was nothing left to hold him here, and when he reached that point, too proud to commit suicide by any of the grisly traditional methods, he waited instead for his own body to call it a day. It could have been a heart attack, it could have been a stroke, but in the event it was cancer, and when it came it was spectacularly devastating, spreading swiftly from his liver to other organs like dry rot, eating away at him from the inside out. And it is Mungo's belief that their father willed this death upon himself. He had, after all, brought a gigastore into existence by the power of will alone. He removed himself from existence the same way. A slow suicide.

None of the brothers has ever laid responsibility for either the old man's decline or their mother's death at Sonny's feet. Not overtly, at any rate. That would be like blaming the deer in the middle of the road for murdering the driver who kills himself swerving to avoid it. All the same, the link between Sonny's birth and their parents' deaths is undeniable, and sometimes it has been easy to make more of Sonny's indirect guilt than fairness might permit. Sometimes, indeed, the brothers have taken vindictive pleasure in doing so. The contempt latent in their nickname for Sonny – the Afterthought – has never been that well disguised and, over the years, as Sonny has increasingly disgraced himself, it has become harder and harder for them to damp down their feelings of resentment.

Mungo knows this because he has had those feelings himself. He has, perhaps, kept them under better control than his brothers, but as he looks as the laughably dressed creature writhing on the sofa in front of him, the words of compassion he spoke just a moment ago ring hollow. What he really wants to say is, 'You killed our parents, Sonny. You may not have meant to, but you did, as surely as if you put a gun to their heads and pulled the trigger. It might have been Dad's decision to let you live at our mother's expense, but if you had been an easy birth, if you hadn't – typically – insisted on making life awkward for everyone, she would have survived and the old man would not have hated himself to death . . .'

And if that's how *he* feels, he who has interceded on Sonny's behalf on more occasions than he can remember, and who has only now abandoned his efforts to persuade his brothers to accept their youngest sibling as an equal, if that is how he truly feels, then the loathing the others must harbour deep down for Sonny must be awesome indeed.

'Bear in mind what I've said, Sonny.' Mungo pushes his hands down on his thighs to lever himself upright. 'Stay put.'

'I don't think he's going anywhere,' says Chas.

They leave Sonny curled on the sofa in a foetal clench of sorrow and self-pity. And Mungo also leaves there, in Sonny's apartment, any last vestigial traces of compassion he might have had for his youngest brother.

Whatever torments Sonny faces now, he faces alone.

31

Septempartite: divided or separated into seven parts

1.21 p.m.
Edgar gazes morosely up at the floor-indicator light as it flicks from red to orange, his chin resting on the push-bar of the trolley he has just hired.

He is not so blindly loyal to Miss Dalloway that he cannot see that what she has asked him to do may well end up costing him his job. His job and, if he is lucky, nothing more. And it seems a terrible shame to be jeopardising what he hoped would be a lifelong career in gigastore retail. It seems, in fact, insane. But to Edgar, as to his fellow Bookworms, Miss Dalloway is more than merely the head of the Books Department of Days. She is an initiate into the Mysteries of the printed word, a Sibyl who speaks in the tongues of quotation, a warrior-priestess steeped in the lore of literature, and to serve her is to serve the ghosts of every man and woman who ever set pen to paper in the hopes of achieving immortality; to earn her approval is to earn the approval of all the poets and authors and essayists whose souls are embedded in the works they wrote.

The floor indicator winks from orange to yellow.

Edgar has no desire to return to the menial level of employment – petrol-station attendant, bar work, telesales – which he endured while waiting for his interview at Days, but there are, he realises, some things more important than a mere job. A tradition – a principle – is at stake. That, surely, is worth any sacrifice. Although he wonders if he will think so tomorrow, when he is signing on for the dole.

The floor indicator goes from yellow to green, there is a soft *ping*, and the same female voice that announces the lightning sales over the public address systems informs Edgar – in less strident, more confidential tones – that he has reached the Green Floor. The lift doors slide apart, and Edgar manouevres the trolley out and sets off in the direction of Electrical Supplies.

1.29 p.m.

'Afternoon,' says the sales assistant in Electrical Supplies, a well-bellied man whose girth strains the waistband of his dollar-green overalls. 'Just that then, is it?'

Edgar lays the spool of rubber-insulated wire on the counter. His throat is suddenly terribly dry. He manages to wheeze out, 'Just this, yes.'

The sales assistant runs his scanning wand over the spool's barcode sticker. 'Staff discount, of course.' He has spotted Edgar's ID badge. 'A handsome five per cent.'

'Handsome,' echoes Edgar. It's an employee in-joke.

'Card?'

Edgar takes out the Platinum and passes it over, deliberately (though he hopes, not obviously) obscuring Mrs Shukhov's name with his thumb.

In the event, as Miss Dalloway predicted, the fact that Edgar is an employee means that the sales assistant does not scrutinise the card. Instead, scarcely glancing at it, he swipes it through the credit register and hands it back.

1.30 p.m.

The credit register flashes the information encoded in the card's magnetic strip down to the central database in Accounts, where Mrs Shukhov's account is checked, its validity assessed, its status confirmed, all in a fraction-of-a-second flutter of silicon synapses.

An anomaly is noted, and a message is sent back to the credit register, scrolling across its two-line readout:

> CARD REPORTED LOST/STOLEN
> SECURITY HAS BEEN ALERTED

Security has, in fact, not been alerted at the time the message is sent, but by the time it arrives at its destination in Electrical Supplies, a second message *has* reached the Security CPU, giving details of the card and the location of the department in which it has been improperly used.

Two seconds have elapsed since the card was swept through the reader. The sales assistant is still returning the card to Edgar. His eyes have registered the message on the credit register's readout but the information it contains has not yet percolated all the way along his optic nerves to his brain. Meanwhile, in the hyperaccelerated world of computer time, a third message is already winging its way from Security to the Eye, fizzing along the fibre-optic connection as a speeding pulse of light.

The message is routed to the first available on-line terminal in the Eye. By now, Mrs Shukhov's card has left the sales assistant's hand and is firmly lodged between Edgar's thumb and forefinger, and the sales assistant's brain has processed the series of hieroglyphs displayed on the credit register's readout and interpreted them as a set of formal symbols denoting concrete and abstract concepts – in other words, words.

A second later the same process takes place between the eyes and brain of a screen-jockey in the Eye. The message from Security, which is important enough to have been highlighted in red and enclosed in a blinking box, is transmuted in the screen-jockey's cerebral cortex into an instruction. His response, when compared with the speed of information technology, is slow.

Standard operating procedure in a situation such as this is for the screen-jockey to locate and alert a guard in the vicinity of Electrical Supplies, which he would do by tapping a command into the terminal mounted on his chair arm and calling up the position of every guard within a three-department radius of that department, as provided by the transponders in their Sphinxes. From the section of floorplan that would instantly map itself out on his screen, he would select the guard closest by, contact him, and inform him of the probable felony in progress.

However, before the instruction to commence typing can begin its journey from the screen-jockey's brain to his hands, it is belayed by the appearance on his screen of a subsidiary message, a corollary to the first from Security.

This one says:

CARD FLAGGED
SPECIAL ATTENTION:
TACTICAL SECURITY OPERATIVE HUBBLE, FRANCIS J.
EMPLOYEE #1807-93N

The screen-jockey, rereading the message, sucks on his teeth, then calls up Link Dial mode and enters the Ghost's employee number – also the call-number of his Eye-link – in the prompt box.

The screen-jockey then leans back in his wheeled chair, bends the mic arm of his headset so that the pick-up is to one side of his mouth, and gropes behind him for the cooler box on the floor that holds several cans of his favourite carbonated drink, a sugar-saturated, highly caffeinated Days-brand concoction rumoured to pack a greater stimulant punch than a fistful of amphetamine.

'Old Hubble Bubble, Toil and Trouble again,' he murmurs to himself as he pops the ringpull on a cold-sweat can. 'Just my luck.'

1.30 p.m.
Edgar is placing the spool of wire in the trolley when the sales assistant says, softly, 'Hold on a minute.'

'What's up?' says Edgar, aiming for innocence but achieving only a querulous falsetto.

'Let's have a look at that card again. I think there's been a mistake.'

Edgar swings the trolley around.

'Wait,' says the sales assistant, baffled, 'I *said*, I think there's been a mistake. Where do you think you're going?'

His first attempt to grab Edgar is foiled by his voluminous belly, which butts up against the edge of the counter, so that even at full reach there is still a gap of several centimetres between his fingertips and Edgar's sleeve. With some discomfort he leans further over, but his miss has given Edgar the opportunity to start pushing.

By the time the sales assistant has made it round to the front of the counter, Edgar is well away, haring down the aisle of fuses, the spool of wire bouncing and rattling around inside the trolley basket.

1.30 p.m.
Across the table from Frank, Mr Bloom is savouring a portion of tiramisu which, if his frequent sighs of pleasure are anything to go by, tastes ambrosial. A Days logo has been stencilled in icing sugar and chocolate powder on top of the portion, and this Mr Bloom has with childlike precision eaten around so that all that remains on his plate is a sagging cylinder of layered pudding topped by twin semicircles, one

white, the other light brown. Frank meanwhile is midway through a cup of espresso.

The two of them have been sharing a long silence which has been interrupted only by the arrival of the waiter to remove their main-course plates and take their orders for dessert. During that long silence Frank has considered, and rejected, dozens of potential topics of conversation. With the awkward business of his resignation out of the way, he has not wanted to waste this opportunity to sit and converse casually with Mr Bloom – an opportunity snatched from his dream of an ordinary life – but it seems that that faculty which others take for granted has atrophied in him. He envies the diners around him the ease with which they fill the air with talk.

He has thought about dredging up some incident from the recent past to twist into an anecdote for Mr Bloom's entertainment, but it is hard to single out an individual event from his life that might remotely be considered amusing. His life seems to have telescoped into one long procession of indistinguishably dull nights and days, sleeping giving way to working, working to sleeping, so that reminiscing is like looking back at an empty road which traverses a succession of low rolling hills of uniform size, a narrowing grey ribbon whose peaks and troughs diminish endlessly into the distance.

He can at least remember the events of this morning clearly enough, and has contemplated giving Mr Bloom a description of his encounters with the ponytailed shoplifter, with Moyle in Matchbooks, and with Clothilda Westheimer at the lightning sale in Dolls. But where is the novelty there? Especially for Mr Bloom, who has been walking these floors for longer than he has.

It has even occurred to him to tell Mr Bloom about Mrs Shukhov's impromptu two-night stay at the Hotel Days, but he has decided that that would be unwise. He has a duty to let his superior know about the breach in security, but frankly his feelings about the woman and his inexplicable, spontaneous gesture in the booth in Processing – what *was* he thinking? – have confused him, and Mr Bloom would detect that confusion in his voice the moment he mentioned her name, and would read more into it than is there. Would jump to conclusions. Ridiculous conclusions. Would say that Frank is exhibiting all the symptoms of infatuation. Which is of course absurd. Frank doesn't even know the meaning of the word infatuation. An infatuated Ghost? Ghosts are men and women with hermetically sealed hearts.

Ghosts keep a lid on their feelings as tight as the drum-skin monofilament net strung over the Menagerie. You may catch a glimpse of an emotion every once in a while, something as frivolous as a blue butterfly or as nobly graceful as a white tigress, but nothing gets in and nothing gets out. The area is cordoned off, secure.

Besides, Processing will file a report. Mr Bloom doesn't have to learn about it from *his* lips.

In the end, saying nothing at all has seemed the course least likely to bore or embarrass either of them. The silence, because it is mutual, is acceptable. But of all the things Frank expected to come away with after this meeting with Mr Bloom, a feeling of chagrin was not one of them. Some kind of catharsis, yes; the lightening of the soul that traditionally comes with confession. Instead, all he has been left with is the lingering, frustrating impression that, although Mr Bloom may have successfully clambered his way up out of Ghosthood, he is still walled in by his work, trapped in a trench too deep to see out of. For Mr Bloom there is still only, and ever shall be, the job. His world is Days.

Which disappoints Frank because he expected more from Mr Bloom, and, perhaps more importantly, because it doesn't bode well for his own future.

'Mr Hubble?'

Frank sets down his coffee cup. 'Hubble here.'

'Mr Hubble, we have an improper usage of a lost or stolen card. Green floor, Electrical Supplies.'

'Well, I happen to be on Green, but I'm off-duty. Why did you contact me?'

'The card was flagged. Special attention you.'

'Who is the rightful owner of the card?'

'C A . . . Some kind of Russian name. Shuckoff?'

'Shukhov.' Frank's throat mic transmits to the screen-jockey a grunt that was not intentionally subvocalised. 'All right. Have you alerted a guard?'

'Not yet.'

'Don't until I tell you to.'

'Okey-doo.'

'Eye?'

'Yes?'

'I'm speaking to you as an individual operative. Have you and I been in contact already today?'

'Yep, we have.'

'Matchbooks?'

'Yes.'

'I feared as much. Hubble out.'

That grunt – a cross between a ruminative hum and an expulsion of breath, Frank's way of saying to himself that he should have known that his moment of recklessness down in Processing would not be without its consequences – alerts Mr Bloom to the bobbing of his Adam's apple. He waits until Frank has finished talking to the Eye, then says, 'Duty calls again?'

'Something like that.' Frank stands up, laying his napkin on the table. 'Do you mind?'

'Not at all. Always the job, eh? Always the job.'

'Let me pay.' Frank reaches for his wallet.

Mr Bloom flaps a hand. 'Won't hear of it. What's the point in having a Palladium if I can't use it to buy someone a meal every once in a while?'

'If you're sure.'

'Go, Frank. Go and do what you do so well. And don't forget to think over what I've said.'

'Donald . . .' Suddenly Frank wants to say a dozen things. Now, at last, when there is no time, he realises how much he has to communicate to Mr Bloom. In the end all he says is, 'Thanks.'

Then he is hurrying out of the restaurant.

1.32 p.m.

Only when Edgar has passed through Horticultural Hardware and is halfway across the Gardening Department does he risk a glance over his shoulder. He is surprised to find that the sales assistant from Electrical Supplies is not hard on his heels. Still he does not slacken his pace. On he goes, the trolley's hard rubber wheels trundling over Gardening's synthetic lawn, which carpets a smoothly contoured fibreglass framework of hillocks, berms and dells. Dwarf cypresses in urns dot the billowing, bright-green landscape, and *trompe l'oeil* murals on the walls and ceiling continue the pastoral idyll, adding details that cannot be reproduced indoors by practical means, such as hedgerow mazes, lily ponds, gambolling nymphs and satyrs, and an electric-blue sky wisped with strands of white cloud and flecked with the tiny black }-shapes of high-flying birds. The illusion has been well crafted. If you squint, the department's physical boundaries seem to disappear, and the parklike vista stretches limitlessly into infinity, the painted perfection betrayed only by the connecting passageways hollowing through to neighbouring departments.

Grecian-style follies – plaster Doric columns supporting plywood porticos – serve as sales counters, and the sales assistants are costumed like characters from a Miltonian masque, the men in shepherds' smocks and broad-brimmed felt hats, the women wearing simple gowns with wreaths of silk flowers garlanded in their hair. Littered about in large, incongruous piles are the items actually for sale: sacks of compost and packets of seeds and net-bags of bulbs and stacks of clay pots; tools and trugs and stakes and canes and gloves and strap-on knee-pads; secateurs and grass-clippers and branch-loppers and apple-pickers. It is in the adjoining Horticultural Hardware Department that automated gardening implements such as lawnmowers, as well as less nature-friendly items such as pesticides and weed-killer, can be found. The Gardening Department is for the hands-on enthusiast who lives for the feel of earth beneath his fingernails and for the Arcadian dream of Nature shaped and tamed by the sweat of Man's brow.

The trolley, having not been designed to perform well at anything above a gentle walking pace, is difficult to control, exhibiting a definite leftward bias. It requires all the strength in Edgar's forearms to keep it running straight and true. His breath is starting to come in hard, short gasps, and his face is bathed in a gloss of perspiration. He runs on through the bucolic tranquillity of Gardening, oblivious to the eyebrows and remonstrations raised by his noisy progress.

For the first time since setting out on this mission, he thinks he is in with a chance of pulling it off successfully.

1.35 p.m.
Entering Electrical Supplies, Frank makes for the main sales counter where Mrs Shukhov's Platinum was used. He introduces himself to the sales assistant and, looking significantly around, asks where the perpetrator is.

The sales assistant shakes his head contritely. 'Ah, well, you see . . .'

'Don't tell me you let him get away.'

'It was just a spool of wire.' The sales assistant is aware that retirement credits are at stake here. 'Hardly the sort of thing to arouse suspicion, you know what I'm saying? And I tried to stop him, but' – he pats the solid swell of his belly resoundingly – 'I'm not exactly built like a cheetah, am I?'

'So he was male, and yet the fact that the card had "MRS" printed on it didn't make you just the slightest bit suspicious?'

The sales assistant gives a hapless shrug. 'He was an employee. He had an ID badge.'

'ID badges can be faked.'

'Like I said, as soon as I realised something wasn't kosher, I tried to stop him. And it was just a spool of wire, remember.'

'Theft is theft,' says Frank. 'Can you at least describe him?'

'Young. Twenty-two, twenty-three – thereabouts. Had a trolly. And a huge forehead. You know, as though his skull has sort of expanded forwards, pushing back his hair.'

'All right.' Turning away from the counter, Frank coughs discreetly into his throat mic. 'Eye? Hubble. We're looking at a male perpetrator, early twenties, with a trolley. Distinguishing feature: big forehead. Possibly an employee, more likely a pro with a bogus ID.'

'Gotcha. Any idea where he is?'

'Somewhere west of Electrical Supplies. Begin a sweep of the area now.'

'On it. Could he be making for the exits?'

'I don't think so. It's unlikely anyone would go to the trouble of obtaining a forged ID and a Days card just to get hold of some wire.' Frank frowns. 'There's something odd going on here, but I'm damned if I know what it is.'

32

Heptane: a hydrocarbon paraffin, seventh of the methane series, having the chemical formula $C_7 H_{16}$

1.41 p.m.

Crouching behind the crescent of hardbacks that screens her desk from the prying Eye, Miss Dalloway locates a section marked by such apt titles as *The Winds of War*, *The War of the Worlds*, *War and Peace*, *The Stand*, and *Mein Kampf*. Book by book she clears away this literary seal, like an archaeologist excavating a tomb, stacking the hardbacks behind her, until she has exposed the cavity within. Oscar stands by, ready to offer whatever assistance he can.

Reaching both arms into the cavity, Miss Dalloway carefully – oh so carefully – eases out a ten-litre steel beer keg. The keg is full and heavy, and she moves it a centimetre at a time, wincing grimly at every slop and lap of its contents. When the keg is clear of the cavity, she squats down, embraces it, and lifts. Carrying it to the desk, she sets it gently down beside the open copy of *Kitchen-Sink Arsenal*, then steps back, letting out a long-held breath. Oscar is curious to know what a beer keg might contain that merits such respectful caution, but decides not to enquire. He has a feeling he may not like the answer.

Miss Dalloway returns to the cavity and extracts a sealed sandwich bag, which she also places on the desk. Inside the bag are a Roman candle, a box of matches, a camera flashbulb, a nine-volt battery and a roll of parcel tape. Oscar recognises items his fellow Bookworms were instructed to buy for their head of department the day before yesterday. But where is the can of paraffin he himself purchased for her? And the fertiliser Colin obtained from Gardening?

He watches Miss Dalloway unscrew the cap of the keg, her movements precise and delicate. As she uncovers the circular aperture in the top of the keg, a sharp, ammoniac smell steals out, stinging his nostrils. Through the aperture he glimpses the surface of some kind of thick brown liquid that reminds him of a chocolate-cake mix.

He can contain his curiosity no longer.

'Miss Dalloway . . .?'

'Not now, Oscar. No distractions.'

The formidable head of Books scans the desktop. Her gaze alights on a perspex thirty-centimetre ruler, which she picks up and inserts into the keg. She stirs the thick brown liquid with the ruler slowly, peering into the aperture every so often. When she is satisfied that the liquid has achieved the desired consistency, she withdraws the ruler and hands it, dripping, to Oscar for disposal. Holding it gingerly by its dry end, he drops it into the waste-paper basket.

Now Miss Dalloway unseals the sandwich bag and lays its contents out in a row on the desk. She tears off a few strips of parcel tape with her teeth and tamps them loosely to the edge of the desk, then uses one of them to attach half a dozen of the matches to the Roman candle so that the matches' heads are in contact with the firework's blue touchpaper. She picks up the camera flashbulb and whacks it against the desk repeatedly until its glass shatters, then tapes the broken flashbulb to the firework and adds more matches to bridge the gap between the touchpaper and the exposed bulb filaments. Finally she tapes the battery securely to the side of the keg. She compares her finished handiwork with the illustration on the open page of *Kitchen-Sink Arsenal* and seems satisfied.

'You may ask your question now,' she tells Oscar.

'It isn't a question, really,' Oscar replies. 'It's more of a . . .' He scratches his plaster cast distractedly. 'Are you making what I think you're making?'

'That, Oscar, depends on what you think I'm making.'

'Well, in the keg – that's fertiliser and paraffin, right?'

'Correct. High-nitrate fertiliser and paraffin, with some salt added to stabilise the mixture. Although it remains, of course, highly volatile. Hence my care in handling it.'

'Yes,' says Oscar, thinking that this has got to be a practical joke, but then remembering to whom he is talking. Whatever Miss Dalloway does, she does in earnest. 'Then that . . .' He gestures at the makeshift-looking contraption she has just assmbled from the Roman candle, matches and flashbulb.

'Is the detonator,' the head of Books confirms. 'Like the deflagrating device itself, concocted from common-or-garden household items, all of which, as you are aware, were purchased on the premises. A neat irony, don't you agree? Days harbouring all the elements necessary for me to inflict my revenge upon it.'

'Neat, yes,' says Oscar, numbly. 'So the clock and the wire that Edgar's getting . . .?'

'Will form the timer with which I will be able to trigger the explosion.'

Oscar barely manages to choke out his next question. 'Miss Dalloway, you're not going to blow up the whole store, are you?'

'Oh no, Oscar,' says Miss Dalloway. She gives a light, dreamy little laugh – a strange sound coming from this particular woman. 'Don't be silly. What I've made here isn't nearly powerful enough for that. No, not the whole store. Just a portion of it. One department. One particular department.'

'Computers,' Oscar whispers.

'My little genius,' says Miss Dalloway fondly.

33

2.00 p.m.

'Attention, customers. For the next five minutes there will be a twenty-five per cent reduction on all items in Third World Musical Instruments. I repeat, for the next five minutes . . .'

Linda was reaching into her handbag even before the echo of the announcement's seven-note overture had begun to fade. Now she pulls out the map booklet, flourishes it open, flicks through to the department index at the back, and on hearing the words 'Third World Musical Instruments' finds T and runs her finger down the column.

Tableware	Red
Tanning Equipment	Blue
Tapestries	Orange
Tea	Orange
Teddy Bears	Green
Telecommunications	Yellow
Theatrical Supplies (see also Costumes)	Indigo
Third World Musical Instruments	Yellow

'Yellow,' she says with hushed excitement. 'It's on this floor, Gordon.'

'Oh?' replies her husband cautiously.

'. . . Instruments is located in the south-east quadrant of the Yellow Floor . . .'

Linda flicks to the double-page floorplan for the Yellow Department, excited to think that she is already a step ahead of everyone else. 'And I have a feeling we're *in* the south-east quadrant.'

'Oh?' says Gordon again, more cautiously.

'This offer will be extended to you for five minutes only.'

'Yes, here we are. Look.' She jabs a finger at the map. 'Next to Clocks. And Third World Musical Instruments is in the Peripheries. It's three departments away. Three departments, Gordon!' She orients the map and points. 'That way. No, wait a moment.' She turns the booklet around. '*That* way.'

'Thank you for your attention.'

'We can make it!' She pulls on her husband's forearm. 'Gordon, it's a *sale*. Come on! You'll love it!'

Around them other shoppers are also consulting their maps and starting to move, gravitating in the direction Linda indicated, breaking from a walk into a run. It is as though a wind is sweeping through the Candles Department, one that only affects people and doesn't disturb the flames that flicker in votive ranks all around, on chandeliers, candelabra and seven-stemmed menorahs. Gordon plants his feet firmly on the floor, determined to resist, to be like those flames, unmoved.

'Linda, neither of us knows how to play any kind of musical instrument, let alone one from the Third World.'

'That's not the point, Gordon. A quarter off – *that's* the point.'

'But if we don't buy anything, we'll save a whole lot more.'

'Please, Gordon.' There is nothing endearing or enticing about that 'please'. Gordon has heard swear words phrased more sweetly. 'I want you to come with me. I want you to see for yourself.'

'And I don't want you to go.'

Linda does a double-take. 'What did you just say?'

That's the question Gordon is asking himself too: *What did I just say?* But he can't pretend nothing came out of his mouth. He spoke clearly enough. 'I don't want you going there to buy something we don't need.'

Linda gives an unpleasant bark of a laugh. 'Very funny, Gordon. All right, I'll see you back here in, what, ten minutes?'

She turns to leave, and Gordon, as if a passenger on his own body, sees his hand reach out and grab hold of the strap of her handbag, and hears himself say, 'I mean it.'

Linda halts and looks slowly round, first at his hand, then at his face, puzzled.

'Listen, Linda. You can't keep doing this. You can't keep buying things just because everyone else is buying them.'

A growing rumble of voices and footsteps reverberates through the departments surrounding Third World Musical Instruments.

'You can't because we can't afford it. If you carry on the way you're going, we'll be paying off our debt to the store for the rest of our lives.'

Linda continues to glare at him, but he has the tiger by the tail. He can't let go.

'We have to keep things in perspective. We don't belong here. We're not a part of this place like everyone else is. Remember what the taxi driver said this morning? He said we looked fresh-faced, innocent. He said regular Days customers have permanently wary and jaded expressions. That's not us. I don't want that to be us.'

Linda's upper lip draws back from her teeth in a sneer. No one, but no one, tells her what she can or cannot do.

'If you go to this sale, Linda, that's it. I'm taking my name off the account. I can do it. You know I can. Quite frankly, I'm beginning to wish we never applied for the card in the first place. It was a mistake. We can be just as happy without it. Being a Days customer isn't the be-all and end-all. Think: we'll be able to buy all those things we've had to do without for five years. We'll be able to live like ordinary people. How about it, Linda? Eh? How about we give it up as a bad idea?'

The blackmail threat clinches it. Linda realises that her husband has gone quite mad.

'Gordon,' she says with acid politeness, 'take your hand off me.'

Gordon does as he is told.

'And wait here. I won't be long.'

She goes a few steps, then stops and turns.

'Oh, and Gordon? You wouldn't dare take your name off the account. You don't have the guts.'

'I do,' Gordon says under his breath, but what is the use in talking to yourself if you know you are lying?

2.01 p.m.

Third World Musical Instruments used to deal, as its name suggests, exclusively in tools of Euterpean expression from the poorer regions of the globe, but, when the Folk Music Department was displaced from the Violet Floor, evolved into a repository for all musical instruments not served by the standard classical repertoire.

Since the department is on one of the lower floors and the discount on offer is larger than usual, the lightning sale is better attended than most. By the end of its first minute a hundred-odd bargain-hunting customers have arrived, and as the second minute ticks to a close another hundred or so find their way in via the department's three entrances. There is jostling and shoving in the aisles, and the occasional strum or hollow bonk can be heard as a Senegalese kora bumps against a Chinese flowerpot drum or a pair of Moroccan clay bongos accidentally strikes the strings of an India israj, but by and large tempers remain in check, the bargain-hunters perhaps inspired by the beauty and fragility of the merchandise to treat it, and each other, with respect.

By the end of the third minute, however, customers are finding themselves crammed around the sales counters with little room to move or breathe, and with the pressure mounting as more and yet more bargain-hunters enter the department it isn't long before the relative orderliness of the crowd disintegrates, to be replaced by animosity, which rapidly gives way to naked aggression. Without warning, several dozen fights break out at once, a spontaneous upwelling of violence. At the majority of lightning sales altercations between individuals are given a wide berth, a pocket of non-interference in which the antagonists can settle their differences, but in this instance there isn't space for the skirmishes to remain isolated. Hence it isn't surprising that some angry blows should miss their intended targets and land on unwitting third parties. Nor is it surprising that these third parties, understandably aggrieved, and feeling that such unprovoked aggression should not go unpunished, but not always able to locate their assailants in the throng, should decide that visiting retribution upon another innocent is better than not visiting retribution upon anyone at all.

And so, like the confusion of ripples caused by a handful of stones being cast into a pond, the violence spreads out through the crowd, strike demanding counterstrike, retaliation triggering further retaliaton, one confrontation sparking off another, chain reactions of violence overlapping and cross-colliding, until in almost no time at all every customer in the department is grappling with another customer, as in a bar-room brawl in a movie western, although instead of a tune plinked on a honky-tonk piano (inevitably truncated when the piano-player, too, is dragged into the mêlée), this fight boasts the rather more exotic accompaniment of drums, xylophones, didgeridoos, maracas, castanets, timbales, flutes, pipes, gongs and miscellaneous other stringed, woodwind and percussion instruments colliding haphazardly with one another and with various portions of the human anatomy, an improvised soundtrack of arrhythmically and sometimes insistently generated notes which no critic would describe as great music but which, as a background score to widespread score-settling, could hardly be bettered.

The Eye, per standard operating procedure, is observing the sale, and a couple of Ghosts and a handful of guards are in attendance, but the violence erupts so swiftly that there is little anyone can do to halt it. One of the Ghosts, in fact, is caught up in the free-for-all almost before she is aware that it has begun. When all is frenzy, when everyone to everyone is a faceless, anonymous enemy, congruity is no camouflage, and the Ghost finds herself besieged on several sides at once. Her principal assailant is a customer brandishing a Jew's harp like a stubby dagger, and although his first stab succeeds only in tearing a slash in the Ghost's jacket, that is enough to convince her to draw her gun. In the madness of the moment, however, the customer, not recognising the sidearm for what it is, thinking it just another unusual item of merchandise, fearlessly swats it out of her hand. The gun hits the floor, is accidentally kicked by a passing foot, and goes skidding under a podium, and the customer resumes his attack. Unarmed, the Ghost is far from defenceless, but in the heave and buffet of bodies it takes her longer than it otherwise might to subdue the customer, and by the time she finally manages to bring him howling to his knees, her face and wrists are bleeding from a number of shallow cuts and scrapes.

The guards, meanwhile, do their best to stem the influx of customers into the department, but they have their work cut out for them. More and more shoppers are arriving at the sale, and for every one the guards prevent from entering another three slip past unhindered. The violence, far from deterring the bargain-hunters, has the opposite effect. If people are fighting, goes the thinking, then the bargains on offer must be worth fighting over, ergo they must be great bargains. And so the demented atonal sonata of strums and bongs and plucks mounts in a crescendo, counterpointed by sporadic splintering cracks of breaking wood and snaps of sundered catgut and human yelps and howls in every register.

One might regard it as a clash of cultures, iktara meeting bodhran, moszmar being deployed against oud, ocarina warding off blows from djembe. One might equally regard it with an ironically zoological eye, as lion drums and monkey drums and guiro frog boxes and cow bells and water bird whistles are used to give vent to bestial urges. And then again, one might simply view the proceedings with world-weary dismay, as instruments crafted to inspire finer feelings – lutes, dulcimers, panpipes, Tibetan meditation bells, Chinese harps and the like – are pressed into service for untranquil, belligerent ends.

Down in the Eye, however, the only emotion evoked by the fighting is glee, as the traditional cry of 'Shopping maul!' goes up and every screen-jockey not otherwise engaged tunes in to watch. The security cameras in Third World Musical Instruments were switched from automatic to manual just before the sale began so that they wouldn't fuse a servomotor trying to keep track of every source of activity in the department, and the scenes they now show – a sea of battling bargain-hunters seething to and fro, display stands being flattened, sales assistants cowering behind their counters while stock scatters and shatters around them – give rise to whoops and cheers. The screen-jockeys start laying odds: how many casualties; how long before the mayhem dies down; whether Strategic Security will resort to a baton charge or gunfire; estimates as to the total cost of the damage. Chairs shuttle back and forth across the Basement chamber as bets are agreed on with a handshake.

Such is the mood, gloating and festive, when Mr Bloom enters, having been alerted as soon as the maul broke out. His arrival brings an immediate calm, like the entrance of a teacher into an unruly classroom. The screen-jockeys scurry back to their posts and adopt attitudes of concentration. Some start muttering into their headset mics as though in the middle of conversation with security operatives on the shop floor.

Mr Bloom glances up at the nearest screen showing the fracas, then looks around the room. 'I trust reinforcements have been called in.'

Straight away half a dozen of the screen-jockeys are contacting guards on the Yellow Floor and on the floors directly above and below.

Mr Bloom turns back to the screens. Reduced to a series of fuzzy black-and-white images, the hand-to-hand combat looks like something out of an old Buster Keaton movie. But there is real pain up there, real anger and suffering, and Mr Bloom wonders briefly but only briefly – if Frank, in his determination to leave Days, might not have the right idea after all.

2.03 p.m.

Linda will probably never realise it, and if she does she would never admit it, but had Gordon not delayed her in Candles she would probably right now be in the thick of the fighting. Instead, the precious seconds he cost her with his sudden, inexplicable lapse into Neanderthal-husband behaviour mean that she reaches the lightning sale after the violence has already taken hold. What confronts her as she rushes in through the connecting passageway from the next-door Periphery, Ethnic Arts & Crafts, is not the rowdy rough-and-tumble she remembers, with such delight, from Ties. What confronts her is naked savagery: men and women with their faces contorted in vicious scowls, beautiful artefacts of teak and bamboo and reed and clay and steel being swung and broken, and blood – blood pouring from cuts, blood speckling the dollar-green, logo-patterned carpet – and the injured staggering and rolling, clutching their wounds. Here, two customers are going at each other with Chilean rainsticks, parrying and thrusting with the rattling lengths of dried cactus like two fencers. Here, a woman is trying to force a nose flute up another woman's nasal passage. And over here, a pair of maracas are being rammed violently up between a man's legs, causing him to sag to his knees in wordless, white-faced agony. This is not healthy, aggressive competition for bargains but nothing less than communal insanity, a rhymeless, reasonless free-for-all. And something inside Linda, something sufficiently uncorrupted by Days, recoils at the sight. While other shoppers push by, eagerly throwing themselves headlong into the throng, she hesitates. She knows that a once-in-a-lifetime bargain is waiting for her somewhere in the midst of the bellicose mob in front of her. She can all but hear it crying out to her above the clang-twang-bang of musical weaponry. Desire sways her forward; caution sways her back.

Then a woman running past grabs the sleeve of Linda's blouse, and, in a spirit of kamikaze comradeship, hauls her into the department. Perhaps Linda is not as unwilling to become involved as she thought, because she allows herself to be dragged several metres before it occurs to her that she might like to make this decision for herself. She digs her heels in and the sleeve tears, but the woman is swallowed up by the crowd before Linda can remonstrate. Her best blouse!

At the edge of the tumult Linda loses the sense of perspective she had in the connecting passageway. At close quarters, all she can see are raking fingernails and flying fists, gouging thumbs and snarling grins. Then something small and wet slaps against her cheek, sticking there. She picks the object off. It is a tooth, still with a shred of gum attached.

That's it. Tossing the tooth aside with a disgusted shudder, Linda begins to pace backward, away from the chaos, moving slowly so as to be unobtrusive, not wanting to catch anyone's eye. As far as she can tell, you don't have to attack anyone in order to be attacked yourself. People already embroiled in the fighting are rounding on newcomers and laying into them as if they are old antagonists in a long-running feud. Still she hears the siren-song of her bargain urging her to dive in and battle her way through to it, but the sound is faint now, and becoming fainter, disappearing beneath the rising cacophony of pain and abused musical instruments.

Suddenly, as though an invisible membrane enclosing the crowd has burst, the fighting spills towards her. A man charges at her with a zither, fully intending to drive one blood-smeared corner of it into her skull. Stumbling backward, Linda catches his wrists and twists his arms aside, so that the zither glances off her temple. There is a hot gush of breath on her cheek. The man is screaming at her, spouting an incoherent stream of obscenities. He brings the zither back up. The trapezoid instrument wavers centimetres from Linda's face. The man's wrists are sinewy, slippery in her grasp, but she doesn't let go. He is bigger than her, stronger, but she is damned if she is going to let him hurt her.

In a vivid flash, she recalls seeing her parents in a very similar pose. She had been lying in bed listening to the argument downstairs rage for the best part of an hour until finally, unable to sleep, she had sneaked out of her bedroom and gone and sat on the staircase. Peering timorously through the banisters, she had seen her father, scarlet-faced, pacing about the living room, snorting and cursing and, between snorts and curses, accusing her mother of all sorts of things: of never listening to him, of failing to understand his needs, of not showing him sufficient respect as her husband and as the breadwinner of the family. Her mother was saying nothing in her own defence, no doubt because she thought the accusations too absurd to merit a response; instead, she simply sat there while her husband worked himself up into a frenzy, until at last, unable to bear her silence any more, he lunged at her as if to strangle her. Reacting with a quickness that suggested she had been expecting something like this to happen,

Linda's mother caught his wrists before his hands could connect with her throat and, bracing them away from her, trembling, arms rigid, she began talking softly, soothingly, to him, the way you do to a fierce dog.

The two of them remained locked together like that, a frozen tableau depicting anger versus reason, until, slowly, as Linda's mother's words penetrated her father's haze of rage, he began to back off. She did not let go of his wrists until she felt sure he had calmed down. She (and Linda) then watched him cross the room to the fireplace, both of them expecting him to say he was sorry, as he usually did at this point, for he was not wholly without a conscience, not entirely a hostage to his own desires. The apologies he tendered after any kind of dispute might have been mumbled and grudging, but at least served as an admission that he had been out of line.

On this occasion, however, he had not yet calmed down and was not about to apologise. His anger had temporarily subsided, but it was seeking a new outlet, and quickly found one.

He snatched down the carriage clock with the cherub feet and weighed it speculatively in his hand. Linda and her mother both realised what was about to happen but both were powerless to do anything about it. They could only look on in appalled disbelief as he drew back his arm and hurled the clock against the nearest wall.

He bent to pick up the clock and inspected it. Even from the staircase Linda could see that the glass covering its dial had a crack in it, a clean, jagged line coming down from one corner like a lightning bolt. Once again her father drew back his arm and dashed the clock against the wall. This time, something inside the clock came unsprung with an audible twang, and one of the cherub feet snapped off. Once more he picked up the clock and, shaking it beside his ear, grinned as its innards rattled. Then he raised it up above his head and threw it to the floor. Glass sprayed out in slivers. Another of the cherubs went flying.

The clock lay on its side on the carpet, a sad, dented, disfigured thing. Linda had to resist the urge to cry out, 'Leave it alone!' Couldn't he see that it (and she and her mother) had had enough? Clearly not, because the next thing he did was raise his foot and stamp on the clock, once, twice, and then again and again, repeatedly.

The clock had been well made, but it could only take so much punishment. It wasn't long before, beneath the pounding of his foot, its casing gave way and gleaming metal movement parts spilled out – cogs, flywheels, escapement, a coil of spring.

Linda's father looked down at what he had done, then up at his wife, his smug, self-satisfied expression that of an infant that has got out of eating an unwanted meal by tipping the bowl on to the floor.

'One day,' he said, 'I'm going to do the same to you, you bitch.' Then he sat down, put his feet up on the coffee table, and switched on the television.

With a quiet, mournful dignity, Linda's mother set to picking up the pieces of the clock, and Linda, tears in her eyes, padded back to her room, and there, in bed, cried herself to sleep.

In the event, her father never made good on his threat. In fact, not once during the course of their marriage did he actually land a blow on his wife, though this was perhaps as much due to her quick reactions as to his reluctance. Nevertheless, the possibility was always there that one day his rage would grow too great to be vented in insults or placated by carefully chosen words, and this meant that Linda's mother had to tread cautiously around the house at all times, a habit Linda herself learned to emulate, even though it was her mother who always took the brunt of her father's temper. He was the sullen, angry planet around which they, two moons, a larger and a lesser, silently circled, and when he finally walked out on them and went to live in another city with another, younger woman, it was as though they had been freed from his gravitational pull. They felt lighter for his absence.

Understandably, Linda grew up fearing men, believing that they were all like her father, liable to turn on you at the slightest excuse. This led to a series of awkward, superficial, unconsummated affairs which earned her a reputation in her social circle as a frigid man-hater. It wasn't until she met Gordon that she at last understood that not all men were made the way her father had been; that some of them could be meek and mild and – yes, no harm in admitting it – malleable.

The memory of the destruction of the cherub clock gives Linda the boost she needs. In the man with the zither's distended, filth-spewing face she sees an echo of her father's, and resentment and revulsion well up inside her, lending her strength. With a grunting shriek, she thrusts him away. He totters back, arms windmilling, and his zither strikes a nearby customer in the neck. This other customer wheels around. He has a balalaika in his hands. He swings it like a club. It smashes the man with the zither square in the face, strings first. A spiky open chord sings out, and parallel slashes across the man with the zither's nose and cheekbones bead crimson and start to run.

Linda starts to run, too.

Her sense of direction has been thrown and she has no clear idea which way the connecting passageway to Ethnic Arts & Crafts lies. She can see nothing except people, but she can detect a current to their movement, a flow. Bargain-hunters are still pouring into the department; therefore, if she heads the opposite way, counter to them, like a salmon swimming upstream, she will get to where she wants to go.

A fine plan in theory, but the inrush of shoppers is an almost solid wall of bodies, pushing her back. She has to force her way through them, wedging a shoulder or a leg into every gap she sees. Several times her feet are swept out from under her and she nearly goes down, saving herself by clinging on to someone's arm or clothing, desperately recovering her footing before the owner of the arm or clothing shakes her off. She knows that if she falls she will most likely be trampled.

At some point during her struggle to reach the exit she hears, dimly, the end of the sale being called out over the PA system, and she entertains the vain, vague hope that, as it did in Ties, the announcement will bring a halt to the proceedings. But no one else seems to hear or, more to the point, to care. The fighting continues unabated, the bargain-hunters keep on coming, and Linda has to carry on pushing against the tide, enduring the knocks and thumps that come her way, gritting her teeth and not retaliating because her goal is getting out in one piece. Everything else is secondary to that.

It begins to seem hopeless. Wave upon wave of bargain-hunters crashes against her. The undertow of their single-mindedness tugs at her. The effort it takes to resist is draining. Linda feels as though she has jumped off the rail of a foundering ocean liner and is trying to swim away against the pull of the vortex created by the sinking ship. For all her striving she doesn't appear to be making any progress. Her reserves of energy are ebbing. It would be easier, her tiring limbs tell her, just to give in and let herself be sucked back into the maelstrom. She has failed to obtain her bargain, whatever it was. Someone who deliberately passes up an opportunity like that (a quarter off!) doesn't deserve to get anything else she wants.

She decides to abandon the attempt to escape from the department and let the flood of bargain-hunters take her where it will.

And in that moment of letting go she thinks of Gordon, who all his life has allowed events to happen to him, who has never once tried to improve his circumstances of his own accord but has invariably adapted, complied and compromised. And for the first time in their marriage she understands why. To choose the path of least resistance has always seemed to her a sign of weakness. The root of her strength has been her willingness to stand firm no matter how overwhelming the odds. But sometimes there is a strength in admitting defeat. Rigid defiance is admirable but not necessarily, in every situation, wise.

She thinks of Gordon, and there in front of her, as if somehow conjured into being by the power of her imagination, *is* Gordon. Gordon extending a hand to her. Gordon shouting , 'Grab a hold, Linda!'

She takes his hand, and he hauls her toward him, and together they form a small island around which the torrent of bodies breaks and diverges. Standing, embracing, husband and wife ride out the onslaught.

34

Fortitude: one of the Seven Cardinal Virtues

2.05 p.m.

Miss Dalloway consults her watch. By her estimate Edgar should have secured the insulated wire by now and be on his way to getting the clock – assuming he hasn't run into difficulties.

Events are for the moment out of her control, and that is an uncomfortable feeling, but Edgar, she reminds herself, is a bright boy. Devoted, diligent. She couldn't have chosen better. Still, the possibility that he might fail is a real one, and she would be a fool not to acknowledge it.

Oscar, standing a few wary yards away from the incomplete bomb, has been busy thinking.

'Miss Dalloway? Forgive me if this sounds impertinent, but you've obviously had this planned for a while, so why leave getting the timer to the last minute?'

'I told you earlier, Oscar,' Miss Dalloway replies. 'I want the store to know what I am up to. I want the powers-that-be watching when I get my own back for the shabby, shameful way in which I and my department have been treated.'

'You mean the brothers.'

'The brothers, Security, the Eye. I want everyone to be looking on when it happens.'

'You want them to see that you're not just some ordinary terrorist.'

'Precisely, my love.'

Yes, that is right. She is not some terrorist. Certainly she has a cause she feels passionately about, as most terrorists claim they do, but her goal today is not to force people into seeing things her way through the indiscriminate use of suffering and fear. Her goal today is to teach the management of Days a lesson it will never forget. She is going to show the Day brothers that they cannot treat their employees like ants; they cannot push them around and step on them with impunity. She is going to demonstrate to them, in spectacular fashion, that running the world's first and (in their father's day) foremost gigastore is a serious responsibility and not, as they seem to think, a boardgame with human beings – human lives – for counters.

That and the prospect of getting her own back on the Computers Department for eighteen months of persecution furnish Miss Dalloway with all the armour of resolve she needs.

Edgar *will* succeed.

He has to.

2.07 p.m.
The lift arrives at the Yellow Floor and Edgar manoeuvres the trolley out. He hasn't gone more than a couple of metres when he spots a guard lumbering towards him. He halts, seized by panic, unable to think about anything but the size of the man. The guard is one of those human beings who seem to have been designed for no other purpose than inflicting physical injury on other human beings. His fists are like hammers, his eyes close-set and compassionless.

Edgar resolves then and there to come quietly. Meek as a lamb. He no longer cares about losing his job; getting through the next few moments with the minimum amount of suffering is all that matters. It isn't that he is a coward. It's just that pain *hurts*.

He stands there as the guard homes in . . .

. . . and rushes past without so much as a second glance.

It is then that Edgar hears the faint, far-off thundering – a sound he has no difficulty recognising. But according to his watch it is seven minutes past two. An on-the-hour lightning sale should be over by now.

Which means that this one must have developed into a maul.

Another guard comes his way, hurrying after the first, and this one Edgar watches go by with considerably less anxiety. There is a perceptible lightening of his habitually gloomy expression as he resumes pushing the trolley in the direction of the Clocks Department, comforted by the knowledge that for as long as the maul lasts Security is going to have more important things to think about than a Bookworm using a stolen card.

2.08 p.m.

The screen-jockey lets out a hiss of triumph and slaps the arm of his chair. He brings his mic round to his mouth.

'Mr Hubble?'

'Hubble here.'

'I got 'im.'

'Where?'

'Down on Yellow. Man with a trolley. Big fucking fore-head. Got to be him. Lift-bank K. moving west now.'

'Good work, Eye. Keep him in sight. Hubble out.'

'All right, all right, my big-browed friend,' the screen-jockey murmurs as he calls up a map of the departments around lift-bank K on Yellow. The position of each security camera is marked by a red dot which is tagged with a reference number and surrounded by a circle denoting the camera's arc of coverage. 'I have you locked and loaded and I'm not going to lose you.' A quick glance shows the screen-jockey the location of the next camera that will be able to pick up a visual of the man with the trolley. A few taps of the keys, a toggle of the joystick, and he has the perpetator in view again, from a new angle.

God, he loves this job! Never mind that the average length of a screen-jockey's career, from training to burnout, is ten years. And never mind that there is a higher-than-average of incidence of cancer and heart disease among Eye retirees. All that is for the future. What matters is moments like this. Pursuit. Hopping from camera to camera. Quick, nervy decisions. Fingers flying over the keyboard. Like a computer game but with real people. All the thrill of the chase but conducted at a safe remove. It makes him feel alive.

'Oh, I'm good at this,' the screen-jockey tells himself. 'I'm so fucking good at this. I'm the best . . .'

'I'm glad to hear it,' says a voice at his right shoulder.

The screen-jockey looks sharply round.

Mr Bloom is standing behind him, one hand resting on the back of his chair.

'S-sir,' stammers the screen-jockey. 'I didn't, um, didn't realise you were . . .'

'Did I just hear you mention the name Hubble?'

'That's right, sir, yes. We're following a perpetrator using a stolen card. Mr Hubble says he thinks he's a pro using a fake employee ID.'

'Mind if I watch?'

'Not at all, sir. But what about the maul?'

'The department entrances have been sealed off. It'll burn itself out soon enough.' Mr Bloom draws up an unoccupied chair. 'Forgive me, I don't know your name.'

'Hunt, sir.'

'All right, Hunt,' says Mr Bloom. 'Where is Mr Hubble right now?'

2.09 p.m.

Frank is on an escalator descending from Green to Yellow. In front of him stands a customer with several bulky carrier bags in each hand, blocking the way. Twice Frank has said, 'Excuse me.' Twice he has been ignored. Aggravating though this hindrance is, he can't quite bring himself to tap the customer on the shoulder, so instead he agitatedly drums his fingers on the rubber handrail and stares daggers at the customer's back.

'Mr Hubble?'

'Go ahead.'

'The perpetrator's reached Jokes & Novelties. Looks like he's going south now into Boardgames.'

'OK, fine. If I cut through Fishing and Photography, I can intercept him in Clocks.'

'That's the good news. The bad news is, there's a maul over in Third World Musical Instruments, so we're going to be a bit short on guards at the moment.'

'That shouldn't be a problem,' says Frank.

The escalator flattens out, the bag-toting customer steps off, and Frank skirts around him and sets off at a lope in the direction of Clocks.

35

The Seven Benedictions of the Jewish Marriage Ceremony: the traditional recital of seven blessings which align the state of matrimony with the history and hopes of the state of Israel

2.09 p.m.
Sensing an easing in the flow of bargain-hunters, the Trivetts start to move towards the exit. Their progress is slow, awkward and shuffling. Neither is willing to relinquish their grip on the other, not just yet.

The fighting rages on behind them as they reach the connecting passageway to Ethnic Arts & Crafts, where they discover that the flood of shoppers coming into Third World Musical Instruments has been pinched off by a dam of human flesh and dollar-green uniforms which plugs the passageway from wall to wall: guards, standing shoulder to shoulder and hip to hip, three deep, impenetrable.

'And where do you think you're going?' asks one of the guards in the front row, as Gordon attempts to steer Linda through.

'Out,' Gordon replies simply but the guard shakes his head and says, 'No, you're not.'

Gordon has to ask, 'Why not?' several times before he is granted the privilege of an answer.

Until the fighting dies down, the guard explains, no one is allowed to leave the department. 'We have to take names when it's over, see.'

'Names?'

'Everyone involved in a shopping maul has to pay for their share of the damage,' the guard says, spelling it out in terms so simple even an idiot can understand. 'It's in the disclaimer form, under "Reparations for Damaged Merchandise". Just stay where you are. You'll be all right.'

'Here, don't I know you?'

This from a guard in the second rank of the blockade. Gordon fails to recognise the man at first, but after a few seconds of scrutiny the penny drops with an awful, chilling clunk.

'No, I don't think so,' he says, unconvincingly.

'Yeah. In Mirrors.'

'No, I really don't think so,' Gordon insists, even less convincingly.

'Yeah, you're the one who was being hassled by a couple of Burlingtons.'

Gordon darts a glance at Linda, but she is busy inspecting the rip in her sleeve and doesn't appear to be paying attention.

'Go on, take their card details and let them go,' this other guard says to his colleague in the front row. 'The poor bastard's not been having a good day.'

Gordon asks Linda for their Silver, and passes it over resentfully for the guard to scan with his Sphinx. The blockade then parts to allow them through.

Emerging on the other side, the Trivetts find a milling congregation of frustrated bargain-hunters, who throw them envious looks, then resume craning their necks to catch a glimpse of the action over the guards' shoulders.

Gordon and Linda keep walking, still holding on to one another, through the masks, totems and clay statuettes of Ethnic Arts & Crafts. Soon they have left the Peripheries behind and are retracing their steps towards Candles, returning to the spot where Linda told Gordon to wait for her because neither is able to think of anywhere else to go.

Gordon decides it would be best to make a clean breast of his encounter with the Burlingtons now, while Linda is in a subdued mood, and he begins to recount what really happened to him in Mirrors, but Linda silences him with a raised hand. 'It's all right,' she says. 'You can tell me about it another time.'

'I only lied a little bit.'

'It doesn't matter. I'd prefer it if you explained something else to me.'

'What?'

'Don't sound so anxious. I simply want to know what you were doing at the sale back there.'

'Oh, that. Well, I changed my mind.'

'Why?'

'I hated being . . . *separate* from you, is the only word I can think of for it.'

'Separate?'

'Because of what you'd gone through at that previous sale. It was like you knew a secret I didn't. So I said to myself, "I'll just go and have a peek in through the entrance and see what goes on," and when I got there, there was all that fighting, and then I spotted you trying to make your way out, and . . . ' The words trail off into a shrug.

'And in you went to rescue me.'

'And in I went to rescue you. Your knight in shining spectacles.'

Linda disengages from him so that she can take a step back and appraise him fully, from head to toe.

'So how are you?' he asks, self-conscious under her scrutiny.

'Oh, bruised, battered, annoyed that my best blouse has been torn . . . but happy.'

'Happy?'

'I wouldn't expect you to understand.' But she says it in such a way that Gordon thinks he does understand.

'Ah,' he says, with a slow smile.

They walk on a few metres in companionable silence, and then Gordon hazards the suggestion that they go home.

Linda surprises him by agreeing, and surprises him even more by adding, 'And when we get there, we'll discuss whether we're going to keep our account or just pay it off and close it.'

A knock on the head, Gordon thinks. *By the time we get home, she'll have forgotten what she just said.*

She reads his thoughts. 'I can change my mind, too, Gordon.'

'Yes, but –'

'Did I look like I was having a good time back there?'

'Well, no, but –'

'There you are, then.'

'But –'

'Gordon, most people don't even get one day at Days. We've had that. We'll always have that.'

'Well,' says Gordon, 'if you're sure.'

'I just want to visit one last department, and then we can be on our way. I made myself a promise to buy two things today. A tie for you was one. The other is that carriage clock I showed you. In the catalogue. Remember?'

Gordon does remember. 'The reproduction of the one your mother used to have.'

'Call it a memento, if you like. A souvenir of our day at Days.' She smiles at him and, despite her mussed hair, despite the tear in her sleeve, despite the raw-looking lump at her temple that is beginning to blossom into a large, prune-coloured bruise, or perhaps because of these imperfections, these chinks in the armour of her appearance, Gordon is won over.

'All right,' he says.

'My knight in shining spectacles.' Linda raises herself up on her toes to give him a brief but warm peck on the cheek, the ghost of which clings long after she has set off in the direction of the Clocks Department.

36

Seven Dials: a conjunction of seven streets in Holborn, London, named after the Doric pillar with (actually) six sundials that stands at its centre

2.17 p.m.

In Clocks, time is divided into infinitesimally small increments, split into thousands of pieces by thousands of timepieces. In Clocks, time does not pass second by discrete second but cascades in a massed cricket-chorus of busy movements, a great fibrillating fusillade of ticks and tocks delivered by everything from slender ladies' wristwatches to stately grandfather clocks, from sleek bedside radio-alarms to curlicued, pendulum-driven ormolus. In Clocks, the arrival of each quarter-hour is attended by a carillon of bells, chimes, cuckoos and digital bleeps, each half-hour by a slightly longer and louder version of the same, and each hour by an even longer and louder outburst. The deafening peals that announce noon and midnight go on for almost a minute.

In addition to the regulation quota of sales assistants, Clocks employs three people full-time just to keep mainsprings wound, replace batteries and make sure every single face and readout in the department is in agreement, the which task they perform diligently, meeting up at regular intervals to check that their personal chronometers have not deviated one iota from complete accord. Even so, it is impossible for so many thousands of clocks and watches to be synchronised precisely. The edges of minutes overlap, and time becomes so blurred and fragmentary that it returns to its true state: a nebulous, unquantifiable abstract. Every-time and no-time.

If you wish to buy a device for monitoring or detecting the passage of time, the Clocks Department is the place to go, but while you are there be prepared for your temporal perception to be thrown off by the staggered succession of thousands of seconds happening almost, but not quite, at once. Be prepared, for an immeasurable period of time, to see time from a number of different angles at once.

2.17 p.m.

Linda finds the cherub carriage clock more easily than she expected, almost as if led to it by an instinct. It is beautiful. Its brass casing has been burnished to a golden shine, and the cherubs that serve as its feet are exquisitely detailed. You can see the strain on their faces as they blow into their trumpets. You can make out every feather in their stubby little wings. It is her mother's clock, reproduced in every detail, perfect in every part. The past resurrected. A memory made real.

She motions to Gordon to come over and have a look.

2.17 p.m.

Gordon comes over and has a look.

'Well?' his wife asks him. 'What do you think?'

He wants to say that the cherubs appear ridiculously uncomfortable, as if they are being squashed by the clock, the breath whistling out of them in trumpet-shaped puffs. He wants to say that he doesn't think it will look good in their house. But he knows how much the clock means to her.

'If you like it, I like it,' he tells her.

Linda removes the clock reverently from the shelf.

2.17 p.m.

'Alarm clock, alarm clock,' Edgar mutters as he cruises an aisle specialising in bedside horology, searching for the second and final item on Miss Dalloway's list. The end of the mission is in sight, and its successful completion seems likely – no, not just likely, inevitable. He is very much looking forward to returning to Books a hero and receiving his head of department's praise, which, other than the chance to serve her well, is all he could ever ask for from her. Once he has made this purchase, all he has to do is go north through two departments, and it will be over.

There. A straightforward wind-up alarm clock. Brass bells. Narrow Roman numerals on a white dial. That should do the trick.

Edgar pops the clock into the trolley and sets a course for the sales counter at the end of the aisle.

There is a soft thudding of rubber-soled footsteps behind him, slowing to a halt. Someone speaks to him.

2.17 p.m.

'Tactical Security. Stop where you are and turn around.'

That the perpetrator hesitates suggests to Frank that he is someone who, by nature, abides by the rules. That he then starts to run suggests that he is determined, not to mention desperate.

'I said stop.'

But the perpetrator does not stop, and Frank's Ghost Training takes over.

In a single fluid motion he draws his gun with one hand while his other hand slips into his wallet, slides out his velvet card sheath and extracts his Iridium. He inserts the card into the slot beneath the barrel and zips it through. The green LED winks alight, and the gun ceases to be an inert configuration of metal parts and becomes a coiled steel trap waiting to be sprung. He can sense the bullets within the clip within the grip within his fist, all thirteen of them impatient to be chambered and released. Suddenly he is holding death in his hand. Suddenly he has power over the perpetrator, the ability to change him at a distance at the touch of a trigger, to transform him from intact human to bleeding, anonymous meat. It is frightening and thrilling. Thrilling because it is frightening, and frightening because it is thrilling.

He draws back the slide, lets it go – *ker-chunk* – and extends his arm. Arm and gun must become one. That is what he was taught. The gun must be an extension of himself, another body part. It comes back to him now even after all this time when the gun has just been a weight he has worn, an object that has hung beneath his left armpit and every so often butted against the Sphinx in his pocket as if to remind him it is still there. It comes back to him like a forgotten name to go with a remembered face. This is what he must be prepared to do if he is to retain his Iridium lifestyle. This is the ultimate price of his employment. This, a few kilograms of oiled steel, is duty.

His left hand rises to cup the bottom of the grip.

Barrel-tip sight covering target. Legs apart in a shooting stance. Aim to wound. Shoulder or thigh.

He calls out the statutory warning: 'Halt, or I am contractually obliged to shoot.'

The perpetrator slips around the corner.

Damn!

2.18 p.m.

Fuck! Fuck! Fuck! Fuck! Fuck!

The word chimes through Edgar's brain, a tocsin of terror.

Gun. Security. Security man with gun.

Fuck! Fuck! Fuck! Fuck! Fuck!

2.18 p.m.

Linda gives Gordon the carriage clock to hold while she delves into her handbag for their card. She hears someone nearby shout something, and a few seconds later sees a man with a trolley hurtling full-tilt towards her and Gordon.

The trolley whisks past them with millimetres to spare, and Linda, on Gordon's behalf as much as her own, says very loudly and pointedly, 'Well, excuse *me*.'

2.18 p.m.

Gordon is about to chip in with a wry comment to the effect that *someone* seems to be in a hurry, but then he catches sight of a second man coming towards them, a man brandishing a gun, and the words die on his lips.

2.18 p.m.

Frank thinks the bespectacled customer with the bandaged hand is going to step out of the way. He is running too fast to avoid him if he doesn't.

He doesn't. They collide. Frank's finger accidentally clenches around the trigger. The world is filled with the roar of the gun.

2.18 p.m.

A knitting needle punches a hole in Gordon's left eardrum. Burning pinpricks sparkle across the left side of his face.

His first thought is: *I've been shot in the head.*

His next thought is a logical extrapolation of the first: *I'm dead.*

2.18 p.m.

At the sound of the gunshot, everyone in the department flinches and ducks, except Edgar, who is too busy running for his life to hear.

Which is why, when he feels an impact in his back like a punch, just above his pelvis and to the side of his spine, he fails to realise what has hit him.

2.18 p.m.

In slow motion, as though someone has cranked down the speed of her life, Linda watches her husband sag to the floor. She watches Gordon's glasses slither down his nose, over his chin, on to his neck. She watches the cherub carriage clock slip from his limp fingers and tumble face first to the carpet.

He isn't dead. She knows that. The gun was pointing past him when it went off. He has collapsed, that's all. Shock. He's fine.

But then the man with the gun bends down beside Gordon and places the barrel against the side of his head. At the same time, inside Linda's handbag, something small, smooth and cylindrical rolls against her fingers.

She acts without further thought. Her hand closes around the pepper spray, and she levers off the cap with her thumbnail.

2.18 p.m.

The idiot! Standing there like a mannequin!

Using his gun hand, Frank feels the customer's neck. A faint but steady pulse. He'll be OK. His left ear will probably ring for a day or two, and the powder burns on his cheek will be sore but won't leave any permanent scarring. Bloody fool. But it was his own fault. He should have moved.

Frank is about to resume his pursuit of the perpetrator when he registers movement at the periphery of his vision. He fleetingly recalls seeing a woman standing next to the man. Now she is lunging at him, her lips twisted in a snarl. He realises, too late, that there is something in her hand. A perfume atomiser? A can of deodorant?

A fine white mist hisses from the nozzles, and his eyes are bathed in liquid fire.

He recoils, bringing his knuckles up to wipe away the scalding, viscous stuff, but that only succeeds in pushing it deeper into his eyes. Tears spring, and they feel like acid. His sinuses squirt a choking mucus into the back of his throat. Coughing and retching, he staggers backward into a display of mantel clocks. One of them tumbles off, striking him on the shoulder and rolling off to land on the floor with a crunch of breaking glass and a tinkle of loosened cogs.

What did she spray him with? His eyelids are swelling, closing, reducing his vision to a narrow slit of swimming opalescence. What was in that can?

2.18 p.m.
'What was in that can?' says Mr Bloom. 'And who is that woman?'

'No idea, sir,' says Hunt. 'Some customer.'

'Quick. Zoom in.'

'But the perpetrator . . . '

'Forget the perpetrator! Get a better visual on that woman *now*.'

The screen-jockey obediently tweaks his joystick and the woman looms large on the screen. She is readying herself to attack Frank again.

'Tell him to move!' barks Mr Bloom.

2.19 p.m.
The screen-jockey's voice, inside Frank's head, in the blinded, burning dark with him, yells out a warning. 'Mr Hubble! She's coming at you again!

'Security!' Frank splutters out. 'I'm with Tactical Security!'

2.19 p.m.
The words 'Tactical Security' mean little to Linda, coming as they do from a man who appeared to be trying to kill her husband. All the same

she hesitates, the pepper spray poised, her forefinger on the button. She knows she ought to give him another squirt for good measure. After all, he hasn't dropped his weapon. Something, though, prevents her. A thought. A suspicion.

The gun.

Who in Days carries a gun except . . . ?

Oh good God.

Oh good heavens above, what has she done?

Slowly Linda lowers the canister. She knows she ought to say something, but what do you say to a Security operative you have just erroneously spritzed in the face with an anti-personnel spray? 'Sorry!' hardly begins to cover it.

The Ghost is seized by a bout of violent sneezing. When the wet nasal explosions have run their course, Linda takes an oft-darned cotton handkerchief from her handbag and holds it out to him. Realising he can't see it, she guides his hand to it. He hesitates, then accepts the handkerchief and blows his nose.

'Better?'

'Acid?' he says hoarsely, circling a finger around his face, which resembles that of a bawling infant's – squinched, scarlet, and soaking wet. His puffed-up eyes are like two split plums, glazed with their own juices.

'Um, no. Extract of jalapeño peppers.'

'Small mercies.' He sneezes again.

Gordon, prone on the floor, lets out a groan.

'That's my husband.' Linda catches herself pointing at Gordon, realising the gesture is wasted. 'I thought you were going to kill him. That's why I . . . you know.' She coughs in embarrassment. 'Perhaps I should see how he is.'

'Good idea.'

Some sort of apology, she feels, is in order. 'I can't begin to –'

The Ghost isn't interested. 'Stay put. Somebody will be along shortly to arrest you. Obstruction of a Security operative in the course of his duty.'

Linda takes this information on board with a stoical nod and kneels to attend to her husband.

2.20 p.m.

Frank expectorates a wad of fiery phlegm into the handkerchief. Clearing his throat to activate his Eye-link feels like gargling with broken glass.

'Eye?'

'Mr Hubble, are you OK?'

'As well as anyone can be who's just had a face-full of pepper spray.' Frank dabs at his eyes with a dry corner of the handkerchief.

'She was carrying pepper spray on her?'

'I don't think she just found it lying around, Eye.'

'Well, don't you worry. We'll have another Ghost there in no time. Unless, of course, you feel up to collaring her yourself.'

'I've other fish to fry. Which way did the perpetrator go?'

'Um, afraid to say I lost him. Mr Bloom was more concerned about you.'

'Mr Bloom?'

'Yeah, he's right here. Want a word?'

'No time. Perhaps later. Right now I'm going after that perpetrator.'

'Leave him to us, Mr Hubble. We'll deal with him.'

'I'm not letting him get away. Which way did he go?'

'Well, last I saw, he was heading north. I'll get another Tactical operative on to it.'

'No,' says Frank, holstering his gun. 'I can catch him. This fellow has put me to a lot of trouble. It's only fair that I should be the one who nails him.'

'But you can't see where you're going. That stuff that woman sprayed you with . . .'

'I know this store like the back of my hand. I could find my way around it blind. But I'm not going to be blind. You're going to be my eyes, Eye.'

2.20 p.m.

Linda picks up Gordon's glasses, without which he always looks so puzzled and forlorn, so babyish, and gently settles them on the bridge of his nose, looping the arms around his ears. Then she inspects the cherub clock. Its glass cover is cracked in two, and its jolted movement has stopped, leaving its hands frozen at eighteen minutes past two. She heaves a sigh, for the clock and for herself.

The greatest day of her life.

Or it would have been, if . . .

If what? If Gordon had moved out of the Ghost's way? She can't blame him for that.

If she hadn't bought the pepper spray from the taxi driver? Possibly. But, even without it, she would still have attacked the Ghost. She honestly thought the man was about to put a bullet in her husband's head. What wife, in those circumstances, wouldn't leap to her husband's defence?

That is what she will tell whoever comes to arrest her, although she doubts it will do much good. The fact remains that she attacked a Days employee, and for that she and Gordon are going to lose their account. They are going to be banned from the premises for life . . . and yet for some reason Linda doesn't care. She doesn't care that she is going to have to explain to Margie and Pat and Bella why she and Gordon are never going to visit Days again (perhaps she will think up a lie to tell them, perhaps not). She doesn't care that she and Gordon may have to move to another street, another suburb, even another city, to get away from the knowing looks and the sly, insinuating comments of acquaintances and neighbours. None of that matters. All that matters is the man lying on the floor in front of her, the sandy-haired, baby-faced, bespectacled man who came to her rescue in Third World Musical Instruments, who appeared just when she needed him, and who, in turn, needed her protection and was given it.

Gordon groans again, stirring. His eyes flutter open. He blinks up at her. Focusing on her face, he braves a smile.

'Not dead then?' he croaks.

'Not yet,' Linda says. 'But when we get back home, I'm going to kill you.'

It takes him a moment or two to realise that she is joking.

37

Christ on the Cross: during the Crucifixion, Christ spoke seven times

2.24 p.m.
There is no pain.

At first, it is a simple statement of fact. Despite the tennis-ball sized exit cavity in his abdomen, all Edgar can feel down there is an awful, unnatural coldness, a freezing-burning sensation like ice. His breathing is constricted, but miracle of miracles, there is no pain.

There is no pain. And as he pushes the trolley from Clocks into Stationery, and from Stationery into Newspapers & Periodicals, and as the pins-and-needles coldness creeps upwards into his chest, Edgar tries not to think about the damage inside him, how much of him may have been ruined beyond repair. He tries to ignore the dark stain slicking over the waistband of his trousers down towards his crotch. Above all, he tries to ignore the hole, with its fringe of gore and shredded shirt, but it is hard to resist looking at it. That is *him*. That is *his* torn flesh. That bulge of something yellow-pink and glistening peeking out of the wound is one of *his* internal organs, which he was never supposed to see.

He is faintly aware of people ahead of him stepping aside, looking perplexed then horrified. He is faintly aware of gasps and little screams arising around him as he goes. But the main thing is that there is no pain.

And then suddenly there *is* pain, and Edgar staggers under the sheer stupefying *wrongness* of it. It feels as though someone has reached inside him and twisted his guts around their fist. His feet become tangled. He nearly falls, but recovers, saved by his grip on the trolley push-bar. Just one department to cross. One department between him and Books. A couple of hundred meters. He can make it.

There is no pain. Now it becomes a silent incantation, to be repeated by the mouth of the mind through gritted mental teeth. *There is no*

pain, there is no pain. And although there *is* pain – fearsome pain, sheets and sheets of it, sweeping through him like wind-gusted rain – the chant sees to it that there is no pain where it counts: in his head, in the brain that drives the body. For as long as his brain insists that there is no pain, his body will not succumb.

And there, up ahead, framed in the connecting passageway to Books – there she is. Waiting for him, her arms folded across her chest. Scanning this way, scanning that. Kurt and Oscar beside her. She knew which direction he could be coming from. Of course she did. She is Miss Dalloway.

Oscar spots him first, and points him out to the others.

there is no pain there is no pain there is no pain

And Edgar can already hear the compliments that Miss Dalloway is going to pour over him like honey.

there is no pain

And then he sees Oscar's jowls sag and his double chin become quadruple, and Oscar says something to Miss Dalloway, and Miss Dalloway's bony hands fly to her mouth.

thereisnopain

And Edgar is no longer breathing. He is hiccuping air in, in, in, but none of it seems to be reaching his lungs. He covers the last dozen metres through a vacuum, through silence, through weightlessness, his legs spasming in an autonomous approximation of running.

There is pain. There is all the agony in the world, and it is concentrated inside him, a vast, white-hot furnace in his belly.

'I made it,' he wants to tell Miss Dalloway, but there is too much pain.

His hands slip from the push-bar. His legs cycle through empty space. The carpet looms like a wall. Newspapers & Periodicals revolves around him, as though he has become the still centre of the turning universe. He is lying on the floor, staring up into striplights. Miss Dalloway is near. She takes hold of his hand, and her face appears above him haloed with light. She is by far the most beautiful thing he has ever seen. Her usually stern expression has melted into one of such sublime, supreme tenderness that he is convinced that she has been transfigured, that she has become a saint. No, not a saint. An angel. She looks how an angel must look to a soul in hell.

He hears the sound of every book he has ever read closing.

And then there really is no pain.

2.25 p.m.

Miss Dalloway lets Edgar's limp hand fall gently to the floor. With the tips of her thumb and index finger, she draws his eyelids down over his empty eyes. With the same index finger she touches his lips, as though to stop any recriminations he might have for her, even in death. Softly shaking her head, she gets to her feet, standing upright but a few sorrow-stooped centimetres short of her full height.

'Who did this?' Kurt spits out angrily. 'Was it the Technoids? Say the word and we'll get them, Miss Dalloway. We'll make them pay.'

'Have no fear, Kurt, the hour of vengeance *is* at hand,' Miss Dalloway replies, her voice as controlled as a laser beam. 'Now, quickly. Go and round up the others. Divide yourselves up into four teams and post one team at each entrance. No one is to enter the department, under any circumstances. Is that clear? No one.'

'Clear,' says Kurt. 'But what – '

'Just do as I tell you.'

Kurt turns and hurries back into the department.

'What *is* going on, Miss Dalloway?' Oscar asks, looking down in trembling-lipped disbelief at Edgar's body.

'The end, Oscar. The bitter end.'

Miss Dalloway strides over to where the trolley coasted to a halt, propelled by Edgar's dying fall, a metre inside the connecting passageway. She inventories the contents quickly. Wire and clock, present and correct. Thou good and faithful servant.

A sob clutches her throat. She forces it down with a hard swallow, takes hold of the trolley push-bar, and orders Oscar to follow her.

2.25 p.m.

Hands held out in front of him at chest height to fend off against obstacles, Frank lurches through Stationery, looking like a mime pretending to be drunk, or a drunkard attempting mime.

The department, to his inflamed, streaming eyes, is a kaleidoscope of distorted shapes and smeary colours. It is hard to tell what is near and what is far, what is sharp-edged and what is soft, what is living and what is inanimate. The Eye helps out with a constant running commentary, alternately coaxing and warning – 'A row of filing cabinets to your left, that's it, a customer a few metres ahead, there, that's good, a ninety-degree turn to the right coming up, you're doing good, Mr Hubble, you're doing fine ... ' – but none the less the pursuit of the perpetrator has become a tortuous succession of stops and starts, bumps and knocks, angles and trajectories, corners and rebounds. At one point the screen-jockey refers to Frank as a human pinball in the world's largest pinball machine, and even Frank cannot be annoyed by the flippancy, because that is exactly how it feels.

Still he perseveres, still he staggers on, with every banged elbow, every barked shin, his determination to catch his quarry increasing.

2.28 p.m.

Her movements urgent yet precise, hurried yet efficient, Miss Dalloway finishes assembling the bomb. Cutting off four lengths of wire from the spool, she strips a centimetre of the insulating rubber from the end of each with her teeth, then uses two of the lengths to join the contacts of the flashbulb to the stem of one of the alarm clock's bells and to the striking hammer. Holding the detonator by these wires, she lowers it into the mouth of the keg until the Roman candle is just above the fertiliser-and-paraffin mixture, firing end pointing downwards. Then she screws the cap of the keg back on so that the wires secure the detonator in place.

The alarm clock is fully wound up and telling the correct time. Miss Dalloway is pleased to note that the Clocks Department's dedication to temporal accuracy remains undiminished. It is nearly half-past two now. A quarter of an hour should do it. She rotates the alarm-setting control until the alarm hand is pointing to the third of the three increments between II and III. Then she tapes the clock tightly to the top of the keg, on its back so that the alarm-setting control cannot be readjusted. The clock ticks softly and steadily.

Now she takes the remaining two lengths of wire and uses them to link the battery to the striking hammer and the bell stem.

The bomb is primed. The final minutes of her life are numbered.

'Oscar?'

Oscar comes to attention. 'Miss Dalloway?'

Unable to resist the urge to hug him, she wraps her arms around his shoulders. Startled at first, Oscar quickly succumbs to the unwarranted gesture of affection, and reciprocates, slipping his good arm around his head of department's narrow waist. She presses his fleshy cheek to the sharp ridge of her collarbone. Oscar breathes in the cool, fresh-laundered smell of her jumper.

'Oh, Oscar,' Miss Dalloway says. 'You've always been my favourite. You know that, don't you?'

Oscar shudders with delight from head to toe.

'And I've always hoped it'll be you who takes over the reins when the time comes for me to step down.'

Oscar thinks he is about to faint with joy.

'Will you do that for me, Oscar? Will you look after my department? Make sure the brothers never try to close it down? Resist them to your last breath?'

Oscar can barely choke out his assent. 'Of course, Miss Dalloway. Of course.'

'I knew I could count on you.'

He tries to raise his head to ask a question, but she simply presses him harder to her chest and starts stroking his hair. If he looks into her eyes, he may realise what her real intentions are. He may try to stop her, talk her out of it.

'I've put in a memo to the brothers exonerating you from all involvement in what I'm about to do, and recommending you as my replacement,' she says. 'Whether those philistines pay attention is anyone's guess, but hope springs eternal.'

'I'll do the very best I can, Miss Dalloway. I'll do you proud. But of course, you'll always be just a phone-call away, should I need advice. I mean, I can never hope to manage everything by myself, not without your help. I won't know where to start.'

Miss Dalloway closes her eyes. No tears. She vowed to herself. No tears.

'You will, Oscar,' she says. 'You will.'

2.31 p.m.

'OK, you're nearly there. It's, I'd say, twenty metres ahead. You should be able to see it.'

Peering out through his swollen eyelids, Frank can just about make out the rectangular opening of the connecting passageway that joins Newspapers & Periodicals to Books, and through it, rows of bookcases. He can also see, in front of the connecting passageway, a small crowd – bloblike bodies on spindly legs, human-shaped silhouettes merging and overlapping. They are gathered around what seems to be a pile of rags but as Frank comes closer the pile of rags glimmers into focus and he sees that it is a supine body, and as he comes closer still he recognises, by the clothing more than anything, the perpetrator. He can discern a wound in the young man's stomach, a dark comet whose tail streaks the front of his shirt and trousers. Frank knows a bullet wound when he sees one.

'That's him, isn't it? says the screen-jockey. 'That's the one we've been chasing.'

'That's him,' Frank confirms.

'Then you must have . . . .'

'Yes.'

It was, Frank supposes, inevitable, although he had hoped that his policy of using his gun only as a last resort would permanently postpone the day. The irony is, another couple of hours and he would have got through a thirty-three-year career without taking a life. Obviously it was not to be, and there is nothing to be gained by dwelling on might-haves and if-onlys.

More to the point, the gun fired when Frank collided with the customer in Clocks, so the perpetrator's death can hardly be considered his fault. He is sorry that the young man is dead. He is sorry that anyone has to die violently. But there you go. Perhaps he ought to feel more than a mild sense of regret, and perhaps he will, later, but right now he is simply relieved that the chase is over.

'Mr Hubble?' says the Eye. 'Mr Bloom says to tell you, "Well done."'

'Tell Mr Bloom that I$^3/_8$ still haven't changed my mind.'

'About what?'

'He'll know what I mean.'

The screen-jockey relays the comment. 'He says there's still two and a half hours to go till closing time.'

Frank had a feeling the answer would be something like that. 'Well, we'll see.' He takes out the handkerchief the woman gave him and has another dab at his face. The excruciating burn of the pepper spray is beginning to subside, to be replaced by an unpleasant but more tolerable itching. He blinks around. The world is foggy and speckled, but getting clearer. 'Eye, I'm going to check the fellow's ID. In the meantime, you have a look for that trolley.'

Frank approaches the body, slipping through a gap in the crowd of onlookers. Kneeling down, he takes out his Sphinx and scans its infra-red eye over the perpetrataor's ID-badge barcode. Barely noticing him, the crowd continues to whisper and coo over the corpse.

A message appears on the Sphinx's screen:

WORKING . . .

Then a picture appears of a young man with a huge forehead that bulges beneath a crop of wavy black hair and overshadows a pair of sunken, mournful eyes – eyes that seem to have known long in advance of the brutal, miserable fate awaiting their owner.

Even with his vision blurred, Frank can tell that the living face on the screen matches the dead face in front of him. He hits a key, and the Sphinx lists the employee's name (Edgar Davenport, as on the badge), number, account status (Silver, and in good order), and the name of the department in which he works.

Frank frowns at the screen, then glances up at the connecting passageway leading to Books, his frown deepening. 'Eye? Do you happen to know if one of the brothers came down to sort out the Books/Computers dispute this morning?'

'I've no idea. I'll ask Mr Bloom.'

A brief conversation ensues off-mic with Mr Bloom, and then the screen-jockey comes back with the reply. 'He says the arbitration went ahead. One of the guards detailed to escort Master Sonny told him that Master Sonny said that the Computers Department should keep the extra floorspace. And he says why do you ask?'

'The perpetrator's a Bookworm.'

'You think there's a connection?'

'I'm not sure,' says Frank, switching off and pocketing his Sphinx.

Frank knows how notoriously militant the head of Books, Rebecca Dalloway, is and he knows too that it is almost entirely her fault that the territorial dispute between her department and Computers has dragged on so long and been so acrimonious. Surely, then, it is more than a coincidence that, on the same day that the dispute is resolved (and not in the Books Department's favour), a Bookworm goes shopping with someone else's card. And it is hard to believe that a

Bookworm would do something like that if his head of department had not instructed him to. A Bookworm doesn't sneeze without seeking Miss Dalloway's permission first.

`'Eye? Run a sweep of Books. I'm betting that the trolley's in there somewhere.'`

2.35 p.m.

Hunt calls up feeds from the security cameras in the Books Department. One by one the images appear on successive screens: unfrequented alleyways of bookshelves, large tables slabbed with books, the sales counters.

Mr Bloom peers at the screens. Everything appears to be normal, except . . . 'The sales counters. No one's staffing the sales counters. Where are they all?'

'There. Look.' Hunt points to a screen showing one of the entrances to the department, just inside which a group of Bookworms are loitering. 'And there.' Another entrance, and another group of Bookworms, all of them carrying thick hardbacks.

'What are they all standing there for?'

'Beats me. They look like they're waiting for someone.'

As Hunt and Mr Bloom watch, a customer arrives. The Bookworms gather round him, words are exchanged, and the customer, with a puzzled and somewhat irritable gesture, about-faces and walks out again.

'They're turning people away,' says Mr Bloom, running a hand over the top of his scalp as though temporarily forgetting that, apart from his foretuft, there is no hair up there. 'Why the hell are they turning people away?'

'Sir?' Hunt points at the screen showing the huge, crescent-shaped stack of books around Miss Dalloway's desk. 'Activity.'

From behind the stack of books a figure has emerged. The long, bony physique is unmistakably that of Miss Dalloway, and in front of her she is pushing a trolley in which sits a squat grey cylindrical object.

'What's that?' says Mr Bloom. 'Get a close-up of that.'

Hunt's fingers are already at work. The image on the screen expands, blurs, comes into focus again. He toggles the trolley into shot, keeping it there by means of delicate taps on the joystick.

'Some kind of barrel?' he suggests.

'Yes, but what's that on top of it?'

'Looks to me like a clock.'

'Coming out of it – are those wires?'

'Maybe strings.'

'No, see the way they hang? Definitely wires.'

Hunt looks at Mr Bloom, Mr Bloom looks at Hunt, each seeing on the other's face the same expression of disbelief that he knows must be on his own.

'It can't be,' says Hunt, in stilled, chilled tones. 'It just fucking can't be.'

'Guards,' says Mr Bloom urgently. 'Get guards there, *now*.'

'But all the guards in the vicinity are at the maul.'

'Then call them up from Orange and down from Green. Do it! And tell Mr Hubble to stay out of Books.'

2.36 p.m.

'Mr Hubble.' The screen-jockey sounds anxious, agitated. 'Mr Hubble, listen. She's built a bomb.'

'What? Who's built a bomb?'

'What's-her-name. The head of Books. I'm not shitting you. Mr Bloom says you've got to stay out of there.'

'You're absolutely certain it's a bomb?'

'Well, it sure as hell looks how a bomb ought to look.'

'And where is she?'

'Heading due east.'

Of course, thinks Frank. *Computers*.

'Mr Hubble? Guards are on their way.'

'They won't get here in time.'

Frank sets off for the connecting passageway to Books.

2.36 p.m.

'He wouldn't listen, sir,' says Hunt. 'He's going in.'

'Tell him not to. Tell him I order him not to.'

'He has a point, though, sir. Guards aren't going to get there for at least another five minutes. If anyone's in a position to stop her, it's him.'

Mr Bloom can see the sense in that. He sighs a sigh of resignation and slaps his hands against his thighs. 'Yes, all right.'

'Sir, something else. Shouldn't we let the brothers know what's going on?'

'Yes,' says Mr Bloom. 'Yes, you're right, we should. Send them a priority e-memo.' He looks up again at the screens and murmurs softly to himself. 'Frank, you bloody idiot. Be careful.'

2.37 p.m.

The first book comes hurtling past Frank's left ear, flapping like a panicked duck. Another follows almost immediately, and also misses him, but a third hits him squarely just below his breast pocket. He hears a glassy crunch and guesses that his Sphinx, which took the brunt of the impact, has been broken.

He reaches into his jacket and draws his gun. The green LED is still alight, the safety still off.

'Tactical Security. I don't want to have to hurt anyone.'

There is a pause. Then someone shouts, 'She said everyone, lads, so she meant *everyone*,' and books start flying at Frank from all sides.

Shielding his face, he wades into the barrage. He glimpses, through the hail of printed matter, Bookworms ducking behind shelves and darting between bookcases. No clear shot. Salvoes of books – novels and memoirs, collections of essays and short stories, biographies and autobiographies, self-help manuals and scientific treatises – rain down on him, their pages riffling and clattering. A spiral-bound children's puzzle compendium glances off his hand. All three parts of a grandiose sword and sorcery trilogy smite his body, one after another in quick succession, like blows from a dull axe. An epic family saga spanning several generations strikes him in the thigh, just missing a more vulnerable region. Slim volumes of verse buzz through the air at him, their narrow edges packing a fierce sting.

'Mr Hubble! Behind you!'

Frank whirls around to find a figure lunging at him, swinging the L-M volume of an encyclopaedia. He fires reflexively, without aiming. The shot punches the book out of the Bookworm's grasp and sends it sailing away, trailing flecks of charred paper from a singed bullet-hole, to land on the floor with a loud clop. The shocked Bookworm stares at his empty hands. Frank's eyesight still hasn't cleared enough for him to be sure of a wounding shot, so he simply lowers his head and charges the Bookworm. Shoulder butts chin, and the Bookworm goes down.

'Left, Mr Hubble! To your left!'

The warning from the Eye comes a fraction too late this time. As Frank turns, a *Complete Works of Shakespeare* crunches into his arm, filling it with numbing, vibrating pain from biceps to fingertip. He fires at the Bookworm, aiming deliberately high. The Bookworm drops the Shakespeare and scurries for cover.

A dictionary spirals out of nowhere to slam into the back of Frank's skull. His teeth clack down on his tongue, and he tastes blood.

That's it. The next Bookworm who attacks him can expect a bullet wherever it goes. If shooting these buggers is the only way to get them off his back, so be it.

He doesn't see the bookcase behind him swaying and tottering until it is too late. Spilling the contents of its shelves in a great regurgitative rush, the bookcase falls, knocking him flat and burying him beneath several hundred kilograms of wood and woodpulp.

The toppled bookcase settles, a last few loose books slip and slither to the floor, and all is still.

38

The Case of the Seven Bishops: seven bishops who protested against King James II's Declaration of Indulgence

2.39 p.m.
Perch leaves his pantry office and heads through the clatter of the kitchen, out and along the corridor to the Boardroom.

He judges his arrival perfectly, with an instinct born of decades of service. Just as he enters by the Boardroom's double doors, the last morsels of a long lunch are being scraped up, knives are being set down on empty plates, glasses and coffee cups drained.

Throughout the meal much laughter has been issuing from the Boardroom, echoing down the corridor to the kitchen, and the atmosphere as Perch comes in is markedly relaxed and convivial. The brothers have treated themselves to a couple of bottles of fine wine to accompany their veal escalope with potatoes au gratin and steamed mange-touts followed by champagne mousse and a selection of cheeses and biscuits, but wine alone cannot account for the merriment. Perch suspects that the real reason is the absence of Master Sonny. There is always less tension in the Boardroom when he is not around.

As Perch covers the distance between the doors and the table, another peal of laughter springs from six sibling throats. Perch is neither so self-conscious nor so naive as to think that he is the object of the brothers' amusement.

'I trust the meal was acceptable?' he enquires as he gathers up the first of the empty cheese plates, Mungo's.

'More than acceptable, Perch,' says Chas.

'I don't suppose there's any more of that champagne mousse, is there?' asks Wensley.

The enquiry is greeted by barracking hoots and pig-like grunts from his brothers.

'My blood-sugar level's low,' Wensley protests.

'Alas, Master Wensley, your third helping entirely depleted our stocks,' says Perch with an exaggerated archness which is calculated to evoke further chortles and jeers from Wensley's brothers, and which succeeds.

'Hey, Perch,' says Fred. 'We were just discussing something. Perhaps you could help us.'

'I shall endeavour to assist in any way I can,' replies Perch, adding Thurston's empty plate to the stack balanced expertly on the spread fingertips of his left hand.

'Do you think it's true what they say about absolute power?'

'Corrupting absolutely?'

'That's it.'

'I cannot for the life of me imagine what could have precipitated such a discussion among the sons of Septimus Day.'

'Let's just say it's an occupational hazard. Here you go.' Fred sets his plate on top of the stack. 'Well? Do you have an opinion?'

'It isn't really my place to have opinions, sir, and those I do hold it is not my place to air.'

Genial cries of, 'Come off it!' and 'Nonsense!' are showered down on him.

'Very well then,' says Perch, coming to a halt between Fred and Sato. 'I shall offer my opinion, but *only* because it was solicited. Power, sirs, is open to abuse if it is not subject to a system of checks and balances, as when, for instance, it is wielded by a dictator who can use oppression to silence those who raise their voices against him and force to eliminate those who would attempt to overthrow him. But does this mean that power *per se* is a corrupting influence? Surely the corruption exists already within the dictator; the flaw is already there, and power merely exacerbates it. Power of one person over another is created out of mankind's willing need for guidance and rule. It would not exist were there not a demand for it, therefore we must assume that it is a good thing, a necessary thing, beneficial to all as long as those in authority remain answerable to those they have authority over. To draw an example from my immediate experience: you, sirs, might be said to have absolute power over this store and every customer and employee in it – and that is some considerable responsibility, given a gigastore's importance to the economy and prestige of the nation it serves. But in order for your decisions to be beneficial to yourselves, they must also be beneficial to everyone under you. To put it at its crudest, any unwise policy you implement will lose you custom, therefore it is in your best interests to ensure that your policies are wise. Which, I hasten to add, they invariably are. In this sense, the absolute power you wield, far from corrupting you, encourages you to aspire to the highest nobility in thought and deed. In short, absolute power makes absolute sense.' He gives a small bow to indicate that he is done.

'Bravo!' exclaims Fred. 'Good man!' He leads a warm round of applause, which lasts for as long as it takes Perch to gather up Sato's plate and proceed solemnly and unsmilingly around the table to Sonny's place, where an untouched main course sits, cooled and congealed.

'Am I to take it that Master Sonny will not be joining us?'

A furtive look passes between Mungo and Chas, which Perch pretends not to have noticed. The other brothers appear oblivious, perhaps busy mulling over Perch's sagacious and not uncomplimentary words.

'It's still possible,' says Mungo. 'When Chas and I left him downstairs, he seemed open to the idea of some kind of solid sustenance for lunch.'

'No doubt he was referring to ice cubes,' quips Fred.

'I could have his meal reheated and take it down to him,' Perch offers.

Another brief meeting of Mungo's and Chas's gazes. Perch is quick to perceive that some kind of deception is going on.

'He seemed quite set on having lunch with us,' says Chas. 'Something's delayed him, obviously.'

'Best leave it here,' Mungo tells Perch.

'Very good, sir.'

Perch has no sooner left the Boardroom than the terminal by Thurston's elbow gives a long, loud beep.

'Priority e-memo,' says Thurston. He removes his spectacles, huffs on the lenses, polishes them with his jacket sleeve, and returns them to the bridge of his nose, then hits a couple of keys.

'Who's it from?' Sato asks.

'The Eye.' Thurston starts to read the message appearing on his screen.

His brothers look on, silent and curious. Chas catches Mungo's eye and mouths the word 'Sonny?' Mungo shakes his head fractionally: the e-memo can't possibly have anything to do with Sonny's trip downstairs.

'Shit,' says Thurston. He rests his thin wrists against the sides of the keyboard.

'Is that a good news "shit" or a bad news "shit"?' Fred asks. 'They sound pretty much alike.'

Thurston does not answer or take his gaze off the monitor. His eyes flick from left to right, rereading.

'It's a bad news "shit",' Fred confirms. 'Shit.'

39

2.41 p.m.

Miss Dalloway, with her trolley, pulls up beside the central sales counter in Computers, a huge square slab of black plastic perched on dozens of spidery steel legs in imitation of a microchip.

'Well, look who we have here,' says Mr Armitage. If he is at all surprised to see Miss Dalloway in his department, he doesn't show it. 'Come to apologise, have we? Declare a truce?'

'I come not to send peace, but a sword.'

'Is that not a keg of beer I see?' Mr Armitage leans over the edge of the sales counter to peer into the trolley. 'A keg of beer would seem to *me* to be a peace offering.'

The word 'beer' gets the attention of every Technoid within earshot. They cluster around the trolley, rubbing their polyester sleeves gleefully until they crackle with static.

'Not beer,' says Miss Dalloway, as, with some difficulty, she clambers into the trolley and squats down facing the push-bar, with her legs straddling the keg. 'Rather, I have here journey's end. The poor man's nearest friend. This fell sergeant. The cure of all diseases.'

'I'm sorry?' Something about the gleam in her eye puts Mr Armitage on his guard.

'Death, Mr Armitage. Pale Death, the grand physician. Pontifical Death, that doth the crevasse bridge/To the steep and trifid God. Death, a necessary end.'

Miss Dalloway slips her arms around the keg, hugging it tight – a mother bird incubating a lethal metal egg.

2.41 p.m.

'Mr Hubble? Mr Hubble? *Mr Hubble?*' Hunt turns to Mr Bloom, batting aside his headset mic. 'It's no use, sir. Either his Eye-link's busted, or he's out cold, or – '

'There is no third option,' Mr Bloom states firmly. 'Where are those guards?'

Hunt checks his chair-arm monitor. 'On their way. The first of them should be arriving in Computers in a couple of minutes, lifts permitting.' He catches a neighbouring screen-jockey peeking over his shoulder, and sees him off with a snarled, 'Nothing better to do, dickwit?'

The other screen-jockey hurriedly returns his attention to his own screens, but the tension in Hunt's corner has radiated out into the rest of the chamber. Something serious is going on upstairs, and everyone in the room is keeping a watchful eye on their colleague and the head of Tactical Security.

'Come on, Frank,' Mr Bloom mutters. 'Be all right. Please be all right.'

2.42 p.m.

The rubble of books stirs. An arm appears.

Bracing his elbow against the canted bookcase, Frank wriggles out from underneath. He hauls himself up on to all fours. He stands unsteadily, his legs sluggishly remembering how they work. He swivels his head from side to side in order to uncrick his neck, then tenderly rubs his chin, which, when the bookcase fell on him, struck the floor, temporarily stunning him. He clears his throat to activate his Eye-link, but does not hear the click of connection in his ear. He tries again, but it is obvious that the Eye-link's delicate circuitry has been knocked out of commission.

A quick glance in front and behind shows Bookworms at either end of the aisle. They are surprised to find him standing, but overcome their confusion quickly enough, and arm themselves for a new assault by plucking books from shelves.

Wearily Frank reaches for his gun, only to find his holster empty. Of course. He was holding the gun when the Bookworms tipped the bookcase over on to him. It is buried somewhere beneath the pile of books, but there is no time to go rooting around for it. The fallen bookcase has left a gap leading through to the next aisle. The Bookworms are closing in on him, thumping books into their open palms menacingly. Frank takes a step to the side, and leaps over the bookcase and through the gap. He jogs along the parallel aisle towards the connecting passageway that joins Books to Computers, hearing footfalls and shouts behind him as the Bookworms give chase.

There are Bookworms clustered around the exit, but they are all peering intently into Computers and don't hear him approach until he is almost upon them. He pushes past them easily, and is soon deep into Computers, heading for the main sales counter, the heart of the department.

And there, sure enough, he finds the trolley, and sitting in it a figure he recognises, even through the haze that veils his vision, as Rebecca Dalloway.

Miss Dalloway is addressing Roland Armitage and the assembled Technoids, delivering some kind of speech. It appears from the casual postures of those around her that no one else knows what the keg contains. Then she finishes speaking and hunches over the keg, and suddenly everyone is backing away.

2.43 p.m.
Those who have ears to hear, let them hear,' Miss Dalloway intones. 'I am become death, the destroyer of worlds. I am the enemy you killed. The foe of tyrants. Look on my works, ye Mighty, and despair!'

There might be more to her speech, but at that moment Frank shoulders past two desperately backpedalling Technoids, seizes the trolley push-bar, and starts to shove.

'No!' shrieks Miss Dalloway.

Frank scarcely hears her. He is scarcely aware of anything except the pounding of his heartbeat in his ears. He is not thinking. Were he thinking, he would not be doing what he is doing. His head, as he steers the trolley in the direction of the Yellow Floor hoop, is not filled with notions of heroism or sacrifice, only with the urge to get the bomb as far away from people as possible. This, to him, seems an objective necessity rather than an act of suicidal bravery.

Spitting and screeching in fury, Miss Dalloway hauls herself over the keg and launches herself at Frank, fingers outstretched, clawed for throttling. Frank jerks his head back. Her nails scrape his neck, her left hand catching the wire of his Eye-link. The Eye-link pops out of his ear and detaches itself from his collar, and Miss Dalloway collapses back into the trolley, clutching a coiling tangle of surgical pink wire and electronic hardware.

The sound of the trolley's wheels changes from a clatter to a clack, marking the transition from carpet to marble. They are out of Computers, out on the hoop. Frank avoids a pot plant and skirts around a group of startled customers. Miss Dalloway tosses the Eye-link aside and stretches over the keg again, groping for the push-bar. Her face is contorted, riven with vertical lines. She rakes her nails across the backs of Frank's hands, ploughing ragged furrows in his skin. When Frank fails to let go as expected, she resorts to trying to pry his fingers free from the push-bar, but his fingers seem glued in place.

The rim of the hoop hoves into view. Frank slews the trolley around, slamming it sideways against the parapet. Miss Dalloway is thrown on to one hip, off-balance. Frank takes advantage of her momentary incapacity and leans over the push-bar, intending to pick up the keg and toss it over the parapet into the Menagerie. It is then that he catches sight of the clock with its straggling wires.

He makes a grab for one of the wires in order to wrench it loose, but Miss Dalloway anticipates the move and, seizing the keg, stands up, hoisting the bomb aloft out of Frank's reach. However, as she does so, the trolley skids sideways and overbalances, and she is tipped backside-first on to the parapet.

Teetering there with her face stretched in an almost comical look of alarm, she clutches the bomb with one arm while her other arm flails out for something to hold on to. Frank's lapel is the first thing that comes to hand, and she seizes it just as she topples and begins to fall.

Unable to brace himself in time, Frank is yanked head-first over the parapet after her.

The Menagerie yawns below him, a lake of lush green. Though he feels a sudden wrench of pain in his elbow and shoulder, it takes him a moment to realise why he and Miss Dalloway are not falling. His arm has hooked itself over the guardrail. Ape-reflex. But the purchase is far from secure, and Miss Dalloway is still clinging to him, and still hugging the bomb.

Seams pop in his jacket. He lashes out at the keg with his foot, hoping either to kick it out of Miss Dalloway's grasp or, failing that, at least dislodge one of the wires. He has no idea how many seconds the clock has left to run.

Then Miss Dalloway's grip on his lapel starts to slip, and for a brief instant her eyes meet his, and he sees in their iron depths how profoundly she feels she has been betrayed, by Days and by life. And then, dimly through his misted vision, he watches her slip away from him and fall.

Still cradling the bomb, she hits the monofilament net, and the net rips like silk to let her through.

She hits the gridwork of pipes, and they buckle and snap beneath her, spurting tropical-warm water.

She hits the jungle canopy, and the leaves seem to absorb her into their moist green intricacy, sucking her out of view.

Frank dangles there for several seconds, staring at the rift in the Menagerie's seal, half expecting plants and animals to come surging out like the contents of a pressurised canister when its casing is cracked. Then, suddenly remembering where he is and what is about to happen, he frantically twists around, bringing his other hand up to grab the guardrail.

His hand never makes it. There is a faint trilling sound from far below, and then his body is borne up on a cushion of air. For a moment the laws of gravity are rescinded. He floats suspended in space, the great dome of Days filling his fogged vision. He thinks he could sail up towards that gleaming hemisphere of black and clear glass, rising like a saved soul towards its eternal, time-telling sameness, for ever.

Then he begins to descend, plunging backwards into heat and flame.

40

The Book of Revelation: the *Apocalypse* of St John the Divine offers a plethora of sevens – seven churches of Asia, seven golden candlesticks, seven stars, seven trumpets, seven spirits before the throne of God (one of them holding a scroll with seven seals), seven vials, seven plagues, a seven-headed monster, and a Lamb with seven horns and seven eyes

2.45 p.m.
Deep in its joists, deep in the lath and plaster of its walls, deep in its very foundations, Days groans.

The basso-profundo *whump* of the blast travels through the store, the shockwave rippling out around the hoops and through every department to the farthest-flung Peripheries. As it reaches the edges of the building it sends a shiver of particles puffing out from the pitted surface of the dried-blood brickwork and sets the window displays' huge panes shaking in their frames, alarming the window-shoppers and the living mannequins. For one brief instant, the living mannequins look directly at their audience, acknowledging their existence for perhaps the first time ever, sharing their fright. For one brief instant, performers and spectators are made equal.

On every floor, display cabinets rattle, merchandise shudders on shelves and in several instances topples over or off, and people let out involuntary gasps and cries.

In the Eye, static zigzags across screens, and a fall of fine grey powder sifts down from the ceiling. In the Boardroom screens also flicker, the ash and ebony table jumps on the spot, and Old Man Day's portrait skews a couple of degrees from true.

The echoes of the explosion reverberate boomingly along aisles and passageways and lift shafts, through all the hollow spaces of Days, like a disturbance in the bowels of some ailing leviathan.

Even Gordon, despite the ringing in his left ear, hears it. He and Linda look at each other, and then at the Ghost who has been assigned to take them down to Processing. She is as startled as they are, and can offer them no explanation.

And Sonny, on his marshmallow sofa, is rudely awakened by what he thinks is a clap of thunder. He hauls himself upright on the sofa with an irritable sigh and focuses his bloodshot gaze on the bright, clear, anything-but-stormy skies beyond the windows.

Slowly the anomaly sinks in.

2.46 p.m.

Up in the Boardroom, Thurston and Mungo stand facing each other, their bodies angled like opposing beams in a vaulted ceiling, their chins jutting, their teeth clenched, their knuckles pressed to the surface of the table, their noses less than a centimetre apart. The slightest of the sons of Septimus Day is dwarfed by the well-developed physique of the largest, but Thurston is far from cowed. His limbs are rigid with rage, the tendons in his neck strain, and his nostrils flare and contract with his rapid breathing. Mungo looks down at him, fiercely intractable, like a stern god confronted by a rebellious worshipper.

'Accuse me all you like,' he says to his younger brother, 'but I have no idea what he did downstairs.'

'What he did downstairs doesn't matter,' Thurston replies, each word like a hand-grenade going off inside a reinforced-steel safe. 'What matters is that *you* talked us into sending him down there.'

'You do yourself and our brothers a disservice. Each of us has the intelligence to make up his own mind. I talked no one into anything. Besides, there's no proof that anything Sonny said or did downstairs led directly to this.' He gestures to the two sets of screens by the Boardroom door, which show two different views of the Menagerie. In both, smoke is filtering up from a section of the tree canopy, filtering through the net and twisting and turning lazily into the atrium.

'Oh, it's a little bit too much of a coincidence, isn't it? Sonny goes down to arbitrate between Books and Computers, and next thing we know the head of Books tries to blow up Computers, and very nearly succeeds. Call me unimaginative, but I can't help but think the two events are connected. Or perhaps you can come up with a better explanation.'

'It would seem to me – and would to you, were you thinking clearly – that the Dalloway woman has had this act of terrorism planned for a long time, and was simply waiting for an excuse to put her scheme into action.'

'An excuse Sonny provided.'

'We don't know that yet.'

'I don't *need* to know that. I can feel it. I can feel it in my bones. In my blood. Only Sonny could screw things up on such a monumental scale.'

'I agree. But the benefit of the doubt –'

'Fuck the benefit of the doubt!' Thurston cries, flecking Mungo's face with stray spittle.

Mungo wipes the spittle off with the back of his hand. He would be angry with Thurston if Thurston were not right. What makes it worse is that Thurston knows he is right, and knows that Mungo knows it, too. Neither of them, though, is willing to be the first to back down.

'Come on,' says Wensley. 'Look on the positive side. According to the Eye, nothing's been damaged except the Menagerie, and no one's been hurt except a couple of employees. We're safe, we're alive –'

'As usual, Wensley, you're missing the point,' Thurston snaps, not taking his eyes off Mungo. 'I don't care about the Menagerie and I don't care about the employees. Those are problems money can fix. Money cannot fix our imbecile of a brother.'

'I trust that that isn't a reference to me.'

In through the Boardroom doors comes Sonny, hands filling out the pockets of his trousers.

He saunters across to the table, offering his brothers a bleary but affectionate grin. For the first time in as long as he can remember, he doesn't feel as though he is walking into enemy territory. He is one of them now. He is their equal.

Which is why he fails to understand the looks that greet his arrival. He has become used to a certain amount of resentment whenever he enters the Boardroom. Outright hostility – much of it originating from Thurston – he is not familiar with.

'Sonny,' says Mungo.

'Mungo?'

'I wasn't expecting to see you here.' Mungo's tone is wary and significant.

'Well, here I am,' says Sonny. His recollection of events between

303

coming up from the shop floor and falling asleep on the sofa is hazy. He vaguely recalls being shouted at by Mungo and then bursting into tears, but the reason for either event is lost in alcoholic amnesia. Mungo's warning to stay clear of the Boardroom for the rest of the day he has entirely forgotten. 'Did anybody else hear that noise just now? Like thunder or something?'

One by one his brothers nod.

'Any ideas what it was?'

'That's an interesting outfit you're wearing, Sonny,' Thurston says.

'This?' Sonny glances down at his suit, which is rumpled from having been slept in. 'Smart, huh?' He pats the golden Days logo embroidered on the breast pocket. 'I thought it would impress them downstairs.'

'Jesus . . . ' says Fred, half to himself.

'And the arbitration, Sonny?' says Thurston. 'How did that go? I must admit, I was surprised you didn't come back up here straight away to report.'

'It went fine.'

'You told the heads of department what you were supposed to tell them?'

'Yes. I mean, I think so. Sort of. No, I did. Yes.'

'You don't sound very certain.' Thurston's spectacles glint dully in the dimmed light. The dark side of the dome now nearly fills all three of the Boardroom windows.

'Well, there was a lot going on. They were both talking so much, I . . .' It was a neat idea. Why be ashamed of it? 'I flipped my card to decide. You know, like at university.'

There is a sixfold intake of breath.

'You flipped your card,' Thurston repeats coldly.

Sonny, all of a sudden feeling like a suspect on trial, fixes his gaze straight ahead. 'I wanted to be fair.'

'And don't tell me – your card fell in favour of the Computers Department.'

'That was the result you wanted, wasn't it?'

'My God,' says Wensley, 'what was he thinking?'

'What was he *drinking*?' says Fred.

'I don't understand.' Sonny's new-found confidence is starting to crumble, and his voice along with it. 'What did I do wrong? All right, so I didn't follow your instructions to the letter, but you sent me down to sort out the dispute, and I sorted it out.'

'And if the card had fallen the other way?' says Thurston.

'But it didn't.'

'But if it had?'

Sonny looks for Mungo, knowing his big brother will back him up, but while Thurston has been interrogating him Mungo has moved out of his eyeline. He turns around to find that Mungo has gone stealthily over to the knife switch, has quietly plucked the ceramic handle of the knife switch from its clips, and is now standing with the handle in his hands, brandishing it like a huge cosh.

All of a sudden Sonny is very afraid.

Mungo wouldn't. Not his own brother. Not his own flesh-and-blood.

So Sonny tells himself, but in the deepening gloom of the Board-room it is difficult to make out what Mungo's intentions are, what is in his eyes.

'Sonny, it was so simple,' says Mungo huskily, apologetically. 'All you had to do was stay in your apartment.'

Sonny shakes his head, wanting to beg Mungo to put the handle back on the wall, but unable to find the words.

'This way is better for all of us,' says Mungo. 'I can't go on protecting you any more. I can't go on helping you if you won't help yourself.'

Tears spill from Sonny's eyes, bright in the unnatural twilight but he makes no move to defend himself or get out of the way as Mungo comes at him, swinging the handle like a baseball bat.

The handle connects with Sonny's cranium with a crack like a log splitting in two. He reels backwards, blood blurting from his nose. Staggering into the table, he just manages to prevent himself collaps-ing to the floor.

Mungo draws back the handle and swings it again, this time striking Sonny on the jaw.

Sonny slams back flat on to the tabletop, moaning and clasping his chin. His eyes seek out Mungo, staring, blank with incomprehension. Mungo stares back, panting hard.

Chas appears by Mungo's side, holding out his hands. Mungo hesitates, then meekly surrenders the handle to him, expecting that to be the end of it.

But something has been unleashed in the Boardroom, something that has been bubbling beneath the brothers' lives of polite formality, homegrown ritual and quiet paranoia for far too long. Something wild. Something dangerous.

'Hold him down, somebody,' says Chas, and Fred and Sato take up position either side of Sonny and, with the grim efficiency of old-time doctors in the days before the invention of anaesthesia, grab his wrists and pin them to the tabletop with their knees. Sonny searches Fred's and Sato's faces frantically, twisting his head from side to side in the hopes of finding pity or mercy, but there is none. His brothers have come to the conclusion that payment for the trials and tribulations he has brought upon them is finally due, in full. Sonny protests, but his words fall on deaf ears. Chas raises the handle and brings it whistling down on to his sternum.

Although the impact is a savage one, Sonny's ribcage holds. At the next blow, however, a rib gives, snapping like dry bamboo. He bucks and writhes, howling in grinding agony too immense for words.

Chas passes the handle to Wensley.

With three swift strikes, Wensley shatters Sonny's jaw, smashes his nose into a lump of crushed cartilage, and ruptures several internal organs with a blow to the abdomen. Then he passes the handle to Thurston.

By the time Thurston has finished with it, the handle's thick end is coated with blood, hair and fragments of teeth, bone and skin.

Then it is Fred's turn. Then it is Sato's. Sonny no longer has to be held down. The switch handle rises and falls, rises and falls, becoming bloodier and yet bloodier with each blow.

The brothers go about the slaughter with precise, businesslike detachment, handing over the murder weapon in strict rotation after each has taken a few swings with it. Soon they have reduced their flesh-and-blood to flesh and blood.

The Boardroom resounds to the thudding wet impacts of the handle against Sonny's body, and for once the old man's good eye appears to be glittering with something other than disdain.

41

7.0: the pH value of a neutral solution, one which is neither acidic nor alkaline, i.e. pure water

2.51 p.m.

Liquid sounds: the babble of distant voices, the trickle of running water.

Liquid warmth: sweat-pricking heat, the slow drift of humid air.

Chilly dampness down his back and down the backs of his legs.

Softness clenched between his fingers – spongy, fibrous and cool.

Water spattering intermittently into his face.

The faint smell of smoke.

And then – eyelids prised apart – vision. The undersides of palm fronds. Varying thicknesses of green shadow. A tunnel hollowing down through the leaves directly above him, ragged-edged, lit with shafts of hazy yellow light and draped with lianas and dazzling chains of water drops. His path of descent. The net, then the irrigation pipes, and finally the trees broke his fall. Branch by branch the trees delivered him to the ground, slapping his back lustily like midwives.

Myriad aches and sore spots all over him, too many to distinguish one from another. His body one huge dull throb of pain. Whether to get up or not isn't so much a question of being unable to as being scared to. What if he tries to move and can't? The loamy floor of the Menagerie is snug and comfortable. He feels welded to the spot. He could happily lie here all day, half buried in the soil, hidden amongst the undergrowth.

Could. Won't. The Menagerie is not the safest of places. *Here there be tygers.* And God knows what other items of livestock waiting to be collected by their purchasers.

Frank steels himself. Courage. Courage.

He tries to raise his right arm.

It won't budge.

Christ. Paralysed. Christ, no.

Then, with a mighty sucking squelch, the arm springs free of the ground.

He brings his hand up to his face and rotates it on its wrist, articulating the individual fingers. His palm and the underside of his sleeve are caked in moss, soil and dead-leaf mulch.

He levers up his head.

At low level, he can see ferns, grasses and bamboos, their intricate linkings weaving a dense wall of green. Higher up, epiphyte-studded trunks. Higher still, mingling foliage.

Again he smells burning, but around him he can see nothing black or charred or dead. Everything is green and lush and living. He must have fallen some way from the explosion, carried out from the edge of the hoop by its updraught.

It is an effort to stand. The ground does not want to let go. It clings to him like a mother to her child and, even when he has discharged himself from its embrace, still lays claim to him with the weight of earth, plant matter and moisture coating his back.

Frank looks himself over. He has been divided into two halves, one clean, the other filthy. Viewed from the front, he would appear normal; from behind, a muck-encrusted mess. Where he landed there is a body-shaped impression in the ground, lined with flattened plants. Pour in plaster of Paris, let it set, and you would prise out a rough half-statue of a spreadeagled man.

He checks his limbs. All working, some with more complaint than others. He checks his eyes. Everything is haloed with a pale, peach-skin furriness, but his focus sharpens if he moistens his corneas with a few blinks.

He glances around. Which way is out?

If he was on the shop floor proper, he would know without hesitation, but the Menagerie is unknown turf. (*Here there be tygers.*) This is the one part of the store he hasn't tramped through thousand upon thousand of times. Every footprint he leaves here will be a first.

Think.

There are two gates allowing access into the Menagerie from the Basement, one to the north, the other to the south. All he has to do is head for the perimeter wall, follow it around, and he will reach one or the other eventually. Of course, he could simply stay put until a team of Menagerie staff locate him. He has no doubt that they are coming.

Mr Bloom will have alerted them. But with nearly two square kilometres of jungle for them to search, that may take some time. Getting out will be safer if he waits for them, but making for one of the entrances by himself will be quicker.

Walking, the skill which has been so indispensible to his career, has to be learned all over again. He is hampered by snaking ground vines and ankle-snaring weeds; the slippery underlayer of moss and the unevenness of the ground. Each step has to be planned, carefully considered, before it can be executed.

The smell of burning grows stronger, and he discerns wisps of smoke trailing through the air towards him. From somewhere ahead comes the crackle of flames. From overhead, the jabber of customers on all six hoops massing their voices in a chorus of opinions and concerns, and a distant wail of fire alarms. What he cannot hear are birdsong and the rustling of hidden creatures. The bomb has shocked all of the Menagerie's denizens, even the insects, into silence.

As the smoke thickens, tingeing the air grey, Frank comes across trees that are seared on one side. The ground turns ashy. Flecks of soot swarm around him like gnats. Soon he is walking among charred and tattered foliage which hangs from singed branches like torn black lace, although higher up the trees are intact and the canopy is still green and tightly intertwined. Feeble flames lick along ground-shoots, shrub-tendrils and the leaves and petals of orchids, flickering fitfully before petering out – everything here too wet, too full of juices, to burn well. His footsteps crackle as his soles tramp down singed-brittle stems. He accidentally kicks over the furless, flash-fried body of a small mammal. Its blistered flesh gives off a not unappetising aroma of cooked meat.

The smoke becomes chokingly thick, and he decides to turn back, but not before glimpsing the epicentre of the detonation. The trees there are blasted but still standing. The crevices in their scorched bark glow orange, and their passenger epiphytes have been reduced to shrivelled black lumps. But they are still standing. The Menagerie was big enough to absorb the fury of the explosion, and damp enough to snuff out its fire.

Frank retreats from the ghostly, fuming ground zero, heading back into the emerald depths of the unharmed jungle.

Unaware that he has been spotted and is being followed.

2.54 p.m.

It could hardly be called walking. It is more like a cross between a stagger and a lurch – in terms of effort to result, disproportionately strenuous. But still she drives herself on. One foot drags, one arm dangles uselessly by her side. Her body is partially encased in a carapace of melted clothing, burnt hair clings to her scalp in gobbets like tar, and her skin hangs in crisp strips that loop her limbs and sometimes snag and tear and fall away when she bumps against something. Slivers of steel from the beer keg protrude from her flesh. Bone can be seen where bone should not be visible. One eye – her right eye, the one that was not baked to a cinder in its socket by the blast – shines balefully. She hurts beyond hurting. She should not be alive. But she is.

And as she shambles after the Security operative who thwarted her plans, Miss Dalloway stoops and, with the blackened claw that is her functioning hand, picks up a rock.

She knows she is dying. Dashing his brains out will be her final gesture of vengeance and defiance.

2.55 p.m.

Frank loosens his tie. Its silk has begun to wrinkle in the humidity. He undoes the top button of his shirt. Then he undoes the next one down. What the hell. Go crazy. There isn't much point in trying to pass himself off as a smart, well-heeled Days customer in the heart of a replica jungle.

He tries to put out of his mind all thoughts of large, untamed creatures roaming noiselessly among the trees or lurking in the undergrowth, observing him, but with so many shadows around it is hard not to imagine predatory eyes peering out, tracking his movements with calm animal intelligence. There is no way he can blend in here or belong. Even half covered in organic muck, he sticks out like the proverbial sore thumb.

He wishes he hadn't lost his gun. Whether or not he would be quick enough with it to kill an attacking animal, simply having it in his hand would make him feel safer.

Chances are he will make it to one of the gates unscathed. Chances are the animals are more scared of him than he is of them.

An inhuman screech directly behind him halts him in his tracks.

2.56 p.m.

Miss Dalloway understands, at some primal, lightless level far below the surface of conscious thought, that she cannot hope to creep up on her target by stealth. Her only chance is speed and the element of surprise.

Summoning up every last erg of energy left in her body, she makes her final charge. Sheer stubborn perversity coaxes her dragging leg to function properly and lends her the strength to lift the rock above her head. The very air itself seems to be trying to hold her back, like an invisible hand, but she wills herself on, accelerating from a stumble to a run.

Even if her eardrums had not been blown by the explosion, she would not recognise the warcry that issues from her throat as a sound created by her own vocal cords.

2.56 p.m.

Some kind of ape? A bear on its hind legs?

That is all Frank can think as the scarecrow-like tatterdemalion creature comes rushing at him through the trees, howling, its one eye shining with a terrible inner illumination. It does not occur to him that this shaggy, screeching, upright beast could possibly be human.

The rock in its paw begins its arc of descent. There is no time for defensive or evasive action.

Then something slams into the ape-bear creature, knocking it sideways, sending the rock flying out of its grasp. Frank has an impression of muscularity, pale fur, vertical black stripes . . .

The tigress.

The ape-bear is pushed to the ground, supine. It flails at the tigress as she sets her forepaws on its chest to hold it down. It gropes frantically at her pelt for some kind of purchase as she lowers her head and clamps her jaws around its neck, and it continues to resist even after she has torn out its throat with a single sideways toss of her huge white head. Gargling horribly, the ape-bear fights on like a machine that has been shut down but continues to run on momentum alone, its stuttering, spastic efforts growing feebler as the tigress chews further chunks out of it.

It is only when the ape-bear ceases struggling that Frank spots, affixed to its chest, a warped, blistered rectangle of plastic still just about recognisable as an ID badge, and realises what (or rather who) the ape-bear is (or rather was).

That is when he turns away. However, though he can avert his eyes to shut out the sight of the tigress savaging Miss Dalloway, he cannot shut out the sounds of human flesh being consumed. They are sounds that will haunt him for ever.

They cease, eventually. Sated, the tigress turns away from her eviscerated kill.

Frank hears the sound of her paws delicately crushing the undergrowth, coming closer, and he holds himself perfectly still, closes his eyes and longs for congruity. If only he knew how to camouflage himself among trees and vines as well as he does among displays and merchandise. If only he could somehow tune himself out of the tigress's perceptions by immersing himself in the jungle equivalent of the everyman ordinariness which makes shoplifters overlook him so easily. But he cannot. Here, he is the suspicious character, the tigress the Ghost.

The tigress halts in front of him, and extends her blood-pinkened muzzle forwards to sniff. She runs her nose over his right hand, up his sleeve to the elbow and down again, down one leg of his trousers and up again to his crotch. The air moves in and out of her nostrils with an audible hiss. Her musk is earthy, urinary, potent.

Frank wants nothing in the world so much as to run, but he orders himself to stay still, not to move.

The tigress peers up at his face with her azure eyes and makes a noise deep in her throat, like a growl, only softer.

So faint is this noise that Frank will never be sure if he imagined it or not. However, just as he will always remember the sounds of the tigress eating Miss Dalloway, so he will always remember that low, subtle rumble. And he will always wonder if it really was, as he thinks at the time, a purr.

Fur brushes briefly, lightly against the fingertips of his right hand – a brittle tickling – and he parts his eyelids a crack, and there the tigress is, loping away from him with her tail slung low, past the mauled corpse of the head of the Books Department, heading deep into the viridian gloom of the Menagerie, gradually merging her paleness into its darkness, slipping her stripes in among its fretted shadows, becoming a spectral grey tiger-shape, and then becoming a part of the jungle and no shape at all.

3.12 p.m.

Some time later, Frank finds himself sitting on a rock by a stream in a clearing, very possibly the same clearing in which he caught sight of the tigress this morning. Above the membrane of the net, the tiers of the atrium rise, narrowing to the dome. Faces fringe the parapets, many of them peering down at him. The fire alarms have been silenced. Anywhere else, a total evacuation of the premises would be under way, but not at Days. What, and lose a couple of hours of valuable retailing?

A squad of Menagerie staff are crashing through the jungle towards him. He can hear them shouting to one another. Clad in their chain-mesh suits and armed with their tranquilliser rifles, they will escort him out to safety.

The stream burbles over its bed of pebbles in a long, shallow, sinuous curve, here and there bubbles beading and breaking spontaneously on its smooth surface. The irrigation pipes hiss a mist that drizzles down on to Frank's head, plastering his hair into flat, matted rat-tails. Nature has tapped her baton, and the Menagerie's birds have tentatively begun to sing again; the insects have picked up their instruments once more and are starting to play.

In his hand he is holding his broken Sphinx, angled towards his face. He is gazing hard into the cracked glass of its screen. Gazing in delight and mild wonderment.

The Menagerie staff are coming.

He will be out of here soon.

42

> **Seven-day Fever**: an acute infectious disease caused by a spirochaete transmitted by ticks or lice, and characterised by recurrent attacks separated by periods of remission lasting approximately seven days; also known as relapsing fever

4.30 p.m.
The processing itself was not so bad. The dour little Scotsman who officiated was terse but not rude. Unlike many whose jobs bring them into close contact with human failings on a daily basis, he had not entirely lost his respect for his fellow men. He remained essentially civil, and for that Linda was grateful. It was a small shred of comfort; she had not entirely been stripped of her dignity.

In the cramped booth, with the Trivetts seated opposite him and their attendant guard to one side of his desk, the processor listened as Linda recounted her version of the incident with the Ghost in Clocks. She put as sympathetic a slant as possible on what she had done, but under questioning could not deny either that she had smuggled the pepper spray on to the premises or that she had assaulted an employee. Not knowing at the time that he was an employee was no excuse. Nor did it help that her offence had been observed and recorded by the Eye. The Eye did not lie. Morrison (for that was the processor's name) showed Linda the clip of her squirting the Ghost in the face. There it was in smudgy black and white. Incontrovertible.

Spinning the monitor back round, Morrison then told Linda that, in the light of the evidence against her, he had no alternative but to suspend the Trivetts' account permanently and banish them from Days for life. Both of them. Linda because of her misdemeanour, and Gordon because he was co-signatory of their account, and so guilty by association.

Even though she had been expecting this, the words fell on Linda's ears like a funeral knell. Gordon's left ear was still ringing so sonorously that he had to ask the processor to repeat himself several times until he got the gist. He seemed none too upset.

Morrison asked Linda to hand over their card, and used it to call up their account details. With a few brief keystrokes he transferred sufficient funds from their joint bank account to pay off the debt they had run up. There would, he said, be an additional sum to be paid once the cost of the damage done in Third World Musical Instruments had been established. Since the total was going to be divided equally among the four hundred or so participants in the shopping maul, the Trivetts' portion would be well within their financial limitations, although still not inconsiderable.

The unkindest cut came when Morrison gave Linda back their Silver, along with a pair of blunt-nosed safety scissors.

'We prefer our customers to perform this task themselves,' he said.

She almost burst into tears while cutting the card in half. Almost, but not quite.

After that, there was nothing for her and Gordon to do but go out and sit on one of the benches in the main room and wait to be escorted off the premises, and here they have remained for the past hour, accompanied by the guard, a sullen, uncommunicative presence beside them. This is the really humiliating part, sitting here among the criminals and the opportunist fools, although of course Linda does not think that she and Gordon belong in either of those categories. Linda would like to believe that she and Gordon belong to a third distinct group, that of hapless unfortunates.

At last another guard calls their names. Their guard takes them out of Processing and down a narrow corridor, at the end of which lies a short flight of concrete steps. At the top of the steps there is an unprepossessing metal door, secured by a number of locks and bolts. Unlocked, unbolted, the door scrapes inwards to reveal another short flight of steps heading off at right angles.

'Out you go,' says the guard, holding the door open, and out Linda and Gordon go. The door clangs shut behind them.

They are outside. The steps lead up to Days Plaza. Wind buffets them as they ascend to street level, in full view of dozens of window-shoppers. Linda braces herself for jeers and catcalls, but the window-shoppers obviously do not consider the sight of exiled customers coming up nervously into the daylight either a particularly novel one or, indeed, more interesting than the events going on inside their favourite window, although one man, noticing them, is prompted to smile and say, 'Welcome to the club.'

Linda's cheeks flush furiously. She strides off, Gordon in tow.

Taxis are parked in the turning circle outside the nearest entrance, waiting for the closing-time crowd. Linda approaches the first in line, checking before she climbs in that the driver is not the same one who ferried her and Gordon here. That would be too much. The final straw. An embarrassment too far. Although, thinking about it, she wouldn't mind having a few words with that particular taxi driver about the pepper spray he conned her into buying . . .

The driver of this taxi reluctantly agrees to accept cash. 'Reached your limit, have you?' he says.

Linda, ignoring the remark completely, gives him their address, then slides the privacy window between the front and rear seats shut.

'So that's that then,' says Gordon loudly, as the taxi pulls away from the world's first and (emphatically, resoundingly, deafeningly *not*) foremost gigastore.

'It was fun,' Linda replies, nodding. 'For a while.' She longs to take a backward glance but she can't. She mustn't.

'Pardon?'

'I said, it was . . . Oh, never mind. How's your poor ear?'

'Pardon?'

'I said – '

'I heard you that time. I was just joking.'

She punches him gently in the ribs.

'So we've learned our lesson, have we?' he says, reaching along the back of the seat and tentatively placing a hand on Linda's shoulder. When she doesn't shrug it off, as she has been known to in the past, he slowly begins to massage the shoulder, proceeding to the back of her neck. She submits gratefully. 'Never again, eh?'

'Never again,' she says. 'Although,' she adds, 'there is always the EuroMart.'

Gordon stops massaging. 'Linda . . . '

She talks quickly. Best plant the seed as early as possible. 'Once we've paid off what we owe Days, it won't take long to build up enough credit again to apply for an account there. Think about it. We could go on day-trips to Brussels. They do discount fares. Package holidays. We could stay in a cheap hotel . . . '

'*Linda* . . . '

She smiles at him, a little sadly. 'Just a dream, Gordon. Just a dream.'

'Well, as long as that's all it remains.' He resumes massaging.

But as the plan slowly evolves in her mind, Linda thinks that yes, it will be possible. It will take time, but eventually she should be able to talk Gordon round. Patience and perseverance are her strong suits. She will win him over. It may take another five years, it may take even longer, but so what? In the end it will be worth it.

And this time she isn't going to settle for a Silver. When they qualify for an account at the EuroMart, Linda Trivett is going to accept nothing less than a Gold.

43

Libra: the seventh sign of the Zodiac, represented by a pair of scales

5.00 p.m.

Closing time was anounced a quarter of an hour ago, and again five minutes ago, and with the third and final anouncement, at five o'clock exactly, those customers who haven't yet started making for the exits begin to do so. They descend in the hallway lifts to the seven levels of car park and disperse to their vehicles, or file peaceably out of the four entrances with their ballast of carrier bags, emerging into a world tinted saffron by the setting sun. Stragglers, hoping to make one last purchase before they leave, are hustled out of the departments and shepherded towards the exits by guards.

Sales assistants reckon up the day's sales and transmit the totals up to the Boardroom. In the produce departments food is covered or, if likely to rot or go stale overnight, binned.

The heavy velvet curtains are drawn over the window displays, bringing to a close the real-time soap operas. The window-shoppers, glutted on vicarious consumerism, sigh and smile in mild dismay, and gather up their belongings. Those who have homes to go to, go, while those who have made the base of the building their home settle down for the night.

Staff put on their overcoats and make their way down to their cars or out to the train stations and the bus stops. It would, in every respect, have been a typical day, but for the explosion mid-afternoon, which set off a wave of excitement that has yet to die down completely. Employees, like customers, are still exchanging stories about their experiences – where they were, what they were doing, when the bomb went off. Rumours, naturally, abound. The one that holds most currency is that terrorists were responsible. Certain other rumours concerning the Books Department have been widely discounted. Several people know someone who knows someone in Computers who swears that Security has rounded up all the Bookworms and arrested them – but that sounds like just the sort of thing a Technoid would say. It has been mentioned by more than one source that the head of the Books Department was the one who detonated the bomb, and that she was killed in the explosion. But a Days employee trying to blow up the store? Surely not!

All the rumours, factual and fanciful, are duly passed on by the employees coming off-shift to the night watchmen and janitorial staff coming on-shift. The consternation felt in the immediate aftermath of the bomb has, through the mysterious alchemical processes of time, been transmuted into exhilaration. In retrospect, it was quite exciting, really, to have been inside the store during a real live terrorist attack. The night-shift employees are left in no doubt that they have missed out on something thrilling and rare.

A repair crew is brought in, on overtime rates, to mend the Menagerie net. Butterflies and birds are escaping through the rifts caused by the two falling employees, and though the repair crew set to work quickly, Menagerie staff will be busy tracking down and recapturing rogue merchandise for the next week or so.

The lights dim all over the empty store.

5.22 p.m.
Frank closes the door to his locker and picks up the carrier bag containing his mud-caked clothes and shoes. He is dressed in an exact replica of his original outfit, correct down to the cushion-soled brogues and the maroon silk tie. With his hair dried and combed, he looks freshly pressed, new-minted.

He casts his eye around the locker room, not expecting to feel nostalgia and, as expected, not feeling any. But then this isn't necessarily going to be the last time he stands here, gazing on these two rows of unremarkable steel doors with their padlocks and vents.

He turns and walks out into the corridor, where Mr Bloom is waiting for him.

'Everying OK?' Mr Bloom asks. 'The clothes, I mean. They fit all right?'

'They're fine. Thank you for getting them. You will, of course, transfer the cost to my account.'

'I will do no such thing.'

'I insist.'

'Frank, after what you've been through today – '

'Please, Donald.' There is an edge of resentment in Frank's voice. 'I don't want to owe anyone anything.'

'You'll always owe Days.' Mr Bloom sugars the remark with a laugh.

'I think I've paid off that debt,' Frank replies, absentmindedly itching at the parallel rows of fish-scale scratches on the backs of his hands, left there by Miss Dalloway's fingernails.

They walk side by side towards the staff lift, Mr Bloom slowing his pace to match Frank's stiff, awkward gait. Several times Mr Bloom looks as if he is on the point of asking something.

Frank finally saves him the trouble. 'No, I don't know yet about leaving. I'm still thinking about it.'

'That's an improvement, at least. At lunchtime, you were dead set.'

'Don't go looking for significance in my words that isn't there, Donald. All I'm saying is that something has happened, something that . . . Well, I can't really explain it.'

They reach the lift.

'For what it's worth, Frank,' said Mr Bloom, pressing the up button, 'I've put in a recommendation to the brothers to allow you to retire on full pension, no penalties, if you so desire. In fact, I was hoping to have received an answer from them before you left, but obviously they've a lot else to deal with. The insurance company, for one. Still, after what you did for them today, they can hardly refuse. That's how things stand, at any rate. You can stay on, or, if the brothers agree, you can retire with all debts discharged and no strings attached.'

The lift arrives.

'So, what's it going to be?'

Frank steps through the open doors, and turns around, setting the bag of soiled clothing at his feet.

He looks at the only man in the world he might possibly consider a friend.

'Donald,' he says, 'I don't know. I honestly don't know.'

The doors shut.

5.31 p.m.

He steps out into the evening. The darkening air smells sweet, which is surprising considering he is downwind from several hundred unwashed window-shoppers. The sweetness, perhaps, is not in his nose but in his mind, the air smelling that way simply because it is not the air inside Days. It is air that belongs to the whole of the rest of the planet, and the sweet smell is freedom and limitless possibility.

There are reporters at the foot of the steps, and they are interviewing employees as they leave. Some outside broadcast vans are parked in the turning circle; more are arriving. Arc lights probe, cameras jut, boom microphones intrude, as the bombing incident yields to the surgery of telejournalism.

Bidding goodnight to the guards, Frank sets off down the steps. He notes the woman standing at the foot of the steps but, taking her to be one of the reporters, walks straight past her.

'Deliberately ignoring me, Mr Hubble?' says a polite, familiar voice.

Frank stops. Turns.

Mrs Shukhov takes two tentative steps towards him.

'The guard told me you're a creature of habit,' she continues, smiling. 'Always arrives and leaves by the north-western entrance, she said.'

'You,' Frank says slowly, 'have put me to a great deal of trouble.'

She can't interpret his tone. Anger? Or sly mockery? His face offers no clues. 'Well, I apologise if – '

'No. It wasn't your fault. You couldn't have known.' The corners of Frank's mouth give an almost imperceptible twitch.

'Are you teasing me, Mr Hubble?'

'I have no idea. Am I?'

Mrs Shukhov sighs. 'Why do men always have to make things so awkward?'

A thought occurs to Frank. 'Mrs Shukhov, you weren't by any chance waiting for me, were you?'

'A glimmer of intelligence! There's hope for you yet, Mr Hubble.' She takes another two steps towards him. He remains where he is, a stranger to the patterns of this verbal and physical dance. 'I was wondering if you might like to go for a cup of coffee with me,' she says. He frowns. 'If that's all right,' she adds hastily. 'I mean, if I've overstepped the mark, say so. If there's some rule you people have about fraternising with disgraced customers, or if you just don't want to, I'll understand.'

'Let me get this straight. You'd like me to go for a cup of coffee with you?'

'Or something stronger, if you'd prefer.'

'No, coffee would be . . . would be all right.'

'Is that a yes?'

'It isn't a no.'

Mrs Shukhov rolls her eyes. 'Honestly! I'm sure if I looked up "obtuse" in a dictionary, the definition would be just one word: men.'

5.53 p.m.

At the edge of Days Plaza, Frank and Mrs Shukhov cross the road, which is clogged with commuter traffic. The dusk has reached that stage when half the vehicles have their headlights on and half do not. The moon, in half-phase, glimmers in the purple sky, its left side dark, its right mottled ivory. Looking up at it, Frank thinks, *No, Days does not own the night. At least, not yet.*

Up a narrow street on the opposite side of the road he and Mrs Shukhov find a café, with plastic tables and chairs in front taking up most of its allotment of pavement, overlooking a litter-choked gutter. Inside, the café is about quarter full, and a pleasant but not especially enthusiastic waitress invites the two new patrons to choose where they want to sit. Mrs Shukhov selects a booth, and she and Frank slide in on opposite sides of the table and make themselves comfortable on the padded bench-seats.

Frank looks around him at the framed, faded posters of continental beach resorts and foreign landmarks, at the potted plant straggling up a fan-shaped trellis by the door to the kitchen, at the other diners chatting or solitarily inspecting evening newspapers. It would be a lie to say he is not nervous. He hasn't been inside a public café since his early twenties.

'So,' says Mrs Shukhov, resting her elbows on the table.

'So,' says Frank, his mind turning over. Conversation. 'So,' he says again. Then: 'Your eyes. Your eyes aren't as red as when I last saw them. Saw *you*.'

Mrs Shukhov feels encouraged that he is at least looking in the right region. 'That guard – Gould was her name? – Gould went up and bought me a contact lens case, some cleaning solution, and even a bottle of eye drops. At her own expense. What with that and you standing up for me in Processing . . . well, I'm wondering what I could have done to deserve such kindness.'

'So you can see all right?'

'Can't see a thing,' she replies, laughing. 'My lenses are in my handbag. I'm surprised you didn't notice me squinting and peering all the way over here.'

'I'm having a little eye trouble myself at the moment.' The pepper spray's residual itch is still unpleasant. His eyeballs feel sandpapery in their sockets.

'They do look somewhat pink. Perhaps you'd like to use my eye drops.'

'Perhaps.'

'Did you know that, except for our eyes, everything we show to the world is dead?' says Mrs Shukhov. 'Our skin, hair, nails, even the insides of our mouths – we sheathe ourselves in a casing of dead tissue in order to protect our flesh and inner organs from the ravages of oxygen, and the only living parts of ourselves we show one another are the irises of our eyes, seen through our corneas. That's why eye-contact is important, both between strangers and between friends, because that way we can demonstrate to each other the truth of ourselves, the life rather than the death.'

'Interesting.'

'Isn't it? I read that in some scientific journal in Newspapers & Periodicals yesterday.'

'It's good to know you didn't completely waste your time.'

'Mr Hubble,' says Mrs Shukhov, shaking her head, 'I wish you'd hold up a flag or wink or *something* when you're being ironic. Humour as dry as yours is hard to detect.'

'I'm sorry.'

'No, don't be. I like it. I was simply remarking.'

'Actually,' Frank says, rising, 'if you don't mind, Mrs Shukhov, I *would* like to take you up on that offer of eye drops.'

'Of course.' Mrs Shukhov roots around in her handbag and produces a small, conical plastic bottle with the Days logo prominent on its label. 'And please – call me Carmen.'

Frank takes the bottle and heads for the cloakrooms.

The gents cloakroom smells strongly of industrial bleach and pine air freshener, and less strongly of urine. Frank bolts the door and approaches the basin warily. He lowers his head as if in supplication, and leaning on the basin, peers slowly up into the speckled, tarnished mirror.

There is his reflection, just as it was in the cracked glass of his Sphinx's screen. Immediately appearing, without having to be willed into existence. Solid, stable and staring back at him – a reversed Frank in a reversed café cloakroom, large as life, there, inarguably, indubitably *there*.

He looks at himself from the side. He looks at himself down his nose. He looks at himself from up under his eyebrows.

He doesn't want to ask how this miracle has happened, because to question it would risk destroying it, like a boy bursting a soap bubble in his eagerness to capture it. But he knows it has something to do with the white tigress.

The white tigress neither overlooked him nor spurned him. With her sniffing inspection and the elusive purr that followed, she *accepted* him.

She accepted him into the restless green commerce of the Menagerie. She said, in effect, 'Here, and in the forests where I came from, things come and go. Predator preys on prey. Herbivore feeds on plant, carnivore feeds on herbivore. That is how it is. Everything is useful to something else. Dead plant matter, living creatures – everything has its purpose and its place. Everything grows to be destroyed so that something else may grow again. The natural order is an eternal to and fro, a give and take, a buy and sell. And you have known this. All along, though you may not have realised it, you have known this.'

Miss Dalloway tried to kill him. The tigress killed Miss Dalloway.

Give and take. To and fro.

And the tigress accepted him. Understood him. Comprehended him.

And he realises that congruity is not, as he has believed, a curse. He remembers the tigress's camouflage, how she blended into her surroundings, but still remained powerful, potent, lethally efficient. Congruity is a question of fitting in to exactly the right degree, not too much, just enough. Being a part but also apart. There is a balance to be struck, a line to be walked between two extremes, a thin grey area, a narrow shadow of overlap. Over thirty-three years he forgot where it is and how to find it, that's all.

He squeezes a couple of the drops into each eye, and the lingering irritation of the pepper spray is relieved.

With one last glance at himself in the mirror, Frank leaves the cloakroom.

Mrs Shukhov has taken the liberty of ordering coffee for both of them. Two full cups sit steaming on the table. Frank finds himself searching for something that isn't there. He quickly realises what it is. A Days logo. There are no Days logos on the cups and saucers.

He sits and takes a grateful sip. It may not have been made using the finest beans money can buy, but it is still the best coffee he has ever tasted.

Conversations ripple around the café. The street outside is growing dusky. The streetlamps come on, shedding a hard orange light. You can feel it: the city drawing in on itself like a closing flower.

Opposite him Mrs Shukhov – Carmen, her name is Carmen – holds herself erect. Good posture. Handsome features. She is waiting for him to speak. Wanting him to speak.

He thinks he will tell her about his day. It has, even by Days standards, been a hellish one. He thinks he will tell her about the lengths he had to go to in order to keep his promise to recover her Platinum, about his pursuit of the Bookworm, and the bomb. Who knows? Somewhere along the way, using his dry humour, he may even be able to amuse her.

Tomorrow, things may change or things may stay the same. Tomorrow, he may fly off to America or he may simply turn up for work as usual. For now, there is this evening, and a woman who is intrigued by him, who wants to fathom him. Tomorrow, when it comes, will take care of itself.

And Days will always be there.

The thought is strangely comforting.

Days – constant, immutable, enduring, too huge and solid to change – will always be there.

44

Shiva: in orthodox Judaism, the period of seven days of mourning for a parent, spouse, brother or sister

6.00 p.m.
Six o'clock!

Perch leaps to his feet. He was so busy preparing tomorrow's menu and compiling a list of groceries to be bought that he completely lost track of time.

He hastens out of his office. The kitchen is empty and clean. The brothers prefer to cook their evening meals for themselves in their apartments and eat them on their own, a necessary antidote of solitude after spending the entire day in one another's company. Thus the catering staff have, as usual, tidied up and gone home.

Normally by six the only brother left in the Boardroom is he whose day of chairmanship it is, working late to fulfil his duty of collating the sales figures and passing on the total to a press agency which will then disseminate it to the media. Perch intends to ask Master Thurston for the full story about the explosion earlier. A news item on the radio an hour ago mentioned that reports were coming in about an incident at Days. No details had been confirmed as yet, the newscaster said, but she promised to keep the public informed as the story developed. Rather than wait for the media to grope their way slowly to the truth, Perch will get it straight from a Day brother himself – one of the small perks of being intimate with the owners of the first and (what else would he say?) foremost gigastore.

Perch is surprised to find all the brothers present in the Boardroom when he enters but, of course, he hides his surprise masterfully.

The brothers are seated around the table in their respective chairs. The dark side of the dome fills the three windows from corner to corner, from edge to edge, a solid wall of blackness, and the brothers have not switched on the ceiling lights. Perch can barely make out their faces. He can see their eyes, though. All of them turn to stare at him as he comes in, except Master Sonny, who is slumped in his mock throne and seems to be asleep.

Master Sonny still here, too? Extraordinary.

None of the brothers speaks as Perch approaches the table. Their eyes follow him, glimmering in the gloom, but none of them addresses him, which is strange. Strange, too, is the smell that grows in Perch's nostrils as he nears the table, a tangy, clean, metallic odour that is desperately familiar, although he cannot quite place it.

He notes some dark stains on the ash half of the tabletop, like spattered oil. He noticed similar stains on the switch handle as he came in, but dismissed this as an illusion caused by his eyes not being accustomed to the gloom. The stains on the table are definitely there, though, and there are further stains on the carpet nearby. Perch tuts mentally. He will be on his hands and knees till midnight scrubbing *those* out.

He halts a metre away from the edge of the table, Mungo to his left, Sonny to his right.

'I came to see if that will be all, sirs.'

The silence holds for a while, until finally Mungo says, 'Since you ask, Perch, I think we would all like something to eat. Nothing fancy. Could you possibly rustle us up a snack?' His voice seems to be coming from somewhere deep down inside him, faint and hollow as though issuing from the bottom of a well.

'A snack? Certainly, sir. I think there is some cold roast beef in the refrigerator. Will roast beef sandwiches do?'

'Roast beef sandwiches will do fine.'

'Seven rounds?' says Perch, with a brief glance at the sleeping Sonny. There is something odd about the way he is sitting, the way his arms are hanging down, the way his chin is resting on his breastbone . . .

'Absolutely,' says Thurston. 'Seven. One for each of us.'

'Because all seven of us are here, are we not, Perch?' says Sato.

'Of that there can be no dispute, Master Sato,' says the brothers' indefatigably phlegmatic manservant.

'Because the charm of Seven is vital to the continued success of the store,' says Wensley. 'That's what our father used to say.'

'Those were his words, sir.'

'And it mustn't be broken,' adds Fred.

'No, it must not, Master Fred.'

The brothers are talking in the dull, numbed tones of survivors of a train crash, and Perch wonders if they might not be suffering from some kind of delayed shock as a consequence of the explosion.

'If nothing else is required, then?' he says.

His eyes have by this stage adapted to the dim light, and as he turns to leave he takes a good look at the figure of the youngest son of Septimus Day.

Sonny hardly resembles Sonny at all. Sonny is a twisted, mangled, lumpen approximation of Sonny, like a wax effigy left out too long in the sun. His skin is webbed with patterns of blood, the same blood that besmirches the table and the carpet. His dangling hands are horribly misshapen, and the angle at which his jawbone is lodged against his clavicle would, for a living person, soon become unbearably uncomfortable. One eye is lost beneath puffy black lids, while the other bulges alarmingly, veiny and gelatinous. His lips have bloomed like a pair of purple fungi, and his nose lies almost flat against his face, as though it is made of putty and someone has squelched it down with their fist. His hair is clotted with indefinable matter and splinters of bone.

This time, keeping his features calm and inexpressive, the habit that has come to Perch naturally throughout all his years of service to the Day family, is the hardest thing he has ever had to do.

He looks round at the six still-living sons of Septimus Day, and in their widened, white eyes sees fear, and something else besides, something he is reluctant to name.

'Sonny is going to be with us every day from now on,' Mungo tells Perch. 'He's turned over a new leaf.'

'I . . . I see, sir. Yes.'

'I personally will make sure that he gets up in good time and is prompt for breakfast. Do you understand?'

'Yes, sir, I do.'

'Very good. Well, Perch?' Mungo attempts to instil the words with his usual authority, but it sounds like a child's gruff imitation of a grown-up. 'Our snack?'

Perch takes one last look around the table, then closes his eyes very slowly and, equally slowly, nods.

'Of course, sir,' he says. 'Sandwiches for seven, coming up.'

Acknowledgements

Adam Brockbank was involved with *Days* since its inception, and helped shape a handful of amorphous concepts into a plot, suggested ideas, proposed different (and invariably better) ways of doing things, and throughout the writing of the novel offered accurate, insightful comments and criticisms.

On the technical side of things, Lieutenant Hugh Holton of the Chicago Police Department initiated me into the mysteries of handgun use and arranged a memorable and eye-opening tour of his precinct station. Ian Hillier, meanwhile, was kind enough to give me a few pointers on how to go about constructing a homemade deflagrating device. Viva the Kew Liberation Front!

Peter Crowther has been a constant source of support and reassurance, always ready to give me a metaphorical clip round the ear whenever I've started whingeing but also always ready to cheer me up whenever I've really needed it.

Simon Spanton found the book a good home at Orion, and his incisive editing, far from inflicting a death of a thousand cuts, proved to be fat-reducing surgery of the highest order.

John Kunzler and Lesley Plant I have to thank for countless Sunday suppers and Sega sessions. I am equally grateful to the boys at Flying Pig Systems Ltd. for many things, the least of which is calling their company Flying Pig Systems Ltd.

Finally, Susan Gleason took on the unenviable role of being the squeaky wheel that gets the oil, or, as it's technically known, 'literary agent'. It is a task she has performed with grace, dedication and a necessary measure of good humour.

These are the people without whom, etc. etc.

James Lovegrove